Readers everywhere are "Coming Home to Brewster," North Dakota...

Here's what they're saying about *After Anne:*

From North Carolina: "I felt as though the characters were my best friends. The last time I cried this much was when I read James Patterson's *Suzanne's Diary for Nicholas.*"

From Canada: "I laughed and cried. It made me reflect on my life. We all assume we have lots of time and put off telling people what we feel...It was a wonderful book."

From Oregon: "I am a well-educated, voracious reader. I could hardly put the book down. Oprah should know about this!"

From Michigan: "I must tell you that *After Anne* was the best book I have ever read, and I read constantly! I have given it to my best friend...we've grown apart because of being involved in our grandchildren's lives...and I felt this maybe will draw us back close again."

From Oregon: "I was mesmerized by *After Anne* from the moment I began reading...You will laugh, and no doubt cry, aloud. But you can't help but be grateful for having spent time getting to know these wonderful characters."

From Christianbooks.com: "*After Anne* is probably my favorite [book of 2002]. This moving story of an unlikely friendship between two women will have you laughing and crying and longing for a relationship like theirs."

And about book number two, *Finding Ruth:*

From Minnesota: "I imagine you don't read minds, but if you did, you would know that I have been thinking about you and your book *a lot!* It was just excellent. I told my mom that I woke up the other day to a feeling of anticipation—I was looking forward to reading your book. I then had a let-down feeling as I realized that I had finished it! It was actually like a friend. Also, my sign that a book or movie is good is if I continue to think about it afterward. Your book reached that status!"

From California: "I just finished reading the last page of *Finding Ruth.*...yes, the tears went down my cheeks as I read it. *Wow!* You are so clever! Every time I thought, *OK she is going this way,* you went the opposite. But what kept me so on the edge...was your showing me Brewster town. I could see everyone, even their laugh lines."

From Kentucky: "Your book couldn't have come to me at a better time. I struggle with contentment or lack of. Thank you for a touching story that fit quite nicely into my life. I was moved by it and feel certain that your book and I came together for a bigger purpose than just a day's worth of entertainment. If I had my way, your book would be topping all the best-seller lists."

From Indiana: "I chose your book from the new fiction section at our public library without realizing it was a Christian book. God does work in mysterious ways. I could hardly bear to put it down. About two years ago I left a dysfunctional relationship after many years of struggle and strife. I finally put all my faith and my life in a much greater power than myself. My entire life has changed 180 degrees. I am finally in a healthy relationship with someone who feels like home to me, and wherever we are together feels like home, too. It's beautiful to me to find a book that reflects the same truths that I have found."

From Tennessee: "You truly have a gift, a God-given gift. I love your characters, all of them, even the broken ones. Even the selfish ones. Even the unlovable ones. I can't remember the last time a book has made me feel such empathy for a fictitious person, first with Anne and Libby and now with Ruth's friends and family. I feel like I know them personally."

Via e-mail: "Your second book is just as good as the first. I felt such a peaceful feeling after reading such an inspirational book. I look forward to reading your next book whenever that may be. You are becoming my very favorite author."

Via e-mail: "Ruthie's emotions and outlook seemed so similar to mine. Unlike Ruthie, I am not yet 'home,' but your book has touched my life in a way I can't quite explain. I am really struggling with being content and feeling like I belong. Thank you for writing such a heartfelt story."

Via e-mail: "I am a 23-year-old single mom living in Fargo. I finished reading your book *After Anne* yesterday. It was one of the best books I have ever read. Since I loved it so much I just knew I needed to read your next book, *Finding Ruth*. I started it this morning and I just finished it about a half hour ago. Let me tell you, *Finding Ruth* really got to me…You see, I moved away from Fargo five months ago. I moved in with a man I thought I loved and who I thought loved me…boy, was I wrong. I just made my way back to Fargo a week ago, and I am so glad to be *home*. I had wanted to return home months ago…but just like Ruthie, I didn't think it was possible…I wondered what everyone was going to think of me, and I could just imagine the words of failure I would undoubtedly hear. To my surprise, my family and friends have been more supportive of me than I ever could have imagined. While reading your book I found a passage that really affected me. The passage is on page 355 and it states, 'There is forgiveness and redemption for everyone who has made a bad choice. All you have to do is ask, and God, your heavenly Father, will hold out His arms, wrap them around you, and welcome you home.' That really hit my heart…I just want to tell you thanks for opening up my eyes to see that even though I may have felt like a failure in life, I can overcome my bad decisions and move on. I had given up on my faith years ago…and by reading your books I feel like I am ready to find it again. After the past few days reading your stories, my heart already feels softer."

Becoming Olivia

ROXANNE HENKE

HARVEST HOUSE PUBLISHERS

EUGENE, OREGON

Cover by Koechel Peterson & Associates, Inc., Minneapolis, Minnesota

Cover photo © Getty Images/Photodisc Green/Doug Menuez

Published in association with Books and Such, Santa Rosa, California.

BECOMING OLIVIA
Copyright © 2004 by Roxanne Henke
Published by Harvest House Publishers
Eugene, Oregon 97402

ISBN 0-7394-4211-2

Printed in the United States of America

Even though I walk through the dark valley
of the shadow of death
I will fear no evil,
for you are with me
—Psalm 23:4 (NIV)

To Lorren.
You walked with me, too.
Thank you.

Acknowledgements

The writing of a book may take place alone, but it wouldn't happen at all without the help and support of many others. I have many to thank...

First of all, my readers. Thank you for reading my books, for sharing them with friends, church and city libraries, and for taking the time to write and tell me what my stories have meant to you. You are what make the long, sometimes lonely hours at the computer "worth it."

Thanks also to the Harvest House sales reps, both in-house and in the field, and to the booksellers across the nation who have seen to it that my stories get into people's hands. Your work spreads God's message.

Thank you to my mother, Jean Sayler Klein, who has morphed into a one-woman PR firm in a motor home. If anyone should happen to bump into her, consider this a warning: You *will* read her daughter's books! Thanks also to my stepfather, Rev. R.R. Klein, who not only encourages my writing, but also drives the RV.

A big thanks to my sisters, Kim Anderson and Ann Jensen. Also to my special friends, Jackie Baumgarten, Yvonne Englehart, Debbie Turner, and Janel Gaugler...it may take a village to raise a child, but it takes phone calls, e-mails, long walks, talks, and coffee to nourish a writer. You all do it beautifully. Thank you!

Thank you to my wonderful editor, Nick Harrison, whose prayers shape my writing as surely as his editing skills. Thanks also to all the folks at Harvest House...your work behind the scenes does not go unnoticed and is much appreciated!

To my agent, Janet Kobobel Grant, who supported my writing voice at a time when I was beginning to doubt it...long before I became a client. Your words, "No! Don't change it," encouraged me more than you know, and I thank you.

Several people provided insight and facts I needed to make the details of this book ring true. Many thanks to Dr. Albert Samuelson,

Carol Samuelson, RN, and Judy Ganey, RN, for a glimpse into the professional side of psychiatric care. To pharmacists Carla Aipperspach and Cari Silbernagel at Wishek Drug, and to Cindy Gall, RN, and Gina Wiest at the Wishek Retirement Home.

I also want to thank the Mount Hermon Christian Writer's Conference and the wonderful friends I've made there…you know who you are!

And, as always, my biggest thanks to my husband, Lorren, and my daughters, Rachael and Tegan. Life would be dull, indeed, if I didn't have you to share it with!

Brewster, North Dakota. Middle America, USA. The kind of town where everybody knows your name. Where everybody knows what everyone else is doing...or thinking of doing. A place where neighbors run cookies over with the latest gossip. Where the waitress at the café is your next-door neighbor. Nine-man football. A twenty-bed hospital. A grocery store that offers home delivery on Thursdays. All these things can be found in Brewster.

What else can be found there? People with hopes and dreams. People in love and people with broken hearts. Friends and foes. Families and faith. When you get to know the people of Brewster, you'll find it isn't all that different from where you live.

Welcome to Brewster...it's a good place to call home.

Prologue

Libby

To anyone else looking at the photo, my life would have appeared perfect. There I was, my belated-graduation cap slightly askew, matching the wide, crooked grin across my face. Emily had me in a sort of sideways bear hug, her young face mashed into a funny combination of grin and gown. Brian was beaming over my shoulder, somehow snugged into the convergence between Emily's grin and mine. My husband, Bob, had his arm thrown so freely around my shoulders it almost embraced all four of us. Smiles all around. Our perfect family.

I knew better.

I swiped a dust rag over the glass and set the framed photograph back on the shelf above my computer. The photo had been taken four months earlier, in May—a picture, a graduation, that had been twenty years in the making. I paused for a moment, as if to get a better look at the whole picture. But I didn't need eyes to see the memory of that day, a memory of gladness that was seared into my heart. I turned, continuing my cleaning sweep around the room, not needing to look at the photo to know what was there. Someone else would have seen four matching smiles. A family of four without a care in the world. But even on that day I couldn't forget what had come before. I'd tried. For one day our family deserved to celebrate...

"Olivia Willet Marsden, cum laude." The voice boomed over the loudspeaker as I began my walk across the stage.

"Woo-hoo, way to go, Mom!" A ripple of laughter spread through the crowd of supportive onlookers. From somewhere in the middle of the auditorium Brian and Emily cheered wildly. I had no doubt Bob was joining in on the clapping. They deserved this diploma almost as much as I did.

"Congratulations, Ms. Marsden." The university president shook my hand. "Quite the fan club you have there." He smiled, then swept his eyes over my shoulder, ready to greet the next graduate.

I adjusted the gold tassel on my four-cornered hat and made my way down the rickety metal steps and off the stage, a feeling of pride growing in my chest as I felt the soft leather cover of the diploma in my hand. At forty-two, I may not have been the oldest graduate ever to cross this stage, but considering what I had invested to get here, at times I felt as if I were.

I scanned the crowd, trying to spot Bob and the kids. The sea of faces blended into one large mass, all alike, with splashes of color here and there. Where were they? What color was Emily's top? My eyes flitted from face to face, my task seeming impossibly large in the crowded auditorium. Then, suddenly, there he was. Bob, my no-public-display-of-emotion husband, standing up in the crowd, all by himself, his hands clasped over his head in a gesture of triumph.

He knew. He knew exactly what I had gone through to get to that day. He knew exactly how close I'd come to not being there at all. In that gown. In that auditorium. In this world.

I gave Bob a thumbs-up and then threaded my way through the graduates already seated in my row. I was determined to take in every moment of this graduation day. A day that very well could have never happened. I found my seat, smiling at the young man beside me. He looked bored, as if he was here only because his parents had made him come. Part of the price of his college education. I wanted to poke him. *Wake up!* I felt like screaming. *Remember this!* But I didn't. Some lessons are better learned on your own.

I watched the parade of graduates as they passed one by one across the stage to receive their long-awaited degree. What were their stories? What price did they pay to earn the diploma they now held in their hands? I doubted most of those young faces had an inkling of what lay ahead. They were dreaming of jobs and wedding bells, children, and new cars. I highly doubted any of their dreams included the death of a best friend, a wayward child, or depression so deep that life no longer seemed worth living. But what good would my telling them do when their lives were just beginning? Would I have done anything differently if I had known? After all, those very events had led me to my long-delayed college graduation. One of the last missing pieces in the jigsaw puzzle of my life.

So much of that time I didn't remember. Which might have been for the best. But looking at the complacent faces of those around me, I knew the day was sweeter for the struggle. I rubbed my hand over the diploma on my lap, a bubble of pure joy pushing at my throat. I grinned at no one. Or maybe at God. He knew the exact measure of joy that day held for me even better than I did.

He knew just how close I'd come to not being there at all.

How it all began...

Two years earlier

Libby

It started with a pimple. A pimple, of all things. It sounds stupid now. Who would think a tiny, red mound on Emily's arm would start a downward spiral that almost was my undoing? Well, it really wasn't that tiny, and the pimple was just the straw that broke this mother's back.

"Mom! Come here! This is gross!" Emily's voice echoed from the hall bathroom.

I knew enough not to run. With Emily, everything was gross or putrid—or awesome. No in-betweens with Emily. The bathroom was a cloud of bath gel, lotion, hair spray, and any other potion sixteen-year-old girls need for their existence these days.

"Good grief, Emily, open the window. You're going to get lung cancer." I waved a hand in front of my face, trying to clear the air. Emily stood in front of the mirror wrapped in a bath towel, her makeup flawless, every light brown hair sprayed into perfect messiness, her eyes focused squarely on the small lump on her arm.

"Mom, look at this! It's so gross! What am I going to do?" Emily was pointing to a small red bump on her upper arm. Her nose was wrinkled in disgust. "I'm going to die if I have to go to the homecoming dance with a pimple on my arm!"

I ran my finger over the bump, feeling the larger core that lay beneath the skin. Squeezing it five minutes before her date was to arrive seemed like a bad idea. "Let's just put a Band-Aid over it for tonight and take care of it tomorrow."

"A Band-Aid!?" You'd thought I'd suggested we cut off her arm. "Mom, do you know what that will look like? I'm wearing a sleeveless dress!"

I bit my tongue. I knew reminding her that I thought a sleeveless dress was too cold for a late-September dance in North Dakota would do no good now. We'd gone over all that in Marshall Field's dressing room. I lost. I'd learned that with Emily, some battles aren't worth the effort. Let her shiver all night.

"Here, let's try this." I grabbed her makeup bottle, dabbing a spot on her red mark. I topped it with a dab of concealer and finished my handiwork with a press of powder. "Take a look." I stepped away, pointing to the mirror.

Emily inspected her arm, relaxed, and sighed, "Mom, you're awesome!"

"Emily," my husband, Bob, called up the stairs, "Mike's here."

"Mike's here?" Emily whispered, wide-eyed, as if she hadn't expected him until tomorrow. "Already?"

"Right on time," I replied tapping on my watch, trying to keep any hint of accusation out of my tone. Her perpetual lateness was another battle I seemed to be losing. "I'll let him know you'll be down in a minute." I closed the bathroom door, wondering how Emily would ever be ready to go to college in a year and a half.

I walked downstairs. Mike Anderson, Emily's—well, I didn't know *what* to call him—was standing by the front door talking to Bob. According to Emily, they weren't *going out,* they were simply *hanging out.* They'd been hanging out a lot since school had started. He seemed like a good kid.

"Hi, Mike." I suppressed a grin as the smell of cologne hit me full force. He was obviously out to impress someone tonight. As was Emily. I was glad I was long past playing that angst-filled game. "You look nice tonight." He did, in his khakis and white shirt, the sleeves carefully rolled back. Black tie, black shoes. Nice. "How's your job going?"

"Great! Did you hear me on air this afternoon? I got to broadcast until we went off the air tonight. Got to do the football game last night, too." He swiped a hand through his hair, his blond stubble short enough that his gesture did nothing but telegraph his nervousness. His lanky build left him off the roster when it came to the Brewster Badgers' football team, but his gift for gab had landed him a job at Brewster's small country radio station, KBRS.

"No, I didn't, but I've heard you before, and you do a wonderful job. Emily will be down in a minute. Who's playing for the dance tonight?"

"He's a DJ out of Carlton. Blue Smoke or something like that."

"Oh, that's right," I murmured, pretending I'd known. My age showed. I kept forgetting no one hired bands for dances anymore. For the life of me I couldn't understand why the school paid as much to hire a kid to play records—okay, *CDs*—as we used to pay for a live band back when I attended Brewster High.

"How's school? How are your folks?" Bob asked, working his way through the standard list of questions to ask while waiting for your daughter to descend the stairs.

"Fine. They're fine," Mike answered, trying to fill the time as well. "Dad and I got our deer licenses, so we'll be going hunting in—whoa, Emily!" He stopped speaking.

All eyes turned as Emily sauntered down the steps, measured nonchalance in her every move. I didn't remember her dress being quite that red or quite that grown-up the day we went shopping in Carlton. But after four stores and what had to be twenty dresses, with tears, who could blame a mother for saying, "We'll take that one," when her daughter finally said, "This one isn't so bad"?

Apparently Mike didn't think it was too bad, either. "Wow," was all his disc-jockey vocabulary could muster.

It was enough for Emily. She smiled, a look on her face I hadn't seen before. A look I wasn't so sure I was ready to see. "Let me take a picture," I said, my voice high-pitched and unnatural. What did I have to feel nervous about? Emily rolled her eyes but moved toward the fireplace, the standard background for most photos in our family.

They stood stiffly, side by side. I stepped close and threaded Emily's arm through Mike's as if they were mannequins. "Smile," I commanded. A nervous muscle twitched one corner of Mike's mouth as the shutter snapped.

"Don't drive too fast," Bob cautioned as Emily and Mike headed toward the door.

"Have fun," I added, reaching out to touch Emily's shoulder, trying to keep her close a few moments more. My hand slid down her arm as she walked past, releasing the fragrance she'd so carefully layered, touching skin so soft it reminded me of the day Bob and I brought her home from the hospital. Our baby—going out the door practically grown. When had that happened? Emily paused for a split second, adjusting the spaghetti strap on her dress, giving my hand just enough time to pause on her arm, on the small, now hidden pimple. A chill ran through me.

"Are you sure you don't need a sweater?" I asked, holding out a crocheted white silk sweater I usually saved for banking conventions with Bob.

"Mo-om." Emily rolled her eyes, determined to be independent, but threw the sweater over her arm.

As she moved away her arm slid beneath my hand, the small hard lump once again beneath my fingers. "Don't forget your curfew," I reminded automatically.

"We won't," Mike called as they ran down the steps to his freshly washed pickup.

Bob closed the door. "Is it my imagination, or did Emily grow up overnight?"

"It must have been last night," I replied, the image of her gliding down the steps in her red dress still in my mind. "I think I'll wait up."

"Me, too," Bob added, heading for his recliner.

I walked into the kitchen. Maybe I'd get a casserole ready for supper tomorrow night. I glanced at the clock on the wall. Emily wouldn't return for several hours. I might even have time to do a little writing, adding a few pages to the book I'd finally started. The book I'd dreamt of writing most of my life but hadn't started until my best friend, Anne, had commanded, "Put it in the book." Then she died. She'd spent a year battling breast cancer. The best and worst year of my entire life.

Well, I wasn't going to think about that now. I pulled a pound of hamburger from the fridge and a frying pan from the cupboard. I'd get this hot dish put together and then head to the computer. It would be a good way to pass the time while I waited for Emily. I'd already forgotten all about the pimple on her arm. I shouldn't have.

Emily

"Parents can be so weird." I climbed into Mike's pickup as he held the door. What was even weirder was Mike acting like we were on some kind of *date* or something. I tossed Mom's sweater over the seat back and tugged my dress down toward my knees. It hadn't seemed so short when I stood in front of the mirror.

"You can close the door now," I told Mike, as if he needed directions. We'd agreed we were going to the dance as friends. So why did he open the door for me? Like I couldn't do it myself. Like I didn't get in and out of his pickup practically every day by myself.

Why did you spend two hours getting ready for the dance?

Good grief, it was homecoming! And besides, all the football players would be at the dance. Rick Wynn, for one.

I wasn't quite part of the popular crowd, but I wanted to be. Who didn't? Well, maybe Mike. He was different. I could tell that about him from the first day he joined our class way back in fifth grade. I was just learning what the word *popular* meant, but Mike didn't seem to care. He walked into our fifth-grade class as if he were already friends with everyone.

At lunch that first day, he sat with Jonathan Preston. Jonathan always wore thick glasses and dressed kind of shabby and would hardly look at anyone who talked to him. So by fifth grade we all kind of quit trying. And, besides, have you ever heard of a *kid* called *Jonathan?* He was strange, but Mike didn't seem to notice. He sat across from Jonathan, talking like he was his new best friend. Jonathan actually laughed out loud! Practically everyone in the lunchroom turned to stare—we'd hardly heard a peep out of him since first grade. Mike and Jonathan didn't even stop talking.

Somehow that fifth-grade fall, Mike became the unofficial mascot of the Brewster football team, running dead balls on and off the field, getting his head rubbed for good luck between plays. By the end of that year, anyone anywhere near Mike was accepted as a cool kid—even Jonathan. Mike just had that way about him. He was everybody's friend. Mine, too.

In fact, Mike was the reason I was almost popular. If you can call being asked to take stats for the football team popular, that is. I wasn't really all that interested in football, just the football guys. Last year, during sophomore PE, Coach Rollins walked up to me and said, "Emily, Mike Anderson mentioned you might be interested in taking stats for me for football next fall? Are you?"

Was he kidding? Of course! I'd like to be anywhere the football guys hung out. Show me a high school girl who wouldn't. I wasn't sure if my volleyball coach would be thrilled with the idea, but we never had matches on the same night as football games, so I doubted she could say much if I said yes.

I'd tried out for cheerleading in junior high and didn't make the squad but ended up on the junior high volleyball team instead. Coach Swenson said I had a natural ability for setting the ball. That's one thing about a small school like Brewster—even someone like me, who would never have a chance of playing a sport at a class-A school, can turn into a halfway decent player in class B.

I'd really been looking forward to volleyball season in the fall. I attended two camps over the summer and had just started to get the timing down to do some back-row spiking. I was anxious to show Coach Swenson what I'd learned. But the second week of practice, I came down from a block off the net with my right foot at an odd angle. I heard the pop before I felt the pain. As the guy at the sports medicine clinic in Carlton said, "Some sprains can be worse than a break." My ankle still wasn't completely healed, and the season was nearly a third over. There I sat, my big athletic career on the volleyball bench. All I could do was bide my time until my next sport started in mid-November—girls' basketball. Thank goodness I'd said yes when Coach Rollins had asked me to take football stats. Even with a limp I could do that.

I had been excited to be a junior. This year was going to be different. I was going to be popular because of volleyball. But we lost some early key matches while I sat on the bench, and rather than feeling part of the team, I felt I was part of the blame for not being on the court. If I was going to get noticed, I would have to do it as part of the football team…well, from the sidelines, anyway. It was a start.

Football was also why I was glad Mike wanted to go to the dance with me tonight. He was in tight with the football players, and I wanted the Badgers' quarterback, Rick Wynn, to notice me. Rumor had it that Rick and his girlfriend, Hannah Stromme, had broken up last week. They'd been going out for*ever*. Jen told me Hannah was going to the dance with some senior girls, and Rick was going with some guys. If I ever had a chance to get Rick to actually look at me, tonight was the night. Mike had been Rick's friend even before he got the job at KBRS, but now that Mike broadcast the football games, the jocks wanted all the air time they could get. And Mike was the guy who could give it to them.

Gravel crunched under the tires as we pulled into the school parking lot. I flipped down the visor and checked my makeup. Good. Mike practically jumped out of the pickup and raced around to open my door. What was with him tonight? He was acting like he'd never seen me dressed up before. Good grief, we went to the same church. He'd seen me in a dress lots of times.

I stepped down from the high running board of the pickup, suddenly glad for Mike's offered hand. My high heel sunk into the gravel of the parking lot. Tiptoeing across the lot was going to completely ruin my entrance. I hoped Rick wasn't there yet.

The school entryway buzzed with kids as Mike held open the door for me.

"Hi, Emily!" My best friend, Jen, came running over. "You look great! Doesn't she, Mike?" Oh, great. All I needed was Jen fishing for compliments for me. And to Mike. If I wanted anyone to think I looked good it was Rick. Jen knew that. I told her practically every-thing. We walked into the gym. "Your dress looks really awesome," she added.

"Thanks." I smiled her way as my eyes swept the gym. Jen would understand. She knew who I was looking for.

The simple banner the cheerleaders had made for homecoming didn't do much to disguise the fact that it was just the gym, but the colored lights the DJ had set up made the room look much different than it did during PE classes. It was dark and cool and exciting.

"Hey, Mike!" Rick Wynn high-fived Mike while my heart started pounding double time. He was right here. Now. "How did ya like that touchdown last night?"

"Awesome." Mike slapped his hand back. "You looked good run-ning through that defense. Sounded good on the radio, too." Mike knew just what Rick wanted to hear.

Rick hooted and then slid his eyes to me, flashing his signature grin. "Emily Marsden, you're looking fine tonight."

So the two hours had been worth it. "Thanks," I said, trying to match his stare. After a second I looked away. Rick was a senior—totally cool, and he knew it. Instead of making him seem conceited, his confidence added to his charm. I racked my brain for something more to say. "That's your third touchdown this year." *Are you trying to prove you keep the football stats? That was a stupid thing to say.* I could feel blood rushing to my cheeks. I was glad the gym was dark.

"Good to know you're counting." Rick grinned again. "Dance with me later?" My head started doing an idiotic bob even before he added, "That is, if it's okay with Mike. He's *The Man*, you know." He pointed an index finger at Mike.

Mike pointed back. "No problem. If it's okay with Emily." Mike was simply Mr. Manners tonight. What was with him?

"Sure," I replied, my head bouncing like a bungee cord. Miss Cool I wasn't. But I really didn't care if Rick Wynn knew I was excited to dance with him. I was. Oh, I was! How many nights had I tried to study but found myself daydreaming about this very thing? Scribbling his

name in the margins of my notebook. Rick. R.W. Rick Wynn. Eight letters I knew much better than my world history notes.

"Catch ya later, then." Rick tapped me once, softly, on my arm
with his fist.

"Ouch!" I couldn't help it, the word flew out of my mouth. He'd
barely grazed my arm, but it was right on that stupid pimple. It hurt.

"Oh, I get it." Rick laughed. "Playing the delicate female, are you?
Don't worry, I'll treat you gently." A quick frown crossed Mike's brow
as Rick winked and then turned away.

"Wanna dance?" Mike held his hand out toward the dance floor
as if he were some old-fashioned movie star. A slow song was playing.

"I suppose." I followed him to the middle of the gym, rubbing
the tender spot on my arm. Mike put one hand around my waist. His
other hand grasped mine, his grip warm and sure. I hardly noticed
because my arm was throbbing in time with the music.

Mike twirled me around, bumping my sore arm again when my
foot caught on his. "Sorry," he said, taking the blame, "it's my first
night with my new feet."

I should have laughed at his joke; instead, tears sprang to my
eyes. How could a dumb pimple hurt that much? What if Rick saw it?
What if he'd been aiming for it? Maybe he'd just been making fun of
me. I blinked rapidly and took a deep breath. Crying at homecoming.
That was a joke in itself. This was supposed to be fun.

"Are you okay?" Mike slowed his steps into a back and forth
shuffle. "You seem kind of quiet."

"I'm fine." I swallowed my tears. "I guess I'm just kind of tired.
It's been a long week." It had been. Our class had put together our
lame junior class float on Monday and Tuesday night after supper. I
mean, "Clip the Clippers"—how original. I rolled my eyes just
thinking about it. Wednesday night I practiced with the choir for the
homecoming halftime performance. I had played piano accompani-
ment (electronic keyboard for football games) for the high school
choir since my freshman year. I loved it. Playing the piano was the
one thing I was really good at. My mom's friend, Anne, had given me
my first lessons, shaping my ten-year-old fingers into their first chord.

How I loved Anne. How I loved the music she taught me. But in Brewster High, being in choir was not cool, and being in sports was. That's why, if I couldn't be playing volleyball, I was glad to be taking stats for the football team. Thursday I'd stayed up late studying for an English lit test. Just because Mrs. Koenig didn't like football, she had to give everyone a test before homecoming. Friday night was the big game between the Badgers and the Clippers. We won, so Mike, Jen, and I had gone driving around after the game until my curfew at midnight. No wonder I was near tears over a stupid pimple. Being tired always made me feel like crying.

Mike pulled me closer as the song neared the end. What kind of friend-thing was this? I mean, he was *Mike*. Practically my brother. Being so close to him like that felt weird. I wasn't about to lay my head on his shoulder, so I rested my chin on the seam of his shirt. It was going to be a long night if Mike planned to turn this into something more.

Over Mike's shoulder Rick caught my eye. He winked again. I blinked back, never mastering that winking business no matter how much I'd practiced in the mirror when I was eight. Evidently Rick hadn't noticed that dumb pimple on my arm. I smiled to myself forgetting all about my arm, which was still throbbing.

All of a sudden the night didn't seem long enough.

Libby

Homecoming night seemed a million hours long. Of course it wouldn't have if Emily had kept her curfew. I made my casserole, sat at my computer until my eyes were so dry they'd hardly blink anymore, and then paced by the living room window while Bob snored in the recliner, his uneven snorts fraying my nerves even more. Where was Emily?

I looked at my watch for about the hundredth time. Two A.M. We'd extended her midnight curfew for the homecoming dance until one. According to Emily, the dance would end at twelve, but no one ever stayed until the end. They were going to go to Jen's house for snacks when they left the dance. Sure they were. I'd been a teenager once upon a time, too.

"Bob!" I tapped his foot as I paced by his chair. "How can you sleep while Emily is breaking her curfew?"

"Well…umm, I—" He pushed down the footrest and sat up. "What time is it?"

"Two-oo," I emphasized. "In the *morning*."

"She should be home by now."

No kidding. I tried to temper my annoyance. It wasn't Bob I was upset with. "Do you think we should go looking for her?"

"I don't know." He rubbed at his face, then yawned. "She's with Mike. How bad could it be? All they ever do is watch movies and drive around. They probably lost track of the time. You know how kids are."

Yes, I did know how kids were, and that was exactly why I was worried. Just last week, my friend Jan had told me one of the sophomore girls was pregnant. A sophomore! And it was getting almost commonplace to hear of some high school kid getting a Minor in Possession. The kids had it shortened to one phrase, "He got a Minor." As if the kid had graduated from something instead of gotten in trouble. I liked to think I trusted Emily, but who really knew these days?

Bob joined me at the window, looking out at our empty driveway, rubbing his hand across my back. "You know, by the time we drive around town, she'd probably be home. She's probably on her way now." He reached down and took my hand. "Come on." He pulled me toward the couch. "Let's sit here and think of ways to torture her. I vote for taking away her hair spray." I laughed in spite of my concern, taking a seat on the couch close to Bob. He pulled me into his chest. "Or we could make out." His voice was light. Do men never worry?

"Probably what Emily is doing right now," I said. "Thanks for reminding me." I snuggled into the crook of his arm, laying my head on his shoulder. If we were going to wait up, I might as well get comfortable.

"You're kinda cute when you're worried." He laid his head on mine, squeezing me gently to his side. "I love you, you know."

I nodded, smiling into his shirt. I didn't need words to tell him what he already knew.

It had been five years since my best friend, Anne, had died. An event that continued to impact our marriage. Who would have thought her death could bring new life to our relationship? I was learning firsthand how God could use something terrible and somehow turn it into something good. Her death at such a young age had brought Bob and me face-to-face with our own mortality. The day after Anne's death, Bob vowed to quit living for his career. At the time I took his vow with a grain of salt; I'd never known Bob as anything but a workaholic. I had to see it to believe it—and I did. Shortly after Anne died, Bob was asked to step in as president of the Brewster bank, and I thought, *Here we go again*. But he kept his word, making time to attend every one of Brian's football and basketball games all through high school. And he had yet to miss a concert when

Emily played or any of her volleyball games, even this season when she'd done nothing but sit on the bench.

Just a couple months ago the Brewster bank holding company acquired a larger bank in Carlton, and the board asked Bob to become the CEO there. Even with the forty-mile commute each way, Bob rarely missed dinner with Emily and me. Of course, these days we usually didn't eat until seven, and oftentimes Emily had to be back at school in the evening for a meeting. Our dinners might be short, but they were sweet. Well, as sweet as a meal could be with a moody teenager at the table.

But we'd been there before with Brian. Leaving home can give a kid a new appreciation for the place. Now that Brian was starting his junior year of college in Fargo, an almost four-hour drive from Brewster, and had moved out of the dorm, he was finding all sorts of reasons to come home and scour the house for things he could use. A pot here, a pan there, a couple each of my knives, forks, and spoons. My kitchen was starting to look like Mother Hubbard's cupboard. I'd told my friend in Carlton, Katie Jeffries, that I needed a mother-of-a-college-kid shower. Before our last book club meeting, she'd passed the word, and each member came with a gift—something "used" from their kitchen. Potholders with burn marks, old pans with the Teflon partly worn off, and plastic glasses that didn't match. We decided we all needed a shower whether we had college kids or not. I couldn't wait to tell them I'd packed all the stuff in a box and actually given it to Brian. "Wow, Mom, thanks!" he'd said. You'd think I'd passed on a treasure chest.

I had Anne to credit for Brian turning into such a neat young man. Well, Anne and God. Anne's faith in Brian during his middle teen years had seen him through a tentative experiment with drugs. When she asked Brian to be the godfather of her daughter, Jane, Brian began a search to learn what that role meant. I had no doubt Anne would not be one bit surprised if she could know Brian led a Bible study in his new apartment. I still marveled at the faith Anne's friendship had instilled in me. Anne had made loving God seem so easy. I learned it wasn't, but I kept trying.

I tried to remind myself of my fledgling faith now. *Lord, keep Emily safe…wherever she is.* Bob's steady breathing both soothed and annoyed me. If Bob could sleep at a time like this, how bad could it be? But then again, how could he sleep at a time like this? Worries niggled at my mind. Images of kids drinking and car accidents replaced my prayer. I sighed, trying to turn my worry into prayer. It wasn't working. I slid off the couch, Bob rousing just enough to swing his feet onto the seat and get more comfortable. I looked at the clock on top of the piano. Two-twenty. Where was that kid?

I stood at the living room window, arms crossed, trying to hold my fears inside. If anything happened to her, I couldn't—. Headlights from a pickup swept through the living room and into our driveway. *Thank You,* I prayed, relief flooding my body. I almost felt weak. The feeling didn't last long. Anger filled every fiber of my being. Who did Emily think she was to make me worry like this? Did she realize she'd kept me up half the night…make that half the *morning?* She'd be lucky if she left the house the rest of her junior year! I moved to the middle of the room, hands on hips, ready to lay into her.

"Mom, I'm *so* sorry!" Emily burst in the door, apology flowing from her lips. "I'm *so* late. Mike's pickup broke down and we couldn't get it started and—"

"Honest, Mrs. Marsden." Mike poked his head over Emily's shoulder. "It's all my fault. Well, my pickup's fault. That's what happens when you're young and broke and—"

I shook my head, waving him home with a roll of my eyes at the logical explanation. I was sure his mom was as worried as I'd been. No use having both the kids standing here telling the details while the clock ticked away.

"You could have called," I said after Mike had gone. I was surprised at how calm I sounded after hours of worry. The logical excuse had diffused some of my anger. I'd never even imagined car trouble.

"See, I told you I should have a cell phone." Emily didn't waste a second reminding me of her latest quest.

"Emily, we've gone over this before. Cell phones are expensive, and besides, we can hardly get reception in Brewster." I often joked that to talk on a cell phone in this town, a person had to stand out-side, face north, stand on one foot, and hold a piece of tinfoil in the air. It wasn't quite that bad, but close. I was in no mood to joke about that now. "You could have…" I searched for something more. She wasn't getting off the hook this easy.

"Walked," Bob reminded from the couch. "Brewster's not that big." Good point.

"Dad," Emily said as if we should already know, "I'd have been even later if I'd walked. I have heels on." She held up her foot as if to prove her point. "Besides, we were out by the ten-mile corner." Her point solidified, a tiny smile turned one corner of her mouth.

The ten-mile corner. Some things never changed. Ten miles out of Brewster where two highways intersected in the middle of nowhere. An approach off to the side made a perfect spot for kids to drive out to, just to turn around and drive back. Or stop and hang out with everyone else who had the same idea. Kids had done that even when I was in high school.

The steam evaporated from my balloon of anger. What could we do? She was home safe. We all needed sleep. Except Bob.

"Let's get to bed," I sighed. "We have church in the morning." It would be a short night.

Emily slipped her heels off, dangling them from one finger. Bob rose from the couch. "How'd you end up getting home?" he asked.

"Umm…" Emily cleared her throat. "Uh, Rick Wynn went back to town and got some jumper cables and jumped Mike's pickup."

And that had taken almost two hours? Right. A red flag started waving in my brain. My alerted senses caught the faint smell of cig-arette smoke filtering through Emily's layers of Cotton Blossom scent. "Were you smoking?"

"No!" Her tone held offense, as if she'd never consider such a thing. Right. I wasn't that naïve. "Some of the other kids were. I can't help that."

I sighed. I had no reason not to believe her. "Let's get some sleep." Emily brushed past me, heading for the stairs. I didn't want to end the night like this. "Did you have fun at the dance?"

She stopped with one foot on the first step as a big grin covered her face. "It was *great*."

"Good," I replied. I followed her up the steps. On the landing I tapped her on the shoulder. When she turned I wrapped my arms around her and gave her a hug, my anger gone. "I'm glad you had a good time. I love you."

"Love you," she answered automatically, then yawned. "Do I have to go to church?"

"We'll see." At this point I wasn't so sure I would even hear the alarm. She turned toward her bedroom. I reached out and touched her shoulder. "By the way, where's my sweater?"

She froze, her eyes wide. "I think I left it in Rick's car."

Rick's car? "What were you doing in—"

She shook her head. "I mean Mike's pickup. I'm so tired. I'll get it tomorrow."

"You do that. That's one of my favorite sweaters." I rubbed her arm, a goodnight of sorts. The pimple that had caused such a commotion earlier in the evening was a hard lump beneath my hand. I scrubbed at it with my forefinger. "Remind me to squeeze this in the morning."

Emily nodded while she yawned. "G'night."

Ah, the sheets felt soft and cool as I slid my legs between the covers, a good five hours past my usual bedtime. The last time I'd been up this late had been…when? Not even New Year's kept me up this long anymore. Already I couldn't wait to climb into bed tomorrow night…make that tonight. My brain was so muddled I could hardly tell what day it was. I snuggled into bed, hiking the blankets up to my chin, but when my head hit the pillow, my eyes stayed open. *Mike's pickup. Rick's car. Other kids smoking.* Emily's words tumbled around, refusing to be put to bed. There I lay, wide-awake for another hour, an alarm of some sort sounding in my mind.

It's hard to believe now that not even once did I think the cause of my unsettled thoughts could be Emily's pimple.

Emily

I told the truth. I just left out certain parts. The parts I knew would make Mom mad and get me grounded. I slipped my dress over my hips and tossed it on the chair in the corner of my room along with the dirty clothes already there. I didn't know if we could wash a homecoming dress, but Mom would figure it out. I just hoped she didn't notice the beer stain on the side. It wasn't even my beer, but I doubted my parents would believe that part.

I tugged the extra-large North Dakota State University T-shirt Brian had given me for Christmas two years ago over my head. Sometimes I wished he still lived at home, but most times I liked not having to share the hall bathroom with him. If he were here this weekend though, I could ask him what he did in high school when everyone else was drinking? I crawled into bed and laid on my back, staring at the kitten poster Brian had helped me tack on the ceiling when I was a fourth grader. Practically every night I'd think I should get up and tear that thing down, and then in the morning I'd get up and forget about it. It would probably be up there until I got married or something.

I turned on my side and pulled the covers up to my chin. I thought for sure I'd get in trouble tonight for coming home so late, even if the battery in Mike's truck really did quit working. Lucky that it did, too, or I'd have really been sunk.

"Hey, Mike," Rick called as we were leaving the dance, "you going to the ten-mile?"

I'd smiled to myself. I knew Rick didn't care if Mike went or not; I was the one he was wondering about. He'd asked me the same question when we'd slow danced three songs earlier.

"Emily Marsden," he said, taking my hand and pulling me onto the gym floor, "I do believe they're playing our song."

"What song is that?" I asked, trying to identify the notes blaring from the speakers, wondering if Rick knew something I didn't. I glanced over my shoulder. Mike was standing on the sidelines alone. *Of course he's alone. You just walked away from him.* I pushed the guilty thought away. Mike and I were just friends. Even he knew I'd had my eye on Rick since school started.

"Does it matter?" Rick asked. I gave him a puzzled look. He added, "Whatever's playing, that's our song." He winked, then twirled me around and into his arms. I had to lean my head way back to see his face. Rick was really tall up close. Much taller than he looked from the football field when I took stats. I was never going to be able to put my head on his shoulder as I had hoped. I put my head on his chest. It was kind of hard and bony, not at all the way I'd imagined dancing with Rick would feel like. "So," Rick said as he pushed me from side to side, "you and Mike got something going?"

I couldn't help laughing. "Mike and me? He's like my brother or something."

"Just checking." Rick stepped on the tip of my shoe, just missing my toes. He was a lot smoother on the football field than he was on the dance floor. It was hard to get into the music when Rick kept moving a half-beat behind the rhythm. I tried my best to follow and tried to keep my feet away from his. I was glad when the next song was a fast one. Rick leaned forward and talked above the music, "You going out to the ten-mile after the dance?"

"I don't know." I shrugged my shoulders, practically yelling, "We're planning on going to Jen's. Then I don't know. Maybe." I didn't want to tell him I had to be home by one. He knew—he was supposed to be home by then, too. All the Brewster athletes had a school curfew to keep, but it was common knowledge they often broke it, and the coaches rarely checked.

"Maybe we'll see you later," Rick said as he walked me back to Mike's side.

And we had. We stopped at Jen's, mostly so I could tell my folks that's what we'd done, and then Mike, Jen, her boyfriend, Ryan, and I piled in Mike's pickup and headed out of town. I'd been to the ten-mile corner before but just to turn around and drive back to Brewster. I'd never dared stop and join the crowd that often congregated there. Another thing my mom's friend Anne had taught me was to believe in God, and up until this year, hanging out at the ten-mile didn't seem like a way to do that. But I was tired of staying home all the time, watching movies with Ryan, Jen, and Mike. We talked about it and decided that if we went to the hangout together, we'd keep each other away from trouble.

Tonight it seemed like half the high school was there. Of course, in Brewster that meant maybe thirty kids, plus a few from some small towns nearby. Enough people for the four of us to blend right in instead of sticking out like goody-eight-shoes. We piled out of the pickup, Mike using his gift-of-gab to melt us into a circle of kids in no time. I couldn't believe I'd thought the ten-mile hangout had been so forbidden. All the kids were doing was standing around and talking.

"Hi." Rick's voice came from behind me a second before he wrapped his arm around my waist and moved to my side like I was his girlfriend or something. A shiver went down my spine, and not because I'd left my mom's sweater in Mike's pickup, either. I couldn't help but smile inside. Outside I tried to act cool, like this sort of thing happened to me all the time. Mike and Ryan talked about the football game with Rick while Jen and I exchanged smiles with our eyes. Neither one of us had been part of the ten-mile group before. It was exciting. Across the jumble of cars I could see Rick's old girlfriend, Hannah, toss a glance our way. She laughed—jealous, no doubt. I leaned into Rick, his body warm in the cool night. He ran one hand down my arm. Goosebumps jumped to my skin. Rick noticed. "You're cold." I was anything but cold, but I wasn't about to tell him that. "Come to my car," he said. "I've got a jacket." He grabbed my hand and pulled me away from my friends.

We made our way through the cars and kids, stopping to talk to practically everybody. They acted like I'd been here with Rick lots of times. This must be what it felt like to be popular. Fun. Someone handed Rick a can of beer. They held one out to me, too, but I pretended I was too busy holding Rick's hand to notice. It wasn't nearly as hard to fit in as I'd imagined. Rick took a long swallow. Apparently football training rules weren't in effect tonight. As long as the county sheriff didn't show up, no one would get in trouble.

Jason Fyle, one of the football players, walked over to me, his eyes glazed and unfocused. He looked really tired. Or stoned. At least what I thought stoned might look like. He held a beer in one hand, a flat cigarette in the other. "How ya doin'?" He bumped me with his shoulder, his beer spilling onto my dress. I jumped back. My dress was brand-new. "Ya doin' okay?" He gave me a goofy smile, his eyes hardly open. What was I supposed to say when he'd just spilled beer all over me? No, I'm not okay? I bit my tongue.

Rick shoved at his shoulder, pushing him away. "Sleep it off, Fyle." Rick grabbed my hand and pulled me toward his car. His restored Studebaker was parked at the far edge of the makeshift circle. Rick opened the door. "Get in for a little bit. You can warm up."

It felt good to have someone pay attention to me and worry that I was cold. Someone *besides* my mom. I climbed into the dark interior; Rick set his beer on the dash and slid in beside me. I scooted over. How far over should I move? All the way to the other side? Would I seem like a dork if I sat by the door? But then if I sat right by him he might think something else. Rick solved the problem by throwing his arm around my shoulder, pulling me close.

Rick picked up the beer and drained it, putting the can on the floor of the car. He circled his arms around me in a sort of backward hug. "Where've you been, Emily Marsden?"

Dumb question. I'd been in the same school with him for umpteen years. Why hadn't he noticed me until now?

"You're so pretty." Rick's voice sounded kind of weird.

I turned to look at him. He was staring right at me. Man, his eyes were blue. Two swimming pools I felt I was falling into. His head slowly moved toward mine. Was he going to kiss me? Now? I'd barely talked to him until tonight. My dad's words from my birthday party last April floated through my mind, *Sweet sixteen and never been kissed.* It wouldn't be true thirty seconds from now. I lifted my chin just a little. Rick's eyes closed, so did mine.

"Hey, you guys!" Mike was knocking on the car window.

Rick's forehead fell against mine. "Great timing, Anderson," he groaned. He cracked open the door. "*What?*"

"Emily's supposed to be home by one and it's a quarter to. We've gotta go."

"I can give her a ride. We're…talking." He made it sound like we were having an important conversation. Well, we were, without words.

"Emily." Mike shoved his hands in his pockets. He tossed his head in the direction of his pickup, his unspoken offer firm.

"It's okay, Mike. I'll go with Rick." I didn't need Mike to babysit me.

Mike stood there for a second, staring at me. "JD," he said, and then he turned and walked away.

Rick closed the car door and turned toward me. "Jaydee? What's that supposed to mean? You got some kind of code?"

"What*ever.*" I shrugged my shoulders, acting like everyone knew Mike was weird. The fact was it was a code. I couldn't believe Mike even remembered. I couldn't believe I did, either. Bible school, maybe five years ago. What Would Jesus Do? That was the theme, our teachers throwing questions at eleven-year-olds that had us pondering what Jesus would do in different situations. WWJD. Eventually Jen, Mike, and I had shortened the phrase even further. JD. We'd thought we were pretty cool that summer, testing each other, testing our faith, holding each other accountable, even though we didn't quite know what that meant.

I knew now. Obey my parents. Keep my curfew.

"Where were we?" With a finger to my cheek Rick turned my face to him.

I ducked my head. Rick might be used to picking up almost-kissing right where he'd left off, but I wasn't. And I wasn't about to say, "You were starting to give me my first kiss." I rubbed at the damp beer spot on my dress. I wondered if it would come out and if Mom would grill me about how it got there. Somehow the kissing moment was gone. Going home with Mike would have been easier. Instead, I had to figure out a way to tell Rick I really needed to get home. Now.

I'd never broken my curfew before—never had reason to. My parents were reasonable and flexible, molding the time I needed to be home to what was going on, using the school athletic curfew as backup to their own decision. When they told me to be home by one o'clock, it had seemed time enough to hang out with Mike, Jen, and Ryan after the dance. I hadn't counted on Rick Wynn figuring into the equation. I didn't feel like going home one bit.

"Emily?" Rick's blue eyes were fixated on my mouth. He tucked a strand of my hair behind my ear.

I licked my lips, suddenly nervous. I really had to get home. "I've got to go ho—" Rick pressed a finger against my words. When he finally moved his finger I said again, "I really need to go—"

"Shh," he whispered as he stopped my words completely with his lips.

Oh! Oh, my. This was much better than the pillow I'd practiced on in junior high. Rick leaned over me, pushing my head onto the seat back with the pressure of his mouth. Each second seemed like minutes. So what could my parents do? Take away the car keys? Brewster was so small I could walk anywhere I needed to go. Besides, Mike drove me practically everywhere, anyway. I lifted my arms around Rick's waist like I'd imagined doing countless times. Rick pressed his lips harder against mine. Ouch! He was pinching my lips against my teeth. Kissing wasn't supposed to hurt, was it? My eyes flew open. He had to know this wasn't comfortable.

"Rr—rr—ick." I tried to turn my head away from him. Not only did it hurt, I couldn't breathe very well, either. My heart was pounding. I slid my arms in between us, giving Rick a shove. "Stop it!" The words burst from my mouth, using up my last bit of air. I gasped for more. "Don't." I pushed at him again, suddenly wanting to be out of the car.

"Oh, Emily." He groaned and leaned back against the car door. "I'm sorry." He ran his hand through his hair, then shook his head and slumped there for a minute, breathing heavy. "Come here." He reached his arms out toward me.

I crossed mine over my chest. I didn't feel like being close to him anymore. I stared out the side window, realizing most of the other kids had left. How was I going to get home?

JD, Mike's reminder echoed. What would Jesus do? Jesus would probably walk, but then He was used to walking long distances. I wasn't. Ten miles was too far, especially without my sweater and in heels.

"Come here," Rick repeated. He grabbed my hand, walking his way up my arm with his hands, pulling me toward him until I had no choice but to lean into his chest. He twisted a strand of my hair around his finger. "It's just that you're so beautiful..." He let the words hang in the air until I relaxed against him. "I'm eighteen." He sighed heavily. "It's a guy thing. I'm sorry if I scared you. Forgive me?"

I'd heard all about teenage guys and hormones in health class. Supposedly what he said was true. I guessed he couldn't help it. "Okay," I nodded. "But I need to get home." There. I finally said the whole sentence. I started to sit up.

"Just give me a minute, okay?" He rubbed his hand across my back, keeping me close to his chest. "I had fun dancing with you tonight." His voice was dreamy, like he was remembering. "Did you?" I nodded into his chest. I'd felt almost as though I was the home-coming queen walking onto the gym floor with Rick earlier tonight.

His hand continued to circle my back, moving further up and down my body with each stroke. I tried to push myself upright, but he held me close. "I have to go," I reminded. "We both do." He knew the athletic rules as well as I did. If he got suspended from the foot-ball team, the Badgers would be sunk for the season—as well as any chance he had of qualifying for a football scholarship.

"Sure," he answered, not moving a muscle, holding me tight.

I didn't have a watch on, but I knew it had to be after one. I was about to find out what happened when I broke my curfew. I was already late; waiting a few minutes until Rick was ready wouldn't matter much. I closed my eyes, trying to imagine how I'd tell every detail to Jen tomorrow. My eyes flew open. I felt the spaghetti-strap of my dress edge over my shoulder, guided by Rick's finger. I froze. I'd been anxious for my first kiss but nothing more. *Lord, help!* I pushed myself upright almost the same instant Mike pounded on the car window for the second time that night.

"My pickup won't start. I need a jump," he called through the glass.

More than an hour later, after Rick drove to town and tracked down some jumper cables, I made it home. But not before Rick stopped me with a touch on my arm as I was climbing into Mike's truck for the drive back to town. "Do you want to go to a movie with me next weekend?" he asked.

"Yeah," I answered, amazed at how nice Rick had been about helping Mike get his pickup started, and even more amazed that Rick wasn't mad about the way I'd reacted to his kiss.

My bed creaked as I turned onto my other side. I needed to get to sleep. I would have plenty of time to relive this night. If I didn't sleep through the day, that is. I pushed at my pillow, rearranging the feathers. One final thump and it would be perfect. I punched my fist into the soft ball, my knuckles grazing the pillowcase and bouncing onto my upper arm. Ouch! That stupid pimple! Suddenly I didn't have to worry about memories keeping me awake. Just pain.

Libby

That Monday was like any other Monday. Bob off to work, Emily out the door to school, me heading to my computer to work on my novel, a cup of coffee in hand. The only thing different was that I'd called the Brewster clinic and made an appointment with my friend, Dr. Ellen West, to take a look at the pimple on Emily's arm. I'd tried squeezing it the day before, but the hard lump wouldn't budge, and Emily howled like the dog we never let her have.

"Must be a boil," I'd stated, not even sure just what a boil was, other than some old-fashioned diagnosis I'd dredged from the recesses of my memory that applied to all unidentified bumps. Not to worry, I thought, waiting for the computer to boot up. I had no doubt Dr. West would simply nick it with whatever tool doctors used for that sort of thing, and we'd be on our way. I never even thought to pray.

I sipped my coffee and then clicked the mouse, waiting while a blank screen appeared. I had hoped to make some headway on the new chapter I'd started in the novel I'd dubbed *After Anne,* but with Emily's doctor appointment in just over an hour I decided to use the time to do a rough draft of my column for the *Brewster Banner* instead. It hardly seemed possible that I'd been writing *The Wry Eye* for almost seven years. Twice monthly I attempted to chronicle life in a small town with tongue-in-cheek humor. Yesterday, I'd written half the column in my head while I tried to put Emily's late night into perspective. I found out from my friend Jan that Emily wasn't the only high school student who missed curfew Saturday night. I had a feeling several folks in Brewster would identify with my column next week. "Home Sweet Homecoming," I typed.

I paused, arranging the words in my mind in a way that wouldn't get any of the kids in trouble, focusing instead on parents' thoughts as they waited for a child late at night. The words flowed from my fingers, the column practically writing itself—a rare event indeed. Within forty-five minutes I had more than the basics down. I'd tweak it a bit over the next two days and e-mail it on Thursday. I clicked on the Save icon, staring at the words on the screen as they became imbedded in cyberspace. How many times had I sat in this very spot, staring at a blank screen, trying to write anything? My friend Anne probably knew the answer better than I did. She was the one who'd listened to my dreams of writing, listened to me lament my lack of imagination, and lack of discipline, and assured me that someday my dream of writing a book would come true. But then she died.

I pushed my chair away from the desk, marching into the kitchen to dump the cold drops of coffee left in my cup. I had to be at the school in fifteen minutes to pick up Emily. In Brewster we measured driving time in blocks. I had enough time to freshen up a bit before I left.

Powder, lipstick, a spritz of light cologne. That should do it. I caught a glimpse of myself in the full-length mirror as I left the master bathroom. My jeans and white shirt were fine for a day of writing, but rather bland for an errand around town. Even if it was just Brewster, I'd been raised to present a good image in public. Being a banker's daughter and now a banker's wife came with its own set of unwritten rules and looking presentable seemed to be one of them. I opened my dresser drawer and blindly grabbed at a scarf to tie around my neck. Most anything would match jeans. Interesting…I had the royal blue scarf in my hand—the one with bits of metallic silver thread woven in. The scarf Anne wrapped as my Christmas gift just before she died. The gift she never got to see me open or wear. Well, I'd wear it today.

I tied the blue scarf loosely around my neck, remembering the yellow winter scarf Anne had been wearing the first time I met her. I laughed now to think of how I had wanted to yank that scarf tighter around her neck, her natural friendliness a threat to the walls I'd built around myself over the years. I was so sure she would step in and take away the few friends I had. Little did I know that Anne was an expert at knocking down walls…or maybe I should say God was. He just used Anne.

I arranged the scarf, and then fluffed my hair. Anne had done so much more than break down my defenses. She'd shown me that friendship is a gift to be shared, not a possession that needs tight guarding. She also introduced me to a faith I'd never imagined. A faith that I was still trying to learn to live. Anne made it look so easy. It wasn't. I leaned into the mirror, wiping at the corner of my mouth with a tissue. There, ready to go.

I grabbed the keys and hurried to the car—now I was running late. Emily was probably pacing in front of the school. I should have told her to meet me at the clinic. She could easily have walked because it was closer to the school than our house was. Too late now.

Pray.

Where had that come from? I backed out of the driveway, a twinge of worry creasing my brow. I didn't have anything in my life to worry about. It was pretty much perfect. Unless you called a pimple a major catastrophe in the scheme of life. I chuckled. This whole incident might make a good *Wry Eye* column if Emily ever allowed me to write about it.

Pray.

What in the world—? I recognized the urgent command. I'd heard it often during Anne's illness, but at the time I hadn't known what to do about it. I did now. But pray for what?

Okay, Lord. I shifted into drive. *I have no idea why You want me to pray, but I will anyway.* I pressed on the gas pedal and headed toward the school. *I ask Your protection and blessing on this day.* Now what? I drove the three blocks to the school. I'd been right; Emily was there, pacing away. *And I guess give Emily courage because I know she's going to freak out if Dr. West needs to—*

"Where were you?" Emily jumped in the car and slammed the door. "I've got to hurry. Mr. Bender wants me to meet him in the band room during my study hall. He's got some new music he wants to give me to practice for Pumpkin Fest." She threw her backpack into the back seat. "I bet it's some of that stupid German music again." She rolled her eyes. Brewster's annual fall celebration was about as exciting to her as it had been to me when I was a junior. "You should see the cool jeans Jen is wearing today. She got them at Herberger's in Carlton and…"

Emily jabbered on as I drove to the clinic, reminding me of the little girl she used to be. The little girl who told me everything. In fact, Emily had helped forge the bond between Anne and me, reporting, after each piano lesson Anne had given her, all sorts of tidbits about this new woman in town who had seemed such a threat to me at the time. Emily loved her piano teacher and wasn't at all intimidated by my cool reception to her Anne Announcements, as I'd called her jabbering back then. What would our lives have been like if Emily hadn't brought us together?

I pulled up to the clinic, its familiar brown brick exterior bringing another flood of memories of Anne. How many times had I sat here with her while we waited to get just one more bad report on the progression of her cancer? I shook my head. Those days were in the past. Right now I needed to get Emily into her appointment and back to school.

"Emily Marsden?" A nurse led the way as Emily and I formed a short parade into Dr. West's office. "What seems to be the problem today?" The nurse opened Emily's thin file. Unlike her brother, Brian, whose minor medical mishaps had no doubt funded this exam room, Emily rarely entered Brewster's clinic. Other than mandatory shots and one case of bronchitis, Emily was a poster child of good health.

"This," I said, pushing Emily's short sleeve up her arm. I hoped the nurse wouldn't laugh that we'd come to the clinic for a pimple. I tried to give the nurse a look that communicated the gravity of a pimple to a teenager.

The nurse shot me a look back. "Hmm, I see." Was she biting the sides of her cheeks? She jotted a note in the file. *Overreactive mother,* no doubt. "Dr. West should be in in a moment."

I knew better than to believe that. I'd spent literally hours in doctor's exam rooms with Anne. We'd decided the words *in a moment* must translate into *light years* in the Official Doctor Dictionary. Anne and I had come up with all sorts of ways to pass the time while we waited. I resurrected one now. "Emily, what if..." I couldn't believe I was saying those words, repeating the words I'd come to dread every time I heard Anne say them. Anne would pose an innocent question to help pass the time, and I'd find myself pouring my guts out to her, telling her dreams and feelings I hardly knew I had, including my dream of someday writing a novel. Anne had challenged me to do just that when the doctor had said the awful words, "There's nothing more we can do for you."

"Put it in the book," she'd told me that same day. Her story. Our story. Cancer, friendship, and faith on paper. I was still struggling to make sense of that awful, glorious time. I'd found putting it all in a book about as easy as growing in the faith Anne had so effortlessly modeled.

"What if, what?" Leave it to Emily to zap me back to reality.

"What if..." I racked my brain, "...what if Brian called home and said he was engaged?"

Her eyes were like two pool balls rolling into the back of her head. "Get a grip, Mom. He doesn't even have a girlfriend."

The kid had a lot of her mother in her. I'd been the same way with Anne, rattling off a quick answer rather than taking the time to examine any emotions a question might cause. Anne never quit, and I didn't intend to either. "Well, what if he did? What if you had a sister-in-law?"

Her brow furrowed as she bit her lip. Obviously, the idea had never occurred to her. "I guess it'd be kind of cool. I mean, I've never had, like, a sister before." She paused. I could almost see her mind chewing on this new concept. Her eyes brightened. "What would be really cool is if we were the same size and we could trade clothes and stuff! But, man, it would be weird to have Brian at home with like, a *wife*."

Suddenly I was the one biting my lip. I'd never quite thought about *that*. I wasn't sure I wanted to. My stomach tightened. Brian with a wife? Who had started this dumb game anyway? No wonder I always groaned when Anne started in on her questions. Where was Dr. West, anyway?

As if in answer to my desperate thought, I heard a rustling outside the door. "Olivia, hello!" Ellen West wrapped me in a hug. "It's been much too long." Anne had christened me Libby, a name that had made me cringe at the time. Now it seemed odd to have my old friends still call me Olivia. Too formal for the person I'd become since my friendship with Anne. "Hello, Emily." Ellen rubbed her hand across Emily's shoulder, then sat on the stool by her desk. "How's Brian?"

"Doing great," I answered. Ellen had a son, Pete, the same age as Brian. They'd given us a scare and a quick education when they were high school freshmen, getting involved in a little-known drug fad called huffing. Thanks to Anne's faith in him, Brian put that episode behind him. Pete, however, continued to struggle. I almost was afraid to ask… "What about Pete?"

Ellen waved her hand in the air. "We're taking it a day at a time. He says he's clean and he's got a job, so that's the good news." She tapped a hand on the file she'd carried into the room. "It says here you've got a pimple on your arm, Emily. Can I take a look?"

Emily nodded, pulling up her sleeve. "It's been there for a while. I mean, I just kind of thought it would go away, you know? But it hasn't, and sometimes it kind of hurts and—" I couldn't tell whether she was using her words to cover nerves or embarrassment. Probably both.

Dr. West scooted her stool over to Emily and peered at the small lump. "Hmmm." She ran the side of her thumb over Emily's arm, watching as the lump stood firm. "Jump up on the table." Dr. West was all business as she patted the exam table. She pulled a lamp over and turned it on, shining it on Emily's arm. The lump didn't look so small now. How could I have thought it was a little pimple?

"Is it a boil?" I was trying to make it be something simple. *Lord, please.*

Ellen didn't answer my inane question; instead, she fingered the lump, gazing off into a corner of the exam room as if she were palpating her brain for an answer. A cold knife of worry dissected my stomach. Say something.

With the fingers of both hands Dr. West pushed at the sides of the mass, her focused concentration scaring me. Finally, she spoke, more to herself than me. "This is not a pimple. It's a tumor."

Ocean waves crashed in my ears. I was being pulled down by a fierce undertow, drowning in three small words. *It's a tumor.*

No! With leaden arms I grabbed my knees. No! It couldn't be. I'd seen what Anne had endured. I was by her bed as she recovered from surgery. I went with her to chemo treatments and watched nurses poke thick needles into her arms. The dead, gray skin that had resulted from her radiation treatments still haunted my dreams. This could not be happening. It simply could *not.*

"No!" I didn't mean to say the word out loud, but I must have. Ellen stood by my side, her hand steady on my back. I wasn't the kind of woman given to loud expressions of emotion, but suddenly I understood the wails of grief I had seen on news reports from foreign countries. I wished I lived anywhere but here. I wanted to throw my head back and scream, to heave my body over Emily as if the gesture alone could change things.

"Olivia, look at me." Ellen's voice was firm, her calm tone turning my head as if she'd grasped it herself. "I know what you're thinking." She did. She knew exactly what had happened to Anne. I'd told her, more than once.

"You need to understand that not all tumors are malignant. This could very well be what we call a fatty tumor. Nothing more than a lump of benign tissue." With her foot she hooked her stool and pulled it close to me. She sat down, taking my hands in hers. "It's small enough that I think I can remove it now. Emily will have nothing but a couple stitches in her arm."

Emily. I'd been so caught up in my thoughts I'd forgotten about Emily sitting right there, her mouth partially open, her eyes wide as Dr. West talked about tumors and stitches. "Mo-om?" she said now, the word more question than worry.

"It'll be fine." The words spilled from some hidden vocabulary vault that had opened out of nowhere. "You're going to be just fine." I felt anything but fine, but for Emily's sake I pasted a small smile on my face and said to Ellen, "Do it."

The next minutes were a blur as a nurse came in and had Emily slip out of her shirt and into a hospital gown. As quickly, she laid out a tray of surgical instruments and then vanished. I wished I could do the same.

Dr. West came back into the room, explaining as she moved just what would happen next. I wanted to plug my ears. Emily acted as though it were a demonstration in science class, craning her neck to watch as Ellen cleansed the spot and injected the numbing medication. I looked away; Emily was glued to the performance as if it were an episode of *Fear Factor*.

"There. All done." Dr. West snipped the last thread of the four stitches. "We'll send the tissue to the lab and have the results tomorrow." She stood by the open door. "Emily, you might want to go home and relax the rest of the morning. You can go back to school this afternoon if you feel like it. Make sure you don't bump your arm on anything, though. Olivia, I'll call you. Don't worry."

Back to school? Emily could go back to school? Was Ellen kidding? I wanted to drive Emily home and lock her in the house, throw soft blankets over her, and feed her warm milk. Well, Mountain Dew, anyway. Anything to make her feel better, to keep her safe.

"Mom, let's go. I can probably still get that music from Mr. Bender." She winced as she climbed into the car, sending a chill right through me. I now understood why doctors didn't operate on their own family members. I could hardly look at Emily without flinching.

She might as well not even have a bandage on—I felt as if I could see right through it.

Emily wouldn't hear of going home. She was going back to school, and that's all there was to it. She jumped out of the car and ran into the school, no worse for wear. I, however, needed a long vacation. A massage. A clunk on the head. Something that would stop the memories of Anne's last days from taking over my brain, something that would stop inserting Emily's face in place of Anne's as she lay dying of cancer.

I turned into the driveway, the house I'd left hardly an hour ago, belonging to a different woman now. A woman whose daughter might have cancer. I knew what Anne would tell me to do. *Start praying.* I planned to, as soon as I quit worrying.

Emily

The way Mom was acting, you'd think we won the lottery or something. First she called me at school, right in the middle of choir, to tell me the tests had come back negative. Then she made my favorite supper—creamed chicken and dumplings, corn, and a chocolate cake. Good grief. I mean, I was sitting right there when Dr. West said, "Don't worry." So I didn't. Apparently Mom did.

At least the kids at school were cool about it. My appointment with Dr. West hadn't taken much longer than the study hall I would have normally been in, so no one seemed to notice I'd been gone. If they did, they probably thought I had a pass to the library.

"Why'd you leave choir?" Mike slid in across from me in the lunchroom, opening his carton of milk and downing half of it. Didn't guys know the word *sip*?

I cut a small bite of the pepperoni pizza on my plate. All of a sudden I wasn't that hungry. I kept seeing that sharp knife-thing Dr. West had used to cut into my arm. I pushed the pizza slice around with my fork. "My mom called. I had to go to the doctor yesterday."

"What for?" Mike asked, pushing three-quarters of a pizza slice into his mouth. If I wasn't hungry before, he wasn't helping matters any.

"I had a thing on my arm." The image of the jawbreaker-sized glob Dr. West had taken from my arm sort of hung over my plate. I set my fork down.

"Are you okay?" Mike stopped chewing.

"Yeah," I said, a finger of relief walking down my back for the first time. "That's why I left choir. My mom called to tell me everything was fine." It hadn't bothered me one bit to watch Dr. West operate on my arm. It had been numb, so it was kind of like watching a video in health class or something. It was only afterward, when the numbness started wearing off, that I started thinking about what had happened. I kind of wished I'd gone home and rested like Mom had suggested. At least for the rest of the morning, anyway.

"Well, I'm glad everything's okay." Mike started chewing again. "You know, if you'd have told me about it, I could have been praying."

Leave it to Mike to bring that up. I knew I should have been praying last night, asking God that nothing would be wrong with my arm, asking that this additional blow to my volleyball season wouldn't cut me from the team for next year, too, or asking God to help Mom chill out at the very least. But by the time I'd done my homework and instant messaged Jen for an hour, I was too tired to concentrate on much of a prayer. Jen told me that Rick stopped her in the hall at school and asked her when my birthday was. Too bad it was seven months away in April. I fell asleep wondering what Rick would get me for a gift.

And besides, I knew my mom was praying enough for the both of us.

Libby

The tests were benign. Emily was fine! If I had any kind of voice at all, I would have been out in the street singing my little rhyme at the top of my lungs. As it was I did a quick impromptu jig in my kitchen and then called Bob to tell him the news.

"Great," he said, relief flooding his voice. "That's great." I could tell by his tone he was distracted. "I'm in a meeting right now. I'll get the details tonight." His attention had already shifted.

I hung up the phone, a twinge of irritation dampening my joy for a moment. I had hoped to meet Bob for lunch to celebrate the good news. That wasn't going to happen. At least he'd taken the call. Not long ago, banking came before everything else. Bob's job was still near the top of the list, but Anne's death had impacted him, too. He did his best to juggle being a husband and dad with his career. His job as CEO of the banks in Brewster and Carlton was demanding, not to mention the community volunteer positions that seemed to come with the territory. Bob had convinced the board to hire a separate manager for the Brewster office. Even though Bob was still the CEO, bringing Paul Bennett home to Brewster from his high-powered investment banking career in Chicago had freed up a lot of the day-to-day, hands-on decisions that had monopolized much of Bob's time. I knew Bob had the best interests of our family at heart. The fact that Bob had told his assistant to put my call through said volumes about how he'd changed.

I refilled my coffee cup, sitting for a moment to relive the good news about Emily. I sighed. *Thank You, Lord.* A twinge of shame rested on my neck. I should have had more faith. I should have spent more time praying instead of worrying. Would I ever learn to turn these things over to God instead of fretting my way through a long night?

I shook off my regret. I could still celebrate His answer to the few meager prayers I'd managed. I picked up the phone and hit the speed dial for my friend Jan.

"Hi, Jan! Can you do lunch today?"

"I'd love to." She was out of breath as usual. Jan did everything at a frantic pace, including talk. "But I have a hair appointment with Jacob in forty-five minutes, and then I have to pick up Joey from school and drive him over to Carlton for an eye appointment. And to top it all off, Dan is having an open house tomorrow, and I promised I'd bake bars for it. And then there's to-niiight!" By her lilting inflection I knew what she meant.

And for me, that meant no. Jan had spent several years after her divorce as a single mom, raising her son, Joey, by herself. About three years ago, she had married long-time bachelor Dan Jordan, Brewster's only real estate "magnet," as Dan had a habit of saying. She had made no secret of the fact they were trying to have a baby. I tried not to mind her enthusiasm over her new life, but in Brewster there weren't all that many women to be friends with. Especially women who were home during the day as I was. After Anne died, I'd grown to appreciate Jan's spontaneous style of friendship, but today there was apparently no room for me.

"Soon then," I said, not feeling like sharing my relief about Emily over the phone.

Undeterred, I dialed Connie's number.

"Connie? Are you free for lunch today?" I asked, hoping I didn't sound too anxious.

"Olivia, any other time this week would work, but not today." Typical Connie—no excuses, no regrets. I often wondered why I kept trying. With Connie, friendship was on her terms or no terms. But Anne had taught me that God never gave up, which is probably why I kept trying. He kept poking me.

I dialed my friend in Carlton, Katie Jeffries, but got the answering machine. She was a substitute teacher. Who knew where she was today? I hung up without leaving a message, my excitement fading by the minute. I was not going to let this good news pass without marking the day in some way. I pulled a cookbook from the shelf. A chocolate cake said celebration without words.

The cake in the oven, I turned on my computer, thinking I'd use the thirty minutes to pound out a page or two of my novel, but I hadn't written a word by the time the buzzer rang. I pulled the two round pans from the oven, put them on a cooling rack, and sat back down in front of the screen, determined to write something. Instead, Ellen West's call replayed in my head.

"Olivia, I've got good news." Thank goodness Ellen didn't beat around the bush. The few hours I'd slept the night before had been filled with odd dreams. Lying awake and waiting for dawn hadn't been much better. I almost spilled my coffee when the phone rang. "The tests came back negative."

That was all I'd really heard. But now, the rest of what she'd said played in my mind.

"Emily's fine," she'd said, her voice sure. "The lab tests all came back negative." That part I'd heard loud and clear. The rest of her words only now began to filter through. "There were some signs of cell changes. If these aren't caught early, they can mutate into cancer cells. But we got it in plenty of time; the margins were completely clear. Emily is fine."

Mutate? Cancer? A flash of panic coursed through me. I couldn't go through this again. I just couldn't. Why was it I'd heard only the good news?

Because that was the news. She's fine.

But what if she wasn't? What if there were some stray cells? What if they were mutating right now?

Give this to Me.

No. I didn't want to give this to God. I was the mom. It was my job to take care of my child, to protect her.

Protect her with your worry? I'm the Father.

I know.

Give this to Me. She's fine.

I breathed deeply, a surrender of sorts. I didn't think I could give it all to God, but I could try to let Him have part of my worry. *Okay, God, take it. It's Yours. Most of it anyway.*

I slipped out of the chair, determined to celebrate somehow. I'd make creamed chicken and dumplings for dinner. Emily's favorite. I went downstairs and pulled a chicken from the freezer, popping it in the microwave to start thawing. The dumplings could wait until later. Maybe the fact that no one could meet me for lunch was good; I'd work on my novel. I wasn't all that far from finishing it. A few good weeks of writing and I might actually be able to type "The End."

Then what?

Interesting question. Then what? The novel I'd dreamed of writing since I was ten would be done. What would I do when my dream was complete? I shifted in my chair, suddenly feeling empty rather than satisfied.

Why couldn't I ever just enjoy the moment? Why did I always have to worry about what's next?

Really, to anyone looking, my life was perfect. Absolutely perfect. I sat back in my chair, plucking at my blessings like daisy petals. I had a hardworking and handsome husband who made an income we'd never dared to imagine back in our early years. We could pay our bills in full every month. We had two great kids. Brian routinely made the Dean's List; Emily, too, was an honor student. We were all in perfect health. Yes, even Emily. Even our teeth had had no cavities this past year. I didn't have to work, so I had all the time in the world to pursue my writing. I had a close friendship with Katie Jeffries and Jan, and several other friendships were growing.

If it hadn't been *my* life I was reviewing, I might have gagged. Instead, I squirmed. Who was I to deserve all this? Why was I given this life of luxury when so many others had to struggle? I thought of my neighbor across the street, Ida Bauer. She'd been widowed for years and had to be in her eighties, and yet she still worked now and then at the local café. She'd told me more than once, in her German brogue, that her social security check didn't make the ends meet. Why did I have more than enough when she had so little?

I shook my head. Why couldn't I ever accept the gifts God had given me? Why did they chafe at me like cheap underwear instead of the pearls they were? Why did…

A beep from the microwave stopped my thoughts midstream. Thank goodness. I pushed away from my desk and hurried to the kitchen. Cutting up a chicken was a welcome diversion.

I pushed the sharp knife between the leg and the thigh joint, determined to change my mood. I was supposed to be preparing for a celebration. Emily was fine. I ran the knife down the breast bone, slicing away the tender meat. Emily was just fine.

So why did I feel a nagging sensation that something was wrong?

Emily

Something was wrong with Mom. It seemed like ever since I'd had that lump taken off my arm, Mom had been acting weird. One minute she'd be perfectly normal, and the next she'd be sniping like Sami from *Days of Our Lives*. For over a month I walked on eggshells. After school, all I did was ask if I could stay out later with Rick after Pumpkin Fest. You'd think I'd asked to move to Yugoslavia or something.

"No!" she'd snapped. I knew enough not to push it. I went to my room and turned on my radio. Loud. Listening to Mike play country music on Brewster's only radio station was better than waiting for Mom to get over whatever was bugging her.

I flopped on my bed and flipped open my English lit book. Maybe I'd read ahead. We really didn't have assignments for tomorrow, and volleyball practice had been cancelled for Pumpkin Fest. Classes would be casual as kids came and went, fulfilling their duties at Brewster's annual celebration. Most of the high school kids would be involved in one way or another. I would be playing piano while the choir sang in the afternoon. Mike was lucky—he was excused from school all day so he could help Ruthie Hammond do a remote broadcast live from Brewster's Civic Center. Whatever. Everyone in Brewster knew it was just the old high school gym with a fancy name.

I knew the afternoon would be a drag. Singing old German songs to a bunch of retired farmers was not cool, but at least it was an hour out of school. All I really cared about was walking around Pumpkin Fest after supper with Rick. It was a dumb celebration, but what else could we do in Brewster? All the kids would be there. And they'd see me walking around with Rick. It was going to be so cool. I doodled a tiny heart in the margin of my lit book.

"Emily?" Mom knocked on my bedroom door and came in. Quickly I turned the page, pretending I was busy studying. I was still mad about how she'd snapped at me when I'd asked to stay out later after Pumpkin Fest. "Are you studying?" she asked.

I knew she was trying to make up for yelling at me, but I wasn't going to make it that easy. She could have at least considered my request instead of just snapping, "No!"

She sat on the edge of my bed and rubbed my shoulder. "I'm sorry, I—well, let's just say it's been a bad day." She kind of sighed. "I talked to your dad, and you can stay out an extra hour after Pumpkin Fest. How's that?"

One hour, big deal. Pumpkin Fest was always the last Friday in October. It wasn't like it was a school night. But after the way she'd acted before, I didn't dare beg for more. That probably wasn't a good time to bring up the idea I had for getting my belly button pierced, either. I shrugged my shoulders. "Okay."

It was dumb, but I couldn't help it. I was excited to be at Pumpkin Fest. Two old men sat on the stage, one playing the accordion and the other tapping out the rhythm on a trap set, brushing the cymbal much too often. Every song they played sounded the same, kind of like the German songs the choir had sung in the afternoon. I called the tune the Mangled Polka.

I stood at the top of the five broad steps leading down into the old gym, surveying the mass of people wandering through the maze of craft and business booths that lined the gym like corn rows. Rick had said he'd be there. But where? Mostly I saw a field of farmers' caps and white heads. I squinted, finally picking out kids from school in the crowd, too.

"Emily!" Jen waved me over to the long line of people waiting to buy a slice of pumpkin pie. She and Ryan shuffled back to make room for me. "Mike will be here in a sec." Mike? She knew full well Mike wasn't the one I was waiting for. "He's gotta stay at the station until Ruthie signs KBRS off the air for the night from here. Then he said he'd be right over."

I could see Ruthie Hammond pulling down the KBRS sign from her booth. Even if I did tease Mike about playing country music at Brewster's dinky radio station, I still thought it was pretty cool that he got to be a disc jockey now and then. Not many sixteen-year-olds could say that. On a night like tonight, though, he had to stay at the station and work the main controls for the remote broadcast. At least that's how he'd explained it to me. The station went off the air at sunset, and now that daylight savings time had ended, Brewster was dark by suppertime. I was surprised Mike wasn't here already.

I'd offered to do the supper dishes so I wouldn't have to ride to Pumpkin Fest with Mom and Dad. Rick had said he might see me there, and I didn't want to make it look like all I was doing was waiting for him. The night was cool, but I'd walked, hoping Rick would offer to drive me home. If I was a little late and Rick was waiting for me, that would be okay.

But here I was. Where was Rick?

"There he is." Jen waved as the pie line inched forward.

I put a big smile on my face and turned, but it was only Mike. "Hi." I wiggled my fingers at him as he took the place behind me in line that Jen had been saving for him.

"Did you hear any of the broadcast? I thought it went great!" Mike was scanning the crowd as if he expected KBRS fans to be rushing him for autographs.

I used to think Mike had the greatest job in the world, but eventually I figured out that in Brewster, every job was just a job. No big deal. I was even thinking about getting a job myself. The two-month football season was over, along with my stats job, and all the time I'd sat on the volleyball bench hadn't exactly drained my energy. Girls' basketball would start soon, but even then, unless there was a game, I had free time every weekend. Time I could be earning gas money, or at least enough to buy those cute jeans at the mall that my mom said cost way too much. The line moved forward about three inches. "I think I should get a job." At least it was something to talk about while we waited.

"*You?*" Ryan sounded like he'd swallowed a cow. "Your dad is president of the *bank*. You don't have to work."

Jen elbowed him.

I hated Ryan's attitude. Everyone seemed to think that just because my dad worked in a bank, we had free access to the vault or something. Like I could walk in and grab a wad of cash anytime I felt like it. My dad got a paycheck like everyone else in town. Sure, maybe it was a little bit bigger than some—I didn't know for sure— but we lived just like everyone else. And my parents didn't hand over money just because I was the banker's daughter.

It wasn't like I'd never worked before, either. The past two summers I'd helped out at the bank. Dad had me come down and do odd jobs part-time. Filing, stuffing statements in envelopes, even cleaning the bathrooms when they were between janitors. If anyone thought banking was a hot-shot career, they should ask me. I knew better. Dad didn't even pay me minimum wage. He said he didn't want people to think he was pulling rank. They just needed an extra pair of hands over the summer while people went on vacation. He said it would "build my character." I didn't know about that, but even the little bit he did pay me built my bank account. For a while anyway.

"Are you going to work at the bank again?" Jen asked as we took two giant steps toward the pie table.

At least Jen took me seriously. I shrugged my shoulders. "Probably not." Now that my dad was working in the Carlton office, it would feel weird to work in the Brewster bank without him there. "I was thinking of applying at the nursing home." A lot of kids thought working at the retirement home in town was gross, as if old people were aliens or something. But I knew some of the older people from church who lived there, and they seemed normal to me. Just old. What was wrong with that?

"I hope they pay good." As if to illustrate his point, Mike pulled a ten-dollar bill from his pocket. "My treat," Mike said as we finally had our turn to buy pie.

"Hi!" Angie Johnson stood behind the pie table. Her mom owned Vicky's Café, so Angie had a permanent job for Pumpkin Fest, selling slices of her mom's pie. She was a seventh grader and in our church's youth group. Our church wasn't that big, so we had to combine the senior high kids and the junior high kids to have enough people to call it a group. "How many pieces?" she asked. "Anything to drink? Pop? Coffee?" She giggled, her face flushing. "Well, I suppose not coffee." I could tell Angie was kind of embarrassed to be waiting on four juniors.

"Four pieces," Mike said. "And four Cokes." Mr. Big Spender.

"*Your* job must pay pretty good," Jen said to Mike as she tried to balance a paper plate of pie, a fork, and her pop.

Mike nodded. "Since Jack left the station, I've been getting more hours. It's nice in the old pocket, that's for sure." Mike patted his wallet like he was Donald Trump. I rolled my eyes. *Nice in the old pocket?* Sometimes Mike sounded like he was thirty years old.

We made our way up to the top of the bleachers, detouring around Miss Quinn, Brewster's fifth-grade teacher, and Paul Bennett, the new guy who worked for my dad. I hadn't met him, but I knew who he was. I thought he was kind of cute for an older guy.

Speaking of cute, I scanned the crowd, looking for Rick. Even if I did see him, I didn't know if I'd have the nerve to call him over to sit with us. We never had gone to the movie he'd mentioned the night of the homecoming dance. Rick had called and said his dad needed help harvesting their soybean crop. But he had said in school this afternoon that he might see me here. I made sure I sat facing the gym floor so that Rick could spot me. If he was looking, that is.

It wasn't hard to pretend I wasn't looking for Rick; even Mike, Jen, and Ryan scanned the crowded gym as we talked. It wasn't often this many people were together in Brewster at one time. It was exciting in some strange way.

Oh! My fork stopped halfway to my mouth. There he was! All six feet, two inches, one hundred seventy-five pounds of him, according to the football program. I shoved the bite of pie into my mouth if for no other reason than to keep from groaning. He was so cute!

"Are Rick and Hannah getting back together?" Mike asked, his eyes obviously taking in more than mine.

Sure enough, Rick was standing by the Cal's Hardware Store booth, talking to his old girlfriend, Hannah. At least I hoped she was his *old* girlfriend. Neither one of them were smiling. A good sign in my opinion. Hannah reached out and put her hand on Rick's arm. She wasn't begging him to come back to her, was she? Rick shook off her hand and walked away. Good.

Now, if only he would look up into the bleachers. I sat up straight so he could see me if he looked, trying to appear as though Jen, Ryan, Mike, and I were having a blast. Like I wasn't wishing I had a super-strong magnet that would pull Rick my way. I tried to pretend I was totally engrossed in whatever it was Jen was blabbing about.

"…and then my mom said, 'Young lady, you—"

"Rick! Hi-ii!" I stood up and waved, I couldn't help it. He was walking right by the bleachers.

Rick stopped and looked around, not sure in the crowded gym just where his name was being called from.

"Up here!" I waved the plastic fork in my right hand. That was dumb. I stuck the fork in my mouth and waved again. Good grief, that was dumber yet. I looked like an overeager seventh grader. With a fork in her mouth. *Calm down.* I sat down and grabbed the fork out of my mouth just as Rick's eyes found mine. A big grin covered his face. He bounded up the bleachers like he was in some slow-motion movie scene when the hero finally finds the girl he's been looking for all his life.

"There you are." Rick sat down right beside me as if there weren't five feet of empty bleacher next to him. My heart started a double-time drum beat as he curved his arm around my waist, leaning into me. "I've been looking for you." I could feel his warm words fall on my hot cheek. Being super happy felt a lot like being embarrassed.

"Here I am," I said, my voice surprisingly calm—nothing like my insides.

"Do you want to go walk around? Look at the booths?" Rick acted like Jen, Mike, and Ryan weren't even there. As if I were the only person in the whole gym and Pumpkin Fest was just for us.

I wasn't sure if my legs would hold, but I stood up, handing my pie plate and fork to Jen as though it were a bridal bouquet and she were my maid of honor. "Sure," I said.

As he headed down the bleachers, I turned and widened my eyes at my friends. *Can you believe this?* Ryan wasn't even looking at me, but Jen bugged her eyes right back at me. Mike gave me a flat stare, then looked away. What*ever.* Guys just didn't get things like this.

Rick grabbed my hand, threading me slowly through the crowd, leading the way with his confident stride. He stopped by the State Bank of Brewster booth where a sign read, Guess and Win. There was a large jar filled with coins sitting on the table. "Want to make a guess?" Rick asked, his eyes crinkling at the corners.

It looked like a simple game, but I wondered if anyone ever thought about how those coins got in there? Or how they would get out? I knew. Two summers ago, when I'd worked at the bank, the staff had done a similar promotion for a Dog Daze of Summer event one weekend. I'd been the one assigned to unwrap rolls of coins and fill the jar. By the time the jar was full, my hands were black from the coins, mostly dirty pennies. I could hardly lift the jar. That day I learned that money was heavy. Even then it seemed like a cool game until the kid who won it brought the jar back in on Monday. His dad had to carry it for him. The Brewster bank didn't have an automatic coin counter, so guess who got assigned to count and rewrap all the coins?

"No," I said to Rick. I wasn't about to make a guess at this game. For one thing, I didn't think it would be fair if I won, my dad being president and all. And for another, even if I did win, I wouldn't want to be the one to make a bank teller count it all. All forty-two dollars and one cent of it. I still remembered the amount that fit in there, counting the penny I'd found on the floor. "I think it's called insider information or something."

"Is it okay if I guess?" Rick asked. "I mean since I'm with you and all?" I nodded as Rick scribbled his name on the tablet, adding his estimate of thirty-seven dollars and one cent. Could he read my mind? How could he know about the extra penny...missing the total by exactly five dollars?

"Having fun?" Leave it to my mom to burst my perfect bubble. Somehow parents and romance didn't seem to mix. Dad stepped behind the bank booth, pulling more brochures from a box and placing them on the table. Mom straightened the ones that were already there. A swell of pride filled my chest. Dad looked just like you'd imagine a bank president would look. Tall. Distinguished. Honest, too. Mom was pretty, no question. She didn't look at all like she had last night when she'd hollered at me. I didn't know what was up with her lately. One minute she was the mom she'd always been, and the next she'd turn into her own evil twin. I was worried, but about what I didn't have a clue.

Dad checked the schedule of bank staff that had signed up to man the booth. "Peggy will be here in fifteen minutes," he reported. "I'll sit here until she comes. Olivia, if you want to go look around for a bit, go ahead." I knew they weren't worried about anyone stealing the money jar—it was way too heavy for any likely suspect to run off with in this crowd. But, as Dad always said, knowing your customers was important in banking. I was sure he wanted to sit there and talk to people as they walked by.

"No," Mom answered, her voice weird. Nervous-like. "I'll stay here."

"We're going to go look around," I said, anxious to get away before Mom said anything about my curfew. It would make me sound like Cinderella.

"You didn't guess, did you, Emily?" My dad pointed to the money jar.

I shook my head. All my life I'd been told not to register for prizes at Pumpkin Fest or any other city-wide event. *How would it look if the banker's daughter won? There are other people in town who need those prizes more than you.* I could repeat his instructions word for word. Now that I was older I understood his reasoning, but when I was little I hadn't. More than once I'd stomped away from a booth as my dad's words sat on my conscience like a mean angel, taking away my fun.

"You two enjoy yourselves," Dad said as he and Mom settled in behind the table.

I could feel my face flush. *You two?* All I needed was for Rick to think I'd been talking about him like he was my boyfriend or something. I stepped away from the table, but Rick stood still. "Would it be all right if I gave Emily a ride home after this is over?"

My head whipped around like a Tilt-a-Whirl at the fair. Had I heard right? Rick was asking my parents if he could give me a ride home? I couldn't stop a big grin from plastering my face. If I was Cinderella, he was Prince Charming.

Dad glanced at me, then nodded once. "It looks like it's okay with Emily. Just get her home on time."

For once I didn't even mind Dad's reminder. I'd be riding home with Rick! Never in all my dreaming about Pumpkin Fest had I imagined it would end like this. It was like some syrupy but wonderful scene in a romance novel.

Rick rested a hand on my shoulder, his muscular arm a warm weight across my back as we walked through the aisles. We passed Jen, Ryan, and Mike registering for prizes at the drugstore booth, and not even for one second did I wish I could sign up, too.

Rick leaned in close, his breath falling into my ear. "How's my girl?"

Goosebumps tickled my neck. *His girl?*

This was the best Pumpkin Fest ever.

I simply smiled my answer. It seemed much too corny to say, "Perfect. Perfect. Perfect."

Pumpkin Fest had been a nightmare. Until that night, I had easily dismissed the odd, vague symptoms I'd been having ever since the episode with the lump on Emily's arm. The sudden pounding of my heart. A surreal dizziness that struck at the slightest turn of my head. A moodiness that extended far beyond PMS. The first few times they happened, I shrugged them off. I didn't require psychotherapy to understand that some of what I'd been feeling was a delayed reaction to the possibility that Emily might have had a cancerous tumor. Deep down, I knew there were many emotions I'd buried over the years…feelings about my dad's death from cancer when I was a teenager, emotions over Anne's death I'd never let out in the light. I assumed, given time, I'd be stuffing Emily's scare right on top of everything else. I was trying.

But since Pumpkin Fest, I knew something was wrong with me. I walked into the laundry room and lifted the lid of the washer, pulling wet clothes from inside and transferring them quickly into the dryer. My heart was doing the same odd dance it had been doing off and on for weeks. I tried ignoring the thumping in my chest, picking up the crumpled pile of dark clothes lying at my feet and pushing them into the washer. Maybe this wasn't a delayed reaction to Emily's scare. What if something was wrong with my heart? Just the thought sent it racing again. I stood straight, breathing deep, trying to calm myself. Surely I was too young to have a heart attack. But then again, a person reads strange stories about things like that every day. Middle-Aged Mother Found Dead In Dirty Laundry. Even through my worry I could see the humor, but it didn't make me feel any better. I wondered how long I would have to lie in front of my dryer if I collapsed?

My symptoms hadn't started at Pumpkin Fest, but that night was the first time they'd threatened to overwhelm me. Just walking in the door of the Civic Center sent my heart thumping as though I'd stepped into enemy territory. I felt almost paralyzed as I took in the sheer number of people. People who would expect me to make intelligent chitchat.

Bob had tapped me on the shoulder, unfreezing me with his touch, to introduce me to Paul Bennett, his new manager of the bank in Brewster.

"Have you met my wife, Olivia?" It amazed me that Bob could sound so normal when I felt like bolting out the door we'd just entered.

Automatically, I stuck out my hand. "Paul Bennett," I managed to say, repeating his name as though I'd never heard it before, although, of course, I had. I'd been about five years ahead of Paul at Brewster High, not so much knowing him as knowing of him. His mother and I crossed paths frequently around town. She'd kept me updated over the years as to Paul's whereabouts. I didn't have the inclination to chat about that just now, but from somewhere in the recesses of my upbringing, good manners kicked in, overriding my intense discomfort. "Bob's spoken very highly of you. It's good to have you back in Brewster." I managed to smile. At least I hoped it looked like a smile.

"I hear you wrote a book," he said.

My eyes darted to Bob. He'd told Paul I'd written a book? Bob was standing beside me, a proud look on his face. If only he knew how I'd struggled with words lately. The last time we'd talked about my writing, I'd told him I was almost done with the book I'd dreamt of writing for years. "A couple chapters and I'll be done," I'd said weeks ago. But in the past weeks a mental lethargy I could only describe as slogging through Jell-O had taken over my brain. Writing had proven impossible. But I wasn't about to detail my problems to Paul Bennett at Pumpkin Fest. It was easier to simply agree. "Yes. I did," I responded. I hoped almost-done counted for something.

"Congratulations."

I ducked my head. "It's not published yet." There. At least he wouldn't be looking for it on any bookshelves in the near future.

"Well," Bob said, putting his hand in the small of my back, "I guess we'd better join the fray."

I'd almost forgotten that I had a whole evening of socializing to get through. An unknown fear prickled my arms, causing my fingers to tingle as if they were bloodless. How was I ever going to get through three more hours of this?

I shook my head, chasing away the memory of Pumpkin Fest night and the fear that had gripped me. I pushed the dryer start button, sending the clothes into a dizzy tumble. I'd been worried about living through three hours. Those hours had turned into weeks consumed by an unspoken fear and tears that threatened to tumble from my eyes at the slightest blink. Even Bob had noticed, suggesting more than once that I go see Dr. West.

"Olivia," he'd said just the other night, firm in a tone he usually reserved for reluctant loan customers, "if I were feeling the way you say you are, you'd be hounding me to get to the doctor." He stopped, leveling his eyes at mine. "Now I'm telling you."

As much as I resisted the idea of trying to explain my vague symptoms to my doctor and friend, the thought of her input was tempting. But spilling my guts, even to a friend, wasn't my style. I'd get over this, whatever it was...eventually. On my own.

I tugged at the washer knob, sending water flowing into the basket, feeling the burn of unshed tears sting my eyes. This line of thinking was getting me nowhere. I grabbed my car keys from the top of the fridge and walked into the garage. Grocery shopping would keep my mind occupied. Thanksgiving was in two days, and even though the turkey was already thawing in the fridge, I had a shopping list a mile long.

I started the car, shifted into reverse, and glanced into the rear-view mirror. Oh! I'd forgotten to put up the garage door! Quickly I jabbed at the remote, watching as the rising door filled the garage with hazy, winter-morning light. If I didn't get my mind off my pounding heart, I was going to be a danger to more than just me. I carefully backed out of the garage, stopping before the sidewalk and checking both sides to make sure little Erika Frank was nowhere near. All clear. I glided out of the driveway, shifted into drive, and started down the quiet street. A light layer of icy snow lined the road. No wonder none of the neighbors were outside. It was freezing.

Pellets of rice-like crystals tapped at my windshield, sending my heart into overdrive. What if this weather lasted through tomorrow? Brian's last class ended tomorrow at three. He'd be on the road nearly four hours, driving home for Thanksgiving break. The sun would be setting while he drove home, so any melted ice would refreeze. The roads could be even worse by tomorrow than they were now. Once again my heart took up its crazy beat. Worry had become a companion beside me.

As I the neared the stop sign at the intersection that led to Brewster's only grocery store, Magner's, I tapped on my brake pedal, testing the traction. The car began a shimmy-like dance as I tried to steer a straight line, pumping the brake in an effort to stop before I glided onto Brewster's main street, the highway that bisected the town. It was a road frequented by older drivers cruising well under the speed limit, watching for no one, and by cattle trucks that barreled through, not bothering to slow down for our seemingly sleepy town.

I steered to the left, trying to correct my crooked slide toward the intersection. The big Brewster garbage truck lumbered past my windshield, far enough away to do no damage, close enough to coat my palms with an icy sweat. I stomped on the brake as the driver of an empty school bus swerved to avoid my skid past the stop sign.

The car slid onto the highway, my efforts at stopping useless. I gripped the wheel with both hands, determined to hang on to something firm.

Lord, help!

The car did a three-quarter spin, coming to a jolting stop in the middle of the road. I was facing the wrong direction, looking straight into the eyes of Mr. Ost, an older gentleman who could often be found driving around Brewster at two miles an hour in his 1974

Chrysler New Yorker—an armored tank compared to what I drove. He slowly waved his hand for me to continue on as if he'd stopped in the middle of the highway just to watch the show. Well, maybe he had. Goodness knows, I'd performed.

I felt as if I should shift gears or something, but all it took to get back on my way was to shift my toes from the brake to the gas pedal. For once my heart seemed to be pounding at an appropriate rate for the conditions. I actually had reason to be afraid this time. I felt normal, even though I could have crashed.

My feeling of normalcy lasted only long enough for me to glide into a parking spot in front of Magner's and walk into the store. The unexplained apprehension I'd felt at Pumpkin Fest had returned as I took a shopping cart and headed for the canned goods aisle. Crowded shelves lined the space. Colors and labels and brand names I couldn't begin to decipher appeared to jump out at me. How could I possibly shop? I couldn't tell one label from the next. There were too many choices. Too much confusion. Where had this feeling come from?

What was happening to me? I took a deep breath. Cranberries. Yes, I would look for cranberries. Red. That's what I'd look for. A label that was red. How much red food could there be? A lot, it turned out. Tomato soup, tomato sauce, kidney beans. My eyes scanned the shelves frantically. Cranberries? Where were the cranberries? Words and labels twirled in front of my eyes, a psychedelic display. I had to get out. I turned on my heel, swinging my cart in a wide circle. Thanksgiving dinner or not, we could eat without cranberries. Or maybe I'd come back tomorrow. Anytime had to be better than now.

"Oliffia?" My elderly neighbor, Ida Bauer, was blocking my way with a shopping cart. "Are you all right?"

How was I supposed to answer that question? *No! I'm afraid of cans on a shelf. I'm hot and I'm cold at the same time. I can hardly see, and if I don't get out of here I'm going to explode.* "I'm fine," I answered, throwing the nearest can into my cart. How could I feel so awful and sound so normal?

"You don't look so fine." Ida patted my hand, her papery fingers rubbing mine. "Iss it that time for you?"

Time for me? What was she talking about? The only thing it was time for was to get out of here.

"I remember when I vent trew the change. Acht!" She chuckled as she waved her hand in front of her wrinkled face. "You vill be fine." She smiled as she maneuvered her cart around mine. "Dis too shall pass."

The change? I pushed my cart toward the exit, a light at the end of the tunnel. My across-the-street neighbor had dispensed all sorts of advice to me over the years, much of it old wives' tales that had a surprising kernel of truth. I'd learned Ida's seemingly simple philosophy wasn't always so simple. I mulled her words as I abandoned the one can in my cart. The change? Oh! The *change.* Ida was talking about menopause!

A war of emotions took up battle in my brain. Surely I was too young. I'd barely breeched the forty benchmark. Then again, I recalled a recent *Oprah* show on this very topic. Her expert had said perimenopause, the stage before "the change," could take residence in a body almost a decade before actual menopause. I counted backward, a reluctant scholar. Sure enough, that put me right in the target range. Ouch!

As quickly as I flinched at the math, a wave of relief flooded over me. Hormones. What I was going through was nothing but hormones. I felt like laughing out loud. If Ida hadn't just rounded the far aisle, I might have grabbed her in an exuberant hug. There was an explanation for all of this after all.

Suddenly the aisles took focus, each can and label stunningly still. Why, there were the cranberries, whole rows and stacks of them practically at my elbow. I grabbed two and started my way through the store. I made a mental note to call Ellen West and make an appointment. Hormone replacement therapy had been getting a bad rap, so I needed to talk to her about other possible options. I was not going to feel like I was losing my mind one minute longer.

As I joyfully tossed a box of Brian's favorite breakfast cereal into the cart, I made another mental note. I knew what I would say I was thankful for this season when we went around our Thanksgiving table…Ida Bauer.

Emily

It was kind of cool to have Mrs. Bauer eat Thanksgiving dinner with us. When Mom told me she'd invited her, all I could imagine was that our meal would be weird, having a sort of stranger at our table. I mean I'd known Mrs. Bauer all my life; she lived across the street since before I was born, but all I ever did was wave to her or knock on her door to see if she wanted to buy wrapping paper or whatever our class happened to be selling that year. She always bought something. She was nice, but I couldn't imagine her at our dining room table. I thought she'd either sit there real quiet, or tell long boring stories about the olden days.

She was telling stories, but they weren't boring. She almost made me wish I'd been born in a different time.

"Yah, and then my brudder chumped on the back of dat oldt cow and rote her like she vas a horse. She wouldt even pull us on a sledt around the farm in the vinter." Mrs. Bauer covered her laugh with two wrinkled fingers.

My friends would have thought I was nuts, but having a live animal pull me around sounded fun—like a fair ride or something. One you didn't even have to buy a ticket for. Listening to Mrs. Bauer reminded me about asking for a job at the nursing home. Since basketball practice had started I'd forgotten all about it.

"Vell, enough of dose oldt times." Mrs. Bauer laid her silverware on the side of her cleaned plate. "Brian, you tell me vhat your favorite subchect iss at that collegch of yours."

Having Brian home was kind of weird, too. He was in his third year at NDSU and didn't come home nearly as often as he had the year before. When he'd arrived the night before, he hadn't been home more than an hour before he left to meet some of his high school friends who were also home on break. I was hoping he would spend some time with just me and tell me what it was like when he was a junior in high school and people were constantly bugging him to drink at parties and stuff. Or maybe he'd never had the peer pressure I felt. I was also hoping to work into the conversation a question about how guys felt when girls kept telling them no. From what I'd heard, all guys my age were hyped-up on hormones, so maybe Brian could tell me a nice way to tell Rick to back off a little.

I was so excited the night of Pumpkin Fest when Rick had asked my parents if he could give me a ride home. I felt like a homecoming queen or something when I walked out of Brewster's old gym with his arm around my waist. I kind of hoped Rick wouldn't drive straight to my house; I lived only five blocks away—hardly enough time for anyone to see us together at all.

"Where are you going?" Rick wasn't heading toward my house; he'd pointed his Studebaker toward Brush Lake, four miles out of town, the opposite direction of the ten-mile corner. It was too cold to hang out there, but kids often met out there in their cars and talked for a while before heading back to town.

"Your folks won't know Pumpkin Fest is over yet. Let's drive around. See what's going on."

Did Rick know something I didn't? Had the popular kids moved their meeting spot? Maybe there was a place out by the lake I didn't know about. I didn't want to sound like a complete loser.

"Okay," I said, sneaking a glance at my watch. The volleyball curfew was midnight on the weekends. Even if I wasn't playing, I was still on the team. I had about twenty minutes. My parents had said I could stay out an hour after Pumpkin Fest. This was cutting it close. But they'd left early because Mom hadn't felt well, so they wouldn't know for sure when it had ended.

The slightly frozen grass lining the public access to the lake crunched as Rick pulled in and shifted into park. He left the car running, the heater finally beginning to catch up to the cold interior of the car. It was dark, but even I could see there was no one here.

"What are you doing?" I asked, realizing it was a dumb question even as I asked it.

"Enjoying the view," he said, throwing his arm over the back edge of the seat and looking straight at me.

The muscles at the corner of my mouth twitched. I wanted to smile, but I also needed to get home. Why did this happen every time I was with Rick? His words were sweet, but his timing was crummy.

"Well, look fast," I said, trying to make light of the fact that I was supposed to be home by midnight. Rick had been captain of the football team, and even though his season was over and boys' basketball practice hadn't started yet, he knew the school rules I was under.

"Don't worry." He crooked a finger at me, urging me closer. "The coaches almost never check curfew."

Almost never didn't mean *never*. Maybe if I moved closer he'd be ready to leave quicker. I slid next to him, his arm closing any gap between us as he pulled me tight. He leaned down and kissed a spot near my ear. Oooooh. It tickled in a way Brian's brotherly torture-tickling never had. Instinctively, I pulled my shoulder near my ear, gently pushing his face away. He snuggled in closer, nudging my shoulder with more kisses. They felt good, but they didn't silence the clock ticking away the minutes in my head. I needed to be home more than here. If my coach did call and I wasn't home, I could be benched for the first game of playoffs, maybe more, and that could stretch into basketball season, too. After my nonexistent volleyball season, I was determined to make basketball the sport I stood out in this year. I wiggled out of Rick's embrace, a nervous smile playing on my lips. He was going to think I was such a dud, but I couldn't help it. Breaking rules didn't feel right.

"We'd better get back to town."

Rick groaned. Even in the dark I could see him roll his eyes. "Yes, *Mom*," he said as he shifted into reverse and sent loose gravel spinning.

It was a good thing I pressed him to take me home. As I entered the house, Rick's curt, "See ya," still ringing in my ears, the phone rang. I snatched at it, not sure if my mom or dad were waiting up.

"Is Emily there?" I recognized my coach's voice immediately. An intermingled surge of fear and relief flooded my body.

"This is her," I replied, trying to sound tired, as if she woke me up instead of catching me coming in five minutes after curfew.

"Good. Just checking," she said. "See you at practice Monday."

It had been a close call.

Mom's words snapped me out of my memories and back to the Thanksgiving table as she said, "I'm going to get the pie ready." She stood, reaching for dirty plates. Brian was still droning on about life at college as if nothing were more important in the world. I guess even Mom was getting tired of listening to him as she interrupted him to go get the pie.

She looked pretty now in her thick brown sweater with a heavy copper leaf pin near the shoulder. She stirred the leftover mashed potatoes into a tidy ball. This morning had been different. She'd been so wound up. I'd barely stepped out of my bedroom when she started snapping at me. "Set the table!" "Iron the napkins!" The cloth napkins that we hardly ever used. Our late-afternoon meal would include just the four of us and Mrs. Bauer. I didn't think we even had to use the good dishes Mom insisted I wipe off with a dish towel, much less the cloth napkins that would just have to be washed and ironed again. She seemed much more relaxed now. I looked over the remains of the dismantled turkey. No one could have guessed five people had eaten from the platter. Two salads and two kinds of cranberry dishes surrounded the turkey dish. I supposed making all that food was a lot of work. No wonder she'd been so tense this morning. She was probably glad the day was almost over.

"Emily, why don't you help your mother?" Dad handed his plate to me.

I began scraping bits of food off each plate onto Dad's plate as Mom went into the kitchen with the bowl of stuffing and the dish of corn. All Brian had to do was to keep talking about his big life at college. I doubted he had a clue what was happening in my life.

I tuned him out as I stacked the plates. Basketball practice had started since Pumpkin Fest, and I'd discovered muscles I'd forgotten

I had. I was out of shape from all the sitting I'd done the past season. The ankle I sprained so badly during volleyball season had to be majorly taped before every practice, but at least it didn't hurt. I didn't even dare mention the pain I started feeling in my other foot. I was determined to play out the whole season this time around.

If nothing else, being in sports gave me a good excuse when I went to parties with Rick. I was surprised at how many athletes drank, but they seemed to understand when I pleaded "training rules" and turned down their offers. Maybe my sticking to the rules made them feel guilty or something, but at least they left me alone. Saying no was easier when the weather was nicer and we all stood around in the dark at the ten-mile. I blended into the shadows without a drink in my hand. Hanging out in kids' basements was harder. Fluorescent lights didn't hide much. I was hoping Brian could give me some tips on how to stay clean and not seem like a dork.

He always made being popular seem so easy. After his trouble with huffing when he was a freshman, he became some sort of antidrug, antidrinking role model at Brewster High. He even started a Fellowship of Christian Athletes chapter. It had kinda fizzled out after he graduated, so those of us who were still trying to keep the training rules didn't have much support. I wanted to ask him how he had made it through high school without drinking and still get elected homecoming king his senior year. I also wanted to try and work into the conversation a question about how guys felt when girls said no. I wanted to know if there was a nice way to say, "Back off." I just wasn't sure I had the nerve to ask my brother about something so personal.

"Earth to Emily." Brian's old tease brought me out of my thoughts. "You going to help Mom, or what? I want some pumpkin pie. Lots of whipped cream, please."

I stared down at the five dishes that had long been stacked. I must have looked like a zombie standing there with a dirty knife in my hand. Quickly I slid the knife onto the top plate, clattering the rest of the dirty silverware together in my hand. I was tempted to tell Brian he could be helping, too, but snapping at him wasn't going to get him to confide in me about how guys really felt about girls. And besides, it was Thanksgiving. I gave him my goofy smile, the one where I wrinkled my nose and showed all my teeth. He barred his teeth back at me. Same old brother, college guy or not.

I picked up the plates, carrying them down the short hallway that led into our kitchen. The first thing I saw was the uncut pumpkin pie sitting on the counter. Mom was standing by the kitchen window, her face in profile to me, her arms wrapped around herself like she was freezing. I could see that she was crying.

"Mom?" I sounded scared, and I kind of was. I tried to remember if I'd ever seen my mom cry before. Not even at her best friend's funeral had she cried. I remembered. I'd sobbed like a baby during my piano teacher's funeral. My mom had dried my tears with a white tissue, her own eyes tired but dry.

"Mom? What's wrong?" I set the heavy stack of plates on the counter and stood empty-handed, wanting to comfort her but not knowing how. I'd never been in this role before. Moms comforted kids, kids didn't comfort Moms.

Maybe because they didn't know how.

Libby

"What's wrong with me?" The ever present sense of worry still hung with me, even when I was finally getting the medical checkup I should have had weeks earlier.

Dr. West threaded her stethoscope around her neck. She'd already tapped at my joints with a rubber hammer, had me walk a straight line, watched me touch my toes, checked my eyes, ears, and throat, and listened longer than usual to my thumping heart. My friend's all-business attitude didn't do much to quell the fear sitting heavy on my chest.

Thanksgiving Day had sent me into an unreasonable panic that left me no choice but to call Ellen and set up an appointment. When Emily walked into the kitchen and found me crying uncontrollably, she practically burst into tears herself. One part of me knew I should have reassured her all was fine. But I couldn't. All wasn't fine, and I didn't even have the presence of mind to couch the truth in calming platitudes. All I could do was stand there and cry.

The pumpkin pie made it to the table. Eventually. Enhanced by my tears and Emily's repeated assurance, "I'll do it. I'll do it." If anyone else noticed my red, puffy eyes, they didn't say anything.

Bob did later that night as I lay quietly sobbing on my side of the bed. Not quiet enough, apparently.

"What's wrong?" he whispered, moving across the bed and taking me into his arms.

I knew he hated that cop-out answer: "Nothing." But the truth was, I couldn't attribute these tears to anything. His gentle stroke on my cheek only made me cry harder.

"Olivia," he pressed on my arm, turning me to face him. "I want you to go see Ellen. Promise me you'll make an appointment? Seeing you like this hurts me, too."

So, he'd noticed my tears more than he let on. Living like this was no picnic for me, but if it was starting to affect Bob and my kids, I'd swallow my pride. If this was the case of "hormones" I feared, it was long past treating with hot tea and long baths. I nodded at Bob, a promise mixed with more tears.

⁓

"What's wrong with me?" I asked Ellen again.

She didn't answer my question but said, "I'm going to have my nurse come in and draw some blood. After you get dressed, we'll talk." Just like that, she was gone, leaving me alone in the frigid room, my fearful thoughts swirling. A heavy blanket of dread weighed on my chest like wet snow. Was I having a heart attack right now? Should I call Ellen back?

I was relieved to see the nurse enter the room. If I was going to die, at least I wouldn't be alone. "Joy, joy." She didn't need to explain her sarcasm. She held aloft a small tray—a waitress serving up a syringe and two test tubes. Rolling appetizers. I laid my arm flat and looked the other way.

As swiftly as she arrived, she left, commenting only on my strong blood pressure, which had filled her vials quickly. Oh, to have such easily satisfied expectations. I dressed, sliding my sweater over my head along with my worries. Was I ready to be told I was in menopause? With all the controversy, should I even consider hormone replacement therapy? Would this official diagnosis make me an official old woman? I buttoned the waistband of my slacks and sat in the empty chair by Dr. West's desk, drumming my fingertips on the surface. Menopause had always seemed light-years away, something that happened to old ladies far past wanting anything more in their lives, not to me, a woman with a daughter still in her teens, a woman who still had dreams.

I gazed around the small office. Where was Ellen? Claustrophobia nipped at my throat. Had she noticed something in her exam she was loath to tell me? Was she even now arranging for me to see a specialist? The now-familiar thump of my heart beat in time with my fears. She might as well get in here and tell me the bad news.

My eyes fixated on the doorknob, willing it to turn. Was this how Anne felt as she waited for her test results? At the thought of my dead friend, a wave of anxiety pushed its way through my body. How many times had I waited with her in an office just like this, hoping for good news, getting bad? Had she felt as I did now? Cold? Anxious? Sick with worry about what *might* be?

Anne would have been praying.

If I hadn't been so worried I might have laughed. Of course she would have been praying.

You could, too.

I mentally kicked myself. Of course I could. Why did it always take a crisis for me to remember to pray? Anne had prayed as easily as she breathed.

Try it.

In spite of myself, I smiled. If Dr. West heard my internal dialogue, she'd be arranging for a psychiatric consultation. I breathed in deeply, filling my lungs with calming air, filling my mind with thoughts beyond my worries. *Help me to remember to pray.* I exhaled. *Keep my mind on You.* I inhaled. *Not on measly old me.* Instantly I felt calmer. Serene in a way I hadn't for days. Ah, lessons from Anne, and she wasn't even here.

Lessons from Me.

Yeah, You, too.

Dr. West entered the room laughing at something. I took this as a good sign.

"So, am I going to live?" My renewed state of mind allowed me to ask the question I hadn't realized was there.

Ellen West sobered immediately. Not a good sign. She laid my chart on her desk and pulled the stool near me. Once again, my heart took off on a race against itself. She checked the clasp on her earring then said, "I'm puzzled."

Great. That's all I needed. Stump the Doctor was not a game I wanted to play. I wanted answers—today. I was tired of living as a captive in this unreliable body. I opened my mouth, ready to demand answers. Ellen cut me off at the pass. "Many of the symptoms you've mentioned would normally be indicative of menopause, as you suspected. But frankly, I think you're just a bit young to be having those sorts of hormonal upheavals."

"Too young? That's a diagnosis I can live with." She didn't smile at my crack.

"The blood tests will tell us that for sure. But a few other indicators have me more concerned." She tapped a pen at some writing on my chart. "Are you aware you've lost eight pounds since your annual exam, which was only three months ago?"

I hadn't been dieting. In fact, I rarely weighed myself—a habit I cultivated after years of letting numbers on a dial rule my life. When my clothes started to feel a bit snug I made a point of cutting back on portions, eliminated snacks, and tried to add a little more activity to my day. My recent days of spending hours at the computer had left little time for daily walks. Loose clothes never bothered me, only tight ones. My weight loss was a surprise to me, too.

"And then the heart palpitations and mood swings that precipitated your visit here…" Ellen closed my file and leaned forward, all business. "Palpations can be common in women and normally nothing to worry about. But if they are frequent enough to be causing you this much concern, I want to do some further testing." She laid one arm on her desktop. "It's funny—so many women are afraid of getting breast cancer, but heart disease is the number one killer of women."

"I didn't need to hear that." The race was on in my chest again.

Ellen sat straight. "Yes, you did need to hear that. You also need to hear that I didn't detect any abnormalities in your heart when I listened to it today. But I don't want to rule out any possibilities. I'm going to order a twenty-four-hour Holter monitor test for you. A machine will be strapped to you that you'll carry around with you for a day. It will monitor your heartbeat for twenty-four hours, giving us a readout that can tell us if anything is going on in there that I can't hear." Ellen tucked my chart in the crook of her arm. "If that is inconclusive, I'm going to order a treadmill stress test." She leaned forward, touching my knee with her hand. "We'll get to the bottom of this. Be patient."

I nodded, too overwhelmed with words and tests and monitors to form any questions. Ellen stood. So did I.

"You can stay here." Ellen motioned for me to sit back down. "I'll have the nurse come in and get you hooked up." She smiled. "I hope you don't plan on wearing an evening gown tonight. The words *fashionable* and *monitor* aren't in the same dictionary."

I appreciated her attempt to lighten the mood. Unfortunately, heart disease had been the one thing I'd never thought to worry about.

Or pray about.

I determined to do just that as I waited for the nurse. Ellen turned, her hand on the doorknob. "Did you hear? Pete's moved back home." Her troubled son. I couldn't tell by her tone if that was something good or not.

"How's he doing?" When I visited with Ellen back at Emily's appointment in September, she indicated Pete was still on shaky ground. My heart went out to Ellen. It hadn't been easy for her to raise her son alone after her doctor husband had found an attractive nurse to move in with. The Brewster gossips had a field day. The new couple's move to Carlton had been a mixed blessing.

Ellen shrugged her shoulders in reply to my question. "I don't like to lay blame, but personally, I think most of Pete's problems stem back to his dad leaving us. Abandonment issues. If moving back home will help Pete, he's welcome. But I've made it clear—if I find any sign of drug use, he's out." She sighed heavily. "He's going to counseling. Let's hope this time it helps."

"I'm going to pray for him. You, too." The words were out before I'd thought. Me? Hard-hearted Olivia offering prayer? Anne must have been laughing in pure amazement. God, too.

I work in mysterious ways.

"Thanks." Ellen gave me a wry smile. "If it works, I won't charge you for appointments the rest of your natural life."

"Deal," I said. As she left the room I closed my eyes. No time like the present.

~

"How…much…" I gasped, "…longer?" The treadmill belt under my feet revolved at a pace that had my feet wobbling as though I were a marionette being manipulated by an evil string master.

"Just one more minute."

An eternity of seconds until this stress test was over. Fifty-nine. I had to think about something…fifty-eight…to get my mind off this torture…fifty-seven…

The good news is I remembered to pray for Pete. The bad news? I forgot all about praying for myself, which, in retrospect, should have made me worry about my memory, too. Once the monitor was removed, the noninformation analyzed, and my stress test scheduled, I completely forgot I might be dying of heart disease. For one blessed week I was free of all the annoying symptoms I'd convinced myself were anything from too much caffeine to heart cancer. If there were such a thing. I had an occasional sensation of dread when I woke a couple mornings, but once I forced myself out of bed and got busy with my day, I was able to banish the feeling. I even managed to write a column about my ordeal. *BlueCross Blues.* I had no doubt our insurance company was monitoring my health almost as closely as I was.

Writing about it was one thing. Praying? I was kicking myself for forgetting now. Well, put it this way, I *would* have kicked myself if I could have lifted my leg.

I slithered off the treadmill, wondering what they would treat me for first, dehydration or complete exhaustion.

The young nurse made some notations on her chart. "You did just fine."

Fine? She called my wheezing like an old asthmatic *fine?* Easy for her to say with her toned legs and new Reeboks. If Brewster had a YMCA, I would have signed up on the spot. How could a person get so out of shape?

Scratch that. I knew exactly how. Five cups of coffee each morning. Sitting all day in front of a computer. Driving instead of walking the few blocks to get anywhere in Brewster. I had no doubt this test would point to the source of my problem. An underworked heart and possibly clogged arteries. I doubled over, resting my hands on my bent legs, sucking in what felt like all the available oxygen in the room. I could be thankful for one thing. The test was over. By this afternoon I'd know the source of all my angst and be on the way to recovery.

"Follow me." Nurse Perfect Body strutted ahead of me while my spaghetti-like legs struggled to keep up. "Wait here." She pointed to the waiting room, its sagging chairs and old magazines not the soft bed I was longing for. "Dr. West will look this over. We'll call you when she's ready."

I plopped into a chair, my breathing becoming less Lamaze-like by the second. The recuperation capacities of the human body were amazing. I resolved that when Dr. West chastised me for how out of shape I'd become, I would promise to do whatever she recommended. I didn't need a college education to know my body wasn't healthy.

I pushed myself out of the sagging chair and poured myself a cup of coffee. Oh sure, more coffee. That should help. As I sat down I savored the hot liquid, a prisoner with his last meal. I held the cup in one hand and paged through an ancient issue of *Good House-keeping*. How to Get Fit in Minutes. Maybe I should subscribe. I had absolutely no excuse for being so out of shape. How many women had a schedule like mine? I wasn't rushing off to punch a time clock every morning. I had no little children at home. I could easily afford whatever exercise equipment I needed. I turned the page. Beating myself up wasn't going to tone any muscles that I knew of.

I glanced down the clinic hallway. What was Ellen doing, anyway? Calling a personal trainer about this hopeless case in her waiting room? I should have remembered what doctor appointments were all about…waiting. Goodness knows I'd spent enough time here with Anne. What had we done to pass so much time?

What if time, money, and effort didn't matter…what would you do? Like a ghost from the past, Anne's voice whispered in my ear. Her old "What If" game. It didn't surprise me one bit that somehow Anne had found a way to be here with me today. I just wasn't so sure I wanted her probing just now. Frantically I flipped pages in the old magazine. I was not going to play this game. Especially not by myself.

What if time, money, and effort didn't matter…what would you do?

Get a college education. The answer was there whether I wanted to play or not. The college education that had eluded me all these years. Along with writing a novel, it was the one dream I had yet to achieve. My novel was almost complete, and I had already started wondering, *Now what?* Deep down I knew. Anne's questioning brought my longing to the surface.

The embarrassing part was that most everyone I met assumed I had a degree already. Maybe even two. Somehow being known as a writer made people think you were educated. Well, I was. I just didn't have the piece of paper to prove it. And I wanted it.

The old magazine disappeared from my vision as I recalled my crooked path on the way to a degree.

"What college do you plan to attend?" It was the question my dad often asked throughout my high school years. He planted the seed that college wasn't optional. In our family, it was what a person did after high school. The next logical step on the road called *life*. But in my case, that staircase had ended with my dad's early death when I was sixteen.

I recalled the college admission forms I filled out at our kitchen table, missing my dad with each question I couldn't answer myself.

What was our annual income? Even Mom couldn't answer that one, the estate still in limbo, my dad's banking legacy on shaky ground. She was occupied in a way she'd never been before, dealing with lawyers and shareholders that all wanted a piece of the pie. Somehow she managed to hang on to our portion of the bank, but not before I dropped out of two colleges trying to find my way alone.

During my third attempt at college, my second time at North Dakota State University, I met Bob. I didn't have to work too hard to learn the name of the cute young man who sat two rows in front of me in the lecture hall. *Robert Marsden,* our early childhood education professor called him during the first day of class. Only later did I learn that he'd taken the class simply because he was a senior and needed an easy elective credit to finish out his economics degree. He also thought a class about childhood would be a good spot to meet girls. Smart man. No wonder he graduated summa cum laude. But we didn't meet until my roommate arranged a blind date that had left both of us stammering for words as we recognized each other from our mutual class.

The rest was history. A harlequin romance that ended with me pregnant, me dropping out of college for a rushed marriage, and a move back to Brewster. My first love turned out to have a knack for banking. At the time, I thought dumb luck had brought us together. Solving the family business dilemma by falling in love. Looking back, I could see God's hand at work even when I'd strayed far from any path He had planned.

I closed the magazine that lay open on my lap. My life history was about as old as the news in the wrinkled *Good Housekeeping* pages. Daydreaming wasn't going to get me any closer to a college degree. The closest I would get today was the lecture I was going to get from Ellen about whipping myself into shape.

As if reading my thoughts, the nurse interrupted, "Dr. West will see you now."

Just in case Ellen was watching I tried to put an extra bounce in my step as I walked through the clinic corridor. I was hoping she'd think that maybe the test results had been a mistake.

"Hi-ii!" I said as Ellen entered the room, hoping the energy in my voice would counter the dismal results of my test.

At my greeting she glanced up from my chart, her face a picture of pure concentration. "Oh, hi." Obviously she was deep in thought. Probably preparing the get-in-shape lecture she was about to give. She pulled out the small desk stool and positioned herself facing me. She didn't even look at my thick chart lying at her elbow as she began to speak. "The good news is that none of the heart monitoring tests we've done have detected any sort of problem. Your heart appears to be shipshape."

I raised my eyebrows. "Well then, obviously, you need new equipment. I thought for sure my heart was going to explode on that treadmill."

Ellen smiled. "Everyone feels like that. That's why it's called a stress test. We purposely put stress on your heart to test it at maximum efficiency. You did just fine."

At her words a Kentucky Derby of sorts started up in my chest. If my heart was fine, then what was causing my problems? Worry was leading the race, but fear ran a close second. What was wrong? Was it terminal? Maybe that's why she looked so preoccupied when she entered the room; she was trying to figure out how to tell me the bad news. I took a deep breath, bracing myself for whatever she would say next.

Ellen took a deep breath, too. "Olivia."

Oh-oh, this was bad. Anytime a doctor takes a deep breath and then says a person's name as if it were a whole sentence, disaster is ahead. I steeled myself for the worst. Maybe my case was too advanced to offer any hope.

"Olivia," she said again, "I've looked over your tests closely and reviewed the results with a colleague of mine in Carlton. We both agree that your heart is healthy. Your blood tests show that your hormone levels are adequate. Your cholesterol levels are in the normal range. No signs of anemia. Your thyroid tested fine. You don't appear to have any physical problems."

No physical problems? What did that mean? My joints were strong? My heart was fine? My blood was…red? Physically I was okay. "Well then what—"

Ellen held up a hand, cutting off my words. Here it comes. "Olivia, we've been friends for a long time." She paused.

I'd never had a doctor deal the friendship card before. My mind raced along with my heart. I started seeing Dr. West when she started her practice in Brewster, right out of medical school. She was the first female doctor I'd ever seen and had a way of putting me at ease discussing women's health stuff that male doctors couldn't hope to emulate. Brian and Pete had started kindergarten together, and Ellen and I had spent more than one evening together working on Cub Scout projects or filling the bleachers at school events. Over the years, we created more than a doctor-patient relationship. She confided the details of her divorce to me during a stint in the school concession stand; I told her about the years my father was sick and then died as she and I tallied the income from the seventh-grade cake walk. As a single mother and doctor, Ellen hadn't had much time to develop friendships, and until I'd met Anne, I hadn't had much use for them, but I could see now that Ellen was my friend whether I wanted her to be or not. A freezing sensation started in my stomach as I waited for her to go on.

"I know your history, Olivia. I know about all those years your dad battled cancer. The aunt who died of it. Your cousin who was treated for a spot on her lung. I remember how closely you walked with Anne during her battle, too."

Okay, this was it. I had cancer, and she was preparing me for the worst. I clenched my jaw and waited for the "c" word.

"And then this fall we had that scare with Emily. The tumor on her arm that could have been cancer but wasn't." I was glad when she breathed because I couldn't. "You've had a lot of loss in your life."

I'd never thought of it that way, but when she recounted all those people, it only made sense that I was going to join the ranks. No use putting it off any longer. I might as well know what I was up against. "Just tell me."

She dipped her head. A small prayer before the bad news? This was bad. She lifted her head, then said, "I think you have grief issues that you haven't dealt with."

Quiet filled the small space. Grief issues? What in the world was that supposed to mean? A good cry and I'd feel better? I would have laughed if she hadn't looked so serious. I didn't doubt that Ellen had worked long and hard on her diagnosis, but it was too bad her medical degree hadn't served her well in this case. *Grief issues?*

Hadn't she heard when I told her how my heart raced through most of each day? How I couldn't sleep? And she herself was the one who'd noted the weight I'd lost without even trying. Grief issues? Something was drastically wrong with me, and Ellen was telling me I had *issues?* She should have her head examined.

That's when it dawned on me. That's exactly what Ellen was trying to tell me, that my problems were all in my head.

My heart pounded now, anger replacing any anxiety and worry that had been there moments ago. How dare she tell me I was imagining all this? She said she knew me. She didn't know me at all!

I struggled to find words to tell Ellen just how I felt about her lousy diagnosis. If she wasn't willing to get to the bottom of my perfectly obvious physical symptoms, I was going to have to find a different doctor. I opened my mouth, then closed it, a barrage of words too thick to emerge clogged my throat.

"I can tell you're surprised by my assessment."

Surprised? That wasn't the word I would have used if I could have spoken.

She filled the silence. "Sometimes when we have psychological issues that are difficult for our mind to process, they will manifest themselves as physical symptoms. It's our body's way of alerting us that something is wrong."

Something was wrong all right. Her diagnosis.

"If we don't deal with our emotions…" She touched her chest, right where her heart should have been. "…they find a way of making us respond—sometimes whether we want to or not." She reached into the pocket of her lily white lab coat and pulled out a card. "There's someone in Carlton I'd like you to see."

I wondered if she'd thought all along my problems were in my head? Maybe she had that card up her sleeve the whole time she put me through those worthless tests. Some friend. Friend of the insurance industry was more like it. Well, I'd be saving them money after this. I had no intention of *seeing* anyone.

Ellen held out the card, but when I didn't reach for it she laid it on the desk between us, pushing it my way. "I know this kind of news can be difficult to accept."

It wasn't difficult at all. I didn't believe a word of it.

"Sometimes when we start dealing with these sorts of issues, we might start feeling worse before we start feeling better."

We? Who did she think "we" was? As if we were in this together. I knew darn well she meant only me! I was the one she thought had the problem. Well, I had news for Dr. West. Some doctor.

I stood, wishing I had left my coat in the waiting room. My exit would have been much more dramatic if I could have simply stormed out. As it was I needed to turn and pick up my coat, knocking the business card Ellen had laid on the edge of the desk to the floor. The mom reflex in me kicked in. Automatically I picked it up.

Dr. G. Sullivan, M.D., Psychiatry.

This problem was *not* in my head. If I was ever going to get better, I'd have to do it by myself.

Psychiatrist. Ha! I swept out of the office, a diva of righteousness. But even in the depth of my denial, so sure there was nothing wrong with my mind, I subconsciously tucked the card in my pocket. Somewhere safe…just in case.

Emily

"Zone defense! Zone!" my basketball coach, Mrs. Hoberg, yelled from the sidelines. "Watch the screen! Watch the screen!"

My eyes darted to the clock. Fifteen seconds. The Flander team had the ball and led by two. If we didn't do something fast, our fifth game would go in the books as a loss. And we hadn't lost yet.

From somewhere in the crowd I heard a voice boom, "Loose ball!"

Before the words registered, I had the ball in my hands. I glanced around, looking for an open teammate to pass to. The Falcons had us covered. A fast break wasn't my specialty, but it looked like I was going to have to do it now. I pivoted to the left, put my head down and broke for the other end of the court. Ouch! The pain in my foot caused a hitch in my step that I hoped didn't look like traveling. No whistle from the ref. Still driving, I spotted Hannah Stromme coming up on my right, heading toward the basket. She clapped her hands once to let me know she was open. I bounce passed the ball her way. In one graceful giant step she drove into the lane and bounced the ball off the glass and into the net as a shrill whistle pierced the wild cheers coming from the stands. Tie game.

"Foul on the Falcons!" The ref motioned to the sidelines, giving the stats crew the information they needed, and then waved my teammate Kathi Bender onto the court. She snapped from her crouch and ran toward me, slapping my hand as we switched places. Seven seconds left. I could have toughed it out.

"Is your ankle bothering you?" Our assistant coach knelt in front of me as Hannah netted her two foul shots, assuring our victory.

"My ankle's fine." I brushed off her concern, focusing my eyes on the Flander team captain's inbounds pass. My ankle was fine—my other foot was the problem, but I was not about to tell that to the coach. Kathi would have my starting spot in no time. I pretended to watch the game. What I really wanted to do was take off my tennis shoe and throw it as far as I could and then sit down and cry. My foot felt like somebody was pounding it with a hammer.

The final buzzer rang before the Falcons got the ball past half-court. The other girls leaped off the bench, dashing onto the court to hug our teammates. I hung back, trying not to limp as I lined up to do the "good game" slap with the other team.

"We won! We won!" Our team captain, Hannah, twirled me around, sending another wave of pain through my foot. The fact that I was dating her old boyfriend, Rick, hadn't seemed to matter to her as we spent the past weeks together learning to play as a team.

Mrs. Hoberg shook the Falcon coach's hand and headed to the locker room. I grabbed my water bottle and headed that way, too. Some of the players' parents were standing around congratulating the other players and hugging their kids.

"Good game!" Ben Pearson slapped me on the back. His daughter, Steph, played on the junior high team, and they didn't miss a game.

"Thanks." I looked Ben in the eye as my dad had taught me to do when shaking hands, and then I looked over his shoulder. Where were my mom and dad? They usually met me on the floor after a game, win or lose. I looked up toward the bleachers where they always sat. Second row from the top. Dad was standing, talking to someone I didn't recognize. Mom was just sitting there, staring into space as if she didn't even know the game was over, much less that we'd won. She'd been acting really strange lately. Her tears on Thanksgiving Day had scared me, but I'd seen her crying umpteen times since. Now they didn't scare me so much as worry me. I hoped my folks weren't getting divorced or something. They seemed to get along really well, but then so did April Glatt's folks, and they got divorced last year.

My dad caught my eye and gave me a thumbs-up. I waved, but Mom didn't seem to see that either.

Ruthie Hammond was helping Mike roll up the cords they used to broadcast the game. "Good job tonight," she said as I walked past.

"Need a ride home?" Mike asked.

I shook my head. "Thanks, though." It still felt weird to have Rick waiting for me after the games. I'd always ridden home after games with Mike since he'd gotten his driver's license.

I pulled open the door to the locker room; the loud chatter of excited teammates filled the space. As I sat on a bench against the wall and tugged at the laces of my shoes, my foot throbbed. Surely my mom had noticed how I favored one foot when I ran down the court. The least she could have done was come see me after the game. I remembered her blank stare from the bleachers. She wasn't even watching the game, much less me. Did anybody even care that I was hurting?

"You played good tonight." Hannah pulled the ponytail holder from her long blond hair as she sat next to me. "Thanks for that last assist. You could have made the layup yourself."

I shrugged. I wasn't about to tell her that I didn't think I could have pushed off hard enough with my foot bothering me so much.

She bent to untie her shoe. "How's Rick? Are things going okay?"

I shot her a look, wondering if she was hoping things weren't good, but her genuine look of concern caught me off guard, and I found myself smiling back. "Yeah, it's good."

She nodded, toeing one Nike from her foot and then the other. I slipped my ankle brace off of the tape that already held my foot in a vice grip, wondering why Hannah and Rick had broken up in the first place. I wasn't about to ask Rick for the details; I'd rather not plant the idea of pretty Hannah back in his head. And asking Hannah about her old boyfriend who was now mine seemed weird.

"Anybody want to pray with me?" Hannah stood in the center of the locker room, a circle of girls considering her invitation.

This was something new. We'd never prayed after a game before. Silence hung in the air. I knew I should join her. I mean, I believed in

God and all that. I even knew the Bible said you shouldn't be afraid to stand up for your faith, but somehow this felt scary. I'd already prayed about the game and my foot before I came tonight. By myself. Did I really need to pray again? What if I was the only one who joined Hannah? How dumb would that look? Just the two of us in some little prayer club.

If any two are gathered in My name…

The verse Mike memorized in Bible school practically five summers ago and repeated so often that I'd learned it, too, convicted me now. But crouching over on the bench and tearing the tape off my foot felt easier than standing up and joining Hannah.

"I will." Kathi Bender walked over and took Hannah's hand. Soon a chorus of "me, too" echoed in the room. Suddenly, joining the circle was easy. I felt a wave of guilt as I joined the group. I should have been the first to say I'd pray. I mean, if I really believed in God and prayer, I should have been willing to say so rather than hunching over my shoes, waiting to see what everyone else was going to do. Talk about peer pressure.

I bowed my head as Hannah began her prayer. "Lord, thank You for helping us to play our best tonight…"

I always thought peer pressure wouldn't bother me. The previous two years I'd spent practically every weekend with Mike and Jen, sitting at one of our houses, watching PG-13 movies or playing Monopoly. We decided we didn't need to join the party crowd to have fun. Well, movies-for-three every weekend got boring, and how many times can a person buy Park Place before even that's not exciting anymore? We'd finally decided that if the three of us stuck together, maybe going to a party now and then wouldn't be so bad. We watched out for each other, and if someone tried to force us to drink or something, we stood up for each other.

That worked fine until Jen started seeing Ryan. Suddenly the three of us had turned to four, and our little support group, rather than growing stronger by numbers, started falling apart. Jen and Ryan wanted to do things alone sometimes, and it felt too much like a date for Mike and me to hang out, just the two of us. Alone. Mike had been my friend since fifth grade, so I couldn't figure out why all of a sudden being alone with him felt so strange. But it did, as if there was this weird vibe hanging in the air between us. Then, when Rick and I started going out, we began hanging out with more of the kids who partied. Without Jen and Mike around to back me up, saying no was getting harder and harder…and not just to drinking but to Rick, too. I'd been trying really hard to remember what Brian had told me about peer pressure when he was home for Thanksgiving.

Brian had already been home for two whole days—two days when it seemed like all he had done was spend time with his old high school friends. I began to think he didn't remember I existed.

"Hey, Twerp!" Brian had tapped on my partially open door late that Saturday afternoon and then walked into my room. I was lying on my bed, hoping he'd come talk to me. "Can a big brother come in and hassle you?"

I tried to look nonchalant as I scooted over so he could sit on the edge of my bed. I wanted so badly to talk to him, but asking him to have a serious conversation with me had felt too strange. Alone in my room. Like it was some big deal or something.

He sat on my bed, grabbed a pillow, and punched it into a ball that fit between his legs and chest as if it had been made to go there. It was weird and familiar all at the same time to have Brian in my room. He hadn't really lived at home for three years, and when he had, we didn't exactly hang out together. But even though he called me "Twerp" and his "annoying little sister," I knew by his grin and the way he tugged at my ponytail sometimes that he liked me.

"What's new?" Brian looked around my room and then tilted his head and eyed the kitten poster on my ceiling. "Still have that old thing up there, huh?"

"Yeah." I drew a line on the comforter with my finger. I felt like asking him to take the little-kid poster down, but I wanted even more to talk to him. Why wouldn't the words come out? I cleared my throat.

"Is something wrong with Mom?" Brian's eyes drilled into mine.

Okay, we could talk about Mom first. The way she was acting bothered me almost as much as my own problems. I nodded, then shrugged my shoulders. How was I going to explain something I didn't have words to tell? "She's kind of, I don't know…spacey? Like half the time she doesn't hear what I'm saying." Lame. "She cries a lot."

"I noticed." Brian tossed the pillow onto the bed and laid down on his back beside me, folding his arms under his head. "Have you talked to Dad about it?"

I shook my head and then realized Brian couldn't see me. "No." I paused. "Mom's always been so…so…in control. I guess I was scared to say anything. Like if I don't talk about it maybe it will go away." I hadn't realized that's what I'd been thinking, but now that I'd said the words I knew it was.

"I'm going to ask Dad before I go." Brian turned on his side, facing me, resting his head on his raised hand. "So, things okay at school?"

Here was my chance. I took a deep breath, but the words wouldn't come. Just like I'd answered his first question, I finally answered this one with a nod, then a shrug. I wanted to talk, and yet I was scared to.

He poked my shoulder with his finger. "There's nothing you can tell me that will shock me. What's up?"

I did a hundred and eighty degree flop on the bed, turning my face from the ceiling to the bed. It was easier to talk into a pillow. He poked me again. The words tumbled, muffled by feathers, from my mouth. "Did you ever worry about peer pressure?"

"Oh, that." I could feel Brian push himself up. I lifted my head as he slid his back against the headboard, bending his knees to make himself comfortable. I laid my head back on the pillow, facing the wall. He reached over and messed up my hair with his hand. "Know what I call peer pressure?" He waited until I looked up again. "*You* pressure."

My eyebrows crinkled together. I was glad he wasn't asking me what kind of pressure I'd been feeling, but I didn't have a clue what he meant by "you pressure." "Huh?"

"I call peer pressure, *you* pressure. Here, I'll show you." He grabbed my private journal off the top of my messy bedside table and flipped it open.

I scrambled to my knees, grabbing the thin booklet from his hands. There was no way I was going to let him read all the junk I'd written in there about Rick and Jen and my parents.

"You just proved my point," was all Brian said.

I sat with my back against the headboard, cradling my journal on my knees.

"What point?" I finally asked.

"If someone told you to open your journal and read it over the loudspeaker at school, you'd tell them to get lost. You wouldn't think twice about doing that because it would be against what you believe in doing. So, what's the difference when someone offers you a beer, or a guy pressures you for sex? If you know what you believe, saying no is easy."

It took a while for his words to sink in. But he'd been right about my journal—I wouldn't let anyone read those words. Ever. I didn't even have to think about it. So why was it so different when Rick wanted more than a kiss?

"Stop and think about it, the only person putting any pressure on you to go against what you believe is you. If you go against what you believe, who feels crummy? It's sure not the other guy. It's you. But when you do what you believe, you feel stronger, especially when you say, "No thanks," to someone you momentarily think you'd like to impress. There's nothing cooler than doing what you know is right."

It made so much sense when Brian explained it, but it was so much harder in real life.

I felt a tight squeeze on my hand as a chorus of "Amen" echoed around the locker room. "Amen." Hannah's voice broke through my thoughts as a wave of guilt washed over me. I should have been praying along and here I stood, daydreaming. I beelined it for the shower, hoping Hannah didn't expect any comment on her prayer.

Rick was shuffling his feet by the locker room door when I pushed it open. He glared at his watch, the empty hallway emphasizing his point. I half expected to see my parents waiting there, too. Where were they? They always had something to say to me after a game. Especially this year, when we hadn't lost a game, you'd think they'd have some sort of comment.

"What took you so long?" Rick asked.

I shoved my disappointment about my parents aside. What could I say to Rick? We were praying? I was pretty sure the guys didn't do that after their games. I set my bulging duffel bag at his feet, hoping his irritation would vanish while I zipped my jacket. I wasn't in the best mood myself. When he didn't bend to pick up my bag, I knew my wish hadn't worked. I hoisted my duffel bag onto my shoulder and fell into step beside him, my sore foot barely keeping up with his angry pace. Silence hung between us as Rick waited for my apology. For the second time that night I knew I should have been proud to stand up for my faith, but for some reason I felt embarrassed about the thought of telling Rick our team had held hands and prayed…it seemed hokey or something.

"Do they pay you to clean the place up? You're always the last one out."

I wasn't sure if the remark was Rick's attempt at a joke or a putdown. I didn't say anything. He could have at least said congratulations before he laid into me about having to wait. And besides, I knew I wasn't the last one out. Hannah was in a serious-sounding discussion with Kathi Bender in a corner of the locker room when I left. But I wasn't about to mention her name to Rick. I was learning not to get into an argument with Rick. Not that we'd really argued, but whenever it came down to proving a point, Rick always made sure he won. It was easier to give him the benefit of the doubt and pretend his comment was a joke.

"Yeah, the janitor leaves five bucks in my locker and I mop the floor." I nudged Rick's arm with my shoulder. He grinned, the tension between us melting with his smile. He was so cute when he was happy. I handed him my duffel bag. In a fluid motion he swung it onto his shoulder as though it contained nothing but feathers.

"It must be nice to be so strong." I said the words, then realized they sounded like some sort of cheesy come-on. "I mean, girls are usually kind of weak and—" I stopped. I really didn't think girls were weak. "I just meant that guys are usually…" My attempt at explanation wasn't going well. I could feel blood flooding my cheeks. "…stronger."

Rick laughed as he threw his free arm around my shoulder in a walking hug.

Mike rounded the corner as Rick pulled me close. His eyebrows rose in a flash of surprise as he took in our cozy twosome, and then just as quickly he was same old Mike.

"Hey, guys."

"Hey, yourself," Rick said holding me tight.

My first instinct was to duck out of Rick's embrace. Having Mike see Rick and me practically hugging felt almost like running into my parents. But I'd been right all along—Rick was strong, and I couldn't budge. I stood there, a plastic smile surrounding my teeth.

"I forgot one of the extension cords under the bleachers." It was as though Mike needed to explain why he was standing there.

Apparently I did, too. "Rick thinks I stayed in the locker room to mop the floor." I tried to stand straight, to move out of Rick's embrace just a little, but his arm was like a vise.

"Get used to it," Mike said, ignoring my eyes and looking at Rick. "Emily always runs late." He moved toward the empty gym. "Stay out of trouble."

Now I did break out of Rick's grip. Just who did Mike think he was telling Rick I was usually late? As if Mike knew me so well! And then telling me to stay out of trouble! Like he was my dad or some annoying little brother! For all the good it did I stuck my tongue out at Mike's back.

"Come on." I grabbed Rick's hand and pulled him to the heavy double doors that led outside. "Let's go." I had been thinking of asking Rick to bring me straight home. My foot hurt, and I wanted to lay on the couch in front of the TV with a bag of ice. But suddenly, it seemed obvious that while my parents didn't seem to care all that much about me, Mike cared just a little too much. Suddenly defying them and defying Mike seemed like all the medicine I needed.

"Let's go find some fun!"

Libby

I knew I should stay up and wait for Emily to get home after the game. She always had a whole list of things to tell me. Who missed what pass, who was irked at the coach because they didn't get enough playing time, and which teammate got her underwear hidden in the locker room. As it was, I completely forgot to even look for Emily after the final buzzer. I was simply relieved the game was over and I could get out of there. It didn't dawn on me until I got home that I forgot to give her my usual hug of congratulations. It had been all I could do to sit still on the bleacher and wait while Bob talked to a customer of his. I stared into my lap, as if deep in thought, trying to avoid conversation with any of the other parents. I must have looked like a modern version of The Thinker statue as I sat on my perch high above the court, but inside I felt like worms were crawling under my skin. I wanted nothing more than to get out of that gym, yet I felt if I moved I might start running and never stop. Whatever was wrong with me wasn't in my head. Not the way Ellen had intimated. My imagination couldn't possibly make me feel that uncomfortable.

When Bob said, "Let's go," my mind was already halfway to the car.

I looked at the clock on my bedside table: eleven-forty-nine. Emily had eleven minutes and she'd be late for our curfew. One hour and eleven minutes and she'd blow the school curfew, too. A part of me knew I should hold vigil and hold her accountable to our rules, but a bigger part knew if I didn't go to sleep I might fall apart. Sleep seemed the better option.

Bob had been snoring for an hour already. Tonight I was going to give Emily the benefit of the school curfew whether she knew the favor or not. As I snapped off the light and buried my head in my pillow, the restlessness and anxiety I felt earlier in the evening crawled into bed with me. All I wanted was to sink under the covers and go to sleep, to pull the blankets over my head and descend into oblivion or some other place where I didn't have to pretend I felt normal. I snugged the covers around my head, hoping to shut out the world. Instead, I found a whole new universe within my head.

Since Ellen's misdiagnosis, I'd done some searching on the Internet. I had to do something with all the wasted time spent at my computer, trying to write. Staring at the falling leaves on my screen saver wasn't doing a thing to get my novel completed; telling myself I was solving my health problems seemed like a good way to kill time.

I had to admit my attitude toward Ellen softened a bit as I researched. My symptoms ran the gamut from perimenopause to hypochondria. No wonder she jumped on the easy out, batting me off to another doctor when she didn't have a clue what was really wrong.

I flipped over in the bed, so sure laying my opposite cheek on the pillow would solve the anxiety of today. I was wrong. The dark of night only heightened my unfounded fears. Where was Emily? What if I didn't fall asleep all night? What if the pounding of my heart meant it was going to explode right here in bed? Should I get up and walk around? Maybe that would steady my racing pulse. No, activity would worsen it. Lying here had to be better. Argh! My racing thoughts only added to the list of symptoms I'd already charted.

Tomorrow I would get to the bottom of this once and for all. I didn't know what was wrong with me, but I was sure it was not in my head as my former friend, Dr. Ellen West, had intimated. I was going to get a second opinion as soon as I could figure out what kind of doctor specialized in baffling symptoms.

I just hoped I wouldn't have to lie awake and count each second until tomorrow arrived.

The phone was ringing in my dream. *Somebody answer the phone.* It rang again. *Isn't someone going to get it?* My eyes popped open. It wasn't a dream. In the second it took my dream to vanish, my brain ran a scan of all the horrible possibilities. Something had happened to Bob. No, he was sleeping beside me. Brian? Who knew what could happen at a college this time of night. Emily? The clock blinked an answer: one-ten. Even though I hadn't heard her come in, I was certain she was zonked in her bed by now. It had to be something about Brian.

My heart thudded as I grabbed up the receiver. "He-ll-o?" Sleep and fear filled my throat. I coughed and tried again. "Hell-o?"

"Hi." The female voice almost whispered. "Sorry if you were sleeping. This is Coach Hoberg. I'm calling for a curfew check. Is Emily home?"

I said the first thing that came to mind. "Well, uh…I don't know." I rubbed a hand across my eyes, watching as the clock turned one-eleven. "She must be, it's after her curfew." I sounded confused and certain in the same breath. "I guess I fell asleep. I didn't hear her come in." My heart settled into a steady rhythm. Brian was fine and Emily was home. All was well in this mother's realm.

"Could you check to make sure? School policy."

I swung my feet over the side of the bed. "Sure." Irritation rose in my chest as I slid my feet into my slippers. I'd had a hard enough time putting my mental demons to rest tonight; I didn't need Emily's coach calling, a grown-up babysitter, waking me from my deep sleep. Why did a couple of kids breaking curfew in the past have to ruin my sleep now? I shuffled down the hall and peered into Emily's dark room. The shadows from the three-quarter moon outside danced across her bed. Of course she was there. Wasn't she? I blinked, my sleep-clouded brain suddenly alert. Her bed was a rumple of sheets and blankets. A couple of stuffed animals lay on the floor as if tossed there in careless sleep. But in a glance I knew they had been lying there since last night, not tonight. Emily was not in her bed.

A cautious beat began in my chest. She might have come home and fallen asleep on the couch. It wouldn't be the first time she'd spent the night sleeping in front of late-night TV. I started down the steps, my mind already spinning. What would I say to Coach Hoberg if Emily wasn't there?

Sorry I took so long, Emily's right here, sleeping on the couch. The imaginary words stuck in my throat. I swallowed, surprised at how easily the lie popped into my mind. I recalled the numerous times I berated other parents who lied for their children, telling the coach they were home when they weren't, valuing their child's role on the team over any convictions they might have.

After Emily's sprained ankle sidelined her most of volleyball season, I knew how much she was counting on the basketball season to make her mark. Was I willing to let Emily get suspended from the team by telling the truth?

I stopped in the entry to the family room, suddenly not so anxious to peer over the back of the couch to see if Emily was there. Almost on tiptoe I crept forward. The television wasn't on, making the likelihood Emily was lying there that much less.

The couch was empty.

What would I say now? *No, Emily's not here. Kick her off the team.* I turned toward the kitchen, stepping to the phone as if walking the plank on a pirate ship. There was no turning back. What would I say? I felt like a character in a Disney cartoon with an angel on one shoulder and a devil on the other.

Emily should realize the consequences of her actions.

What would the people in Brewster say if she got kicked off the team?

The rules were made to help the team.

Why make Emily suffer when kids through the ages have pushed the limits of the rules? Emily's a good kid.

Emily is disobeying.

Back and forth my thoughts raced. In my heart, I knew what God would have me do. How many ways could a person interpret the proverb I'd read earlier that week? "Lies will get anyone into trouble." I didn't need a college degree to figure that one out. Regardless of what I knew was right, I watched as my hand reached for the phone, the lie ready on my lips.

My search of the house seemed to have taken hours, each step a piece of evidence leading to condemnation. In truth it had taken barely a couple minutes for me to make a sweep of my empty house. I apologized anyway. "Sorry," I said, buying time before I sinned. "Emily's—" The kitchen door flew open, Emily tumbling in right behind her duffel bag. "—right here," I finished, a wave of relief washing over me. "In the kitchen." As if it mattered.

"Great," said the coach. "Have a good night."

I hung up the phone. "Well-ll, young lady," I said, putting my hands on my hips and facing Emily like some nineteen-fifties sitcom mom in a nightgown. "Explain."

"Hi, Mom!" Emily grinned at me with glassy eyes, her hand flopping in a goofy wave.

"You're drunk." There wasn't a nicer way to put it, and I didn't feel like mincing words.

Emily giggled. I hadn't lived in a cave; I knew enough to understand that her giggle could just as well be caused by pot as by alcohol…in addition to pure stupidity. "You might like to know that was your coach on the phone."

Emily sobered in a hurry. Well, maybe *sober* wasn't exactly the word, but at least she still had some of her senses about her. She wiped the dumb grin off her face. "What did you say to her?" Her glassy eyes were wide.

"That I needed to look for you and found you in the kitchen," I responded, half wishing she hadn't burst in just then. Half wishing I had the courage to tell the coach the truth. Then the punishment would have been the school's responsibility, not solely mine. I narrowed my eyes at her. "What have you been doing?"

She shrugged her shoulders, as if that was an answer.

"Tell me."

"Nothing."

"And I'm supposed to believe you did 'nothing' for four hours? The game was over at nine. You're an hour past our curfew and late for the school curfew, too. Where were you?"

"We were just driving around." She stuck out her chin.

"Who's *we?*"

"Rick and me."

A warning pricked my neck. I didn't know Rick Wynn well, but I had the feeling he'd been around a few more blocks in life than Emily. "Driving around *and* drinking?"

She hung her head and shrugged again.

"Oh, that makes me feel good," I said with as much sarcasm as I could muster. "Drinking and driving. How intelligent. Where'd you get it?"

Emily was smart enough not to pretend she didn't know what I was asking. "Rick had someone buy it for us," she mumbled.

Like a bad actress on TV, I shook my finger at her to make my point. "As of right now, you can plan on being grounded for the rest of the season. And you can tell Rick he's not welcome here anymore." Even as I said the words, I knew I was overreacting. Christmas was barely two weeks away, and the basketball season lasted at least until the end of February. Even in my anger I recognized I'd never keep Emily home for two and a half months. It would be as much punishment for me as it would be for Emily. And anything I'd ever read about parenting teens had said forbidding them to see someone was as good as throwing them together. I knew better. But she didn't need to know that right now.

"Mom!" Emily leaned forward, her mouth wide. "That's not fair."

"And I mean it," I countered, turning on my heel. Goodness, I was getting good at this lying business.

Surprising how easy it is to sin, isn't it?

The thought convicted me. I turned back to her. "Emily, I'm tired. I was worried, and I'm angry about your behavior tonight. I can't talk about it anymore. We'll talk about it in the morning. I'm going to bed."

I crawled into bed for the second time that night, marveling at how Bob could sleep through calamity, wondering if I'd sleep at all. Once again I tugged the covers around my shoulders, wrestling more than blankets as I remembered the lie I'd been ready to give the coach.

I thought you were a Christian.

Yeah, I thought so, too. That was what made my near-deception worse. *Forgive me, Lord?*

From down the hall I could hear Emily making a mad dash into the bathroom. The sound of her vomiting made me feel sick, too.

Emily

"Set the table and then go do your homework." Mom had her back to me and didn't even bother to look away from the potato she was peeling. She was acting as if I was a leper or something. "Dad's going to be a little late."

I knew better than to throw my duffel bag onto its usual spot near the door. Ever since that Friday night a little over a week earlier, my mom had turned into the Wicked Witch of Brewster. Good grief, I wasn't the first kid in town to ever drink in high school. I wondered if my mom had thought to be thankful I hadn't started drinking in junior high like half the kids in my class.

I set my duffel bag in the laundry room and hung my coat on the doorknob. I half expected Mom to holler at me about that, too. She yelled at everything I did these days. Christmas vacation was only one more school day away, but so far I hadn't done much right in her opinion since that Friday night. I put my backpack on top of the dryer and grabbed three dishes out of the cupboard, not concerned that they clanked together as if they might break. Who cared? I dealt the dishes out like cards, daring Mom to yell at me. Three glasses, three sets of silverware, fork on the left, knife and spoon on the right, napkin beside the fork, just like she'd taught me when I was five. I was tempted to switch the arrangement to bug her, but I was already in enough trouble. Sometimes she still treated me like a little kid. I mean, none of my friends ever got grounded for three weeks, or if they did, their parents never stuck to it. I knew my mom, and she'd make sure I sat home every minute of my sentence.

"Is there anything else?" I made sure my voice was like syrup so she couldn't accuse me of being sassy. As it was I was grounded through Christmas vacation. Some vacation that would be.

Mom glanced at the table. "No, that's fine. Go do your homework."

I bit back a reply. What else was there for me to do? I grabbed my backpack and climbed the stairs to my room, switching on my CD player and cranking the volume knob. If she told me to turn it down, I wouldn't hear her.

I flipped open my chemistry book and tried to understand what Einstein, or whoever invented this Greek, ever saw in the stuff. It didn't take long for me to roll onto my back and stare at that dumb kitten poster still hanging on the ceiling above my bed. I knew when Brian got home from college for Christmas break he'd probably tease me about it. I could stand some teasing; it would be a relief from all the tension in the house these days.

"Do you realize the position you put me in?" Mom had sounded more sad than mad. "Do you?"

What was I supposed to say to something like that? Yes? No? I'd hung my head, the only position I could come up with to look sorry enough to satisfy her.

Like a tag-team partner, my dad had picked up where Mom left off. "Emily, we were very disappointed in you last night."

I'd hung low all that Saturday, waiting for the ax to fall. The one my mom seemed to be lugging around all day. I was pretty sure she hadn't forgotten about the night before, but when she didn't say anything by noon, I started hoping that maybe middle-aged forgetfulness had arrived just in time. I wasn't about to bring Friday night up myself. I wasn't feeling so hot after spending half the night on the cold tile in the bathroom. And the idea of Cheerios for breakfast pretty much turned my stomach all over again. I was kinda sure that was what a hangover felt like, and I vowed never to feel like that again.

I hoped Mom wouldn't tell Brian what I'd done during their usual Saturday morning phone call. I'd had all night to remember the conversation we'd had at Thanksgiving about peer pressure—and then kick myself for not listening to him. Not only did I feel sick to my stomach, I also felt sick about what I'd done. Brian had been right, but I didn't need him to tell me so.

Even though I'd only had two beers, they were apparently enough to make me feel crummy. Rick had practically downed a whole can in one long swallow when we parked on a country road outside of Brewster, and then he offered me a sip of his second one. It wasn't like I'd never tasted beer before. I had. But just a swallow or so. I guess I was thirsty after the game. One sip turned into one can. Then two. I knew I was being stupid. I was breaking the rules, but just then I didn't care. Besides, who would know?

God will, I remember thinking.

I shook my head, clearing the memory from my mind. I flipped myself over on the bed, determined to finish my chemistry homework. Daydreaming wasn't going to solve any equations. As I rearranged myself on my comforter, my eyes landed on the daily devotional book that was practically buried under the junk on my nightstand. Mom had put the devotional in my Christmas stocking last year, and I vowed to start the year anew. I read the inspirational paragraphs every night until…? How long had it been since I'd opened that book? I wasn't so sure I wanted to know. Sliding forward on my elbows, I shimmied to my nightstand, carefully sliding the book from beneath a pile of CDs, hair clips, a bottle of lotion lying on its side, and an unread *Brio* magazine. The book looked mostly unused. I cracked the spine to where I'd left a photo of Mike and me to mark my spot. Our arms were thrown around each other's shoulders, our grins goofy. We looked like we didn't have a care in the world. When had that been? I looked at the date in the devotional: March twenty-third. March? I hadn't opened this book since March? A wave of embarrassment flooded over me. Had it really been that long since I'd read a nightly devotion?

I remembered the first devotional book I'd ever gotten. It was sort of a belated Christmas present from Anne. She'd already had my gift wrapped in pretty silver paper, but she died before she could give it to me. About a week later I found her gift lying on my pillow one night. Mom explained that Anne's husband, Kevin, had brought the gift over that morning. I'd ripped the wrapping open, sad and excited at the same time. I loved Anne almost like she was my mom. Anne had told me about God at the same time she was teaching me about middle C. When I opened the cover of the children's devotional she picked for me, I read her last note to me. "Always play for Him. Your prayers are music to God's ears."

Even though I was only eleven, I promised Anne and God that I was always going to pray, always going to think of God and Anne when I practiced the piano. I read that first devotional every night from January first to December thirty-first, not missing a day. The next year my mom put a devotional in my Christmas stocking. "In memory of Anne," she wrote in the front cover, and she'd done it every year since. I read those books faithfully, too, but as the years went by, skipping a night had gotten easier and easier. Sometimes I was too tired, sometimes I forgot, and sometimes I just didn't feel like it. I thumbed through this past year's almost-new book. How could I have forgotten my promise?

That was more than five years ago. You were just a little kid then. You've changed. Grown up.

Yes, I had grown up. But did people ever grow out of a promise to God? Or to someone who died? I didn't know, but I didn't think so.

I knew I would never read the whole book before the new year, but I was pretty sure Mom would give me another devotional this year, and I vowed to read it. Every night. I climbed off my bed and pulled out a large cardboard box from under my bed. I took off the cover and put the devotional in beside the other books Mom had given me over the years. I saved them all. They were safe in my box, along with two of Anne's best cookie recipes I helped her bake and a rolled and unrolled piece of sheet music I played for Anne's funeral. "Jesus Loves Me." And it wasn't just the beginner version of the song, either. I couldn't believe I was only eleven then and that I'd had the nerve to play in front of all those people. But I had known Anne would be proud. So I did—crying the whole time but not on my fingers. Even my little-kid brain knew that tears would make my fingers slip on the keys. After the funeral, I found this box and put the music inside. It hurt my heart too much to think of playing Anne's favorite song without Anne around, and besides, if I ever needed to play it, I knew it by heart.

I put the cover back on the box, keeping the photo of Mike and me out. I pushed the box under the bed with my foot and lay back on my floor, holding the photo above my face. I tried to remember exactly when it had been taken. Obviously, sometime in March or before. We were still sophomores. Those days seemed more like years ago than months. The picture was taken way back before I sprained my ankle in volleyball, long before I even dreamt of actually going out with Rick. Back when Mike and I were still like best buds. Things had sure changed in just a matter of weeks.

I wondered what Mike would say if he knew I'd been drinking? Not much, that was for sure. Or maybe too much. Maybe that was why I'd been avoiding him.

I knew teenage drinking was wrong. I'd heard plenty in Quest class about the dangers of alcohol on undeveloped teen brains. But I thought I'd be okay if I was careful. I didn't need some know-it-all health teacher, or Mike, telling me what to do. Lots of people did it and were fine. I also knew all about the sex-stuff, too, and that some of the things Rick and I had been doing alone in his car weren't exactly "approved." I closed my eyes, remembering how his arms had felt around me that night a little over a week ago. When Rick kissed me, I really didn't think about what was right and wrong.

I opened my eyes. The romantic feelings vanished as Mike's face stared at me from the photo I was still holding. Was he accusing me of something he didn't even know I had done? I got off the floor, pushing the offending photo into the stack of junk on my dresser.

You can hide from Mike. You can't hide from Me.

Ouch. I picked a stuffed animal off the floor and swatted it like a volleyball across my room, trying to bat the incriminating thought away.

"Emily, phone." Yes! Just what I needed to quit thinking about this stuff. At least Mom was still letting me talk to my friends.

I carried the receiver down the hallway and into my room. My parents still wouldn't let me have a phone in my room, but they did get a longer cord after I stretched the old one into something that resembled a sick-looking snake.

"Hi!" I didn't care who it was; I was just glad to talk to someone besides my mom.

"Hi, Emily. Did you ask your mom about ungrounding you for the movie tomorrow night?" Jen didn't waste a minute getting to the point. Ryan was going out of town for an early Christmas celebration with his grandparents, and Jen already had an agenda of things she wanted me to do with her over the weekend. The movie was just the start of her plans. Shopping at the mall in Carlton, lunch at Space Aliens, and shopping for Ryan's Christmas gift were all on the list, too.

"I'm not gonna be able to go." I didn't even need to ask. Mom hadn't shown one sign of easing my punishment all week.

"Have you asked? I mean, it's Christmas. How can she be mean at Christmas?"

"You don't know my mom."

"She'll let you at least go shopping, won't she? Tell her you have to buy *her* gift."

"I'll ask, but don't hold your breath."

Jen sighed, letting out her breath as if she had been holding it. "She's not going to make you stay home for New Year's, is she? That would be the *worst*."

I hadn't thought that far ahead, but when I stopped and counted the days of my grounding, they wouldn't be over until two days after New Year's Eve. Argh!! There was *no way* I was going to sit home with my parents on New Year's Eve! Anger rose in my chest. Rick had already talked about going to Carlton for a special dinner that night, and I had no doubt we'd find something to do until midnight. He was patient when I told him I was grounded for coming in late. I didn't tell him that my mom had figured out I'd been drinking with him. It had never occurred to me I'd still be grounded by New Year's. I knew my parents wouldn't let me do anything on New Year's Eve. *Nothing!* I felt like screaming.

"Emily? Are you still there?" Jen tapped at the phone.

"Yeah, sorry, I spaced out for a minute."

"What about New Year's? Do you have anything planned with Rick? Mike's gonna hang out with Ryan and me and maybe Kathi Bender. Hannah is having a party later, and she said anyone could come. You want to?"

Jen had to be out of her mind. Like I'd bring Rick to Hannah's house.

"As if."

"Oh, sorry, I forgot they used to go together." How could she forget something like that? "You and Rick seem like you're made for each other." There, that was better. "So what are you going to do?"

I wasn't about to tell Jen I was still going to be grounded for New Year's Eve, because I didn't plan to be. One way or another, I was going to have fun on New Year's whether I had permission or not.

I knew I was being a witch, and not just to Emily. I just hoped I could shake my weeklong bad mood before Brian walked in the door from NDSU. He wouldn't have much of a break if his mom was acting like Scrooge.

I pulled the last sheet of Brian's favorite Christmas cookies from the oven, letting them cool a minute while I breathed in the spicy fragrance. Maybe a little aromatherapy would help my frame of mind. I grabbed the spatula and began transferring the brown rounds to a cooling rack. I didn't have to be the Ghost of Christmas Past to know what was causing my bad temper. I was well aware that Emily thought her drinking and curfew violation had set me off on a Grinch-like tangent, and I wasn't proud of the fact that I'd let her—and Bob—think just that. My mysterious symptoms of the past few months had intensified, and the second opinion I'd received from a doctor in Carlton set my irritability in concrete. He was no better a diagnostician than Ellen West. Now what was I going to do?

I broke off an edge of molasses crinkle, juggled it between my hands as it cooled, and popped it into my mouth while it was still plenty hot. Why not? A burned tongue was just another excuse to stay crabby. I nibbled on the rest of the cookie, images of my trip to Carlton dancing in my head like sour sugarplums.

"I don't know what you were expecting to hear from me." Dr....I had to look at his name tag...Potter intoned. He looked over the top of his half-glasses. "I've looked over the test results Dr. West sent over from the Brewster Clinic, and I concur with her assessment. Although some of your symptoms could be interpreted to indicate the start of perimenopause, I don't see any specific indication of that in the tests

Dr. West ran." He closed my file as if that said it all. "There doesn't seem to be anything physically wrong with you."

The familiar anger was rising in my chest. These doctors were all in cahoots. "But—" I stopped myself and took a calming breath. My dad's voice echoed in my mind: "You'll catch more flies with honey than vinegar." I poured on the syrup. "Your reputation as an internist is stellar, Dr. Potter. I thought you would have access to tests that Dr. West wouldn't know about." Dr. Potter seemed to bite back a smile. I certainly didn't need condescension. "But then with the availability to the Internet, I guess Dr. West would be as up-to-date as you. I'm sorry if I assumed more than I should." There.

Dr. Potter pressed his lips into a straight line. "Frankly, I'm not one to rerun tests if I don't feel a need, and in your case I think Dr. West covered all the bases." He leaned back in his chair. I could almost feel the hand patting that would come next. "I know that experiencing symptoms and not having a specific diagnosis is frustrating. We all want a pill that will make whatever we think we have go away. Unfortunately, getting well is not always that easy."

I took a deep breath, determined not to let the tears of frustration fall. How many doctors did I need to go to before someone would listen to me? Couldn't they hear me when I said I felt lousy? If it wasn't perimenopause, what was it? I cleared my throat while I waited for my frustration to morph into aggravation. "Then why am I feeling so…so…" I couldn't think of a better word. "…crappy?" Maybe that would get his attention.

Dr. Potter draped his stethoscope around his neck. Obviously this appointment was over. "Mrs. Marsden, I'm only a doctor, not God. If I can't find reason for an illness, I can't treat it. And, frankly, I don't think you are ill. I know your symptoms feel very real to you, but sometimes when we are experiencing inner turmoil, our bodies…"

Did I really have to sit here and listen to his lecture? The same one Ellen had given me? Did they teach this in medical school? Stumped 101…tell the patient it's all in their head. I bided my time, waiting for him to quit talking. Two could play this game.

"Thank you," I said, shaking his hand, the polite little woman who hadn't listened to a word of his canned speech. If he wasn't going to pay attention to me, I wasn't going to pay attention to him.

Oh, that's really mature of you. You came here for a second opinion, and now you have it. Just because it wasn't what you wanted to hear, does that make it invalid?

I drove the forty miles back to Brewster conversing with my conscience. Part of me discounted everything the two doctors had told me. How could not sleeping and weight loss be in my head? Part of me considered their words carefully...even the words I'd claimed not to hear. *When there is trauma in our lives, we often delay experiencing it until much later, when our minds are ready to process the pain. Until we do, our bodies can send us complicating signals, alerting us to the need for attention.*

The only attention I needed was someone who would listen to me!

I'll listen.

Yeah, sure. I knew God would listen, but I didn't have any trauma to process! I leaned forward and turned up the radio, but even that wasn't enough to drown out Ellen's words of a couple months ago. "You've had a lot of loss in your life...I think you have grief issues."

I did not! I slapped at the steering wheel with my gloved hand. I was perfectly fine!

If you're so fine, then why are you running to the doctor? To two doctors?

I pressed on the accelerator, anxious to put this day behind me. Evidently I was going to have to handle this by myself—just like I had most everything in my life. When my dad died, I muddled through alone. When Anne was sick, I was there for her, alone. I simply had to get through this by myself, too.

I was there.

Well, of course God was there. I knew that. Didn't I?

Trust Me.

Of course I trusted God, but He wasn't telling me what was wrong with me.

Sometimes people are My messengers.

I pulled into the driveway, easing the car into the garage as I considered the thought. If God used people to deliver a message, how was I supposed to know whether the message was from God or from some charlatan? Say, from some quack doctor? I pushed the gearshift into park and turned off the car. What a waste of an afternoon. I could have spent my fifty dollars on fortune cookies for all the answers I'd come home with.

And I had no more answers now. The trappings of our Christmas celebration were scattered around the living room. Bob was sitting in his recliner, paging through the political cartoon book Brian gave him. Brian was on the phone in the kitchen, calling long-distance to wish his new girlfriend merry Christmas. Emily had gone to her room to try on the brand-name jeans and red sweater we gave her. The small Black Hills gold cross Mike had given Emily at the church program sat in a small box on the couch. I tucked it under the tree and then started filling a garbage bag with empty boxes and paper as if it were Santa's sack.

"Church was nice." Bob put down his book. He pushed himself out of the chair and bent to retrieve a curl of gold ribbon under his feet. "Here." He tossed the coil along with a crumpled piece of wrapping paper into my bag.

I squished the paper down, remembering the Christmas Eve service we'd attended five years ago, the day of Anne's funeral. We'd buried my best friend that afternoon, but I couldn't bury the emotions she left me with. All the rest of that day I felt restless, unable to sit still, much less cry. On an impulse I now knew was God's prodding, I dragged my family to a children's Christmas Eve program at a church in Carlton—the same church I stopped at impulsively one day during Anne's illness, seeking answers but finding none that day. My answer was waiting for me that night as small children acted out the story of Jesus' birth. They told of His arrival to save the world, to save *me*. He had, then and there. A Christmas miracle I'd have called hackneyed if it had happened to anyone else.

Unfortunately, the road to redemption wasn't as smooth as Anne made it look. At my insistence, Bob and I had decided to join a church in Brewster, the same one Anne had belonged to. Was that any surprise? I knew Anne had to be smiling somewhere. Brian and Emily had jumped into Sunday school with both feet. Well, Emily with both, Brian dragged one foot for a while just to make sure we knew he was a teenager. Eventually he became president of the youth group two years running, and the rest was history, so they say. His walk with God appeared as effortless as Anne's. Mine, however, was another story.

I tried to study the Bible on my own, but accumulated a lot of questions with no one to talk to about them. I joined a nondenominational women's group, Sarah's Circle. The name seemed fitting since Anne had once shared with me the skepticism of Sarah in the Bible. God had told her she'd get pregnant at something like age eighty-nine, and she'd laughed. Sarah sounded a lot like me, wondering if God knew what He was talking about. I wasn't much different most days. Reading my devotions and searching for direction, trying to pray while wondering if the coffeepot was perking. I tried to hear God's voice when the phone wasn't ringing. Like Sarah, I'd laugh too if God actually said something to me.

I'd gone to that group looking for answers. Who was God? How did I know what He wanted for me? Most of the women in the group seemed like they already had all the answers. Or were too busy to need any. They were more interested in getting through the lesson and getting home than in discussing how I, personally, could discern God's voice.

I didn't last long. I'd never been much of a joiner, and when the time spent discussing "important" business—whether to have a May Day Basket exchange or not—exceeded our study time, I knew my time in the group was over. In the meantime, I hobbled along on my own, now and then using my monthly pre-book-club dinners with Katie Jeffries as a makeshift Bible study. The arrangement wasn't ideal, but it was the best I could do. I found out depending on God wasn't nearly as easy as Anne made it look.

I tied the top of the garbage bag and handed it to Bob. He knew the drill. Out to the garage until garbage day. Goodness knew I tried to depend on God, but most days *my* way seemed much more tangible than God's.

I wrapped my arms around myself, surveying the clean living room. Some gifts still needed to be put away, but that could be done another time. The multicolored lights on the tree cast a soft glow over the room. We'd had a good night.

"Shoulder rub?" Bob came back into the room, flexing his hands, demonstrating the additional gift he was offering.

I didn't need to be asked twice. I took a place on the floor in front of his recliner, and he settled in behind me, kneading my knots away with firm strokes. "Mmmmm."

"You did a good job making Christmas feel special." Bob worked his fingers up my neck. I rolled my head into the pressure. "I know things haven't been…" He paused. "…easy for you lately."

So, he'd noticed. Bob's philosophy over the years had been to let my moods pass before speaking. He was probably afraid of upsetting me more by asking rather than ignoring. Tonight I liked knowing he'd taken note.

"I'm okay," I said, a small lump pushing its way into my throat. "Okay" was a wild overestimation of the way I'd been feeling, but Bob was right, tonight had been special. I didn't want to spoil it by talking about my vague troubles. I leaned my head against his hand, a hug of sorts, then let him continue offering comfort in the way he knew best.

The children's pageant at church had begun our evening and seemed to touch us all. It had been more meaningful by its innocence. Bob had clasped my hand as the miniature Mary and Joseph made their way down the aisle. Brian was unexpectedly misty-eyed when the small innkeeper shouted at the top of his lungs, "No room!" He'd draped his arm over the back of the pew, giving me a gentle hug and a choked-up smile. Emily had participated in the youth group part of the candlelight service, appearing almost angelic in her white robe and pale candle. She was as much unlike the grump she'd been for most of the season as could be. I thought she'd even smiled at me. A truce for the night, anyway.

So we made it through the holidays, one big, happy family. Well, make that one small, somewhat cordial family. Brian left early to head back to his apartment in Fargo. His girlfriend, Aimee, was no doubt as much of a draw as his part-time job. As much as I didn't want to admit it, Brian's childhood room was no longer the place he felt most at home. The transition had been seamless, as it should be. It was just hard for a mom to acknowledge sometimes.

I sank onto the couch, pulling the novel my friend Jan had given me at lunch two days ago onto my lap. "Brain candy" I called the lightweight story. Just what I needed after saying goodbye to Brian and almost three weeks of struggling with Emily's foul mood—and mine.

I opened the book to the third chapter; it wasn't hard to remember that the hero and the heroine didn't like each other…yet. All the books Jan passed my way had the same plot. I traced my eyes along the page, finding myself thinking about Emily instead of Countess Emmaline. I'd eased up on Emily's initial three-week punishment. She was still grounded for the three weeks, but I did let her spend a day in Carlton with Jen. Even juniors in high school had last-minute Christmas shopping to do. Bob and I had also agreed that she could get together with Jen and Mike for a gift-exchange on the twenty-sixth, but the New Year's Eve plans she'd tried to finagle had been nixed. She'd taken the news surprisingly well.

"So I can't do anything for New Year's Eve?" Emily pushed the peas on her plate into a short row. She sounded matter-of-fact, as if it really weren't that big of a deal.

"We think you need to stay home." I knew better than to add that Bob and I would be home all night, too. She didn't need to think we were guarding the prison. Who knew? Maybe none of her friends had plans and she really didn't care if she stayed home.

"I can't even go driving around with Mike?" It was almost as though she was pretending to beg, saving face or something.

"Emily," Bob cautioned, "you're still paying the consequences from another night of driving around." He didn't add *and drinking,* but we all knew it was that, too. "Let's start this new year off right."

If it had been a movie, loud sappy music would have swelled just then. As it was, Emily knocked her peas out of alignment and sighed loudly. "Some New Year. Yippee."

Some New Year was right. Emily had headed for her bedroom shortly after the special New Year's Eve supper I prepared, turning her CD player just loud enough to let us know she was there by protest. Bob and I exchanged glances and laughed. What else could we do? We were as grounded as she was.

After dishes, Bob grabbed my hand and pulled me into the family room. "Might as well make out," he said, his eyes twinkling, "she won't be down the rest of the night." He pushed a movie into the tape player and leaned over to kiss me as the action-adventure flick started playing. Mr. Romance, he wasn't, but I'd keep him. I kicked off my shoes and tugged off my socks. He might not be Mr. Romance, but Mr. Expert Foot Massager was a good substitute.

Happy New Year.

I woke with a start. The movie had rewound itself, and some loud, late-night New Year's show had taken its place. It didn't take long for me to wake up enough to hear Emily's music still pounding away. Did she plan to torture us the whole new year? No doubt she had fallen asleep just as Bob and I had.

I slipped out from under Bob's arm, walking to the television and turning the sound way down. I stood for a moment, trying to figure out just where this raucous celebration was taking place. Certainly nowhere near Brewster. New Year's celebrations could look surprisingly foolish when you weren't a part of them. I snapped the television off; Bob's gentle snoring played backup to the rhythmic bass coming from Emily's room. I had to agree with Emily. Some New Year.

I shuffled into the kitchen, noting that the clock on the stove quietly showed that more than an hour had passed in this new year. Time I'd slept away. I unbuttoned the waistband of my slacks, wishing I had changed into my nightgown before Bob and I sat down to watch the movie. In spite of my recent weight loss, sitting on a couch for a whole evening didn't make waistbands any more comfortable. I rubbed my hands across my face. I still had to wash off my makeup and get ready for bed. Ugh. I sure didn't feel like doing any of that at this hour. I poured some milk into a mug and popped it into the microwave, punching three minutes onto the display. Hot milk—my mother's recipe for most any ailment. It would have to stand in for champagne tonight.

While I waited for the milk to heat, I stared out the kitchen window. Snow fell lightly earlier in the evening, but now the wind had picked up, creating the first blizzard of the year. The wind howled as it pushed ice crystals past the window, practically obliterating the light from the streetlight on the corner. I rubbed at my arms. Something about being safely inside a warm house made a North Dakota blizzard feel like a comforting blanket. But only if you were watching from the inside. I hadn't lived in this state my whole life not to know blizzards could be deadly if you were caught unaware.

The microwave dinged; my instant celebration was ready. I turned from the window as a pair of headlights bounced down the street outside. No doubt some foolish kids out testing their mettle against Mother Nature. I held the mug of hot milk to my mouth, blowing gently across the surface. Breathing in the soft aroma was almost as comforting as sipping it. I took a few swallows and headed for the stairs. Time for bed.

I stopped at Emily's door, knocking lightly in case she really was still awake. You never knew with teenagers. I didn't need to start the new year with an argument about respecting her privacy. The only response was the steady thumping of the CD. Slowly, I opened the door; Emily's usual array of clothes, stuffed animals, and a magazine or three littered the floor. I'd given up the clean-your-room battle long ago. Her standards were certainly not mine, but as long as she kept her door closed, we had peace in the castle. After Anne died, I learned to go to war only over more important things than messy rooms. Funny how death can put life into perspective. I sighed.

Setting my hot mug on the messy dressertop near Emily's door, I tiptoed into her dark room, hoping I wouldn't break a leg on my way to her CD player. The lump that was Emily remained inert. Forget tiptoeing—I might as well march through with a tuba for all she'd hear. I made it to the machine, fumbling to find the power button in the green glow of the display.

I squinted at the CD display, pretty sure I'd found the power button. I took a chance and pushed it. Sure enough, blessed silence. Darkness, too. Complete darkness. I hadn't realized how much light the CD player had given off until it wasn't there anymore. The blizzard raging outside took care of any light I might hope for from the moon. I stood, stranded in a sea of mess. Okay, I told myself, you got in here without falling; you can get out. I picked up one foot and set it down, suspecting I could be standing on Emily's Christmas sweater as well as carpet. At least it was solid. One more careful step. Then another. I reached the end of Emily's double bed, wondering why I hadn't thought to turn on the hall light before I came into the room. Gingerly I set my left foot down, feeling the coolness of a magazine page a millisecond before I put my full weight on the foot. A millisecond too late to keep from slipping on the glossy pages. Whump! Right on the bed. Right on top of Emily. I braced myself for her scream.

Silence. Only this time I didn't consider it blessed. Rather than landing on Emily, I came to rest on two pillows that formed an expert imitation of her sleeping body. Or they had until I uncovered them, a poor magician revealing a secret the audience wasn't meant to discover.

"Bob!" I screamed, not one bit concerned about being quiet any longer. "Get up here!"

I flipped on the overhead light, the glare revealing what I didn't want to see. An empty bed. Evidence of a daughter's defiance.

As I waited for Bob to stumble up the stairs, I stared at the empty bed as if it held some sort of clue. The only thing it revealed was that Emily was gone.

Bob hurried into the room, stopping in his tracks when he saw the two pillows that weren't Emily. "What on earth…"

Oh, this was going to be some new year, all right. Some new year.

Emily

If I had known sneaking out was going to be that easy I would have done it two weeks ago. As it was, I laid awake in my room for a good fourteen days plotting my escape. I debated the merits of jumping from my second-story bedroom versus tying my sheets together and shimmying down the outside wall, a trick I'd filed away from a fire escape video I watched in fifth grade. In the end all I had to do was walk down the stairs on the pretense of grabbing a Coke. My parents were snuggled on the couch. Two prison guards asleep on the job.

I had my pillows lined up and tucked in for the night before ten, my CD player set on continuous play since after supper. All that remained was to close the door as quietly as possible. I grabbed my jacket and tiptoed out the kitchen door. A gust of wind grabbed my coat as I tried to shove my arms into the flapping cloth. Already I was wishing for a scarf. Mittens and boots would have been nice, too, but everybody knew that to be cool in Brewster a teen didn't wear anything that might look practical. I had no doubt I looked cool…*freezing* was more like it. I tugged the thin hood of my jacket over my head. I'd never actually used it before and was surprised at how much protection it offered. If only I could see. I pushed the edge of the hood back a bit, only to have the wind blow it completely off. Wow, it was seriously cold out. I tugged the hood back on and held it in place with already stiff fingers.

The next step of my mission was to find Rick. I'd told him I planned to sneak out as soon as I could after ten. I'd worried that my parents might try to stay awake until midnight and that I might have to resort to the window escape. But they conked out by ten-thirty. All my worry and plotting for nothing. I ran toward the curb, jumping snowbanks with my Sketchers as best I could. But a snowbank is different from a snowdrift. The sidewalk was covered. I had no choice but to step into the middle of the deep snow. Ice crystals filtered over the top of my socks, settling cold and damp around my ankles. Already I was imagining the warmth of Rick's car. I planned to stick my feet right in front of the heat vent as soon as he picked me up. Where was he? I stood on the curb, squinting into the wind, then turning my back to it, wondering which direction he'd be coming from. He'd said he would be driving around my block, watching for me after ten. I hoped he could see me in the swirling snow.

I stomped my feet, trying to stay warm, looking first one direction and then the other, willing Rick to hurry up. If my parents had let me have a cell phone I'd know exactly where Rick was right now.

No you wouldn't. He doesn't have a cell phone, either.

It was easier to blame my parents—his, too. Easier to blame the town of Brewster for being stuck in the middle of nowhere in North Dakota where cell phones barely reached. I felt as if I lived in a Star Trek zone. If we lived in Carlton, I would have tons of stuff to do and wouldn't have to resort to driving around and drinking for entertainment. I might never have even gotten grounded.

Even as I paced on the curb, trying to keep warm, I knew my thoughts were just an excuse. The kids in Carlton did the same things we did and also complained about having nothing to do. But getting mad helped warm me and also helped me ignore what I'd just done. Snuck out of the house. Disobeyed big-time.

In addition to imagining what my parents would think, I could feel Brian's disapproval, almost hear his words about "you pressure." I glanced back at my house. It looked warm. An invitation of sorts. I couldn't blame anyone for tonight except me. I could still go back…

I blew on my fingers, trying to bring some feeling into them. The wind shoved the hood from my head again. I yanked it back up and started walking in the direction of Brewster's main street, the highway that cut through the middle of town, the wide road that everyone cruised to see and be seen. No, I would not spend New Year's Eve alone! If Rick stood me up, certainly someone would be around to pick me up out of this blizzard. I gathered the flimsy hood tighter under my chin. Man, it was cold!

I stomped through the deep drifts on the sidewalk with a picture forming in my mind. The new devotional book Mom had given me a week earlier lying on my nightstand, waiting for January first. What had happened to my resolve to start over? I didn't want to think about that right now—I just wanted to be warm. Where was Rick? He wouldn't stand me up, would he? I couldn't walk outside much longer, or I'd freeze to death.

I peered into the wind. I could see the dim glow of headlights about two blocks away. Already I felt the approaching warmth. Ah, my prince, coming to rescue me. My brain must be freezing to think something so dumb. I jumped up and down, waving my hands. I wasn't about to let him miss seeing me.

As the vehicle neared, even a blizzard couldn't hide the fact it wasn't Rick's low-slung Studebaker. This was a pickup, high enough to buck snowbanks, which is just what it was doing. From down the block I could hear the driver revving the engine, gearing up to plow through serious snow. Flakes flew as the truck bucked through a bank that had formed in the intersection. Mike's green Ford emerged out of the flurry.

Mike? He was supposed to be Rick, but at this temperature I wasn't going to be picky. I waved both arms above my head, praying they'd see me and stop.

"Emily?" The electric window on the passenger side of the pickup slid down. Mike leaned toward the steering wheel, peering around Austin Vetter and Scott Dosch, Brewster athletes. They were all grinning. "Did you get locked out of your house? What are you doing out here?" Mike knew I'd been grounded, but he didn't know my punishment was still in effect. For all he knew it could have been over.

"Rick was supposed to pick me up, and I didn't want him to ring the doorbell and wake up my folks…" The wind whipped my lie away. "I don't know what happened to him. Maybe he got stuck or something."

Mike scooped his arm in one big *get in* motion. I didn't wait to be asked twice. Scott jumped out and I piled into the middle of the warm pickup cab, scooting over so Scott could fit back in. Sorta. Austin and Scott played football for a reason. They were big. They'd switched to basketball after the football season, but even I could tell they belonged on the field. When they weren't warming me up, that is. I was thankful for their warm bulk on either side of me.

"We'll drive around and see if we can spot Rick." Mike gunned the engine and took off down the street. "Hang on, here's a big one." Mike gripped the wheel with both hands as his truck hit the drift. I held my breath as snow plastered the windshield. In a second we'd left the drift behind as Austin and Scott hooted approval. I was quiet, glad I was inside the pickup as Mike sped toward another snowdrift. My socks clung to my ankles, cold and damp. Standing outside in this blizzard had been stupid.

Before long, we had driven most of Brewster's main drag. Except for one other vehicle full of kids, the streets were quiet. Clusters of cars here and there appeared to huddle around late-night celebrations. The Johnsons had closed Vicky's Café for a party of their own. It looked like Dan and Jan Jordan were having a small party, too. Jan was a friend of my mom's, and as we drove by her house I wondered why she hadn't invited my parents to her get-together. Oh…maybe she had. Maybe my folks had stayed home on account of me. Suddenly, as cold as I'd been moments before, I was flushed. Hot with shame. I unzipped my coat. "What do you think happened to Rick?" Changing the subject was easier than thinking about my folks asleep on our couch while their friends were having fun.

Austin patted at his parka, trying to shift the bulk to make more room in the crowded cab. "I'm guessing in this weather his folks didn't let him come to town."

I'd never given a thought to the fifteen miles Rick would have had to drive from his farm to get to town. But wouldn't he have called if he wasn't going to make it?

And don't call! My parents might think something's up. The words I'd e-mailed Rick yesterday scrolled through my mind. I never even thought to check my e-mail. I assumed anyone I wanted to chat with was doing something more exciting on New Year's Eve than sitting at their computer. I suddenly knew Rick was sitting at home just as I should have been. Just as I wished I still was.

Funny how quickly my adventure had lost its intrigue. The whole point of sneaking out had been so that I could spend the New Year with Rick. Not so funny was the way I felt now. I pasted a smile on my face and looked at Mike. "What were you guys planning to do?" Pretending to have fun was almost worse than being stuck at home.

He shrugged one shoulder. "The usual."

That meant driving around Brewster until everyone almost died of boredom. If I were in my room, I could be listening to my favorite CDs, reading a book, chatting on-line, or even having a bowl of ice cream. Instead I was stuck spending New Year's Eve the same way we spent practically every night in Brewster. Driving around. Some New Year.

"We stopped by Hannah's party," Austin said, "but when they pulled out the karaoke machine we split." Austin and Scott started an off-key version of "Girls Just Want to Have Fun."

Their performance would have been funny if I'd been in the mood. I wasn't. I leaned forward and turned the heater fan to low; in spite of the blizzard raging outside, the pickup was positively claustrophobic. We slammed into another snowdrift. I reached across Scott, bracing my hand against the frosty side window. I didn't wish I was back outside in the cold wind, so the only option I had was to ride along. *Girl's just pretend to have fun,* I sang to myself as we bounced through the deserted streets of Brewster.

Mike whipped the truck around a corner sending all four of us into a unison sway, first left and then right. The pickup fishtailed and then straightened. "Whoo-hoo!" Scott yelled. "Do that again."

"Wait," Mike said, pressing on the brake, "is that a car stalled up there?"

"Maybe it's Rick!" My heart started a tune of its own until I realized that the likelihood of Rick being stuck on this side street in Brewster's two-block warehouse district was next to none. None of us ever drove this short road.

The guys peered through the glass into the swirling snow. "Yeah, that's a car," Austin said. "It looks like that new guy's car. From the bank." He looked at me as if I were an expert on anything to do with the bank. "You know, that guy who drives the silver Bug."

Oh, great. Just what I needed—my dad's new loan officer seeing me. As Mike eased the pickup alongside the VW, I pushed myself into my coat, hoping that Paul Bennett was like most adults and thought all teenage girls looked alike. Besides, maybe he wouldn't see me in the dark.

While I debated the possibility of diving under the dashboard, Mike jumped out of the pickup cab and knocked on the window of the Bug.

"Need any help?"

Mike was probably just as surprised as I was to see Ruthie Hammond, his boss from the radio station, behind the wheel of Mr. Bennett's VW. What were Mr. Bennett and Ruthie doing stuck in a snowbank together in a blizzard? I couldn't help it—I leaned forward for a better look. Mr. Bennett was leaning around Ruthie to talk to Mike. His eyes caught mine, and I quickly moved back into the seat. If I hadn't snuck out, I would have relished the thought of going home to my parents with this news. Already I couldn't wait to tell Jen.

In less than a minute Scott and Austin had joined Mike and Mr. Bennett, and they had the round Bug pushed out of the snow and were piling back into the truck. Mike banged his shoes against the running board as he climbed back in.

"I told them we'd follow them until they get to Ruthie's place." He put the truck into gear. "A small car like that could get hung up again. Kinda dumb for them to be driving this road in the first place."

Yeah, kinda dumb. Kinda like this whole fiasco of a night had been. I fished at my sides, finding the bottom edges of my coat buried between Scott and Austin. I tugged them out, matching the ends of the zipper together.

"After you go by Ruthie's, why don't you drop me off at home? I'm kinda tired," I said.

"Swing by Hannah's first," Scott said, "I wanna see if Kathi's still there."

Oh-hh! I hid my smile. So Scott was interested in Kathi Bender. Interesting, especially since Jen had hinted that Mike might like her, too. I couldn't wait to get home to e-mail Jen. Mike tooted his horn as Ruthie and Mr. Bennett stopped safely in front of Ruthie's sister's house, where she was living now. Then he headed down the block toward Hannah's. No wonder the streets of Brewster were so quiet—all the kids in town appeared to be at the Stromme's. Mike double-parked as Scott jumped out. Austin gave me a small push, then flipped his body over mine in a move more suited to wrestling than exiting a vehicle.

"I'm gonna go see what's going on," he said, swinging out of the cab and closing the door on the howling wind.

It was Mike and me. Alone. With me sitting practically next to him, now that Austin had so abruptly left. I inched toward the door.

Mike looked past me to the glowing windows of the house. It was easy to see this was where the action was in Brewster tonight.

"You wanna go in?"

Part of me did. I knew Jen was there and probably half the school. Knowing the Strommes, I was sure her parents were home, and if I'd had permission, my folks would have had no qualms about letting me attend a party there. But another part of me knew the night had been over a long time ago—before it had even begun. My soggy socks were just one reminder that I should have never left home in the first place.

"No." I shook my head. "I think I'd better get home."

Mike nodded, then shifted into gear, driving much slower than when the other two guys filled the space between us. Now all that hung in the air were the remnants of our friendship, threadbare from lack of use.

"Mike?"

"Emily?"

We spoke in unison, breaking off, laughing nervously as we each gave permission for the other to speak first.

"You first," we said together, as if our minds worked alike. Awkwardly, we laughed again. How could we be so much alike and yet feel so far apart?

"I'm driving, you talk." Mike solved our stalemate.

I threaded my fingers together, twisting them uncertainly, not at all sure just what I'd meant to say.

"I wasn't supposed to leave home tonight." The words fell from my mouth. Confession. My attempt at remaking the still-young new year. If anyone would be on my side, Mike would.

"I wondered," he said without judgment.

"I snuck out to meet Rick, and then when he wasn't there..." Mike knew the rest. I looked at my lap. "I thought tonight would be fun. Instead, I've felt crummy all night."

Mike nodded as he guided the truck around a snowdrift. "Yeah, God does that sometimes."

There was a time when Mike's reminder might have made me angry, but not tonight. I felt my disobedience heavy on my shoulders even without his words. What he said was only the truth.

"I really need to get home."

"Almost there." Mike doused the headlights as he turned the corner, gliding to a stop in front of my house. He shifted into park and then stared out the window.

The wind had died down; only an occasional gust twirled the snow outside. A bright moon cast blue shadows across my front yard.

"I suppose I'd better go in." I put my hand on the door handle.

"Emily?" Mike turned my way. "I want to say something, so you can't say you didn't know." He filled his lungs, then exhaled before he spoke. "I've liked you since I moved to Brewster in fifth grade. You were my best friend practically before I even knew the difference between boys and girls." I couldn't help but smile. Those days didn't seem that long ago tonight. "You're still my best friend whether you know it or not. And, well…" he paused, looking me in the eye, "…I just want you to know that…" He stopped, dipping his head for a moment, lifting it to look squarely in my eyes. "I still like you."

Oh. I knew what he meant. Not "like you" like when we were still little kids. *"Like* you," like…well, I knew *exactly* what he meant. I blinked at Mike. What was I supposed to say? Rick was my boyfriend. Mike knew that.

Of course he did, but he'd told me his feelings anyway. That was so like Mike, being honest even when not saying anything would be easier.

I knew what he wanted me to say…*I like you, too.* I doubted he expected the words, but he probably hoped to hear them all the same. Saying them wouldn't be fair when he'd been so honest with me. I did like Mike, but not in the same way I felt about Rick. At least I didn't think so. Right now I felt nothing but confused.

"As long as I'm telling you everything," Mike went on, as if my mind hadn't been wringing for words while he waited, "I might as well tell you that I was driving by your house on purpose tonight."

My eyes widened. "You were?"

"Everyone was at Hannah's except you, and I kinda figured Rick wouldn't make it to town in this weather. So…" A wry smile played on his lips as he shrugged one shoulder. "You never know…"

Never in all my plotting about how to spend this New Year's Eve had the idea of spending it with Mike crossed my mind, but now that I had, I knew that if I had been bent on disobeying, there were a lot worse things I could have done than spend the evening with Mike. Who knew what might have happened if Rick had been the one driving past tonight? Rick had been pushing for more from me for weeks now. I'd known full well when I'd left the house tonight what the evening might have in store. Even then, I'd still left.

Mike's feelings for me felt so honest. Simple in a way my relationship with Rick wasn't. Suddenly I knew just the words to say to Mike. I opened the door of the pickup and turned to him as the cold winter air hit my face. "You never know…"

I got out of the truck as Mike's eyebrows shot skyward and a big, goofy grin covered his face. I couldn't help but grin back at my friend.

I could hear his "Happy New Year" in my mind long after he'd driven down the street. I stood on the curb, thinking about how this night had turned out so differently than I had planned.

I use all things for good.

God might have had this evening figured out long before I had ever left the house.

I turned toward the sidewalk leading to my kitchen door, wondering if God had worked on this next part at all. Very slowly I put one foot in front of the other, taking one careful step and then another, marveling how in all my planning and plotting about how to get out of my house, I'd forgotten entirely about figuring out how to get back in.

Libby

Logic told me Emily was safe. Even in a blizzard she could knock on most any door in town, and someone would recognize her and pull her inside the warmth and protection of their home. But logic wasn't fueling me. I panicked.

"Where do you suppose she is?" My throat was tight, my voice shrill as I pulled at the pillows that were supposed to be Emily. I tossed them to where they were supposed to be, near the head of the bed.

"Well, she didn't drive anywhere." From somewhere in the mess that was Emily's dressertop, Bob held up her set of car keys.

"Is that supposed to make me feel better? That she's not inside a warm car but wandering outside in this weather?" I had no idea why turning on Bob made my panic feel justified, as if he was withholding information on purpose. In my mind's eye I pictured Emily stumbling through the streets of Brewster in a gauzy, tattered dress that she'd never dream of owning, much less wearing. Her lips were blue as she wrapped a thin shawl around her shoulders, gazing at some imaginary lantern in the too-far-to-stumble distance. If only my imagination worked as well when I tried to work on my novel.

"I suppose I'll drive around and look for her." Bob's tone held no panic, only his lack of enthusiasm for taking a drive after one A.M. In a blizzard, no less.

I looked out the window. "At least the wind has gone down." I followed him to the kitchen. "You know darn well she didn't wear any boots, and knowing her she didn't even take a scarf. What was she thinking? Well, obviously, she wasn't. Make sure you have the heater on high. She's probably a Popsicle if she tried to walk anywhere." As

Bob grabbed his keys off the top of the fridge I added, "And don't get stuck. I don't need to be worrying about you, too."

In no mood for my harping, Bob leveled his gaze at me. Okay, so he wouldn't purposely go out and get stuck. But still…It wasn't easy, but I clamped my mouth shut. Nothing I could say would improve the situation.

Panic continued to dog me as I paced from the living room into the kitchen, then back again and again, a labyrinth with no soothing center. Who was Emily with? What was she doing? When had she snuck out? Where could she be? I was asking the questions any crackerjack investigator would ask, but I had no perpetrator to interrogate. I had only my overactive imagination to fill in the blanks.

No question she was with Rick. The young man she'd admitted to drinking with only weeks before. Probably toasting the new year with sloppy kisses…or worse. Once again, my mind flew into overdrive, imagining my baby, my youngest, with some testosterone-driven, drunken athlete overpowering her in the back seat of his polished Studebaker. I could almost hear her cry for help.

I stopped in my tracks, yanking at a kitchen chair and throwing myself into it. What was almost worse was the thought that Emily might not be fighting off Rick's clumsy advances. Maybe she snuck out of the house in hopes of them.

I stood once again and resumed my pacing. This just couldn't be happening. Where had my talkative, tell-mom-everything young daughter gone? She had turned into a secretive teenager, apparently. One that would defy us rather than accept just punishment.

Normally, my anger would have kicked in by now, pushing away fear and doubt, but tonight this wee hour held only worry and uncertainty. Was our punishment just? Was making her stay home on New Year's Eve too harsh? Were we wrong to expect her to obey? What had we done wrong? Maybe I wasn't meant to be a mother. But if I wasn't meant to be a mother, why did I feel that if anything bad happened to Emily tonight I'd rather be dead than hear the news?

The familiar squeak of the kitchen door interrupted my frenzied thoughts. I'd been so lost in panic I hadn't heard the garage door or Bob's car.

"Did you find her?"

I knew I sounded frantic, but I didn't care about that. I ran into the kitchen expecting to find Bob taking off his coat, telling me Emily was dragging her frozen feet out in the garage. Instead, there stood Emily, stock-still in the doorway, the empty garage framing her homecoming. No wonder I hadn't heard the car drive in. Bob was still out looking for her.

Emily stared at me for one long moment, as if debating the merits of turning around and going back outside against staying and facing me. Apparently I won out over the subzero temperatures. Her face crumbled, and she threw herself into my arms as though she were three instead of sixteen.

"Mo-om, I'm so sorry. I—" Her loud sobs drowned out whatever else she meant to say.

I wrapped my arms around her and let her cry, surprised to find tears coursing down my face, too. My baby was safe. That was all that mattered.

"Rick was—" Emily sucked in a chestful of air, squeaking out words between sobs. "So cold—pickup—stuck—Austin—Scott— pushing—party—" She drew in a long shaky breath and added, "It was supposed to be fun, but I feel awful." Again she broke into huge sobs.

My tears dried as cold fear filled me. I tried to piece together the words of Emily's night. Rick picked her up? And then they got stuck? It was cold and Austin and Scott showed up? Austin and Scott who? And what were they pushing? Rick's car or Emily's body? Had they ganged up and assaulted her? What happened at the party? Did they force her to drink? To swallow some sort of pill? What happened that was so awful?

I took a deep breath, trying to calm myself. I wasn't going to get any answers by making them up. Only Emily could tell me what really happened.

"Let's go sit on the couch." I kept my arm around her as we walked into the living room, snuggling together on the sofa pillows as if ready for a bedtime story. This was a bedtime story all right, just not the kind I ever imagined I'd want to hear. "Emily…" Surprisingly, my voice was soft and assuring, not at all how I felt. "…you need to start over and tell me what happened tonight." If those boys had hurt her, I was going to see that they *paid* for harming my daughter.

I held Emily close as she recounted the details of the night. How she'd tiptoed right past the couch where we sat now, letting herself out on her New Year's Eve adventure while Bob and I were sound asleep. The particulars of her night were nowhere near the grim fantasy I had imagined. And yet, her innocent night of getting stood up by Rick, driving around with Mike, watching as the boys pushed Paul Bennett and Ruthie Hammond out of a snowbank, and dropping Austin and Scott off at Hannah Stromme's party did nothing to calm the wild thoughts racing through my brain. I could barely hear the facts over the roar of what could have been. I stroked her hair as she finished her story, only an occasional hiccup interrupting her tale.

"Some new year," she concluded, lifting her head to look into my eyes.

"Some new year," I agreed, tucking a strand of damp hair behind her ear as I wondered just what this new year held for us. It was going to have to start out with a punishment of some sort for Emily's disobedience. But then what? I'd learned that night that no amount of vigilance could protect Emily from what lurked outside our house.

I had yet to learn that no amount of vigilance could protect me from what lurked within my mind.

Emily

I opened my locker and automatically smiled at the photo of Rick and me I had taped inside the door. Then I remembered I wasn't smiling at him that day. Not even his picture. I was still mad at him for standing me up on New Year's Eve. I pushed my lips into a line and tossed my lit book into my locker, pulling out my chemistry book with the same hand. Ugh. I didn't feel one bit like sitting through another boring class today.

The first day of school after New Year's had always felt sort of exciting—finding out what everyone did for Christmas and what neat gifts they'd gotten, but this year I almost wished I had the flu or something. Rick was mad at me because I was mad at him and Jen was crabby because Ryan had told her he wasn't sure they should keep going out. The only person who seemed to be enjoying the new year at all was Mike.

"How's it goin'?" Mike clanked his locker shut with his hip, grinning at me from his locker, four down from mine.

I shrugged my shoulders. "It's goin'."

"Did your folks find out you went out on New Year's Eve?" Leave it to Mike to get right to the point.

I nodded, pushing my locker closed with my hand. I looked around to see if anyone else had heard Mike's comment. Jen was the only other person I'd told about the New Year's dud.

"Well…?" He fell into step beside me as we headed to chemistry. "Are you dead meat?"

I couldn't help but smile. Mike had a way with words that always caught me off guard. I bumped him with my shoulder, giggling. It was the first time I'd laughed in the new year.

"I'm here, aren't I?"

"Well, yeah, but your parents would get put in jail if they didn't let you come to school. Maybe this is their cover for locking you in a closet when you get home." He walked backward in front of me, wiggling his fingers in front of my lips as if coaxing words from my mouth. "Come on…you can tell me. Tell all and I'll sneak into your house in the dark of night and kidnap you from the trolls who are holding you hostage." Even Mike couldn't keep a straight face anymore. He laughed out loud as he spun on his heel and walked beside me again. "Really, what happened?"

"Nothing," I said, knowing full well he'd never believe me.

"Sure—and I'm the King of…of Flander." The dinky little town fifteen miles from Brewster. Funny.

"It's true." I stopped at the door to the science room, wanting this conversation to be over before anyone else from my class overheard it. I didn't need the whole school to know the disaster my New Year's Eve had turned out to be. "They didn't punish me." Mike's brows furrowed in question as I continued, "Actually, they apologized for not allowing me to go out." I tossed my head, pushing my hair away from my face. "Go figure."

Mike followed me into the science room, stopping by my desk as I slipped into the seat.

"And the captives shall go free," he said smiling, tapping one finger on the back of my hand before he walked to his desk near the back of the room.

I pulled out my notebook and a pen, waiting for Mr. Morgan to start class. I had no doubt what Mike had said was some Bible verse he'd found. It was weird, though. I didn't feel free at all…especially when I remembered what had happened New Year's Day. Or really, what *hadn't* happened…

"Emily, we need to talk to you about last night." Dad was standing at the foot of the stairs as I came out of my room sometime near noon on New Year's Day. "Your mom and I will wait for you in the kitchen."

I headed into the bathroom and splashed warm water on my face. I was kinda glad they weren't going to beat around the bush and make me wonder all day just where I stood with them. I went back into my room and slipped into the same jeans I'd worn for my little adventure. I had a bad feeling that Mom and Dad weren't going to think it was little at all. I tossed a sweatshirt over my head and walked downstairs to meet my fate.

Dad was reading the newspaper at the head of the table; Mom had her hands clutched around a cup of coffee so hard her knuckles were white. This didn't look good. I pulled out my usual chair at the table and sat down. Dad slowly folded the paper. I took a deep breath, and as I released it words tumbled out of my mouth.

"I know I blew it last night. I'm sorry. I shouldn't have snuck out, and if it makes you feel any better I really didn't have all that much fun. I was with Mike and you know Mike, we just drove around and didn't do nothing."

"Anything," Mom corrected. She glanced at my dad, then relaxed her death grip on the cup. "Sorry…it's what you get when you live with a writer." She looked down at her hands, almost as if she couldn't stand to look at me.

My dad took off his reading glasses. "Emily, your mother and I have talked this over…at length."

Mom looked at Dad again and then looked out the window.

Okay, so what was up? Usually when I did something wrong, Mom had a million things to say and Dad would just sorta sit there. But today, Mom couldn't bring herself to talk to me or something. My heart started pounding.

Dad took a sip of his coffee.

"This might be hard for you to believe, Emily, but your mom and I were teenagers once upon a time. Last night we were so intent on upholding the punishment we'd given you, we forgot just how important being with your friends is." He held up a cautioning finger. "That doesn't mean what you did was right. It wasn't, and it could have been dangerous, too, considering the weather, but we realize we might need to give you a little more freedom. You're growing up, and maybe we've been holding on a little too tight."

Mom sighed, a catch in her throat that sounded like she was crying inside. This was so weird, as if I'd snuck out last night and returned in a different time zone. Make that *world*.

"We've decided we need to take part of the blame for last night. Your mother said you two talked when you got home, and you fully understand what you did. We're going to chalk this up to mistakes on both our parts. Hopefully, we can all learn from this and start the new year on a better note. Olivia, do you have anything to add?" Dad picked up his glasses, obviously done.

Mom practically whispered. "About the job."

"Oh, yes." Dad set his glasses on top of the newspaper. "Along with giving you more freedom, we also expect you to take on more responsibility."

Ah-ha, I knew there had to be a catch. My finger traced along a grain pattern in the tabletop as I waited to hear what it was.

"We know you're busy with basketball right now, but we think it would be a good idea for you to get a part-time job. That way you can start paying for some of the gas for your car, and for some of your clothes. Those sorts of things. How does that sound?"

How did it sound? It sounded like my parents had their brains sucked out during the night. If I didn't know better, I'd swear there were two aliens sitting at the kitchen table with me. My normal parents would be grounding me for life for sneaking out last night, not telling me to be away from home more by getting a job. They also would have forbidden me to speak to my friends until I graduated from college or got married, whichever came last, and they would have made sure my phone conversations were monitored by the FBI until I shriveled up and died. This whole conversation was super-weird. Of course I wasn't going to tell them that.

"It sounds…okay." I didn't want to sound too excited yet. I was still trying to comprehend what my dad had said.

"So I'm not grounded?"

Dad looked at my mom, who was still staring out the window, and then he picked up the paper. "No, you're not."

"And I'm not getting punished for last night?" I still couldn't believe it.

"No."

"Do I still have a curfew?" Maybe they'd simply decided to wash their hands of me. Suddenly I hoped not. As much as I'd begged for freedom, now that it was being handed to me it felt kinda scary.

A half-smile crept onto Dad's face. "Yes, that you still have, but we've decided to let you follow the school's curfew on the weekends."

One whole extra hour. Twenty-four hours ago, I wouldn't have thought much of it if they'd told me I could stay out an extra hour…big, hairy deal. But now I was sorta glad they kept some rules. As much as I complained about my curfew, I was secretly glad I had a reason to tell my friends I had to get home sometimes. More than once I'd been uncomfortable with what was going on, and accusing my parents of being monsters gave me a good excuse to leave.

"So the chemical formulation of copper is…" Mr. Morgan's drone worked its way through my thoughts, bringing me back to chemistry class. I looked down at the blank piece of paper in front of me. I hoped I hadn't missed anything important. If I had, I knew Mike would let me borrow his notes. I glanced over my shoulder to the back of the room where he sat, head down, writing fast. That was Mike, someone you could count on.

Now all I had to do was figure out when to start talking to Rick again. He called me New Year's Day, explaining that the weather had kept him home, offering to come over and watch a movie or something that night. But after the talk with my folks and finding out I wasn't getting punished, well, I almost felt as if I should punish myself. I felt guilty for sneaking out, for disobeying, and I kind of thought Rick should shoulder part of the burden I was lugging around. Being mad at Rick at least made me feel as though I were paying some kind of price for my bad behavior. Besides, I didn't have the nerve to ask Mom and Dad if Rick would even be allowed in our house. He hadn't been over since that night Mom found out I'd been drinking.

I looked up at the classroom clock as the second hand swept around the dial. This class was fifty minutes long—usually fifty minutes too long, considering it was the last class of the day. But today I wished it lasted longer. It wasn't that I was worried about seeing Rick; I was pretty sure we'd be talking again by the end of the evening. And it wasn't the thought of our first basketball practice after the Christmas break—always harder because of the laziness of the days before. It was the thought that after class, after practice, I was going to have to go home and see my mom.

I closed my chemistry book and waited for the bell to ring, feeling the tightening of my stomach as I thought of the hours to come. Ever since New Year's night, I had turned into the invisible daughter. It was almost as though Mom didn't see me even when we were in the same room. Half the time she dabbed at her eyes with a tissue, as if what I'd done was so disappointing to her the tears wouldn't stop; the other half she'd be staring at her computer screen, not typing a word…just staring. She was spooky, and even worse, I didn't know what I could do to make things better.

The bell rang and I stood, pulling my backpack over my shoulder. The way my mom was acting was worse punishment than being grounded. If they had grounded me, I could have paid my time and been done. Punishment over. Free and clear. The way things were I had no idea how I could make amends for what I'd done. I didn't have a clue how to patch up the black hole in my mom's heart. The hole I'd put there.

Libby

I still didn't know what was wrong with me, and it was getting worse, not better. I pulled another tissue from the box and blew my nose, determined to get my column written this morning even if I had to do it through tears. I tossed the tissue into the garbage can at my side, not missing the irony that I was attempting to write a humor column while crying.

I placed my hands on the keyboard, squinting at the handwritten notes I'd scribbled earlier at the kitchen table. I was glad to have my annual year-in-review column to fall back on. Plucking highlights from the past year's news and adding a satiric comment was much easier than reinventing the wheel with a brain that was no longer fully functional.

In the week since New Year's Eve, I'd lost control of my thoughts and my emotions. I could barely force myself through the motions of each day. I pulled myself out of bed, my cocoon from the world, and pushed myself through a routine until I could climb back under the covers. I had no idea what was happening to me, and the uncertainty made it worse.

I took my hands off the inert keyboard and pressed my fingers over my eyes, the momentary darkness a comfort. If only I could call Anne. She would know exactly what would bring order to my thoughts.

Prayer.

Of course that's what Anne would be doing. She would be praying. I took my fingers from my face, my eyes falling on the silver pen Anne had given me as a birthday gift years ago. I rolled the cool metal between my warm fingers. The gift had been her way of encouraging my dreams of writing. But how was I supposed to write or pray when I could hardly think?

Maybe another cup of coffee, a dose of caffeine, would jolt my brain into action. I pushed away from the desk and headed toward the kitchen. If only I had a diagnosis. Some illness, some disease… something to blame for the way I was feeling…then I could cope. I knew how to research, how to tackle a problem that had a source. If only I could find one. But I somehow doubted any medical book listed "Unknown Mysterious Illness" between its thick covers.

I blew on the coffee, sipping slowly. The steaming, dark liquid was not the soothing comfort I had hoped. Nothing was these days. Not even the commotion of Emily's basketball game the previous night had been able to snap me out of the fog that enveloped me.

"Defense! Get your hands up!" Bob rarely raised his voice at anything, but with the Badgers two points behind and only a minute left in the game, apparently yelling seemed the only way to help from the bleachers. I only wished I could muster the enthusiasm to get involved.

I sat on the bleacher next to Bob, high above the wooden floor, listening as the ball bounced rhythmically across the gym. The voices that echoed through the cavernous space sounded fuzzy, like static from a bad telephone connection. But the connection wasn't from a bad phone line; it was in my brain. The harder I tried to focus on the game, to keep my eyes on Emily as she darted between the opposing players, the more difficult it became to ignore the fact that there were two of me watching her play.

Yes, two of me. One shell-person sat on the bleachers, clapping her hands occasionally only because some part of her knew she should, all the while hoping she was clapping for the right team and no one would notice if she wasn't. The other me, the one that felt almost more real, hung invisibly somewhere high above the gym, watching the other Olivia as she watched the game, understanding all the while that a high school basketball game was a highly unlikely place to develop a split personality. Both of me would have laughed if they weren't so scared.

I shook my head, shaking my thoughts back to the kitchen and my cooling cup of coffee. I popped it in the microwave, tapping my foot as ten seconds counted down. No one yelled "Happy New Year!" at the end of this countdown. In fact, the new year held no happiness at all. Something had happened to me New Year's Eve, something that combined all the symptoms of the weeks and months before and condensed them into a cement block that had taken up residence on my chest. At the *ding,* I pulled the hot cup from the microwave and breathed in a huge lungful of air, hoping to dislodge the brick that had settled New Year's Eve as I cried along with Emily.

That night was the first time I had noticed the two Olivias. One Olivia, the one who was the in-control mother, led her daughter to the couch in the living room, put a warm arm around her daughter's shaking shoulders, and stroked her hair as she cried out her fear and disappointment. *Pat her shoulder,* that Olivia said. *There, there, everything will be okay.* She wasn't sure just who she was trying to comfort, her daughter or herself.

The other Olivia, the one who stood across the living room by herself, watched the mother and daughter, sizing up the fact that the mother had no sure way to protect her vulnerable child. She had raised her as best she could, and now the daughter had to go out into the world, armed only with the meager rations her mother had provided. They didn't seem to be near enough.

I knew feeling that there were two of me didn't make any sense, but try telling that to my brain. I blinked my eyes, hard, trying to merge the two of me. One fully comprehended what was going on with her daughter and understood this was the way of life, and the other me realized I had absolutely no control over what happened to my daughter.

A wave of cold panic was no comfort at all.

⌒

I spread mayonnaise on four slices of bread and added a thin coat of mustard. Bob wasn't crazy about mustard, but I had to do something to make the sandwiches more palatable to my dulled taste buds. I peeled several slices of deli roast beef from the one-pound package, piling Bob's sandwich high. I hoped he wouldn't notice the difference in the other half sandwich I put on his plate. I couldn't possibly choke down more than one half. I set the sandwiches on the table, covering each plate with an unfolded paper napkin. No sense drying out the bread and making it even harder to swallow.

I poured two glasses of skim milk and set them on the table by the plates. Now that Bob worked in Carlton, he rarely came home for lunch, but he had a meeting at the Brewster bank and would be joining me at noon. I glanced at the clock on the microwave—twelve o'clock sharp. He'd be here soon.

I hurried into the bathroom and pushed a brush through my hair, smoothing the brown strands I'd barely combed that morning. I dabbed a bit of eye shadow on each lid, hoping Bob wouldn't notice that I'd spent most of the morning in tears. Somehow I'd written my column, but I planned to read it over after lunch before I e-mailed it to the *Brewster Banner*. Who knew what words my muddled brain might have put there?

I patted at my nose, hoping the loose powder would cover the redness. I stared into the mirror; nothing was going to hide the red rims of my eyes. Just the thought caused another round of tears to spring into the corners. What was *wrong* with me? If I didn't find out soon, I was going to lose my mind.

There's someone in Carlton I'd like you to see.

Ellen West's words from my doctor appointment at Thanksgiving time rang in my ears. At the time I'd been upset that she hadn't found something physically wrong with me, so sure that my pounding heart and loss of appetite were clues to some obvious ailment. I was no longer so certain. My roller-coaster emotions seemed to be pushing me to a precipice I didn't want to reach. My mind was no amusement park, and the ride was no fun at all. As I'd been doing all morning, I blinked back tears.

Bob's voice came from the kitchen. "Olivia, I'm home."

Oh, great. I held my hands under the faucet, wetting them with cold water. I pressed my fingers carefully against my eyes, hoping the coolness would somehow dampen the tears but leave the eye shadow intact. It certainly wasn't a secret to Bob that I'd spent most of the new year in tears. I tried more than once to explain my crying jags, but how do you explain something that's a mystery?

I took my fingers from my eyes, grabbing a tissue and dabbing away the excess moisture. For a couple days Bob had accepted my excuse that I was upset over what Emily had done. He even offered to add a punishment to her relaxed rules if that would make me feel better.

Bob was the one who had suggested not punishing Emily for her late-night escapade, reasoning that she needed to experiment with freedom while still under our watchful eye. College was a little over a year away; better for her to have us to buffer any problems she encountered now.

I'd been little help that night as we lay in bed discussing our options. Actually, I just cried and Bob talked, trying to soothe me with reason. I had a suspicion that part of the reason he suggested we not punish Emily was that enforcing her punishments usually fell on me since I was home with her more. And the fragile state I'd been in recently didn't lend itself to maintaining discipline. That thought alone caused a new wave of tears. I couldn't tell Bob I wasn't crying about Emily. Who knew where my tears were coming from? I certainly didn't.

They had continued to flow long beyond explanation—a whole week after the fact. I knew I wouldn't be able to use Emily as an excuse any longer. My real worry was that Bob would insist I see a specialist. He wouldn't have to spell it out—I'd know he meant a psychiatrist. What would I say then?

I took a deep breath and hurried down the stairs, pasting a smile on my face.

"Hi!" My voice didn't give a thing away. So far, so good. "How was your meeting?"

Bob was already seated at the table. I slid into my spot across from him, noting that he hadn't answered my question. He reached across the table and took my hands, bowing his head. I did, too. Ever since Anne's death we'd started saying table grace. Funny how quickly it had become a part of our routine.

"Amen." Bob squeezed my hands, then swept the napkin off his plate. "Mmm, looks good." Three sandwich halves outlined his plate, surrounding a small stack of potato chips and five mini dill pickles.

I picked up my napkin and put it in my lap. I didn't feel at all hungry for the lone half of a sandwich on my plate.

"Did we run out of chips?" Bob asked. "Here, have some of mine. He picked a few up and held them out.

"No, that's okay." I picked up my sandwich. "I'm not very hungry today. I'll probably have some fruit later." Probably not. Eating was beginning to feel as though it were a mandatory military march. *One-two, take a taste, three-four, get it down with haste.* I only ate because I knew I had to. I swallowed the bite of dry sandwich. Lately everything I forced down tasted like cotton balls. "You didn't answer my question. How was your meeting?" Maybe distraction would take Bob's mind off my nearly empty plate. Maybe a conversation would take my mind off my troubling emotions. But even as I said the words a lump filled my throat. I swallowed at nothing, trying to keep the tears inside at least until Bob went back to work.

"I wanted to talk to you about that." Slowly, he placed his half-eaten sandwich on his plate, leveling his gaze at me. "How would you feel about moving?"

Moving? *Moving?*

"As in leaving Brewster?" The words squeaked from my throat.

Bob nodded, his eyes assessing my reaction.

The knot that had been in my throat tightened. I was suffocating. I put down my sandwich and quickly sat up as straight as I could, taking in a lungful of air. No, I was okay. Air was flowing through my nose, down my airway, filling my lungs. I was fine. Just fine.

So why was an elephant on my chest? I breathed deeply again, hoping if not to push the elephant off, at least to move him over just a little bit to a spot where I could breath without straining.

"Olivia, are you okay?" Bob half rose from his chair.

"Fine." I waved him down. "Just something caught in my throat." My voice sounded as though I were being strangled from behind. I coughed, trying to clear away the imaginary crumbs that were my vocal chords. What was happening?

A sip of milk, that would help. I grabbed at my glass, pushing the liquid down my throat. It did help a bit. I could breath again. No, I couldn't. I pulled air through my nostrils, telling myself that as long as I could get air I would be okay.

"Any thoughts?" Bob finished off a pickle in one bite and picked up another sandwich half.

How could he keep eating? Couldn't he see I was dying over here? How could he suggest moving as though it were as simple as packing for a picnic?

"Just a minute," I said, pushing myself away from the table, coughing to keep up my ruse. "Bathroom," I added, hoping Bob could decipher the cryptic sentence that fell from my mouth. I hurried up the stairs, bypassing the half bath on the main floor. I wanted the familiar comfort of my master bath. It was also the farthest room in the house from where Bob sat.

Ah, I pressed a cold washcloth against my face. *You're going to be fine. You're going to be fine.* I repeated the mantra. *You're going to be fine.* It was better than thinking about how I really felt. I took the washcloth away, looking into the mirror. My eyes were wild, as if I were a trapped animal. How could Bob even think about moving *now?* My hands shook as I ran more water over the cloth.

When the kids were little, I had begged Bob to move us to a bigger town. I told Anne about my dream of browsing a bookstore whenever I had a whim, about joining a writer's critique group. I'd have sacrificed my eye teeth to move before. But now? Now, when the only place that felt safe was this house? When every trip to the grocery store turned into an excursion of epic proportions? The thought alone made my head spin. I grabbed onto the counter, hoping the cool marble surface would steady my world. I couldn't tell Bob my fears. He would think I was nuts.

If the shoe fits...

"There's someone I'd like you to see."

If the shoe fits...

Maybe I was losing my mind. I sank onto the cold tile floor as sweat beaded on my upper lip. My hand trembled as I moved to wipe it off.

"There's nothing physically wrong with you." The doctor's words were hardly comfort now. Were they proof enough that I was losing my mind?

I leaned back against the porcelain bathtub, letting its cool veneer seep into my overheated body. How was a person to know if she was going crazy? I'd always thought that people who were labeled "mentally ill" were too far gone to know they were.

If I hadn't been diagnosing myself, I might have chuckled. For some reason I had always found some humor in those common phrases: *I'm losing my mind. I'm going nuts.* Not funny now. Not one bit. I brushed my hair away from my face, the tepid breeze from my hands small relief from the heat.

Would I know if I was going crazy? Could part of a person be sane while another part crumbled? As quickly as the furnace that was masquerading as my emotions had heated my body, it turned off, sending icy chills through my limbs.

I needed help.

"Olivia, are you okay?" Bob's voice filtered through the bathroom door.

Bob. I'd forgotten completely about my husband downstairs. But now he was no longer in the kitchen. Now he stood four feet away, only a thin piece of wood separating him from his wife.

His crazy wife.

A second ago I had wished for help, but now all I wanted to do was hide the fact that I might need any. I coughed loudly, keeping up the pretense as I rose from the floor. I grabbed the wet washcloth lying on the counter and swiped at my face as I opened the door. "Man, I really must have swallowed wrong."

"I was beginning to wonder if I should dial 9-1-1." Bob patted my back.

"That's all I'd need, the Brewster ambulance crew here because of a bread crumb. And the bathroom's not clean." I folded the washcloth and hung it on the towel rack, marveling at how easily I could pretend.

Bob chuckled. "That's what I love about you, Olivia, you're quick. You can make anything seem like it's not a big deal. Even choking. Sometimes I'd love to see what's in that mind of yours."

Believe me, you wouldn't.

"Sorry, that department is closed for the day."

Bob chuckled again. Let him laugh, goodness knows I wasn't doing much of it these days. He could chortle for the both of us.

"So," he said, stepping aside as I walked out of the bathroom, "do I even dare ask again what you think about moving?" He quickly added, "Or will it send you off on another coughing binge?"

I waved my hand in the air as if his words were silliness. If only he knew. I sat on the edge of the bed.

"Why are you bringing this up?" Maybe if I knew the facts I could deal with them. Maybe the thought was simply his way of making lunchtime conversation.

Bob took a seat in the overstuffed chair near the bed. I bit my tongue as he sat on a pair of his slacks I'd been meaning to take to the cleaners. Wasn't that thought itself evidence I wasn't crazy? Surely someone who was on the edge of sanity wouldn't be thinking about the dry cleaners. Would she?

Bob cracked his knuckles, a nervous habit he'd brought with him into our marriage. You'd think after twenty-one years I'd be used to it. I wasn't. It was metal marbles clanking inside my head.

"Please don't do that."

"Sorry." He gave me the same bashful grin he always did at the reminder. "At our meeting today…at the bank," he prompted, plunging in as if I hadn't practically just died in the bathroom, "the board entertained an offer for a buyout." He cleared his throat as mine closed tighter. "I've known about the possibility for a while. Ever since we bought the bank over in Carlton, I've anticipated this might happen. John Weber, the CEO at First Northwest, has been dropping hints that they might like to take a look at acquiring our two banks. It's an attractive package now that we've expanded. I didn't want to say anything until we had a firm bid, but yesterday their lawyer sent a package tendering an offer. That's why I called the special meeting today."

And to think I'd thought it was a routine board meeting. Somehow a roast beef sandwich, chips, and dill pickles didn't seem the proper fare to conclude discussion of a several-million-dollar deal.

"What did they decide?" I forced the words from my lungs as the elephant sat back down.

"Well, they didn't. Not today anyway. This kind of deal takes time." As if that reminded him, he looked at his watch. "I've got to get back to Carlton," he said, but then he put his arm over the back of the chair and continued. "I wasn't sure how some of the stockholders would feel about selling. Some of them take great pride in the fact that they own part of a bank. In a mostly family-held corporation like this, a decision of this magnitude can be touchy. A couple of the older stockholders are ready to start divesting their shares; they're ready to take the money and run. Well, hobble, anyway," Bob cracked. Even in my current state I saw the humor. "A few of the middle-aged stock-holders recognize that in this economy, the investment they have in the bank is about the only sure thing they have right now. They want to hang on. It's complicated."

"So I don't have to start packing yet?" How could I sound almost jovial when another pachyderm had just settled onto my chest? Maybe the term *funny farm* had been invented by someone like me. Someone laughing at the zoo animals sitting on her body as white-clad attendants dragged her, kicking and screaming, out of her home.

"No, not yet," Bob confirmed. "But I wanted to get your thoughts. I mean, I certainly don't have enough shares to sway a vote, but they will listen to my counsel. If we sold the bank, I wouldn't be CEO any longer. The new owners might offer me a position of some sort, but I'm guessing it wouldn't be anything close to what I'm doing now. I'm not so sure I'd want to stay in that capacity. I know you've mentioned moving in the past and I'm wondering…would you still be up for it?"

The only words I could muster were, "Emily's a junior."

"Yeah, I know. I thought about that, too." Again Bob glanced at his watch, this time slapping his hands on his knees and rising. "I've got to get back over to Carlton—I have an appointment at two." He leaned down and quickly kissed my cheek. "We don't have to decide anything right now. These things take time. We've got our annual strategic planning meeting at the end of February. If anything happens, the details won't get hammered out until then. But think about it, okay?"

Think about it? *Think about it?* I wondered if I would ever think about anything else. The thought seemed to have entered my brain and expanded as though it were some mutant sponge from a dank pond, sucking any other thoughts from my gray matter. Bob walked out of the bedroom, leaving me sitting on the edge of my bed, the edge of life as I knew it.

"Mom? Are you here?" Emily's voice drifted from downstairs.

I leapt off the bed as if I'd been shot. What was she doing home at this time of the day? I looked at the clock. It couldn't possibly be almost six o'clock! She couldn't be done with school, home from basketball practice. What had happened to the day?

"Up here," I called, dashing into the bathroom, wiping sleep from my eyes. "I'll be down in a second." I patted at my messy hair. The last I remembered, Bob had left the bedroom and an icy chill had taken over my body. I'd pulled at the afghan folded near the end of the bed and then…and then…well, then Emily was home. I paused at the top of the stairs trying to compose myself, trying to act as though four-hour naps were part of my regular routine.

"How was school?" I asked, nonchalantly entering the kitchen.

"Fine." Emily closed the oven door and looked in the fridge. "What's for supper? I'm starving."

Ah, supper. I knew there was something I should have been doing in those four hours besides trying to avoid reality. What was I going to serve for supper? "Pizza?" I asked, saying the first thing that came to mind. Obviously we wouldn't be having slow-roasted pork tonight.

Emily closed the fridge, a quick line of worry wrinkling her brow. "Are you okay?"

"Fine," I said, pulling the menu from Brewster's only pizza place from the drawer, silently thanking God Brewster *had* a pizza place. Even if they didn't deliver, we could go pick it up. I knew the fact that we were having pizza on a week night didn't escape Emily's scrutiny. I was usually a stickler for well-rounded, balanced meals. At least during the week. Tonight would be a rare exception. She'd have to adjust.

As I ran my finger down the menu, searching for some combination that appealed, my brain began working over Bob's question, "*What would you think about moving?*" A feeling I could only call *doom* filled my body. My heart started pounding while a cool layer of sweat glazed my skin. My hands tingled as if I'd slept on both of them, pins and needles pricking like insects. Is this what dying felt like? A vague part of my brain wondered what Ellen West would think when she read my obituary. Would she believe *then* that there really had been something wrong with me?

"*Sometimes when we are experiencing inner turmoil, our bodies…*"

"*There's someone I'd like you to see…*"

I handed the pizza menu to Emily. "Pick out whatever you want and call Dad to pick it up on his way home. I'm not feeling well." A wave of dizziness engulfed me. Was I going to pass out? Quickly I pulled out a chair and plopped down, resting my head on my knees.

"Mo-om?" Anxiety tinged Emily's word.

"I'll be okay," I said upside down. But would I? I didn't feel one bit okay. "I think it's…it's…" I grasped at a straw: "…menopause." At least I still had the sense to assure Emily. And what would she know about menopause? I could suffer in clear conscience that she wouldn't intervene.

"Should I still order the pizza?" She sounded on the verge of tears.

Slowly I sat up, testing for vertigo. There, it had passed.

"Yes, but just get a medium for you and Dad. I don't feel much like eating." Quite the diet I was on today. Maybe I could turn it into a column: The One-Bite-of-Sandwich and Glance-at-a-Pizza-Menu Diet.

"I'm going to go lie down." Tentatively I stood, hoping the bout of dizziness was gone. So far, so good.

As I climbed the steps, I hung onto the stair rail just in case. All I needed was a broken leg or concussion on top of all my other ailments. I planned to crawl into bed but found myself veering into the walk-in closet instead. Even as I told myself a good night's sleep would take care of whatever was ailing me, I rummaged through the jackets hanging in my closet. I knew exactly which black blazer I was looking for, exactly which pocket to look in. I pushed my hand across the satin lining. There it was. I grasped the small business card in my trembling hand. *Dr. G. Sullivan.* For all the forgetting I'd tried to do, I'd remembered well.

I slipped out of my clothes and into my nightgown, all the while clutching the white card in my cold hand. I crawled under the covers, hoping Emily wouldn't tell Bob I was suffering from menopause. Emily might fall for my diagnosis, but Bob never would.

⁓

I looked at the clock as Bob climbed into bed. Almost midnight. He checked on me earlier, rousing me from a dead sleep just enough to ask if I needed anything.

"No, I'm fine," I mumbled, slipping back into my troubled dreams.

Now I lay awake, staring at the clock as Bob's steady breathing played a backbeat to my anxiety. Two A.M. According to the card I still clutched in my hand, I only had six more hours to get through before I could call Dr. G. Sullivan. The vertigo I'd experienced earlier in the evening played tag with my racing pulse. I had to do something. I couldn't go on like this.

I turned onto my stomach as if trying to turn my back on reality, but my new position did nothing to dispel my worry. I couldn't believe it had come to this. I, Olivia Marsden, was going to be calling Dr. G. Sullivan at daybreak. A psychiatrist. If I still had the nerve, that is. If I still had enough of my wits about me to make the call. I punched at the pillow, careful not to crumple the card I grasped like a lifeline.

Dr. G. Sullivan. I only hoped he had answers, because I no longer had a clue.

Into the Shadow…

Dr. Sullivan

> Patient exhibits increased signs of paranoia. Discussed one incident of possible hallucination since last appointment. Also discussed coping techniques. Follow-up appointment in one week.

I released the Dictaphone button and closed the file on Phillip Grogan. I knew most people in Carlton would be shocked if they knew the successful restaurant owner had battled post-traumatic stress syndrome since his stint in Vietnam more than three decades earlier. I shook my head. So many years of trying to stifle his fear. He was feeling empowered as he fought his terror head on. But the battle still raged. My job was to give him the weapons to fight with.

I sighed, loosening my tie for a moment. This business of psychiatry was an inexact science at best. Progress was hard to quantitatively measure. For not the first time, I wished I'd gone into another branch of medicine. Surgery, for instance. There, a doctor was *doing* something, and results were observable and measurable. Rarely did I feel one of my patients was completely cured. "Management of symptoms" was the goal in my branch of medicine. Hardly a comfort for those who came to me with their illnesses. That's why I infrequently told a patient the goal up front. Sending them running was not the objective.

I looked over my morning schedule. Already I'd seen two patients. Mr. Grogan and Julie Diede, who had been my first appointment. A young woman who had been beaten by her husband and had been referred to me by the safe house where she'd taken refuge.

Anger rose in my chest as I recalled the scar on her cheek, still not completely healed after a month of appointments. Even her gait revealed the way her spirit had been crushed by her unloving husband. How could a man like me expect to heal a ghost?

Lately, I'd been questioning my choice of career more and more. After twenty-seven years in the business of healing, I'd grown cynical. Had I done any good for anyone? I wasn't at all sure as I watched patients shuffle through my door, their problems weighing them down as if they wore cement shoes.

I tried to remind myself that healing wasn't completely in my hands. My patients had a responsibility to themselves, too. Clients didn't help matters when they refused to take the medication I prescribed or, when they did start feeling better, stopped taking the medication altogether, thinking they no longer needed it. Would a diabetic quit taking insulin because their glucose level read normal? Convincing people that brain chemicals functioned in a similar manner was difficult.

I wasn't the Great Healer, but many people came into my office assuming I was. There had been a time when I turned to God, asking for His help in my practice as I determined the proper treatment for patients, but I was long past believing His hand could help my clientele. I gave up on Him completely when He abandoned me.

Well. I wasn't going to think about that now. I sat up straight and tightened my tie. My next appointment was probably tapping her foot in the waiting room. Of course, most of my patients tapped their feet—more in agitation than impatience. I smiled at the inside joke. My colleagues would get a kick out of it. *Get a "kick" out of it.* I smiled to myself at the pun. I was on a roll this morning.

Elaine, my secretary, knocked softly on the office door before she entered.

"Here's the new patient information for your next appointment." She laid the file on my desk, exiting as quietly as she'd entered. What was it about a psychiatric office that made people act as though it were a church? My old carpeting was certainly no hallowed ground.

I picked up the file Elaine had put squarely on the upper left corner of my desk. She hadn't taken long at all to understand that order was important to me. That was one of the factors that had kept her employed by me for nearly twenty years. My eyes scanned the intake information on the familiar form. Olivia Marsden. Housewife. Early forties. Insurance. Not that it mattered, but psychiatry didn't come cheap, and I had expenses, too. And who knew what was on the horizon concerning—no, I'd vowed not to think about that at work. *Focus, doctor.*

Mrs. Marsden was lucky to get a new-patient appointment this time of year. There weren't many psychiatrists in a town the size of Carlton, and my days were booked well into the New Year. "Happy Holidays" was a misnomer in my profession. The holidays took their toll. Many of my old regulars made an appearance in my office this time of year. I was never sure if they were attempting to brush off the old or usher in something new. Maybe a little of both. But it was discouraging to understand there never was a real "fix" for most people. All I had to offer were my listening ears and a prescription. Not much in the whole scheme of things. Only a cancellation had left room for Mrs. Marsden today.

Olivia Marsden…hmmm. I rubbed at my chin. Marsden? Marsden? The name rang a bell, but which one? Oh well, I couldn't think of it now. If a connection existed, it would come to me at three o'clock in the morning, no doubt.

I made a quick assessment of the information on the back of the page. No compromising health problems. No family history of mental illness. Married. Two children, a son in college, a daughter in high school. Husband a banker.

Ah-ha! That was where I'd heard the name. I'd visited with a Robert Marsden at the bank in Carlton recently. Nice man. I wanted some advice about my retirement portfolio. My portfolio looked fine, but my plans felt empty. What with Margaret—no, I wasn't going to think about that now. *Focus.* I riveted my eyes back to the form. Mrs. Marsden was from Brewster…they could be related. *Marsden* wasn't a very common name in this area, and many people from Brewster commuted the forty miles to Carlton for work. Jobs were certainly scarce in a town the size of Brewster. No doubt Mrs. Marsden was a bored banker's wife on the verge of empty-nest syndrome, panicking at the thought. A prescription and advice to sign up for volunteer work should take care of her problems.

I threaded my fingers together and pushed my arms out straight, cracking the knuckles. If my assumptions about Mrs. Marsden were correct, this would be an easy appointment. Her problems couldn't be too daunting. Money might not buy happiness, but it certainly came close. It allowed a certain ease, no matter what else seemed to be wrong.

This should be easy. I reached toward the intercom, "Elaine, you can send my next appointment in now."

Libby

I wiped my sweaty palms against my black pleated skirt. The fact that I was wearing the matching suit jacket didn't escape my notice. The same black jacket where I'd safeguarded Dr. Sullivan's business card all those weeks. I brushed at the shoulders of the jacket and tugged at the hem of my light blue sweater. I wondered if all of Dr. Sullivan's patients dressed up for their appointments. By the looks of the waiting room, they should.

I reached for a magazine on the cherrywood coffee table. A current issue of *Psychology Today.* What a surprise. Either Dr. Sullivan didn't read it, or he read very quickly. In all the appointments I'd been to with Anne, I'd never ever seen a current issue of any magazine. I begrudgingly gave Dr. Sullivan a second point, this one for having up-to-date magazines. I'd already been forced to give the first point to his secretary, who had taken my frantic phone call so calmly that I hung up the phone and wept. Tears of pure thanksgiving. She made the event I dreaded, a phone call to a psychiatrist, seem like the most common occurrence in the world.

I'd lain in bed that morning, feigning the flu, watching as the clock ticked by the minutes. My carefully plotted plan to call Dr. Sullivan the second the clock struck eight A.M. had been foiled as I impatiently waited for Bob to leave for work and for Emily to run out the door to school. For the first time in weeks, I was anxious to get up. Looking toward the phone call I planned to make as though salvation of some sort were on the other end.

I dressed carefully, pulling on gray knit slacks and a matching turtleneck sweater, as though Dr. Sullivan would judge my competence over the phone by what I was wearing. My side-zip, black leather boots hugged my feet, making me feel secure, as if my feet were firmly planted somewhere even when my mind wasn't. A touch of makeup, and I was ready to make the phone call.

No, I wasn't. I paced past the phone, looking again at the card in my hand, the phone number memorized hours ago. I poured myself a cup of coffee, vowing that after the fifth sip I'd make the call. Okay, the tenth sip.

Maybe another cup would make it easier. I poured a second cup, my hand shaking as if on caffeine overload. The comforting warmth soothed for a millisecond, but my heart took up its crazy beat in short order. I hadn't been this nervous since the blind date I let my roommate arrange in college. That was the second time I'd been at NDSU, the first time I'd met Bob.

I gulped the hot coffee—liquid courage. Now. Now I'd call. In one swift motion I set down the cup and picked up the phone, punching at the numbers with one clammy finger. One ring. Pause. My heart pounded. What was I going to say? I'm going crazy? I need help?

I hung up the phone, grabbed my cup, and downed another dose of black medicine. Why, in all those hours I'd lain awake, hadn't I thought about what I'd say when I made my desperate call? I closed my eyes, rehearsing possible opening lines. *Hi! My name is Olivia*— No. *Hi!* was too cheery sounding for someone as miserable as me. The doctor might not let me make an appointment. And I wasn't so sure I wanted to say my name right off. If the doctor sounded even remotely like a quack, I wouldn't make an appointment. No need to leave a clue to my identity.

Good morning. Maybe I shouldn't say *good.* People who were in need of a psychiatrist would be weighed down with negative thoughts, wouldn't they?

Oh, good grief! If I kept this up, I could bypass the psychiatrist altogether and drive straight to the state hospital.

Are you taking appointments? There, that was noncommittal enough. My hand reached again for the phone, paused in midair, and then detoured back to the handle of my coffee mug. How could making a simple doctor appointment be so hard? It was just a simple phone call, but somehow it felt like defeat. Giving in. Surrendering. Admitting I could no longer help myself.

I paced in front of my kitchen cabinets. The other me, the one who now was my almost constant companion, hung near the ceiling, watching my antics with an amused eye. *All dressed up and no where to go,* she chanted as I paraded past my dining room table and into the living room.

If only someone would make this call for me. I marched past the old upright piano in the corner and turned on my heel. *If I had an appointment, I'd keep it.* I walked around the coffee table. *But how can I get an appointment if I can't make the call?* I paced by the end table near my favorite chair, my eyes landing on the Bible I'd kept there since Anne had died. I stopped in my tracks. Anne would have dug into that Bible long ago, seeking guidance from a source more reliable than my frantic wonderings. I sat in the chair and picked up the thick book.

During the two years right after Anne died I'd read the Bible from cover to cover, soaking up the words Anne had used as her daily lifeline. In the following years I hadn't been quite so diligent, making halfhearted attempts at Bible studies I purchased solely on the rec-ommendation of a store clerk in Carlton. Usually I barely made my way past the third lesson before time and interest waned.

My knowledge of the Bible was hardly deep enough to know where to turn now. I flipped open the deep blue cover, letting the thin onionskin-like pages fall open at random. Hardly scientific, but I doubted God put much stock in science anyway.

I closed my eyes in quick silent prayer, something I hadn't done nearly enough of these past months, then opened them and focused on the page before me. Matthew nine, verse twelve: *"People who are well don't need a doctor! It's the sick people who do!"*

I laughed out loud for the first time in months. God couldn't get much clearer than that. Obviously, I wasn't well; if God thought I needed a doctor, maybe I did. I closed the thick book, letting its reassuring weight comfort me for a moment, and then set it aside and strode to the phone.

"Dr. Sullivan's office. How can I help you?"

A secretary? Of course. I hadn't realized that a secretary would answer the phone. In all my imagining, I somehow thought the doctor himself would pick up the receiver, expecting me to enumerate my problems sight unseen. What now? Surely a secretary wouldn't expect me to spill my guts. "I'd…uhhh…I'd…mmmmm…" Suddenly my palms were sweaty again. Words left me.

"Are you calling for a new patient appointment, or a follow-up visit?"

Her voice was soft, calming in a way I hadn't expected. As if she'd done this before. A lump formed in my throat.

"New patient," I managed to say.

"Let me check." I could hear a page turn. "Oh good, here." She spoke more to herself, but if her tranquility was any indication of Dr. Sullivan's competence, I was glad I called. I could use some of what she had. Her voice was a bit louder now. "He had a cancellation for the day after tomorrow, eleven o'clock. Will that work for you?"

Whenever it was, I'd make it work.

"Fine-*e*." My voice cracked. Almost forty-eight hours until my appointment. Somehow I'd had a wild hope that I'd get in that day. Disappointment pushed at my throat. I breathed deeply, steadying myself before I answered the rest of her questions.

"Dr. Sullivan will look forward to seeing you," the secretary said in her soothing voice, as if people called psychiatrists every day.

Well, I supposed they did. I had called and miraculously lived to tell about it. A wave of relief flooded over me. I had an appointment! Someone was going to help me. All I had to do was get through the next forty-eight hours, and I would be on my way to feeling better.

"Take care now," Miss Pleasant Voice said, sounding as if she really hoped I would.

Slowly I hung up the phone and headed back to the chair by my Bible. I held the heavy book next to my chest and wept tears of thanksgiving. I was going to be better soon. Finally.

The next evening I confided in Bob, fumbling my way around the word *psychiatrist* as if it were a swear word and we were in church.

"I have something to tell you," I said the night before my appointment with Dr. Sullivan. My back was to Bob as I scrubbed at a crusty frying pan in the sink. Emily was in Carlton at her CNA class. "I made an appointment yesterday." My throat closed off the rest of the words I planned to say.

Bob was carrying dishes from the table, scraping food into the sink, and loading them in the dishwasher as if this were any ordinary night. Eventually he noticed my silence, noticed my tears falling into the sink, breaking bubbles as they landed. He stepped behind me, his backward hug breaking the dam that held my words.

"I'm going to see a psychiatrist tomorrow," I sobbed. "I don't know what's wrong with me. I'm sorry."

"Sorry for what?" Bob turned me in his arms, cradling my head against his chest, letting my wet hands dry on the back of his cotton shirt. My tears were staining the front of it. He put his hands on my shoulders and held me away from him, just far enough to look into my brimming eyes.

"You have nothing to be sorry about. We both want you to be well." He pulled me to his chest again, holding me tight. "We'll get through this." Minutes later, when my tears had dried and he released his hold, he offered a gift. "I'll drive you tomorrow."

I teared up again, his concern making me brave.

"Thanks, but I'll be okay alone."

Fourteen hours later I looked up from the magazine I was only pretending to read, eyeing the woman behind the desk. She looked exactly as I'd imagined her: blond, angelic hair in soft curls around her face, her countenance a mix of efficiency and empathy. She hadn't blinked an eye as she looked over the form I filled out. I put a check mark beside just about every symptom offered on the menu that was masquerading as a medical form.

I chalked up Dr. Sullivan's third point. Anyone who hired someone so compassionate deserved a point…even if no one but me was counting. I decided to be generous and chalk up a fourth point.

The waiting room was a picture of tranquility. I'd sworn if it appeared even the slightest bit tacky or sleazy I would be out of there, but the dark brown leather sofa and the burgundy, tapestry-like fabric on the side chairs softly whispered, "Sit here."

The score was Dr. Sullivan, four; Libby Marsden, one. I gave myself one point just for showing up.

I gazed out the window. The hollow January sun lit the brick wall of the medical complex next door as if it were a faded photograph. It looked much like I felt: dull, lifeless, a façade. I sighed…well, that was why I was here. Hopefully, within the hour I'd have answers to the feelings and questions that had plagued me for so long.

I planned to make the most of this appointment. Maybe, if things went well, one appointment would be enough. It certainly had been after Anne died.

Anne's death had cloaked me like a heavy winter coat—one that didn't do a thing to keep out the midnight chill that had settled in my limbs. Calling someone for help then showed how muddled my thinking had become. I picked a counselor out of the yellow pages. One who advertised that she *specialized* in loss. As though it were an item on a grocery shelf. I was hoping she could pluck the despair from my heart. Toss it far away like a welcome scrap for some scavenging animal. I'd certainly pay good money for that.

After only a few minutes in the counselor's office, I realized that nothing and no person was going to make the pain go away. Not even someone who specialized in loss. I left quickly and had not gone back.

I closed the unread magazine. No use pretending to read when my mind wandered so widely. Certainly people who worked in a psychiatrist's office were trained to see through pretense anyway. Why pretend? I planned to tell this doctor as much as I could as fast as my lips could shed the words. The faster I told him what was bothering me, the faster he could cure me. Yes, maybe one appointment would do it this time around.

I pulled back the sleeve of my jacket to look at the time just as the secretary said, "Dr. Sullivan will see you now."

As if I'd been shot, I jumped from the chair, but then I forced myself to pause and gather my wits about me, so to speak. Who knew what psychiatrists analyzed when a patient walked through their door? A good first impression couldn't hurt. As I walked toward the door to the doctor's inner sanctum, the thought occurred to me that I could still turn on my heel and make a mad dash for my car.

"People who are well don't need a doctor! It's the sick people who do!"

Okay, okay. The promise I'd made to God after reading that Bible verse propelled me past the secretary and into Dr. Sullivan's nicely lit office. Even before I noticed Dr. Sullivan, I saw the couch, sitting innocently along the far wall. Surely I wouldn't be asked to lie down. I thought of every cartoon I'd ever seen that included a psychiatrist. Always a couch. Always a patient lying down. I hoped with all my heart I could sit in one of the two chairs near Dr. Sullivan's desk.

"Mrs. Marsden." Dr. Sullivan unfolded his lean body from the chair and held out his hand. He reminded me of someone. My mind scrambled to make the connection. Who? I couldn't place the familiarity. His handclasp was firm, not at all clammy like mine.

I wondered if he noticed? Of course, he had to. That was his job, wasn't it? He'd better notice everything about me for what he probably charged. Thankfully, Blue Cross would be paying for this appointment, but still, I wanted my money's worth regardless of which pocket the money was coming from. I tucked my damp hand into my jacket pocket, clutching the tissues inside. I made note of the fact that wondering about the cost of this appointment was proof that I wasn't completely removed from reality. I chalked up another point for myself. Four to two.

"Have a seat, please." Dr. Sullivan motioned to the burgundy leather chairs.

I took the one closest to me; Dr. Sullivan sat in the other. So, this was how it would be. With one index finger I worried the brass nail heads that outlined the arm of the chair. I doubted I was the first patient to discover this soothing technique. I was surprised they weren't worn off completely. Again, I tried to assess who this doctor reminded me of. Something was familiar about him.

Dr. Sullivan adjusted his navy blue tie. "How are you?"

Oh, my. My mind froze. *How was I?* Was his question a casual inquiry? A simple way to greet me? Or was I supposed to dive right in and spill my guts? Was I supposed to murmur *fine* as if we'd just passed on the street, or should I start off telling him about the pit that was playacting as my stomach? I certainly hadn't expected to be stumped by his first question, but I was. I shrugged one shoulder, then wavered my hand, indicating the wobbly path I'd walked of late. Let him analyze that. After all, that was what I was paying him for, wasn't it?

Dr. Sullivan pressed his lips into an understanding smile, almost bowing his head as he acknowledged my gesture.

"I guess that's why you're here," he began. "So, Mrs. Marsden, why don't you tell me what brought you here today?" He held a clipboard against his crossed knee. No doubt he already knew all about my pounding heart, my sleepless nights, and the episode of dizziness I'd experienced two days ago. I supposed he wanted to hear me tell all the gory details. Out loud.

I cleared my throat.

"Could you call me Olivia? Or Libby? Mrs. Marsden makes me feel so old. Like my mother-in-law or something." The second the words were out I wished them back. What sort of psychological implications could that request have?

Patient doesn't like to be called Mrs. Marsden. Unhappy marriage? Latent feelings of hostility against mother-in-law?

Dr. Sullivan smiled. "Olivia, it is." He didn't make a notation on his clipboard. Whew. Then again, maybe he figured there was plenty of time after I left to report my sweaty palms, nervous gestures, and the fact that I hadn't even said hello.

"I guess I should say hello first." There, that took care of that. I forced what I hoped was a friendly smile, picked up my hand and wiggled my fingers in a tiny wave. He wiggled his fingers back at me, an amused expression crinkling his eyes. Okay, so that was dumb. I clamped my hand back onto the chair arm. I had no doubt Dr. Sullivan would be busy all afternoon making notes about his odd new patient.

"Sorry," I mumbled. "I've never..." my words trailed off, an unexpected lump pushing its way across my vocal chords.

"How about if I ask you a few questions to start? That might be easier."

I nodded my reply, pulling out the wad of tissues I'd stuffed into my jacket pocket as I'd left the house. I'd never dreamed I'd need them just to say hello. I dabbed at the corners of my eyes.

"I suppose you're used to this, huh?"

"I am." Discretely he reached over to the desk and slid a box full of tissues my way. "Professional strength," he added.

I looked up and saw that he was smiling. I smiled back, relaxing for the first time since I'd opened my eyes this morning.

"Why don't you start by telling me when this all started?" Dr. Sullivan rearranged the papers on his clipboard, putting a blank sheet on top. His Mont Blanc pen was poised for action.

"Well, ummm..." Where to start? My mind raced through the years. When *had* all this started? Did he mean the physical symptoms that had absorbed all my energy the past months? Or was I supposed to dive right in and tell him any suspected trauma from my past in the hope it held a key to my current distress? One thing for sure, trying to catalog the past chased away the tears. "Gosh." I pushed my hair behind my right ear, something I often did when I was writing. Trying to think. "I've been having these...well...weird symptoms. My heart pounds. I can't sleep, but then sometimes that's all I want to do. I've lost weight. *Without trying,*" I added quickly, just in case he thought I was talking about a successful diet plan I'd concocted. He made a note. "I'm crabby all the time—when I'm not crying, that is." The words alone brought the tears right back. I dabbed at my eyes, again. "See?" As if I needed to offer proof.

Dr. Sullivan nodded, an understanding look in his eyes. Encouragement.

I took a deep breath, forcing the next sentence out fast. "I thought I was starting menopause and went to two doctors but neither one agreed with me and one gave me your card and then two days ago I almost passed out when I was talking to my daughter and I don't know what else to do." Like a marathon runner at the bottom of a hill, I stopped to refuel, filling my lungs for the last portion of the journey. "You're my last hope-*e*."

There. I'd said it, the thing I'd been thinking for two days. The other me, the one who wasn't crying but was sitting in Dr. Sullivan's black leather chair across the desk from me, watched as tears took over and I sobbed silently in the burgundy leather chair next to Dr. Sullivan. I pulled two tissues from the box and wiped my wet face.

There went the makeup I'd applied so carefully, trying to make a good impression. I wrapped the tissue around my index finger, running it under each of my streaming eyes. The other me made a note to buy waterproof mascara. How could one part of my brain be mush and the other be thinking about mundane things liking buying mascara? Maybe I was crazy. A sob escaped my lips. The other me felt a twinge of embarrassment at the show of emotion, but the me in the burgundy chair cried for both of us.

Dr. Sullivan put his pen in his shirt pocket and waited patiently while I cried more tears. While I blew my nose, he studied the notes he'd made, then he folded his hands across the clipboard and spoke.

"I know your symptoms are puzzling to you. And not finding answers in the medical arena only adds to the confusion. I'd like you to take a short test, and then we'll discuss the outcome. All right?"

I recognized he wasn't asking permission, but nodded anyway. He handed me a pen and a small pamphlet he pulled from under the papers on his clipboard.

"Put a check mark by what applies."

My eyes scanned the short list of statements. Ten sentences that would tell me my fate. I wasn't sure if this was the sort of test I wanted to pass or not. I squeezed my left palm against the tissues I held in my hand as I read the first statement.

I am sad most of the time. Oh, yes. I checked the box, wondering what in the world Dr. Sullivan would be able to diagnose from a simple sentence like that.

Number two. *I don't enjoy the same things that used to give me pleasure.* I thought of the school gym where I used to love to climb the bleachers to watch Brian and Emily play ball. That climb was Mount Everest these days. I checked the box and then read the next two statements as if they were one: *I can't sleep at night. I want to sleep all the time.* It seemed impossible, but they both were true. Maybe it was a trick question. I checked both boxes and moved on.

Food has lost its appeal. Yes.

I could eat all the time. Finally, one statement I could answer no. This test was no mental challenge, that was for sure. I hadn't paused once to contemplate an answer. Maybe there were extra points for finishing quickly.

I have physical symptoms that don't go away. Duh, what had I been running to doctors about? Yes!

I have no interest in sex. Poor Bob. I was sure he would love to answer this question for me.

I feel afraid and irritable most of the time. My pounding heart? My perfect imitation of a snapping turtle? Yes to it all.

This questionnaire had apparently been designed to ferret out my exact symptoms. I mentally patted myself on the back. I intuitively knew if I didn't give up, if I pursued my ailments, someone would be able to tell me what was wrong. I was beginning to think I should have come to Dr. Sullivan as my first choice instead of my last. I could hardly wait to hear what the diagnosis would be after all these months of suffering. I had no doubt he would refer me to a specialist of some sort once he realized my symptoms were real and not a figment of my imagination.

One question left. *I am afraid I might harm myself.* Ah, the one statement even I could figure out what they were asking…and why. Suicide. Of course a psychiatrist would throw that question into the mix, the one question that would give him fodder for months of analysis. Thankfully, that was one symptom I did not have. No.

I handed the pop quiz back to the doctor, setting the pen on the edge of the desk as if I were being timed.

"There." If there were points for swiftness, I wanted them.

"I see you didn't have any trouble with any of the questions." Dr. Sullivan took the paper. "I'm sure you're wondering what I can gather from this small amount of information."

"It had crossed my mind," I replied.

As he looked down at the quiz, I slid back the sleeve of my jacket, wanting to take note of the time. If this was a timed test I wanted to document my results for myself. I hadn't noted a starting time, but certainly we'd visited for at least thirty minutes before he'd given me the exam. I could get a guesstimate from that. Eleven *twenty?* How was it possible that only twenty minutes had passed since I'd walked into this office? I felt as if I'd been sitting here for hours! Maybe he wouldn't even charge me for a full hour once he passed me off to whatever specialist he deduced that I needed.

Dr. Sullivan's head bobbed as he contemplated my answers. Probably deciding which of his colleagues to refer me to. Dr. Sullivan tapped once on my test with his finger.

"As you can see the screening test for depression is fairly simple," he said.

Depression? This was a test for depression? I'd been duped. A stab of anger rose in my chest. As quickly, it was replaced with resignation. *You've duped yourself long enough.*

I sagged into the chair like a deflated balloon. In my heart I knew what the doctor had diagnosed was true. I'd known it for days, weeks, maybe even years if I thought back far enough. A melancholy cloud had enveloped me for as long as I could remember. That is, until Anne had come along and, with a great gust of friendship, blown away my cover as if it were mere mist. Until Anne, I'd built such a thick wall around my emotions, I thought I would always be strong enough to withstand the jabs of the outside world. Apparently I wasn't. Not anymore. A new wave of tears filled my eyes, spilling over in an odd mix of acquiescence and relief. I was tired of being the sole sentinel in charge of holding my world together.

"Olivia?" Dr. Sullivan's gentle voice interrupted my thoughts. "It's important that you answer one more question for me." He paused while I sat up straight and dried my eyes. When I gave him my watery-eyed go-ahead he asked, "Do you believe that nothing is physically wrong with you?"

I tapped my fingertips against each other as I contemplated his question. Already I knew the answer. I didn't have any excuses left, but to say yes was to admit I was no longer in control of my body, no longer in complete control of my mind and emotions.

As if you ever have been.

My life had been a card trick. Sleight of hand had held me together for more than forty years. Smiling when I felt like crying. Saying, "Sure, I can do that!" when I really didn't want to at all. Attempting to be the perfect wife, the perfect mother, when perfection was never attainable by anyone…especially me. The game was over. Either that or I no longer had the will to play. Saying yes to Dr. Sullivan's question would be the end of the game, the start of…of what?

My heart started pounding as though I were in starting blocks, waiting for the gunshot that would start the race of my life. My ears hummed with a silence louder than any roaring crowd. My vision narrowed, eyeing only the other me who sat silently across the room, her arms folded across her chest, waiting. Waiting to see what I would say.

"Olivia," Dr. Sullivan spoke again. "I need to know if you still feel you are ill, or if you are willing to work with me on your depression." He asked the million-dollar question again. "Do you believe that nothing is physically wrong with you?"

I looked once again at the other me. She stared back for one, long moment, and then, slowly, she nodded. I did, too.

"Yes," I finally said so faint I wasn't sure Dr. Sullivan heard my reply. I cleared my throat, gaining confidence now that I'd said the brave word out loud. "Yes."

"Good," he said, uncrossing his legs and shifting in his chair. "Then let's get to work. You need to know one thing before we get started." He paused as if debating whether I could handle the information he was about to tell me. I realized my hands were clutched together, white-knuckled. I unclasped them as Dr. Sullivan went on. "As we begin this emotional work, I want you to understand that you will probably feel worse before you start feeling better."

Feel *worse*? How could I possibly feel worse than I already did? Again my heart thumped as if it would pound itself out of my chest. I felt scared, as if I should get up and run. But even in the midst of my panic, I knew the time for running was over.

"You need to remember," Dr. Sullivan assured, "that you didn't get this way overnight, and you won't feel better overnight. But I want you to know…," he paused while he clenched his fist, punctuating his next four words with four soft thumps on the surface of his desk. "*You*," thump, "*will*," thump, "*get*," thump, "*better*," thump. "I want you to remember that."

What then? What would happen if I wouldn't, if I couldn't function without the melancholy protection that had protected my heart all these years? A feeling of suffocating terror clutched at my throat. I couldn't breathe. I—I—

Trust.

The simple word entered my mind as fear threatened to sweep me away. *Trust. Trust.* The word was soothing in a way my jumbled thoughts weren't. I breathed deeply, a small bit of calm settling in my chest.

Trust. There it was again. But trust in what? In my sloppy emotion? In Dr. Sullivan?

Trust. Where was this assuring word coming from? Even without knowing the source, my heart began to quiet.

Oh-hh. Recognition dawned. I'd heard that voice before. It was the same voice that had urged me to pray for Anne during her illness, even at a time when I hadn't known she needed my prayers. The same voice that had told me to pray for Emily before the appointment with Ellen West when she'd diagnosed her tumor.

Trust. Trust in God.

Of course. I breathed deeply. Life-giving air filled my lungs, sending oxygen and assurance to places within me only He could touch.

Trust.

If all God was asking of me was to abide by one single word, maybe that much I could do. *Trust.* I would cling to that word. Cling to His instruction. He'd led me to this office with a verse from His Word. I just had to trust that He would lead me to a place of healing as well.

Emily

"Well, Emily, does the job sound like something you would like to do?" Cindy Pearson raised her eyebrows, hopefully. It was no secret around town that the Director of Nurses for the Brewster Retirement and Nursing Home was always looking for people to add to her staff. Even high school kids like me. Turnover was high in Brewster's largest industry—old people.

I thought over the duties Mrs. Pearson had told me would be part of my job. Depending on which shift I worked, I'd be responsible for waking the residents, helping them wash up for the day and get dressed, getting them to meals, and getting them ready for bed. None of the tasks seemed too hard.

"Yeah, I think so," I said, agreeing just like that to what I considered my first *real* job. What choice did I have? My folks were following through with their New Year's plan that I get a job, and even though Dad had backed down and offered me a job at the bank, I wanted to prove to them, and myself, that I could get hired on my own merit and not just on the fact that I was the daughter of the CEO.

"When should I start?"

"First, you're going to need to get trained as a Certified Nursing Assistant. CNAs we call them." Cindy paged through some papers on her desk. It was weird seeing Mrs. Pearson in her nursing uniform. Her daughter, Steph, was a seventh grader and played on the junior high girls' basketball team. Her parents, Ben and Cindy, never missed a ball game, junior or senior high. I was used to seeing her in a Brewster Badgers sweatshirt. It was going to be strange having Cindy as my new boss. "Here we go." Cindy pulled a sheet from beneath the pile.

"CNA classes will be offered in Carlton starting next week. You're going to need seventy-five hours of course work before you can start on the floor."

Seventy-five *hours?* I'd never earn any money.

Mrs. Pearson seemed to read my mind. "You do get paid while you attend classes. You'll start at six seventy-five an hour. Once you complete your CNA training, you'll make eight dollars an hour. Since you're only going to be working part-time, you won't be eligible for any benefits."

I wasn't sure just what kind of benefits a full-time worker would get, but I hadn't even dared to ask how much I would be earning part-time. I was glad Cindy had told me. Quickly, I did the math. Even if I could only work two shifts a week until basketball season was over, I'd make about a hundred dollars a week. Wow. I felt rich, and I hadn't actually earned a penny yet.

"If you'd like, I can schedule you to get oriented on the floor while you're attending the CNA classes. That will give you an idea of what you'll be doing and let you get to know the residents. It's sort of a job-shadowing system that will help you feel more comfortable with the facility and meet some of the other staff."

I nodded, a nervous feeling twirling around my stomach. What if I couldn't remember what I was supposed to do? What if whoever I followed around, watching her work, didn't want me there? How was I ever going to learn the names of the eighty residents who lived here, much less all the people I'd be working with? What if—"

"You'll need to stop at Wal-Mart when you're in Carlton and pick up a uniform. Be sure and give me a list of basketball games and practices so I can schedule around them." Cindy stood up, placing her palms against the small of her back, leaning gently from side to side. "Occupational hazard," she stated as she twisted back and forth. I stood up, too. "That's one of the things you'll learn in class—how to properly lift a resident so you don't injure your back." She straightened. "I want you to remember that your first job is being a student. We don't want your work here to interfere with your grades, so if you ever need time to devote to your studies, let me know and I won't schedule you to work. Any questions?"

I had a million of them as she talked, but just then I couldn't think of a one.

"Uh-uh," I mumbled, feeling suddenly overwhelmed by what was ahead of me.

"I think you'll enjoy working here, Emily." She handed me some papers I needed to fill out in order to start work. "Once you get to know the residents, you get pretty attached. It doesn't seem so much like work when you are caring for people who feel like friends." She walked around the desk and put her arm around my shoulders as she walked with me to the door. "You'll see," she said, her words comforting the anxious butterflies that were swarming in my abdomen.

As I headed through the spacious foyer leading out of the retirement home, a feeble voice called, "Emmie?" I stopped, seeing Mrs. Stoltz sitting lopsided in a wheelchair. She'd been my Sunday school teacher when I was in fifth grade, never quite understanding that my name was Emily, not Emmie. I'd thought she was ancient even then. Only now did I realize I hadn't seen her in church in ages. I wondered how long she'd lived here. "Come closer," she said, her voice shaky and filled with air. I took three tentative steps her direction. She grabbed my hand, squeezing with strength I would have never guessed could come from someone who looked so frail. "Did you come to visit me?"

I shook my head, then realized she couldn't see all the way to my head at the angle she was sitting. I squatted down beside her chair.

"I got a job here," I blurted, excitement filling my words even as my stomach churned with nerves. "I'm kind of scared, though." I didn't know why I was telling my old Sunday school teacher information I was reluctant to admit even to myself.

"There's no reason to be afraid of us old folks. Look at me..." She waved a trembling hand toward her chest. "I'm not going to wrestle with anyone except the Devil." She chuckled and patted at my hand. "You just remember those Bible verses I taught you. Let's see..." She rolled her soggy eyes skyward, then repeated, "What time I am afraid I will trust in Thee."

Normally I would have thought an old lady quoting Bible verses was kind of corny, but her soft, tremulous words recalled a time when I'd memorized that very verse for myself...to earn a gold star.

"I remember," I told Mrs. Stoltz, remembering also the way she'd looked when she had stood in front of my class—regal, a bit holy, and a lot loving. Suddenly, I saw that her wheelchair didn't make her one bit different from the way she'd been six years ago. "I'll be seeing lots of you," I said, squeezing her hand, unexpectedly glad I was going to be working here.

"I got the job!" I gushed, opening the front door so Rick could come into the house and share my excitement. It was the first time he'd been over since before New Year's. My parents had relaxed their ban on Rick being here around the same time they'd given me my non-punishment on New Year's. All I had to do was ask, and Mom gave me a distracted, "I suppose."

A frown crossed Rick's brow so quickly I thought I might have imagined it.

"That's good," he said, stepping inside, his voice not sounding overjoyed. "I wouldn't want to work around old people like that, but I suppose someone has to. How much do you get paid?"

"Six seventy-five to start." It seemed like a fortune next to the nothing I'd earned so far this year. But after talking to Mrs. Stoltz, I had a feeling there was going to be more than a paycheck to make my new job fulfilling.

"Hmmm," Rick murmured. "I don't suppose you'll get too many hours, what with basketball and all." He shrugged out of his letter jacket and hung it on the doorknob.

"Mrs. Pearson said she'd schedule me around games and practice times. I start CNA training in Carlton next weekend. Cool, huh?"

"Next weekend?" He shot me a look. "I thought we were going to the movie on Saturday. Like we always do if there's not a game."

"The classes are only until five. I'll be back in Brewster in plenty of time for the movie." What was with Rick? Couldn't he see how great this was? I was going to have my very own job. I was going to become a Certified Nursing Assistant. Who knew, maybe once I had the training, I'd decide to major in nursing when I went to college. The world seemed open to all kinds of new possibilities. I decided to keep that thought to myself for tonight. Rick didn't appear to be in the mood to celebrate.

Neither had Jen. I barely got in the house before I called her with the news.

"Oh," she'd said, totally bored. "That's nice, I guess." She sounded distracted, then giggled. I was pretty sure she was playing Tetris while she was talking to me.

Ever since Ryan had broken up with Jen, she'd been weird. Almost like she expected me to break up with Rick so we could hang out like we did back in junior high. I wasn't about to do that; I'd waited too long for a boyfriend to dump him just because Jen was in a funk. She'd get over it eventually. In the meantime she started hanging out with Mindy Werre, who was totally uncool in my opinion. Everybody knew the only reason she had guys chasing after her was because she dressed like she had a gig on MTV. I knew the only reason Jen was hanging with her was to make Ryan jealous. From what I could see, it wasn't working. The way she was acting, I was even more glad I had Rick.

I grabbed his hand now. "Come on, I'll tell you what I get to do for my job." He shuffled his feet as I pulled him toward the living room.

Normally, my parents didn't allow Rick to come over on a week-night, but they were just as proud of my new job as I was and said I could invite Rick over to tell him the news. But now that I'd told him, he didn't seem all that glad. The nervous churning that had stopped after my conversation with Mrs. Stoltz started up again.

"Is something wrong?" I asked as we walked into the living room to watch TV.

"No." Rick sat on the couch, grabbing my hand and pulling me down beside him. He put one arm around my shoulder. "I just don't want your new job to interfere with the time we get to spend together, that's all."

"It won't," I replied automatically, even as I realized it probably would. With basketball, homework, my new job, and the certification classes, I didn't have to be a math genius to figure out that something would have to give.

Rick took the remote from my hand and began clicking rapid-fire through the stations. His silence conveyed more than words of congratulations ever would. A sudden stab of panic jolted through my stomach into my chest. What if Rick decided he didn't want to go with me anymore because of this job? Lots of girls in school didn't work and would make sure they had plenty of time to spend with the star of the boys' basketball team.

I looked at Rick out of the corner of my eye. His unsmiling profile etched itself in my mind. I wasn't going to lose Rick over this. I just wasn't. Maybe I'd have to quit my job if things didn't work out. I snuggled in close under Rick's heavy arm, thinking of all the girls in school who would trade places with me in a nanosecond. I wasn't going to let a dumb job come between us.

"*We think it would be a good idea for you to get a part-time job. We expect you to take on more responsibility.*" At the memory of my parents' words and their insistence about me finding a job after that New Year's mess, a worm of fear crawled around the moths already crowding my stomach. I crossed my arms over my chest and repeated Mrs. Stoltz's words to myself. "*What time I am afraid, I will trust in Thee.*"

I knew Rick would laugh if he knew I was repeating a Bible verse to give myself a guarantee that our relationship would stay strong, but right now I didn't care what it took. And Bible words were just as good as anything else I could think of.

Libby

I held the green-and-vanilla capsule in the palm of my hand, rolling it around as though I were some sort of pill inspector looking for a flaw. The fact that it was a pretty green didn't make it any easier to swallow.

It's not cyanide. Just take it.

I closed my eyes and tossed the antidepressant toward the back of my throat, washing it down with a quick gulp of water. There. Swallowed. Gone. I took a deep lungful of air as if pausing to mark another milestone on this odd trek I'd begun.

Okay, it's done. Get on with your day. I'd found my little pep talks more and more necessary lately. Dr. Sullivan had told me I might feel worse before I felt better. He was right. That was exactly how I'd felt the next few days after my appointment. Worse. I looked in the mirror, the dark circles under my eyes bearing witness to the hours I hadn't slept last night. *Wash your face. Get dressed.*

I forced myself to walk out of the bathroom and over to my dresser. Dr. Sullivan had emphasized the importance of keeping up my daily routine. "It's part of the healing process," he'd said. If this was healing, I wasn't so sure I wanted any part of it. I tugged a black sweater from the drawer, then walked to the closet and pulled a pair of khakis from a hanger. My feet felt like lead blocks as they slipped into my black loafers. I threaded a black belt through the loops. One. Two. Three. Four. Five. Six. There. Buckle up. I'd found myself counting all kinds of things of late. It was soothing in a way thinking wasn't. Ten steps from my bedroom door to the landing at the top of the stairs. Fourteen stairs separating the upstairs from the downstairs. One mug from the cupboard, three heaping tablespoons of coffee into the filter. I slowly counted the beige tiles that made neat rows along the backsplash of my kitchen counter until the coffee was ready to pour. Seventy-three. There'd been more the day before. Maybe I'd counted slower today. Maybe these pills were helping in some way I had yet to fathom.

I breathed in the heady aroma of the freshly brewed coffee. At least one thing still gave me pleasure. Mmmm. I took a sip. One. Two. I should eat something. I opened the cupboard where a mini-store of cereal waited to be poured. Six boxes, none appetizing. I closed the cupboard, wondering about the nutritional value of coffee. I'd work at the computer and eat at lunch. Promise.

I topped off my cup and headed to my computer. The *only* reason I had bothered to get dressed at all today was because I had a lunch date with Katie Jeffries, and explaining my way out of our monthly lunch date would be more work than suffering through it would be. Thank goodness she was coming to Brewster for lunch. I didn't think I had the energy or focus to make the forty-mile drive to Carlton to meet on her turf.

I flicked on the computer, listening to the familiar hum while it booted up. Not long ago, the only counting I'd done was to count the days until my monthly lunch with Katie. A trip to Carlton was always a welcome break from the confines of Brewster. And lunch with Katie was always fun. Our discussions ranged from books to politics, religion to family, and anything in between that we could squeeze into our afternoons of gabbing, eating, and shopping.

Half the fun of our monthly lunches was selecting a new restaurant to eat at each time we met in Carlton. Today I was glad the only choice in Brewster was Vicky's Café—no choices to overwhelm me in that department. I often made lunch for Katie at my house. But lately, Bob and Emily had been lucky to get the bare basics. I wasn't about to force Katie to mutter polite phrases about a lousy lunch. We were eating out. The only thing I was worried about was carrying on an actual conversation.

Up till now I'd been able to maintain the illusion that my life was normal—well, as normal as any middle-aged housewife on the verge of empty-nest syndrome and menopause can be. Goodness knew, Katie and I laughed about our foibles often enough. I hadn't felt the need or desire to confide my latest struggles with her, but I knew today I might be forced to. Dr. Sullivan had advised me to tell a few close friends that I was on antidepressant medication. "Sometimes they will notice subtle improvements in your mood before you do," he said. So far I hadn't noticed a thing. Maybe Katie would offer the encouragement I craved. The elephant was back on my chest and anxiety flowed through my body like a tide…rising, falling, high, low, never really gone, sometimes threatening to pull me under altogether. I wasn't sure I had the energy to hide it all from my perceptive friend.

I set my coffee mug on the warming contraption Emily had given me for Christmas a few years ago. At the time I'd thought it one of those gifts I'd use for a time just to please her and then pack up for Goodwill. It had turned out to be almost as valuable to me as my computer; cold coffee was not at all my cup of tea. In spite of my funk, I smiled. Even if my brain felt like mush most days, the fact that I could still crank out a good pun on occasion gave me a small measure of comfort. Maybe I wasn't as bad off as I thought.

I pictured the small, oval, peach-colored pills sitting in a brown vial in my makeup drawer. Dr. Sullivan had prescribed them along with the Prozac. "This should assist with the anxiety," he'd said, writing out the prescription for Alprazolam. I had yet to take one. I had a hard enough time choking down the antidepressants I was averse to swallowing. In my inner core, I still thought I could beat this thing on my own. If I could just figure out what "it" was.

I clicked through the start-up menu, working my way through the pages to my work in progress, the novel I'd started out writing like gangbusters a year ago, the novel that was progressing like a slog through stiff Jell-O these days. I stared at the cursor, winking at me, urging my fingers to move it along the page. I scrolled back, rereading the mere paragraphs I had written in the preceding weeks. The words lay on the screen, dull icons meaning nothing.

I clicked to a clear page. If I couldn't work on my novel, maybe I could eke out a few paragraphs that I could call my column for next week. Again the cursor beckoned to be moved. I put my hands on the keys, then moved them to my lap, where they lay inert.

"Libby? Are you ready?" Katie's quick knock followed by her lilting voice jolted me out of my chair like a lightning bolt.

You're so lazy, and now you're late, too.

It couldn't possibly be close to noon already. Katie had said she'd pick me up for lunch when she pulled into town. Something must have happened to have her on my doorstep hours ahead of time. I glanced at the clock. Eleven-fifty-six! Impossible. Where had the morning gone?

A blank computer screen accused me. I knew exactly where the morning had gone. Nowhere. My mind did a fast rewind of the lost hours. I'd spent them worrying about my mental health, fretting over my physical health, agonizing about my lack of energy, my inability to write, the way I'd failed Bob as a wife and my children as a mother. Now, I was proving what a lousy friend I was. I'd worried almost three hours away and had accomplished nothing but wasting an entire morning.

See, I told you you were lazy.

"Be right there," I called, remembering I hadn't put on a drop of makeup. It had been effort enough to simply wash my face this morning. "I need to hit the bathroom. Give me a sec. Pour yourself a cup of coffee. Sit down. Sorry." I waved Katie into the kitchen as I dashed upstairs. Being ready on time would have been easier than making these lame excuses.

"That's okay," Katie said as I rushed past, "your writing is more important, anyway."

If she only knew how lazy you were.

My fingers scrambled through my makeup drawer, editing my routine to the bare essentials. Concealer for the dark circles under my eyes, another quick swipe to cover the redness of my nose. My hand shook as I reached for a powder puff, an attempt to camouflage what was left. As I leaned into the mirror, stroking mascara onto my eyelashes, a sense of doom enveloped me. Cold fear pricked at my sternum. What was going on? As if having lunch with Katie were anything to dread. A feeling of numbness spread from my chest down into my arms. My fingertips turned to ice. Was I having a stroke? I grabbed the edge of the sink with both hands, the mascara wand falling into the sink, planting a black smudge on the porcelain. *Oh, dear God, help me.*

My eyes darted wildly around the small room. Should I yell for Katie? Should I sit on the floor in case I passed out? The numbing sensation sent tentacles into my head. The ringing in my ears blocked out any other sound. Maybe this was the end of the world. Maybe I was dying. Whatever the truth, I wished it would hurry up and be over. I leaned down, resting my forehead on the cool edge of the sink. There, that was better, a steady hand on an icy slope. No, I was sliding away. *Lord, what's happening?*

My mind raced, sure something awful was about to happen. Soon. Very soon. The unnamed fear clutched my throat, suffocating me. The harder I tried to breathe, the tighter the vise inside my neck became. *Breathe, Libby, breathe.* I fought against the tidal wave that threatened to carry me away, to pull me under where there was no air. *Breathe. Breathe. Just breathe. All you have to do is keep breathing…*

Gradually the noose loosened its grip. I lifted my head. Whatever had happened was over. Sort of. I could breath again, but I felt unsteady and weak. I didn't know whether mere seconds had passed or hours, but I assumed it hadn't been too long or Katie would have investigated. My hand trembled as I returned the mascara wand to its holder and then to its spot in the drawer. How was I ever going to get through lunch? My heart thudded at the thought of sitting in Vicky's Café, pretending all was well. Ha! This was going to be a performance worthy of an Oscar nomination.

I glanced in the mirror; a ghost stared back. As I fumbled to grab my compact of blush, my eyes fell on the small cylinder of pills lying by my powder. *These should help with the anxiety.* I sucked in a deep breath. So that's what this had been, an anxiety attack. I fumbled at the lid, cursing the child who'd been the reason for this puzzle that sealed relief from my hands. Finally, I popped the stubborn lid off, spilling the entire contents of the container into my hand.

Oval baby-aspirins were what I held. I remembered the familiar shade of orange from my own youth as well as my kids'. I hoped whatever these pills contained was more than baby strength. I read the label: *Take two as needed for anxiety.* I tipped all but one pill back into the brown plastic. One tablet should be enough. I held the pill in my now steady hand. My symptoms had all but disappeared. It seemed I'd weathered the worst. Surely, now that I knew what had happened, it wouldn't happen again. Or, if it did, I'd have the comfort of knowing what to expect. My tough German upbringing kicked in. I tossed the remaining pill back into the bottle. *I can do this myself.* I tossed the vial back into the drawer, bumping it closed with my hip.

"Ready," I called to Katie as I raced down the steps. "Let's go eat. I'm starving." I wasn't, but I wasn't about to let on to Katie that I was anything but a-okay.

Katie sat back in the booth while Vicky Johnson, the owner of the café, refilled both of our coffee cups.

"Was everything all right?" Vicky's eyes were fixed on my half-eaten hamburger.

"Fine," I muttered, forcing a laugh. "Guess who's been doing all the talking?" I hoped Katie wouldn't chime in with the truth that she'd had to practically drag conversation out of me.

"It's a good thing you two came in late for your lunch." Vicky rested the two coffeepots on the edge of our table, taking a mini-break. "I was swamped earlier. Finding help has been so hard since that telemarketing operation opened. You wouldn't be in the market for a job, would you?" She eyed Katie.

Katie laughed. "Me? Oh my, believe me, you wouldn't want me waiting on your customers. I'm the original klutz at school." She paused, then added, "I'm a substitute teacher in Carlton."

"I'm sorry. I should have introduced you." I felt my cheeks flushing. I was so used to knowing most everyone in Brewster and having them know me that I assumed Vicky knew Katie, too. Either that or my brain had turned to Swiss cheese. "Katie Jeffries, Vicky Johnson."

Vicky set one coffeepot on the table and stuck out her hand. "I've seen you in here before with Olivia. I wasn't sure whether you were company or new in town. Nice to meet you." She picked up the coffeepot, smiling. "Well, now that you've turned down my job offer, can I get you anything else?"

Katie lifted a finger and pointed to her chest. "I have to have a piece of your banana cream pie. I can't get anything nearly as good in Carlton."

Vicky's eyes quickly surveyed the pie cabinet that hung on the wall across from our table. "You're in luck, one piece left. Olivia, would you like another kind? I've got apple and sour cream raisin."

The thought almost gagged me.

"No," I managed to croak. "I'm fine."

Vicky refilled the cups of the four other customers in the café as she left to get Katie's pie. I noticed my neighbor, Ida Bauer, step into the café. I hoped against hope she wouldn't join us at our table. I was having a hard enough time carrying on this charade of normalcy with just Katie.

"So, tell me…" Suddenly serious, Katie set her heavy cup into the thick white saucer. "…what's going on?" She clasped her fingers together and placed her chin in the crux, staring into my eyes. I could tell by her tone that her question wasn't simply idle curiosity. Evidently my career as an actress was over.

Always a trooper, I kept up my part. "Oh, Brian was home over the holidays." She already knew that. "Bob's been busy at work. Year-end stuff." She'd pulled that information out of me already, too. "And Emily…" I trailed off; I'd already mentioned Emily's new job, too. I hung my head, averting my eyes, dipping low to take a long swallow of coffee, hoping Katie wouldn't notice the tears I'd held back for over an hour.

She reached one hand across the table and placed it over mine. "What's wrong?"

I blinked rapidly, looking at the ceiling, trying to dislodge the stone that rested in my throat. Katie pulled a napkin from the small dispenser that rested near the wall of our booth and handed it to me.

"I've got all afternoon," she said.

"It might take longer than that," I croaked, dabbing at my eyes.

Katie moved her hands back as Vicky placed her pie on the table. "I'll be back with more coffee later. Enjoy your time together." If Vicky noticed my tears, she didn't comment. I blew my nose into the thin tissue. I imagined Vicky saw a lot of things in the lives of the people in Brewster as she served up meals and coffee. I hoped she had learned discretion.

Katie cut the point off her pie and chewed slowly. She took a sip of coffee, then another bite. "Any time you're ready," she said in no hurry at all.

I nodded as a new wave of tears filled my eyes. If I didn't get myself under control I was going to be the talk of Brewster when the three o'clock coffee crowd arrived in an hour. I doubted they knew much about discretion at all. I tugged out a second napkin and dried my eyes. Deep breaths helped, too.

"I've been—" I took another deep breath, trying to force the hard words out, thinking just how to say it. "I've been seeing a…a… doctor."

Katie's fork clattered onto the plate. "Oh, dear Lord…no. You're not—you don't have—?"

She didn't have to say *cancer* for me to know what she thought. She knew all too well what I'd been through with Anne. Katie, too, had felt the fear of possible breast cancer when her mammogram had come back with an abnormal spot. All was well in the end, but we'd shared the waiting and our dread of the illness hitting us someday. For some reason just now, breast cancer seemed almost preferable to what I was going through. At least there was a way to treat it. Cut it out. Take treatment. Something to *do* to try and beat it. As much as the idea appealed some days, I couldn't very well cut out my brain.

There's treatment for you, too, if you'd take your medicine as pre-scribed and follow Dr. Sullivan's suggestions.

I pushed the thought away. Medicine for the brain sounded like an oxymoron. If I was aware that I was having an emotional problem, I should be able to think my way through it. That was the only cure that made sense. How could pills make me think any differently?

Katie was staring at me, wide-eyed. My short journey into my thoughts had probably led Katie to think I was searching for the right words to tell her my bad news. I hadn't thought my halting words would lead Katie to think I had cancer. Quickly I shook my head. "No. No. Not that."

Katie sighed deeply. "Thank You, God." She picked up her fork, then set it back down. "What are you seeing a doctor for?"

Again I dipped my head, retreating into my coffee cup. Why were the words *depression* and *psychiatrist* so difficult to say? Katie waited. *Oh man. I'll just say it and let her think I'm nuts.*

"I've been seeing a psychiatrist." *There.*

"Oh, thank goodness." Katie forked a triangle of pie into her mouth.

"Thank *goodness?*" She *did* think I was crazy.

"Oh no, not like that." Katie spoke around her bite, then held up a finger while she quickly chewed and swallowed, smiling the whole time. "Oh, gosh—I didn't mean it the way it sounded. I meant I'm glad it's not cancer. Do you want to share any of the details, or is it private?"

How easy it would have been to brush off her question by repeating, "It's private." How much harder it was to offer the truth, that Dr. Sullivan had asked me to share this…this *secret* with close friends.

"Actually…" I tore a small piece of bread from my hamburger bun and rolled it into a pea-sized worry stone. "My doctor did tell me to share some of the details of my appointment with friends—with you," I added quickly. Katie continued to eat as though psychiatry confessions were something she heard every day. Her eyes urged me on. Where to start? At the beginning seemed like a good spot. "I'd been having these weird symptoms for a few months and—"

"Months? And you never said anything?"

What could I say? I kept talking. "I went to a couple doctors, and they couldn't find anything wrong. Eventually I was referred to Dr. Sullivan—he's a psychiatrist in Carlton."

"You've been coming to Carlton without calling me?" Katie gave me the stern, substitute-teacher look she had mastered.

"Sorry. I wasn't sure I wanted anyone to know. And besides, I haven't been the best of company. I'm sure you noticed today."

"I could tell you had something going on," was all Katie said, offering compassion with her words. "How are you feeling now?"

"Awful." That word wasn't hard to say. "I feel this constant sense of alertness, as if I were a small insect waiting to be stepped on and if I don't keep a watch out something's going to smush me. I'm dreading something, but I don't have any idea what it is. But if I let my guard down, I feel like it will be worse. Whatever 'it' is."

"Wow, that's crazy." Katie slapped her hand over her mouth. "I didn't mean—"

I couldn't help but smile. "Don't worry, I've thought of every cliché possible. You can't imagine how many references there are to losing your mind…until you think you might be."

Katie grew quiet. "Really?" she asked, no judgment in her tone. "Do you feel that way?"

"Some days," I answered truthfully. "I don't know what to think anymore. The doctor's tests proved nothing was physically wrong with me. The only option I had left was Dr. Sullivan. He started me on some medication…" Admitting I was taking an antidepressant was still hard; I'd been raised to solve my problems myself.

"And?" Katie urged.

I ripped off another piece of bread and worried it between my fingers. "And I'm supposed to tell a few people. Dr. Sullivan said sometimes the people around me will notice a change in my mood before I do. He thinks I'm depressed."

Her brow wrinkled. Concern filled her words. "Are you?"

I shrugged. "I don't know what to think anymore. Obviously, if I'm seeing a psychiatrist I'm grasping at straws."

"Don't talk about it like that." Now Katie was using her teacher voice. "I'd say you're reaching out for help. Trying to feel better is no crime. Have you been praying?"

I shrugged, thinking of the mere minutes I'd spent in my prayer chair lately. "I try. It's hard to concentrate. My mind feels so...so... muddled."

"Well then," Katie reached over and squeezed my hand, "I'll just have to pray for you." She paused. "More than I already do, that is."

A feeling of warm relief flooded through me, a different sort of tears rimming my eyes this time. "Thanks," I said, suddenly grateful I'd gone out for lunch after all.

My talk with my friend Jan was a different story.

"I only have a half hour—talk fast." Jan slid into her usual spot at the head of my kitchen table, dropping her shoulder bag at her feet. "I'm having my nails done before lunch, and you know how Sally hates it if you're late."

Actually, I didn't know. I'd only had my nails done once—on a convention trip I'd gone on with Bob. The spouse's program had left me with tons of free time. The organizers must have assumed all bankers' wives liked to do was shop. I didn't, especially in unfamiliar stores. At Bob's prompting, I made a manicure appointment at the hotel salon, expecting to relax and enjoy being pampered. Instead, the attention made me feel awkward, self-indulgent in a way that made me want nothing more than to dash back to my hotel room and read a book. But I did know Jan valued her manicures, and her command that I "talk fast" might actually make this whole ordeal easier.

I'd wrestled long and hard with Dr. Sullivan's second request that I tell a few more people about the medication I was on. He'd reiterated that since he didn't know me well, noticing small changes in my disposition would be difficult for him. He wanted the assessment to come from those who knew me best.

Bob had been in this from the start, but I had the feeling he saw me too closely and too often. If my mood was improving, the change would probably be so gradual he wouldn't notice any sooner than I would. I debated about telling Emily I was on medication, but she was so caught up with her new job that I didn't want to spoil her enthusiasm with my talk of depression. Frankly, I was glad she had CNA classes to keep her busy—not that she wasn't busy enough with school and basketball. I remembered well the extra energy I'd had as a teenager. It was a bit like the anxiety I felt almost constantly now, except it had fueled me back then instead of paralyzing me. Emily had energy to burn; she didn't need to waste it worrying about me.

As if she'd read my mind, Jan said, "I hear Emily's going to be working at the nursing home." She brushed the long nails of one hand through her mane of hair. "I don't know where these kids get the energy. It's all I can do to keep up with Joey." The seventh-grade son she doted on was the only good thing that had come from her first marriage. "And Da-*annn*." Her third husband. She fanned her fingers in front of her face. "If I don't get pregnant this month, I don't know what it will take." She giggled.

I was a grown woman, but still I blushed. Jan's lack of convention always took me by surprise. I hoped I was doing the right thing by telling her about my recent struggles. Jan had a way of looking at life that made the harsher realities of life disappear. Some would call her Pollyanna, but I was slowly learning her attitude was infectious in a good way. I only hoped she could stop talking long enough to listen. I opened my mouth, ready to spill my news—

"And what's with Jen and Emily these days? They used to be joined at the hip. I hardly ever see them together anymore." With a flick of her head Jan tossed her hair over her shoulder. "Did they have a fight? It wouldn't surprise me. You know teenage girls. I remember when I was in high school, there were these two cliques…" She was off to the races, her words circling the track of my kitchen with no finish line in sight.

Slowly, I closed my mouth. I tried to listen, but my thoughts wandered. Now that Jan mentioned it, what was up with Emily and

Jen lately? Jen hadn't been over in ages, and the phone messages I took weren't from her. Jan was right; teenage friendships were fickle. I knew that all too well. I cringed, remembering the awful days that had made up my high school years. The class clown who never gave up taunting me about being the banker's daughter, assigning me a position I had no clue I held. I didn't have the social skills back then to bat his taunts back, to deflect them as foul balls…or as jokes. My classmates had followed this strong young man's lead, teasing or ignoring, but never befriending. Finally a blind date, set up by my roommate my sophomore year in college, restored my faith in mankind—or in one man, anyway. Bob. The thought of his blustered bravado at my dorm room door, "Hello, uh…hi, uh…I hope this is the right room, uh…you're way cuter than I thought you'd be. Don't we have a class together?" still sent my heart reeling.

Ah, first love. No wonder Emily and Jen weren't spending much time together these days. Jen had Ryan, and Emily had Rick to take up the few free minutes they had. A worm of worry threaded through my thoughts. A part of me was glad Emily had Rick to occupy her free time and to confide in, but I hadn't forgotten that Rick had encouraged Emily to drink that one night. Brought her home drunk. I was hoping our firm talk with her had been warning enough that her time with Rick would be over if that kind of behavior continued. In spite of my worries, I was all too aware of the fact that I had been no great shakes as a mother lately. I hoped Rick was a better listener than I'd been lately.

"Oh my, look at the time." Jan pointed at the clock hanging on the wall. "It's almost time for me to run and I've babbled and babbled and didn't even give you a chance to talk. I'm going to shut up now." She crossed her arms over her pink sweater and clamped her mouth shut. Then she opened it. "That's one of my New Year's resolutions, to listen more. Okay, talk." She bit her lips together.

I might have laughed if what I'd had to say wasn't weighing so heavy. I ran a finger along the edge of the table, stalling, wishing I hadn't drunk the last drop of coffee before Jan breezed in. I could use fortification now. Well, I wasn't about to make the same mistake

I had when I'd told Katie, hesitating and pausing in a way that had led her to assume I was practically dying. I'd already decided to give Jan the bare minimum. I took a breath and plunged. "I haven't been feeling well, and the doctor I'm seeing put me on some medication." I clasped my hands together, holding them steady in front of me. "He wants me to tell some of my friends. He thinks that you might notice improvement before I do and that if you do it will encourage me." I paused. "I mean, it will help me know the medicine is working."

Jan sat nodding, arms crossed, her lips tucked between her teeth as if a cork about to pop.

"That's it," I said, opening my palms to show I was holding nothing more. She was quiet. "So, I guess I just want you to tell me if you notice anything different." More silence. I wished she'd talk. Say something. Anything. "That I'm seeming better, I mean." I had no more to say. I folded my arms, just like Jan.

"Are you done?" The dam broke and the words fell out.

I nodded.

"Whew," she sighed, as if it had taken all her effort not to talk. She bent over and picked up her purse, rummaging until she found a lipstick. Pressing her lips shut for all of a minute obviously required a touch up.

I wondered if she'd even heard a word of what I said. Suddenly, I was regretting that I'd told her. Where had my words gone? Evaporated into thin air, apparently. Fresh tears clogged my throat. I pushed back my chair, anxious to have Jan leave so I could cry alone.

You fool, you should never have told her.

Jan smacked her lips against a tissue, tossed it into her purse and zipped it shut. She looked up. "What are you seeing the doctor for?"

Her question took me by surprise. I thought she hadn't heard, but she had. I blinked rapidly. Whenever I thought I had Jan figured out, she did something to change my mind. Okay, I'd take the chance and tell her the hard part.

"The doctor thinks I'm depressed."

As I spoke, Jan stood, tossing her purse over her shoulder. She sat back down, crossing her arms on the table, leaning forward. "Who isn't depressed these days? Just the other day I felt so down in the dumps. Of course, I'd gotten my period the day before and what with trying to get pregnant and all it just made me feel so down." On and on she went with her idea of empathy.

Tears were streaming down my face before she finally closed the door. *That's what you get for trusting someone. You should have known better.* I snatched a box of Kleenex from the kitchen counter and headed to the couch, cradling the tissues in my lap, a cardboard box of comfort absorbing my hurt. I tried to pray, but thoughts of my failures as a mother intruded. I was no better as a wife. And what kind of friend was Jan, when all she could do was take my depression and turn it into a story about herself? I was nothing but a failure all around. A moan of anguish escaped my lips. Harsh sobs racked my body. Why was I even bothering to think about her?

Because she's practically the only friend you have.

I sobbed harder. Some friend.

You should have never become friends with Anne. Then you wouldn't know what you were missing.

My heart ached as I cried from a place deep inside. Would I ever find a true friend again?

You have Me. Softly the words filtered through my self-pity. *You have Me.* The gentle words from God caused more tears to flow, but these felt different, warm and soft in a way my earlier tears hadn't been. Healing.

"I'll just have to pray for you then. More than I do already." Katie's words mingled with my tears, giving comfort when moments before I'd had none. Hot tears poured down my face. Katie. In my self-absorption over Jan's rebuff, I'd forgotten about my dear friend, Katie. She'd been the one to step into the gap Anne's death had left in my life. Calling to invite me to her book club. Offering to come pick me up, all the way from Carlton, when I lamely protested I didn't want to drive that far. She was the one who insisted we set up a monthly lunch date, "So we don't forget to be friends."

You're a lousy friend, my conscience chided, always finding a way to pick at the scabs that encrusted my faults. *You'll be lucky if she*

doesn't hightail it out of Dodge now that she knows how sick you are.
Fear gripped my chest. Katie wouldn't do that, would she?

Neither will I.

I bowed my head, pressing a tissue to my dripping nose. *Oh, Lord, don't leave me. Don't, please don't…I—* My mind went blank, unable to pray, unable to focus on anything but my misery. Would my tears never stop?

"I'll just have to pray for you then. More than I do already."

My only hope was that Katie really was praying for me. Hard.

Dr. Sullivan

Clinical note: Olivia Marsden. January 23 office apt. Continues depressive episode. High levels of generalized anxiety. 20 mg Prozac for depression, .50 Alprazolam for anxiety as needed. Client states not eating or sleeping well. Generalized complaints about lack of daily focus. Discussed importance of maintaining routine. Mrs. Marsden appears healthy, well-groomed. No suicidal intent.

I sat forward in my chair, reviewing the notes I'd made after Mrs. Marsden's last appointment. The appointment today would be our third, and I had yet to put a finger on her case. By all appearances she was the picture of the content banker's wife. Impeccably groomed, as if she were attending a formal luncheon rather than a doctor's appointment. In spite of her depression and anxiety, she continued to function fairly well in her daily life. Her marriage seemed secure, her children behaved well. Her life certainly wasn't the shambles most of my patients were dealing with.

I picked up a pen and tapped it on my desk. Oftentimes, by the time patients reached my clinic, they'd managed to bungle just about every area of their life in a way that had me scratching my head and wondering how I was going to clean up the mess.

I scratched my head now, wondering why Mrs. Marsden's seemingly perfect life had begun to crumble. I tightened my tie, pushed my chair back, and walked to the door. There she sat, reading a book she'd brought along, back straight, ankles crossed, not exhibiting the hopeless slump depressed patients usually assumed in my waiting room.

"Mrs. Marsden, you can come in now." She looked up as I took one step back, motioning her into my office with my open palm.

"Libby, or at least Olivia, please," she reminded. Her regal manner made me want to address her more formally. She pulled a metal bookmark from the back of the book and marked her spot, smiling at me as she stood. Her fresh fragrance followed her into my office. I couldn't help but appreciate her effort. Many times my clients appeared in my office wrinkled and unshowered. Not Mrs. Marsden...Olivia. I thought of my wife, Margaret. It had been a long time since I'd smelled her similar perfume. I breathed it in. *Not the time to think of her now, Doctor.* Quickly, I strode to my desk and lifted Olivia's file.

She placed her book on the edge of my desk. "How was your week?" she asked as she took her usual spot in the leather chair next to mine.

"Oh. Uh, fine. It was fine." I wasn't used to patients asking me the questions. "And yours?"

"So-so." She crossed her legs, then uncrossed them, folding her hands in her lap. "I can't say I feel any better since my last appointment. Worse, maybe."

So, she was going to jump right in. "In what way, exactly?"

"I still can't sleep worth beans. I don't have an appetite. I feel cranky all the time; the tears are right here—" She crossed her neck with the flat of her hand. "And...I don't know...I feel like I've got a sword hanging over my head waiting to fall all the time. Even now."

I made a note. Mrs. Marsden was still having trouble identifying her feelings as anxiety. *Odd, the Alprazolam and Prozac should have helped diminish that by now. Maybe I should up the dosage.*

"I did what you asked." She spoke hesitatingly. "I told two of my friends." She paused. "About the medication."

"And?"

"One responded well and one didn't. It was kind of terrible, actually." Olivia raised one brow, one corner of her mouth turning up as well, irony painted on her face.

"What do you mean by *terrible?*"

She gave a small chuckle, relaxing a bit in the chair. "I'm assuming telling my friends was supposed to *help* me in some way. But you've got to know Jan to fully appreciate her reaction." Olivia crossed one leg over the other, sitting back. "She pretty much blew me off. Said everyone was depressed. Why should I be any different?" Olivia crossed her arms defensively. "Not quite the sympathy I was expecting."

I set her file on the edge of the desk, turning to face her fully. "That's one of the major misconceptions about depression." I wondered how many times I'd have to repeat this information in my career. It was getting old. "The general public calls any sort of low feeling *depression*. I'm sure you've used the term yourself." She nodded. "The human body naturally goes through periods—mood cycles if you will. No one is ever going to live life on a mountaintop, but just because they are in a valley does not mean they are depressed. It's natural for people to feel down in the dumps at times, especially after events that might be expected to trigger a downward mood swing." I ticked some of the reasons off on my fingers. "Losing a job. The death of a loved one. A break in an important relationship. Poor health. There are a multitude of reasons people might feel low. It's natural. The resulting sadness after these adverse circumstances serves as a coping mechanism that helps the mind slowly process the change. When the person doesn't start feeling better in time, when all they can see is the valley, intervention is sometimes necessary."

"But nothing like that has happened to me!" Olivia's frustration spilled out. She uncrossed her legs and leaned forward. "That's what's so aggravating. I can't figure out a *reason* why I should be feeling so awful. I've got a great husband. Most days," she added with a small smile. "Two wonderful kids. A beautiful home. No financial worries. I've got friends." She stopped. "Even if Jan is a clod sometimes." A corner of her mouth turned up. "I'd like to be making more progress on my novel, but I do have fulfilling work. By all measures my life is perfect. Well," she smiled wryly, "as perfect as life is going to get on earth."

My antennae went up. Did her reference to life on earth mean she'd been thinking about life not…here? I leveled my head, making my words soothing, inviting clarification, not panic. "Can you explain what you meant by that last statement?"

"What statement?" She looked completely puzzled.

"What you said about life *here on earth.*"

She leaned back her head and laughed, not something patients often did in my office. It was a chortle so clear and free of hidden meaning I couldn't help but smile along. She raised her head, amusement coloring her eyes. "I meant that I understand life on earth will never be heaven. It's not supposed to be and I don't expect it to be." She paused, dipping her head to add, "I'd *like* it to be, but I don't expect it. My task is to learn to live with it. Do you know what I mean?"

"I'm not sure."

"I'm not thinking about suicide if that's what you're getting at."

"I was." Checkmate.

Slowly, she pushed both sides of her brown hair behind her ears before she spoke, a gesture that indicated to me she was about to reveal something. "Dr. Sullivan, I think you should know that I am relatively new to faith. My friend, Anne, taught me what Christianity was about simply by being my best friend. Even when I tried to push her away, she never gave up on me. She died before I learned that was exactly what Jesus was offering me, too. Unconditional friendship. I know now, but sometimes I have difficulty translating that kind of love into everyday life. Do you understand what I'm saying?"

"I do," I said, thinking of Margaret. What I didn't understand was why a loving God would allow this…this…separation between us. I made some scribbling motions on the tablet in front of me. *Focus, Doctor.* It wasn't often a patient's words sent me off into my own dilemmas, but for some reason Mrs. Marsden had a way of doing just that. "And how are you trying to deal with that?" I needed to turn the focal point back to Olivia. "Translating your loss into daily life?"

"Oh-h." She sounded surprised. "I lost my friend, but I gained so much from knowing her, from coming to faith, that I can hardly count it as a loss. Do you understand?"

Why did this woman keep asking me questions? I shifted in my chair, discomfort trying to squeeze in beside me.

"I do understand that loss, in time, can bring one to a place of greater understanding." In my case, I hadn't reached that spot yet, but Olivia certainly didn't need to know that.

Seldom did my patients in the throes of depression see the bigger picture. I mentally scratched my head again. How could this woman function on such a high level and yet be so emotionally miserable? She didn't fit the classic profile, that was for sure. All I could do was listen, hoping something she said would be the clue to the puzzle that made up Mrs. Marsden's life.

"What bothers me," she went on, "is that if I am a woman of faith, why can't I find comfort in my faith now?" Mrs. Marsden didn't beat around the bush. She tackled the big questions head-on. "Why can't I see God working?" Did she really expect *me* to answer these questions of hers? "Why can't I *pray?*" She stopped, her eyes imploring me for a response.

"Maybe this is a time when others are praying for you." The answer tumbled from my lips. It was definitely no advice I'd ever learned in a classroom. Where had those words come from? A strange chill traced a finger along my spine. Was anyone praying for me? For Margaret?

"Oh." She bent her head, resting the bridge of her nose between her fingers for a moment. When she looked up a peaceful smile had replaced the furrow that had creased her face earlier. "You're right. Just the other day, my friend Katie said she was praying for me." She shook her head slightly. "I keep forgetting. I'm not used to needing…" She paused, looking down at her hands. "…other people." She repeated my words as if tasting them, trying them on, seeing if they fit: "Maybe this *is* a time when others are praying for me. I'm going to try and remember that." She reached out and touched the tips of her fingers to my knee. "Thank you."

When was the last time I'd been touched? Other than a hand-shake, I didn't think a patient had ever laid a hand on me. And my secretary, Elaine, knew not to bring personal issues into work. Nothing that would encourage closeness of any sort. Not that I encouraged it. Ethics and all.

Ethics? Ha. You didn't encourage Margaret's touch, either. Now she— I was not going to get into that. Certainly not now. Not ever, if I had any say about it. Things went along much better when I didn't think about the past. *Physician, heal thyself.*

If only I could.

Libby

I stepped over an icy ridge of snow in the parking lot and climbed into my car. My third appointment with Dr. Sullivan was over. This appointment had produced no magic pill. For some reason I kept hoping. I still hadn't figured out who he reminded me of. Maybe that mystery was the only reason I kept returning. I stared at the reminder card in my hand. One week. One whole week to plod through until I could see him again. I felt my mood begin its usual post-appointment slide. The slippery slope of depression. No one yelling in excitement at this amusement park. Only shrieks of pure terror. I shook my head at the ghastly image. I wondered what Dr. Sullivan would say about my alternative Disney World?

I slammed the car door and inserted the car key into the ignition. The stiff coldness of the steering wheel seeped through my gloves as I waited a moment for the engine to warm up. *Now is a time when others are praying for you.* At least I had the consolation of his words to cling to until next week. And the consolation of Katie's head bowed on my behalf.

I stepped on the brake and shifted into reverse, looking over my shoulder before pressing lightly on the accelerator. Some days I'd almost have welcomed the distraction of a fender bender—anything to take my mind off myself and the implosion in my brain that focused all my thoughts like a spotlight on my misery.

I backed out of the parking space and shifted into drive. Where to now? I could swing by Katie's and see if she was free for a cup of coffee. I pressed down the blinker, circling the parking lot to reach the exit. Once again I hadn't told Katie I'd be in Carlton this afternoon. For all I knew, she could be teaching today. No use crossing town to find an empty house. Besides, my conversational quota for the day had been used up in Dr. Sullivan's office. Even though I spent most of every day trying to force my brain into coherent thought, when I walked into Dr. Sullivan's office my verbal skills were at their sharpest. I had this wild notion that if I talked fast and furious, examined every possible contributing factor, I just might stumble upon the one thing that would bring relief to my tortured soul. So far, my verbal spewing hadn't done anything but tire me out. The thought of trying to carry on a conversation, even with Katie, seemed like far too much effort.

I pressed on the gas pedal, easing into traffic, driving mindlessly. I didn't want to head straight back to Brewster and my same old gloom. Maybe I'd go walk around the mall for a little bit. I needed to fill my antidepressant prescription. The sample pills I'd started with were almost gone, and I wasn't about to fill my prescription at Brewster's small pharmacy. Even though the pharmacist was the model of discretion, I had a hard enough time admitting to myself I needed to take these pills. I wasn't anxious for anyone in Brewster to know I was on antidepressants and anxiety medication. Then again, I wasn't actually taking the anxiety pills. I hadn't mentioned that to Dr. Sullivan.

Filling my prescription in Carlton was as close to home as I wanted to get. I decided to make a wide swing through my favorite store, Marshall Field's, to make the trek to Osco Drug more palatable. Who knew? Maybe I'd find some bauble on a shelf that would dispel the shadows for at least a few moments.

I switched lanes as low January clouds spit dry snowflakes across my path. Except for our New Year's blizzard, the winter had been relatively snow free. Bob was already fretting about that. The Brewster farmers needed moisture now if crops and pastures were to grow in the spring. A poor harvest would mean the farmers wouldn't have money to pay back the loans the bank had made. I tapped on the brakes, slowing down to make the turn into the mall parking lot. Everybody had something to worry about. Things that were of more import than my imaginary misery. Once again I felt the melancholy that had lifted in the doctor's office settling heavy around my shoulders. Cold comfort.

I slipped into a parking spot near the mall entrance. Wrapping my black leather coat around me, I ran into the mall, a biting wind tossing my hair into the air and nipping at my ears. A scarf. I'd shop for a scarf. Something thick and fluffy that I could wrap around my neck and snuggle into up to my cold ears. I headed for Marshall Field's. Surely they'd have what I decided I needed. A little retail therapy before I filled the prescription that I hoped would provide a more conventional cure.

Familiar with the layout of the store, I threaded my way past the makeup counters and socks to the winter gear. Having a purpose felt good, even a minor one like buying a scarf. I stopped to look at the purse section first. Handbags weren't my thing, but just looking was fun. I picked up one and then another, smoothing my hand over the soft leather, testing the snaps and zippers as if I were truly in the market. I opened a black purse, the smell of new leather pungent and satisfying. I lifted it closer, closing my eyes and inhaling again, imagining the possibilities of a new life with a new purse...another me, a woman whose only concern in life was whether to use her brown leather handbag or her new black one.

"May I help you?" A stylish older saleswoman stood across the display table, eyeing me suspiciously.

What must she think of me with my nose in a purse? Maybe I was losing my grip. Quickly I put the purse back on the table. "Actually, I started out looking for a scarf. To go with my coat." I waved my hand in front of my body as though I were Vanna White showing off a prize and not the Crazy Purse-Sniffing Lady.

"The scarves are over here." She led the way. "They're kind of picked over from Christmas. But the good news is they are all on *sale*." The magic word. She stopped by two small shelves of neatly folded scarves. Not much inventory, but all I wanted was one. "This would go nicely." She pulled a scarf I hadn't noticed in my quick scan from the bottom of the pile. Yellow. Canary yellow. The exact same color of the scarf Anne had been wearing at the football game in Brewster the first night we met. The night I decided I hated her before she'd even said, "Hi-yi-iii!"

Instant tears clogged my throat as I remembered Anne, scarf wrapped loosely around her neck, walking down the sidelines of the Brewster football field. I hadn't had an inkling that night what this new person in town would mean in my life. No clue her friendship was about to change me, change my family, in ways I was too blind to imagine back then. I'd long before abandoned the image of the person Anne thought I could be. But somehow, softly, she'd done it. Knocked down the walls I'd built against friendship as if they were made of mist. I barely had a chance to glimpse myself as the person Anne was helping me become, and then she was gone. I was left half-formed, with only tears to fill my mold.

It wasn't Anne's image of you, it was Mine. You are becoming—

"Ma'am, are you all right?" The saleswoman had her hand on my arm. Her veneer was gone, and all I saw was genuine concern.

I rummaged in my pocket for a tissue. "Bad day," I croaked, wiping at my eyes.

"I didn't think it was the scarf." She squeezed my arm and then let go. "I know our selection is poor." She smiled and began folding the bright yellow scarf. "But not worth crying over. As I tell my grand-kids, 'A good nap can solve a lot of problems.' I'm sure after a good night's sleep, tomorrow will be a better day for you." She added the folded scarf to the top of the short pile. "There." She patted it for good measure. "Have a good—*oops!* Sorry, they practically brainwash that into us. You take care, now." Her eyes met mine. She meant it.

"I'll take it." The impulse felt good. "I want that scarf." I pointed, as if she didn't know.

"Nothing like yellow to brighten a North Dakota winter." Her eyes crinkled. "Will there be anything else?"

I smiled. "I doubt there's anything else in the store that could move me quite like this scarf."

She laughed, thinking I was kidding. Little did she know how true my words were. "I'll ring it up then."

"Please. And don't bother with a bag. I think I'll wear it."

I wrapped the soft, bright scarf around my neck. Twice. Once for Anne and once again for the promise God had just given me.

It wasn't Anne's image of you, it was Mine. You are becoming— It wasn't an interrupted sentence. It was a promise.

You are becoming… Who knew where this odd journey was taking me? Who I would be when it was over? Obviously, God did.

I stepped out into the cold January afternoon, snuggling my chin into my scarf. If I hadn't had hope when I entered the mall, I had it now. I was going to cling to those three precious words.

Repeating my new mantra to myself, I scurried across the snow-covered parking lot to my car. *You are becoming…* I stopped at the car door, fumbling in my purse for the keys. Man, it was cold outside! The temperature must have dropped ten degrees since I entered the mall. Where were my keys? I pulled off my glove and stuck my hand to the bottom of my handbag. Tissues, loose change, assorted junk, a pen, and old mints. No keys. I pushed my hand into my coat pocket. Nope. I pulled my other glove off with my teeth and checked the other pocket. My teeth were chattering together. Where were they? I threw my purse on the hood of the car and patted myself down as though I were a cop, frisking for weapons. All I needed to find was one key. Just one. As if I could feel my car keys through my lined, leather coat, anyway. Argh! I closed my eyes, leaning my head against the side window of the car. *Think.* Mentally, I retraced my steps. They had to be in my purse. I always put them there. I opened my eyes, ready to search again. There. The keys were hanging from the ignition inside my securely locked car.

One hour and one locksmith later I slid into my cold car. I tried repeating the mantra that had given me comfort, given me hope, earlier this afternoon. *You are becoming…* The words hung in the frozen air as I started the car. I shifted into reverse, backing out of the parking spot, more than ready to be back in Brewster. I shifted into drive. *You are becoming…* Funny, they didn't sound at all like hope anymore.

Hope? You call half a sentence hope? My harsh inner critic beat at my brain as I turned onto the highway for home. *Who knows what you are becoming? Probably crazier!*

Some hope.

Emily

"Mom! Where were you?" I threw my pen on top of my English lit notes. I'd been waiting for her to come home for hours. Well, it hadn't been hours…just since basketball practice, which had gotten over early. Mom was almost always home. If not, she left a note on the kitchen table. But not this time. I hoped she'd been to Carlton and brought Chinese take-out home for supper. I scanned her hands. No little white cartons. No fortune cookies. But that was okay; I had my own good fortune to tell. "Guess what? It's just the coolest, most awesome thing that ever happened to me! I can't believe it! You'll never guess." I took a breath, imagining all the possibilities my mom might suspect. I knew she'd never ever guess. But it would be fun to have her try before I spilled my news. "Go ahead, guess. I know I'll have to tell you. It's unbelievable. Cute scarf." I interrupted myself. "Can I borrow it sometime?" I didn't wait for an answer. I was too excited. "Three guesses."

Mom stopped unbuttoning her coat. "You got engaged!"

I didn't want to smile, but I couldn't help it. Her guess was an old joke from way back when I was little. Every time Mom and Dad left to go to a banquet, a convention, or whatever, Mom would leave Brian and me with her standard instructions: "Get to bed at a decent hour, listen to the babysitter, and don't get engaged until we get home."

I rolled my eyes now, secretly happy she remembered our game. "No-o-o, guess again."

"You got an 'A' in chemistry?"

I grinned. "No, but good try. One more."

Mom slipped out of her coat, unwinding the cute yellow scarf from her neck. She was so pretty. The prettiest of any of my friends' moms. They all said so.

"Ummm, let me think." She opened the closet door, hanging her coat on a hanger, draping the scarf carefully around the neckline. She closed the closet door and stood still, staring at the door. Just staring. It creeped me out. She'd been doing a lot of that lately. Staring into space and just sort of checking out for a while.

"Mom?"

She shook her head a little bit. "Still thinking," she said, distracted-like. She opened the closet door and felt in each of her coat pockets and then checked her purse. She frowned, walked into the kitchen, opened the fridge, and grabbed a lump of hamburger.

I had a feeling she wasn't thinking about her next guess at all. I could already feel my enthusiasm begin to drain away. Jen had almost completely ignored me when she found out, and Rick, instead of bear-hugging me like I thought he would, had said something I didn't even want to remember now. My mom was my last hope for someone to share my news. "Just guess, okay?"

"Emily, I'm sorry, I just can't think right now." Mom pulled a frying pan from below the counter and set it loudly on the stove. If I acted like that she'd yell at me. Mom stood there a second, her back to me, and then she turned. "I'm sorry," she said again. "I was at the doctor today, and then I ran to the mall. I just remembered I forgot to do an errand while I was there. I'm distracted. What was your news?" I could hear the fake enthusiasm in her voice.

I didn't even feel like telling her anymore. Let her read it in the *Brewster Banner* for all I cared. I bent my head over my homework. She probably wouldn't even notice if I didn't say anything more.

My whole life felt like it was falling apart. Jen had more or less dropped me as a friend. Not that I wanted to hang around her and Mindy, but I'd been friends with Jen practically since we were born. Not telling her everything every day felt weird. I saw her in school, throwing back her head and laughing at anything one of the guys said, checking to see if I saw that some cool guy was talking to her. Now, it seemed, she didn't care what I thought about anything.

Then there was my job at the nursing home. Well, for the few hours I worked I could hardly call it a job. I was having a hard time fitting the CNA classes in around my game schedule, much less finding time to job shadow in the few free hours I had. I was tired from going to school all day, hitting basketball practice as soon as the final bell rang, and then hopping in the car and getting to Carlton in time for class at seven. I'd had two evening ball games since the CNA classes had started, and the instructor had agreed to let me make up the missed class time by self-study and watching a video. When I was going to find time to do that, I had no idea. Probably on Sunday afternoon. The only time I had to spend with Rick. Or nap. If I didn't get called in to work, that is.

And what was I going to do about basketball? My foot hadn't gotten any worse after Christmas break, but it hadn't gotten any better, either. The coach was starting to comment on the fact that I often limped off the court and favored my opposite side when I drove in for a layup, a practice that was causing me to miss more layups than I made. "Mid-season is not the time to switch your approach," Coach Hoberg had said as I hobbled to the locker room one night. I nodded, glad that the assistant coach stepped in and motioned Coach Hoberg aside. I had a feeling if something didn't change soon, my great basketball season might be spent on the bench.

I closed my eyes, shutting out the lit book in front of me for a moment. I wished I could shut out everything about this suddenly rotten day. Tonight was a rare night when basketball practice had let out early and my Carlton class had the night off. I'd been looking forward to getting to bed early all day. After what happened in school this morning, I thought sleep might be the last thing I wanted by tonight, but now I couldn't wait to put my head on my pillow and zone everything and everyone out. Rick included.

"Did you hear?!" I'd practically jumped over to Rick's locker between classes.

"Hear what?" He rummaged for the book for his next class, not bothering to look at me.

I put my hand on his back. "I got nominated for Snow Princess!" I squealed like a game show contestant who won the grand prize.

"Oh, that." He stood, tucking his book in the bend of his arm. "Yeah." He sort of smiled, but not really. Not like I was.

"Don't you think it's cool that you're up for Senior King and I'm on the court, too? For the juniors," I added, as if he didn't know. If I wouldn't have looked so stupid, I would have done my own version of an end-zone dance right there in the hall. Nominated for Snow Princess! Never in my wildest imagining had I dreamt my vow to be popular at the start of this year would lead to the possibility of being Brewster's Snow Princess. Granted, it wasn't Queen; you had to be a senior for that. But this was as good as it could get for me. A nomination for Snow Princess and Rick Wynn for a boyfriend. Someone pinch me.

Jen would…if we were still friends. A stab of loneliness cut through my elation. The junior class had only twenty-one kids—ten girls and eleven boys. The fact that Jen had been left off the court was almost as unbelievable as me being on it. She'd been a favorite in our class until lately. Being on Snow Court would be a lot more fun if Jen and I were doing it together. Only three junior girls were up for the honor, and Jen wasn't one of them. But having her nominated might have been more weird than fun. Would she finally start acting normal around me? Or would I feel her cold shoulder each time we were together? Maybe it was better this way. Besides, I had Rick.

"Come on," I nudged him with my elbow, "aren't you excited?"

"It's not a big deal." He started walking down the hall; I followed a half step behind. I could see the envious eyes of other girls as they passed us in the hall.

I caught up to him. "It's a big deal to me!" Just because he'd been Snow Prince last year didn't mean he couldn't be excited for me.

"Whatever."

"Hey, Em, congratulations! Good luck!" Hannah Stromme squeezed my arm as she walked by. It was no secret she'd probably get voted Queen. She was without question the most popular girl in school. I'd quit worrying about her and Rick getting back together. Rick didn't seem one bit interested in her. And even though Hannah would sometimes ask how Rick and I were doing, I got the impression she was more concerned about how I felt about Rick than how Rick felt about me. I genuinely hoped she'd get voted Queen…and me, Princess!

"Thanks!" I grinned back at her. "Good luck to you, too." The voting was in a week. I had a whole week to dream.

Rick rolled his eyes. Guys didn't have a clue how important these things were.

"Hey, Em, you're the hottie!" Jason Fyle was heading toward us. A big grin covered his face, framed between the two thumbs he had pointed up.

So fast I hardly saw it happen, Rick dropped his book on the floor and had Jason shoved against the wall. "Leave her alone," he growled in Jason's face.

"Back off!" Jason shoved Rick away.

"What's going on here?" Mr. Morgan, the chemistry teacher, stepped into the hall.

I was wondering the same thing.

Rick glared at Jason, taunting him with his eyes.

Mr. Morgan put a hand on each of the guys' shoulders, turning them away from each other. "Get to class."

Rick bent to pick up his book, then tossed his chin at Jason as he put his arm protectively around my shoulder. "You're *my* princess," he said into my ear as we walked down the hall. He pulled me closer. "Remember that." He wasn't smiling.

~

I opened my eyes. My literature notes were a scribble in front of me. I hadn't wanted to think about what had happened in school that afternoon, but I had. I had a feeling some girls might like the way Rick had called me "my princess," but something about the way he'd said it and what had happened with Jason sent a strange chill creeping down my spine. I didn't like the feeling at all.

I could hear hamburger sizzling in the pan as my mom pushed it around with a wooden spoon. My stomach growled. I wanted to ask what we were having for supper. I was starving. But I wasn't going to give her the satisfaction of talking to her. Obviously she'd already forgotten I even had news to tell. I plopped my elbow on the table and pushed my chin into the heel of my raised hand. If she didn't care enough to ask, I wasn't going to tell her. Let her feel stupid when she read about it in the paper. *Emily Marsden, the Snow Princess Candidate Nobody Wanted.*

Libby

"My week? On a scale of one to ten, ten being awful?" I looked up from my lap, squarely into Dr. Sullivan's eyes. I wanted to make sure he fully understood what I was going to say next. "It was a twelve." I held his stare, waiting for him to break eye contact. I'd been coming to this plush office once a week for a month now in order to get better. If anything, I was getting worse. I was tired of feathering his lavish little nest with my insurance premiums and getting nowhere. I'd decided this was the day to let him know just how I felt. "It was a *twelve,*" I repeated, continuing to stare. I might as well have said, "So, what're you going to do about it?"

He bent his head. Ha! I'd won that contest. I looked back down at my lap, my small victory somehow hollow. Dr. Sullivan made a note on my chart. Then looked back up, catching my gaze. "Do you want to tell me what made this week a twelve for you?"

"Yes, I do!" My voice was filled with challenge. *Make me better!* I took a breath, ready to enumerate my terrible seven days. Come to think of it, maybe I didn't want to relive the past week. I closed my big mouth. I didn't relish pointing out my many shortcomings since my last appointment. Tears welled in my eyes, one large drop spilling over and marking my hand. A hot, wet coal burning with anguish.

"You might feel better if you tell me what happened. Then we can discuss how you might have had a better week."

Mr. Rogers. Finally it came to me. Dr. Sullivan reminded me of Mr. Rogers. With a tie, a sport coat, and a bit of an edge. Kindly, yet keen. Mr. Rogers' death had felt like losing a dear friend; seeing similar qualities in Dr. Sullivan felt like finding one. He was an understanding neighbor who challenged me while he walked through this journey with me. Surely Mr. Rogers would be compassionate about my many failings.

So will I.

Another warm tear dropped on my hand. Ah, yes. Jesus, too. My befuddled mind was so wrapped up in my problems that it kept forgetting Someone else was on my side. How could I forget that? Forget Him?

A small sob escaped my lips. I was nothing but a failure.

You're Mine. I created you. I knit you together according to My plan.

Some plan! Look how I treated Emily. The biggest event of her life, and I had to read about it in the paper.

I grabbed two tissues from the box on Dr. Sullivan's desk, pressing them to my eyes. I remembered all too well the evening Emily tried to have me guess her big news. I'd been so wrapped up about the fact that I'd forgotten to fill my Prozac prescription, I hadn't even noticed that I hadn't finished playing her guessing game. That night, long after Emily was in bed, her news untold, I rose from my sleepless tossing and stood in her doorway, wishing I could redo the whole miserable day. I watched her sleep as I used to in the days when impatience tucked Emily under her covers at night as often as I did. Time and again I'd been irritated at the whining of a two-year-old, the rambunctious energy of a three-year-old, the unrelenting questioning of a four-year-old who kept her mother from plotting the short story she was trying to write in her mind. How many nights had I stood vigil by her crib, by her twin bed, and now by her double bed, wanting to gently shake her awake? Wanting to take her in my arms, to answer all her questions, to listen to whatever it was she'd been so excited about telling me. I'd stomped on her excitement with my selfish preoccupation.

Forgive me, Lord, I cried that night.

You're a terrible mother. You don't deserve a child like Emily, a husband like Bob, or a son like Brian. It's a wonder Anne didn't die from your poor example of friendship. Once again, my inner uncertainties took over, berating me, beating me into a pit of self-doubt. *No wonder you don't have any friends.*

I'd sobbed in Emily's doorway, much like I was crying now. I was aware of Dr. Sullivan's assessing eyes. Maybe now he'd see just how much pain I was in.

I see.

I knew God did. Why couldn't I feel it?

"I just don't understand," I said, raising my wet face to the doctor. "I try so hard to remember God's promises, to claim them as mine—" I had to pause as another wave of emotion swept through me. "But then I get caught up in counting all the ways I've failed my family and I…" Once again, tears interrupted me. "…forget," I finished on the edge of a sob.

Dr. Sullivan sat quietly, waiting while my tears ran their course. At one time, I couldn't cry. My tear ducts had been stopped up as though they were fortified like Hoover Dam. I called those the Drought Years. The years I wandered through a dry desert, through a landscape that was as parched and featureless as photos I'd viewed of the Sahara. I hadn't had reason to cry because I hadn't let anything or anyone get close enough to matter. I'd even kept Bob at arm's length, letting him do the loving while I made sure my heart was good and protected from any sort of attack. As if love were the enemy.

And then Anne had come striding over the sand dunes, or rather the Brewster football field sidelines, as though she were some female version of Lawrence of Arabia, taking my defenses by storm. Anne had created an oasis of friendship in my life. An oasis that had destroyed my defenses. Wind on sand, blowing away resistance as though it were mere dust. Watering my soul, the essence of God's love for me springing up like fresh grass. Why couldn't I grasp that love anymore?

"If I'm a child of God, why can't I act like one?" There, I'd said it, what had been suppressed for days. I certainly didn't expect an answer from Dr. Sullivan; I simply needed to say it. The rest of my week spilled from my lips. Finally. "I forgot to fill my prescription after my appointment last week, and then I locked my keys in the car. I came home distracted and in a bad mood. Emily had some big news to tell me, and I didn't even notice. Completely blew her off. Only after she was asleep did I remember she wanted to tell me something. By then it was too late."

I'd pulled myself out of bed the next morning, something I hadn't done for months, to see Emily off to school. She still wasn't talking, even when I'd taken my hand and turned her face to mine. "What was it you wanted to tell me last night?" I'd asked at the door.

"I forgot." She'd shrugged as if it had been nothing. Nothing at all.

Maybe it had been, I told myself later. I pushed the guilt of the previous night away, sitting and staring at my computer as I did most days, accomplishing nothing. Nothing at all.

"Then I called the editor of the paper. The *Brewster Banner*," I reminded Dr. Sullivan. Even though I'd told him about my twice-monthly column, I doubted he subscribed. "I told the editor I couldn't write a column this week. The only other time I've done that was after Anne died." I paused, briefly recalling the short blip the *Banner* editor had run back then explaining the repeat of an old column was due to a well-deserved break for the writer. Kind words for a shadow-filled time.

"Emily never said a word all week," I went on, Mr. Rogers' comforting silence inviting me to fill the air. "Then Bob asked me again how I felt about moving and I *lost it*." I clamped my mouth shut and eyed Dr. Sullivan, not sure if he'd understand it was simply an expression. Before he considered slapping me in the hospital, I hurried to explain, "I started ranting about how I couldn't move. Wouldn't move. That all he ever thinks about is himself and his end-all business. I told him, 'I have a life, too! How about thinking about *me* for a change?'"

Dr. Sullivan didn't look shocked. Not anywhere as surprised at my words as I'd been when I'd said them. Even as I'd spouted my rage at Bob, I recognized the sham I was perpetrating. How many years had I wished to move from Brewster? I'd even told Anne of my fantasy to move to New York and be a writer. How many nights had

I lain awake, plotting the possibilities of Bob getting a job as a banker on Wall Street? It had been pure fantasy, but fantasy I'd actually prayed about, hoping God would hear and send our family on its way to a new promised land.

After I yelled at Bob, I stomped to the bedroom, throwing myself dramatically on the bed, the other me silently laughing at my forked tongue. Shame washed over me as I buried my head in the pillow.

"Telephone," Bob had called minutes later, his voice as even as if it were any normal night. "It's Katie."

"I don't want to talk to anyone," I screamed, making sure he knew I meant him, too. I had no control anymore over my words, my emotions, my thoughts, or my actions. Who had I become? I'd turned my head into the pillow and cried myself into an uneasy sleep.

"I'm so miserable," I concluded, my sordid tale finally told. My tears were dried, my throat scratchy. I looked to Dr. Sullivan, certain I'd find revulsion written on his face. I already knew there was no hope for the likes of me.

He lifted the lapel of his sport coat, pushing his expensive pen into the corner of his shirt pocket. Then he folded his long-fingered hands together over the clipboard on his lap. *Say something,* I silently urged.

"Discontent is the cutting edge of growth, you know." Dr. Sullivan tapped the tips of his index fingers together.

I certainly hadn't expected those words. "Say that again?"

"You're an intelligent woman, Olivia. I'm surprised you haven't figured out that our discontent often pushes us into new territory. It causes us to grow in ways that can be painful, but are ultimately for our good."

I cocked my head. "Like Job?"

Dr. Sullivan unfolded his hands and adjusted his tie. "Who?"

"Job, the man in the Bible whom God allowed Satan to test."

"Oh, well. Yes. Ummmm."

My mind was sifting through the basics of the story. "Job had a very nice life going for himself when God stepped in and let Satan test Job's faith by making him miserable, taking away everything Job thought was important. In the end, God gave him back even more." I stopped talking. I'd never thought of what I was going through as a test of faith. That my current misery might lead to something better. How had Dr. Sullivan put it? "Could you say what you said again?" I pushed my hair behind my right ear as though to hear better.

He shifted in his chair and repeated the words as though they were now a question, "Discontent is the cutting edge of growth?"

"Yes, that." The words played in my mind. Somehow the phrase put a spin on my troubles that made them just a bit bearable. For today, anyway. Possibly I was moving toward something good in all my misery.

You are becoming... There was that promise again.

"I need to ask," Dr. Sullivan said, "you mentioned you forgot to refill your prescription. You are taking your medication, aren't you?"

I nodded. "I made a trip back to Carlton the next morning and got it refilled," I said in a small voice. I didn't add that I tried the antianxiety pills for the first time the night I blew up at Bob. Well, *pill,* not pills. Half a pill to be exact. After I stood in Emily's doorway and cried out my regret, another feeling had risen to take regret's place. I didn't have a name for it; I only knew it felt like impending doom. At first I couldn't breathe. A weight pushed at my chest and then at my back. Nausea pushed at my throat. I ran down the stairs, thinking if I could just stick my head outside I'd feel better. I'd put my hand on the doorknob, then pulled it back as if I'd been shocked. What if what I feared was standing right outside the door? What if I opened the door and invited doom inside? Even as I wrestled with my nighttime demon, I understood my fear was irrational. But it felt so real. If I opened that door I would die. Or at least it felt like I would.

You're going crazy. This is Brewster, North Dakota. There is nothing, no one, outside that door.

I knew that and yet I didn't. My mind screamed, *Don't open that door!* All the while I realized my thoughts were foolish. My ears rang as if gongs were being pounded on either side of my head. My vision blurred as fear blinded me. *Oh, God, don't let me die! Help me. Please. Help me...*

I didn't know how long I'd stood there, praying, willing myself to breathe. Eventually my vision cleared, silence returned, and sweat coated my body. I reached up and brushed damp bangs from my face, testing…if I moved, would it happen again? The feeling of doom had passed, sort of, but I was left with another fear, the fear of it happening again. What if I was alone when this sensation came back? What if I was driving? What if…? The fear of fear itself closed in. I couldn't go through this again. Ever. I wouldn't live. I knew I wouldn't.

I climbed the steps to my bedroom, feeling my way along the dark hall, into my room, past my familiar dresser and bed, past my peacefully sleeping husband, into the master bathroom. I switched on the nightlight I kept in the outlet near the sink. I reached into my makeup drawer, knowing exactly where to put my fingers. They grasped the small brown vial I'd saved for a moment like this, a time when I could no longer cope on pure grit. I shook one pill from the plastic and into my trembling hand.

You're weak if you take it. Don't. You should be able to handle things by yourself. You don't need a pill. You need to get tough. Don't take it.

The memory of the previous hour hounded me, nipping at my back with fangs of fear. I placed the pill on the counter, pinching the small oval between my index finger and thumb. With my other hand I grabbed a metal nail file from the drawer and sawed along the faint line in the middle. I'd take half. Only half a pill would mean I still had some control. Shadowy fingers of terror plucked at my neck. Hurry. I jabbed at the pill with the sharp point of the file. There. It broke in two, small grains of medicine salting the counter. I threw one half into my mouth, forcing it down without water. I dabbed at the crumbs, licking the bitter treat from my finger.

Wimp. Weak. Pathetic.

I switched off the nightlight, clawing my way back under the bed covers. I lay on my back, forcing my eyes to stay shut. Did I feel anything? Was the pill dissolving? When would relief course through my bloodstream? Would it? The other half of the pill, the one I hadn't taken, hung in my mind, a beacon.

"Olivia?" Dr. Sullivan's touch on my knee startled me. Good. Let him see that this is how my days were spent. Lost in thought. Absorbed in worry and self-doubt. "I'm going to change the dosage of your medication."

"I don't know how much longer I can take this." My voice was flat. I didn't mean the medication. I meant the emotions.

He seemed to understand. "Sometimes it takes some adjusting to get the proper levels into your system. Don't get discouraged; we're going to keep working until we get it right."

"I only hope I live that long."

Dr. Sullivan's quick stare penetrated. When would I learn that my attempts at macabre humor didn't play in a psychiatrist's office?

"It was a joke." I smiled wanly. "A bad one. But I was wondering…" I twisted my hands together, playing with the question I'd been toying with for weeks. "What about…what would…?" I paused, feeling the full weight of my question, the very thing I'd feared my whole life, now looming as my only hope. "What about the hospital? Would that help me?" My question hung in the air, a soiled sheet on the line. Had I really asked about being admitted to the hospital? As a psychiatric patient?

The other me suddenly appeared, laughing hysterically. She was well aware of the irony. The thing I valued most in this world was my mind, and I was finally admitting I had no control over it at all. It was a cruel joke, to be sure, but she laughed all the same.

Dr. Sullivan tugged at his chin. "The hospital is not a place you want to be," he remarked softly.

But I did. At least I thought I did. I closed my eyes, quickly drawing up the image I'd created in my mind during my long, desperate nights. A clean, glowing corridor. White. Pure white. Simplicity. Quiet. A place where worry could not hide in dark corners, waiting to pounce when I wasn't looking. A magic shot. A secret pill. Something that would chase away the demons that haunted my days and my nights. I didn't know how much longer I could carry on with this charade that was my life.

"You don't belong in the hospital," Dr. Sullivan said. "Not now."

How much worse do I have to get? The thought alone was enough to cause my breathing to become shallow. The threads of panic started to snap at my neck. If something was worse than this, I couldn't begin to imagine what it would feel like. I didn't want to. I nodded meekly. I had no choice.

"Okay." The voice wasn't mine. It was the sound of the other me, the alternate me, who could pretend so well that all was fine. Even when the real me knew, without a doubt, that my world was crumbling from within.

Dr. Sullivan

"I'm going to remember what you said," Olivia remarked as she stood up, brushing at her deep brown slacks. "About this being a test of faith, of sorts."

"But—I didn't—"

She kept right on talking, stuffing her ever-present wad of tissues into her pocket. For not the first time in my career, I kicked myself for not buying stock in Kleenex years ago. She pulled another tissue from the box as though her hand felt empty without the flimsy comfort. "I'm going to try to think of this as something…" She paused, searching for a word. "…beneficial," she finished, a small eye-glint of triumph marking her word.

She glanced at her watch. "I'd better get going." She walked briskly to my office door. "The Snow Princess coronation is at the Brewster High gym right after lunch, and I won't miss that." She turned, giving me a wry smile, both eyebrows raised as if seeking my affirmation.

"Yes." I nodded, following her to the door. "You need to be there." I stood with one hand on the doorframe, watching Mrs. Marsden's confident stride move her away from me. No one looking at her would ever suspect the inner turmoil that brought her to my office each week. If I didn't know better, even I would assume she was a pharmaceutical rep sitting in my outer office rather than one of the more hard-to-classify cases I'd run across in my career. I only hoped this new dose of medication would bring about the chemical balance I was seeking. Catching the eye of my next client, I held up one finger. "Be right with you."

I closed the door, wanting a few minutes to record this appointment before seeing my next patient. As I circled around my desk, I thought about Mrs. Marsden heading back to Brewster on a road I should know better considering how close it was. The forty miles between Brewster and Carlton somehow appeared shorter when a big town was on the other end. I couldn't imagine that the drive back to Brewster held any more allure for Olivia than it did for me. Miles of time filled with self-recrimination was not something anyone would anticipate. I sat in my chair and picked up the Dictaphone. Maybe today was different. Olivia did need to be at her daughter's big event. The remorse she expressed over reading in the paper that her daughter, Emily, was a candidate for Snow Princess would have more than made up for her earlier negligence. If only Emily had seen her mother as I'd observed her today. Unfortunately, Olivia had been unable to share her regret with Emily. But, knowing sixteen year olds, I doubted Emily would have listened to her mother's apology anyway.

Swiveling my chair to gaze out the window, I pressed the record button.

> Clinical note: Olivia Marsden. January 30 appointment. Patient highly distressed. Complained of outbursts to husband. High agitation over missed sharing of important event with daughter. Several episodes of panic disorder past week. One severe. Patient inquired about hospitalization. Increased Prozac to 60 mg. Alprazolam to 1.0 mg.—three times daily. Patient appears well groomed. Daily routine uncompromised by depressive episode. No suicidal intent.

I released the record button and placed the microphone back in its cradle, laying my head against the soft leather of my high-backed chair. Ice crystals hung outside my window, shimmering in the cold January sun. Their sparkle was deceptive, offering a kind of hope I knew would dissolve with the slightest touch. Much like what I did each day. Trying to hold out hope for patients whose lives were as fragile as crystal.

For not the first time I puzzled over Mrs. Marsden. On the outside she appeared strong and confident. Most anyone looking at her would agree to change places in a second. What the outside world didn't see was what perplexed me. How could she be so high-functioning, verbal, and competent in her daily life, and yet still be so tormented with anxiety and depression? I couldn't help but marvel at the effort she must have made to keep up appearances. Each week when she appeared in my office, just by the looks of her, I expected her to flash me a smile and remark, "I'm better!" The medication should have started working by now. And even without medication, depression was cyclical; I kept hoping her cycle would soon pass.

The way she could articulate her problems, her episodes of anxiety, her low moods and feelings of failure, were counter to any depressive patient I'd seen in my practice. Most were practically struck dumb by overwhelming sadness. Hardly able to speak of their misery. Agitated to the point of nervous foot-shaking or pacing. Unable to sit still and describe their anxiety. Her question about the hospital today had surprised me. Olivia didn't fit into any of these molds and certainly not the mold of the psychiatric hospital patient. She spoke eloquently and sat calmly, even when she cried. Her inner core held her together, even when she felt as if she were falling apart.

But then, maybe that was exactly why her case was causing me to lose so much sleep. I twisted back to my desk, closing the cover on Mrs. Marsden's file. I didn't need to review the notes I'd made. I didn't have to be a doctor of psychiatry to know that the reason I was puzzling so long over Mrs. Marsden's problems was to avoid contemplating my own. What I hadn't put in the notes is what was really on my mind. Why I really wanted these few minutes alone.

"These troubles are a test of faith, of sorts…" If they weren't her exact words, they were close.

Quit mincing words, Doctor. Exact words don't matter…intent is what counts. Face it.

"If I'm a child of God, why can't I act like one?"

There. Those were her exact words. The words I'd been trying to avoid thinking. I removed my reading glasses and laid them across the vanilla file folder. *If I'm a child of God…?*

I scrubbed at my face. I could hardly be called that. Not anymore. Not the way I'd treated Margaret. Not the way I'd behaved since…

I sat back in my chair, allowing my eyes to travel around my office. Several framed diplomas lined the wall. The first article I'd written for *Psychiatry Quarterly* was framed, as well. An award from the North Dakota Mental Health Association stood on a nearby shelf. What did any of it mean now that I had no one to share them with? My eyes roamed the shelves, noting the many books and diagnostic manuals, as well as the small golf trophy I'd won at the regional psychiatric conference in Arizona three years earlier. Margaret had loved the warm weather there in the middle of a miserable February in North Dakota. Why hadn't I taken her there again? Why had I thought a week off to simply *be* with my wife wasn't time well spent? Why hadn't I grabbed her hand and spent a half hour walking along the desert path near our casita with her instead of heading to the convention hall, where I drank a scotch and water I didn't need and talked with a software salesman about a computer program I needed even less? Why hadn't I—

I pushed my thoughts and my eyes away from the memory. Again my eyes traveled the shelves. Expensive trinkets took the place of family photos. The family we never had. Even the photos of Margaret were now put away. There, in that drawer. My eyes fixed on the brass handle. One tug could bring her back to me.

I rose from the chair, crossing the room and pulling at the drawer. There she was. My Margaret. I picked up the silver-framed photo. It had been taken at the picnic area at Brush Lake near Brewster our first summer in Carlton. I'd just finished my psychiatric residency. How excited Margaret had been when my first job offer brought her back to North Dakota. She was raised on a ranch in the western part of the state and longed to escape the confines of whichever city my schooling brought us to.

"Carlton?!" She clapped her hands like a little girl when I told her.

Our whole future lay before us that summer, and here it was, captured again in framed faded color. Flowing blond hair. Crinkled green eyes. Her arms thrown in the air in a pose any model would envy. Look at me. I am a woman in love. In love with the outdoors. In love with life. In love with my husband. I recognized that smile. Her head tilted just so. Smiling the way she always used to. As if I were so much more than just the man on the other side of the camera. As if I were a man who would never betray his marriage vows.

"If I'm a child of God, why can't I act like one?"

I felt the full weight of that question, heavy on my shoulders. Mrs. Marsden wasn't the only person struggling with that thought. The difference between Mrs. Marsden and myself was that she dared to ask the question aloud while I pushed it so deep in the recesses of my psyche that most days I didn't even know it was there. Except the days like today when Olivia Marsden brought the question front and center.

Physician, heal thyself.

What amazed me about Mrs. Marsden was how she could be in such anguish and still struggle to find God in the midst of her pain. I'd done nothing but run the other way from God ever since—

"Dr. Sullivan?" My office assistant, Elaine, knocked softly and then peeked around the door. "Mr. Reed has been waiting for some time now." She practically whispered, "I just don't want you to get too off schedule. You have that banquet to attend tonight and—"

"Yes." I slipped the framed photo back into the drawer. "Thank you for reminding me." I pushed the drawer closed with my knee. "Send Mr. Reed in, please."

"If I'm a child of God, why can't I act like one?"

I reached out my hand to greet Mr. Reed, motioning him to the same chair Olivia Marsden had just left. I breathed a sigh of relief as I took my customary place next to him. I knew Mr. Reed's laments wouldn't shake loose any old memories the way my previous client had. If I was lucky, I'd concentrate hard enough during this next hour that the words that haunted me now would be completely forgotten.

"If I'm a child of God, why can't I act like one?"

Forgotten. Remember?

You need to forget, Doctor. Forget.

Quickly, I reviewed my notes from Mr. Reed's last appointment. Another part of my brain tumbled with the conundrum…could the mind be told to remember to forget something?

If I hadn't felt so troubled, I might have been pleased to wrestle with the catch-22. Certainly a topic for another article in a respected medical journal.

"Dr. Sullivan?" Mr. Reed interrupted my thoughts. "Could we get started? I need to get back to work."

"Of course." I cleared my throat while pulling my pen from my pocket. Unprofessional. These intrusive thoughts of mine were wholly unprofessional.

"If I'm a child of—"

"Yes, let's get started. Tell me about your week." I'd think about this later.

Emily

"And the Snow Prince is…" Brent Will, the student council president, held an envelope in the air. Everybody cheered. The three junior guys up for Prince jokingly held hands, pretending they were dying of excitement. "Drum roll, please." At Brent's words the crowd laughed. There were no drums.

Leave it to Mike, one of the three candidates, to whir his tongue in an uncanny imitation of percussion that only those of us on stage could hear. I looked at the other candidates standing in a line on either side of me. Their faces were plastered with fake smiles. Even Rick's. None of them even seemed to hear Mike's attempt to lighten the mood. Win or lose, Mike would still be Mike.

My palms were sweaty, and I pressed them tightly against the soft fabric of my emerald green dress, hoping the moisture wouldn't leave a hand-sized stain that everyone would see. I knew being so nervous about being up for Snow Princess was silly. In a school the size of Brewster High, almost all of us had a chance at some sort of recognition. But mine usually came for playing piano for choir, not for something that seemed more like a fairy tale. Being crowned Snow Princess was an event based on popularity, not practice. *Hurry up!* Brent was milking his moment at the podium.

"Miiiii-ke Anderson!" Brent called the name as though Mike were the MVP of the Super Bowl. The other two guys collapsed in phony tears, hugging Mike in a poor imitation of the losers in the Miss America pageant. Mike stepped forward, bending his lanky frame to receive the flimsy crepe paper crown.

"Speech! Speech!" The student body set up a chant. Had there ever been any doubt Mike would be elected Snow Prince? Mike was everybody's friend, kindergartner to senior. Of course, in a school the size of Brewster, knowing everyone by name was easy. What was hard was to get them all to like you. Mike had.

Mike reached up to adjust his tilting crown. From the side where I stood, I could see the familiar glint start in his eye as he spoke into the microphone, "As Prince, I would like to free you from the tyranny of the teachers." A low chuckle rippled through the gym. "But, alas, my powers are limited. I am only a lowly prince next to the senior who will be my king." He turned and bowed to the five senior guys waiting for their turn to be crowned. Chuckles turned into laughter. This was vintage Mike. "But I urge the future king to be kind to us peasants, for we are many in number with our eye on the crown. Power to the peasants!" He thrust his fist into the air. A roar went up from the student body. Mike tapped at the air with both hands, settling the ruckus. He dipped his head, and when he lifted it the impish grin was gone, replaced by a confident smile. "On a more serious note, I'd like to thank all those who voted for me and wish the Badgers good luck in their games this week." There was a smattering of clapping as Mike concluded, "Victory is ours, sayeth the Lord!" He stepped back from the mike, index finger raised, his eyes lifted to the high ceiling of the gym. Hoots and cheers rang through the gym. There was no counterfeit in his action. Everyone knew he meant more than winning a couple basketball games. Mike could clown with the best of them, but he was dead serious about his faith. Only Mike could get away with proclaiming his faith at a school assembly and still be considered cool.

A tiny finger of guilt scratched at my stomach. What had happened to my New Year's resolve to read my new devotional book each night? I'd been so focused on my relationship with Rick, my non-relationship with Jen, my homework, and my CNA classes, that prayer and Bible study hardly ever crossed my mind. Maybe part of the reason things between Jen and me were so strained was because I hadn't been praying for her. Not at all.

My eyes scanned the auditorium. There was Jen, high in the bleachers, sitting by Mindy. I could hardly tell from this distance, but she seemed to be looking right at me. She looked away, mumbling something to Mindy. A snide comment about me, no doubt.

That wasn't nice. You have no idea what Jen just said.

True, I didn't. But imagining she'd said something mean was easier than admitting how much I missed her friendship. The real truth was Jen should be up here with me. We both knew it. We'd been friends since before kindergarten. We did everything together. Tiny Tots Twirling was where we met. Some other little kid had knocked Jen in the head with the end of a baton when we were practicing the pancake twirl, and I was the one who hugged her tears away. We'd been buddies ever since. Until now. I looked away from where Jen was sitting. It was easier when I didn't remember.

Mike turned from the podium, his eye catching mine. A sly smile turned up one corner of his mouth. "Good luck," he mouthed. I mouthed back, "Thanks."

"And our Snow Princess is…" Once again Brent held up an envelope. I could see the elementary girls sitting on the bottom rows of bleachers near the foot of the stage gazing up at me and the two other junior princess candidates. The little girls giggled, fidgeting with excitement. They obviously dreamed of standing here someday. I remembered well my own years of imagining myself on this stage. Now I was here.

Brent tore his thumb along the crease of the white envelope. "Who will be Prince Michael's princess?" More giggles from the elementary kids. Hissing from the older kids. I rolled my eyes, annoyed with Brent's theatrics; I just wanted the suspense over. The two girls on either side of me clasped my hands. Damp joining damp. Unlike the guys who were trying to be funny, our grasp was nothing but nerves.

Brent pulled a slip of paper from the envelope, read it, and slipped it into his pocket. He lifted a sparkling rhinestone crown from a shelf under the podium and walked behind Brenda, April, and me. I could hear the smirk in his voice as he hovered the crown over each of our heads. "Who-oo-oo will it be?" Kids in the audience clapped as the crown hung for a second over each of our heads.

My heart thudded in my chest. I didn't think I wanted to be princess this bad, but suddenly I did. *Please let it be me!*

Brent got to the end of our small row, playing the crowd with suspense as he bounced the crown once more over each of our heads. I took a deep breath, the muscles in my cheeks vibrating with hope. My eyes floated over the faces that were following the moving crown as though it were a Ping-Pong ball. I felt my hair lift just a bit as Brent teased the top of my head again. I looked to the far wall of the gym, wanting nothing more than for the anticipation to be over. There was my mother, elegant in black, standing stiffly along the back wall of the auditorium. I had no doubt her eyes were focused on me. My dad was standing beside her, his hand around her waist, his eyes on me, too. They'd both come. I closed my eyes. Suddenly, it was enough. The fact that my parents were here made whatever was going to happen okay.

I felt Brent behind me again, pausing where he hadn't before. My eyes flew open just as he set the crown firmly on my head. *I was Snow Princess?* I was Snow Princess! My hands reached up to steady the crown. Now I knew why every queen pageant I'd ever watched had the winner grabbing her head. She was checking to make sure the crown was really there.

Brenda and April hugged me from either side. "Congratulations," they said in unison. It didn't matter if they meant it or not. I was Snow Princess!

"Kiss! Kiss!" The chant started from the back and was quickly picked up by the overexcited elementary kids. "Kiss! Kiss! Kiss!"

Mike stepped forward, bowing from the waist, taking my hand and twirling me around once as if to show off me and my crown from all angles. As I turned I caught a glimpse of Rick's face, his eyes squinted, his lips pressed into an unhappy line. My bubble popped. Mike tipped me over backward, his arm supporting me from below. I grabbed at the crown with one hand, holding it tight to my head. From my upside-down view I could see Rick still frowning. As quickly, Mike pushed me upright, dropping to one knee as if I were a real princess and innocently kissing the back of my hand.

"Ahhhh…" A collective sigh filled the gym. I could pick out Jason Fyle's voice calling, "Chicken!" I shot a quick glance at Rick. His eyes were searching the crowd, looking for Jason, his fists a knot at his side.

Not sure what to do, grateful to Mike for playing his part so well, I gave him an awkward curtsy. My real-life prince. This afternoon, anyway. Mike nodded, his eyes over my shoulder, appraising Rick. Had Mike seen something more in Rick's frown? Something I hadn't? Maybe he hadn't been *playing* the prince; maybe he had saved this princess from sure disaster.

"Oh, Emily!" My mom held me a little away from her, her hands warm on my shoulders, eyes shining as she took in the sparkling crown on my head. "I'm so happy for you!" She pulled me into a hug. For this moment, thankfully, she seemed to have pushed aside the dark mood that had her snapping at all of us lately. The Mom I remembered was here. I squeezed her back. Through my closed eyes I could see the flash from a camera.

"Here." Dad handed Mom the camera as he pulled me into his arms. "My princess," he whispered in my ear. The way he said it made me feel like snuggling farther into his arms, not at all the way I'd felt when Rick had growled it in my ear in the hall last week. "I'm so proud of you," my dad said, hugging me once again as Mom snapped a picture.

"Let me get one of you and Mike." Mom motioned Mike to my side. I could see Rick off to the side of the stage, grouped for pictures with the Senior Court. He hadn't gotten crowned Senior King, but I had a feeling that wasn't what had put the scowl on his face. I wasn't going to do anything to make him madder. I crossed my arms across my chest in a very un-princesslike pose if I'd ever practiced such a thing.

"Emily, stand straight," Mom coached.

"Here." Mike grabbed my hand and fell to his knee, imitating the pose he'd struck during the coronation. "My dearest damsel," he clowned. "Surely you are the fairest in the land. Next to Queen Hannah, of course. Second fairest I declare thee!" I couldn't help but laugh. Luckily, Mom captured my one true laugh of the day on film.

⌒

Please don't let Rick be mad. Please let him be happy for me. If I had forgotten about praying in the weeks just past, I was making up for it now.

"One more." The editor of the *Brewster Banner* repositioned Hannah's dress, stepped back, and pointed his camera. The Senior King and Queen sat on band stools while Mike and I stood on either side of them. The gym had emptied while parents and the newspaperman regrouped us for photos. "Smile. Got it. Thank you." Just like that it was over.

"See you at home, Emily." Mom waved from the steps leading to the stage, her big smile a sort of apology for the misunderstanding we'd had over all this. "Have fun!"

"Thanks." I waved back, forgiving her finally, a generous princess. "Remember I have practice after this, then class in Carlton tonight." I was glad I would be busy all night. It would give me more time to figure out just what was up with Rick. He was glaring at me from across the stage, acting like he didn't even care that I was crowned Snow Princess. Almost like he was mad that I got it. I turned my back to him. Maybe he was upset that he didn't get Senior King, but at least he could be glad for me. I had a suspicion that most of the kids had voted for Collin Ritter for King because his dad had had a heart attack last week. I couldn't help it if the kids hadn't voted for Rick. I had, and I planned to tell him as soon as we were alone.

"You look very pretty." Mike stood across the two empty stools from me. Hannah and Collin had left. "In that crown...and...dress... and all." He pushed his hands into his back pockets, biting the inside of his cheek. Mike, my friend who was never at a loss for words, couldn't seem to find them now. "Very pretty," he added, looking over my shoulder. I remembered all too well what he'd said to me on New Year's Eve and felt myself blushing. Obviously, his feelings hadn't changed in the month since. A month when I'd all but ignored him, caught up in school, my CNA classes, and Rick. Unlike Jen, Mike had remained my friend, no matter how often I forgot to treat him like one. I could make up for that now. I looked down at my hands, then reached one out to Mike. "Thanks," I said, smiling up at him, waiting for him to touch my hand and reconnect our friendship.

He took a small step backward, his eyes darting from my face to somewhere behind me. "I like your hair like that, too." He backed up one more step. "Hey, Rick."

Rick's arms circled around me from behind, claiming me as his. A delicious thrill went through me. He was happy for me after all.

Mike nodded at Rick and walked off, leaving my hand reaching into thin air. I moved it to Rick's thick arm.

"Congratulations." Rick said into my ear. He didn't sound much like he meant it. Not like Mike had.

I turned to face him, taking his strong hands in mine. "I'm sorry you didn't get King." There, maybe that would help him feel better. In all honesty I was glad he hadn't gotten elected. I wasn't sure how I would have felt having Rick holding Hannah's arm, King and Queen, a couple like they'd been last year at this time, Prince and Princess. But I didn't have to worry about that. Rick was my boyfriend now.

Rick shrugged one shoulder. He reached up and brushed a strand of my hair off my cheek. "Can I come over tonight? Give you my real congratulations?"

Oh, so that was it. He felt too shy to show how he really felt here at school where someone might see. I couldn't help but grin at him.

"What time should I come over?" Rick touched my nose.

The smile fell from my face as I remembered…it was a school night. I had basketball practice, and then I'd be rushing straight to Carlton for class. I wouldn't get back to Brewster until at least ten o'clock, and by then my folks would never let Rick stop by.

"Oh, Rick," I said. "Gosh…" I was stalling for time while my brain thought of a way to explain this to him in a way that wouldn't make him mad. Ah! "I have class in Carlton tonight, and by the time

I get back, it will be past curfew. I have a game tomorrow night, and coach is letting me stay out until ten only because of class." Rick knew the athletic rules. Nine o'clock curfew the night before a game. "And you know my folks…" He knew how strict they were about my curfew, especially on school nights.

His brows knit together. "You don't want to see me, is that it?" He dropped my hand. "You'd rather hang out with Mike, I suppose."

"No! That's not it at all." I looked over my shoulder, wondering if Mike had heard. Except for the janitor and a couple of coaches at the end of the floor, the gym was empty. I grabbed Rick's hand and held tight. "You know it's not."

"You have time to take pictures and talk to Mike but no time for me."

How could he think that? Couldn't he tell how much I wanted to see him tonight? I tried to explain. "I want to see you, I really do. It's just that—"

"You don't have time for me now that you're the *Princess.*" His voice was mocking as he pushed my hand away.

"Rick, that's not true." I tried to reach for his hand but he crossed his arms over his chest.

"You're too good for me now, huh?"

"What are you *saying?*"

"I don't know how you got elected princess, anyway. If people knew what you were really like, they would have never voted for you."

My mouth dropped open. Speechless. What had gotten into him? This was supposed to be one of the best days of my life, and he was ruining it completely.

"You walk around school saying…" His voice rose to a high-pitched whine, "'*Hi-ii!*' to everybody in sight." If his imitation was supposed to make me sound snotty, it worked. "Don't you think people can see through you? You're so…so… *fake.*"

A lump pushed its way into my throat. I wanted to turn and run away, but my new shoes felt like they were glued to the floor. I clamped my mouth shut. His words hurt, but maybe they were true. Hadn't I just been thinking about how I'd ignored Mike? And maybe it hadn't been *all* Jen's fault that we weren't hanging out much anymore. I'd been giving her the cold shoulder right back. Maybe Rick was right. Maybe I was a fake. A snotty fake.

"Maybe you don't want to go together anymore." Rick's face was hard.

Instant tears sprang to my eyes. "No!" The word came out loud, echoing in the now empty gym. How could this be happening to me? "I do want to go with you, Rick. I do! I'll skip class tonight." I was desperate. "We can go driving around or something." He couldn't come over—my parents would have a fit if they knew I was missing my class to see Rick. "I'll drive. Okay? I'll pick you up."

"Oh, sure. You're going to come out to the farm and pick me up. Right. Just forget it." His arms came down from his chest and pushed against my shoulders as he turned and walked away.

I stumbled backward, the heels of my new shoes scrambling to find a grip on the shiny floor of the stage. Something in my sore foot popped loudly. Ouch! I wasn't sure which hurt more: my foot or Rick's harsh words. I was too stunned to call after him. Too shocked to cry. *Lord, please don't let him break up with me. Please!* What had I done to make him act like this?

You're a fake, remember? You say you're a Christian, but you forget to pray until you're desperate. You don't have time for God, much less Rick…or any of your friends.

I watched as Rick stomped off the stage, heard the clank of the broad handle on the gym door as Rick shoved it open, and listened as the door slammed shut. Leaving me alone. The snotty fake Snow Princess.

Rick was right. I didn't deserve this crown. I reached up and pulled the sparkling stones, *fake* stones, from my head. I didn't deserve Jen or Mike as friends. Maybe I didn't deserve Rick, either. And I certainly didn't deserve to have God answer a frantic, last-ditch prayer.

The tears came then. Hard and hot. Splattering on the rhinestone crown I held in my shaking hands. Everybody thought I was the

Snow Princess, but I knew better. I was a nobody. A worthless, fake, nobody.

⁓

I pulled the car into the driveway, making sure Dad could get his car out of the garage in the morning. I shifted into park, letting the car idle while I waited for the song on the radio to be over. I was wishing I could listen to Mike broadcast on KBRS, but the station went off the air at sunset each night. Mike had a knack for getting me out of a funk, even if I just listened to his goofy chatter over the radio. I could use some of that tonight.

I stared out the window, watching as ice crystals danced around the halo from the streetlight on the corner. I didn't want to go inside. The thought of the dark quiet of my room made me feel afraid. Too much space to fill with memories of this awful day.

Basketball practice had helped me forget for a little bit. The coach ran us hard and made us move so fast, all I could think about were the plays we were running and how badly my foot was hurting. But the second practice was over, all my teammates wanted to talk about was how Hannah and I had felt when we got crowned...*Awesome! Still can't believe it!*...and what everyone was wearing to the dance Saturday night. I got busy and untied my shoes, leaning way over and tugging at the laces until they practically fell from the tie-holes, taking my time ducking from the conversation. I wondered what they'd say if they knew the Snow Princess might not even be at the dance?

I didn't want to think about it in the locker room, and I didn't want to think about it in the car. Song over, I turned off the car, not feeling one bit like getting out into the cold February night. *Funk* was a good word to describe the way I felt, a good word for the whole day for that matter. The tears that had pushed at my throat all through CNA class fell now. How was I ever going to get to sleep when all I could think about was losing Rick? What was I going to do in school the next day when everyone would act like it was supposed to be the second-best day of my life? Could I pretend to be sick? Not go at all? No, then I wouldn't be able to play in the game that evening. Even though my foot was still throbbing, a reminder of the whole, awful day, I knew I couldn't use it as an excuse to miss school. Coach always told us that we played as a *team*. I couldn't let my teammates down, pretending to be sick or injured. A couple of aspirins and some tight taping would take care of my foot. But I wasn't sure how to mend my broken heart.

I laid my head back against the seat, wishing I could talk to someone. But who? I closed my eyes, my mind sorting through all the people I knew. Who would be the one person to understand? *Mike.* I pushed his name out of my head. If Rick knew I was thinking of confiding in Mike, we'd be done for sure—if we weren't already. I pulled the sleeves of my coat down to cover the fingers of each hand. The cold outside air was working its way into my car. I'd go inside in a minute, after I found someone who cared…at least in my mind. Who would listen to me?

Peg. The name of Mrs. Stoltz's roommate at the nursing home appeared in my mind, bringing comfort just at the thought. I'd never met anyone who listened better than her.

Well sure, she can hardly talk.

There was that snotty voice again, reminding me that maybe Rick's accusations were true. I closed my eyes, tucking my chin into the warmth of my scarf, remembering the day I'd met Peg. "Grandma," I'd called her that first day. The same name I called all the old women at the nursing home if I didn't know their names. Mrs. Stotlz, my old Sunday school teacher, was the only resident's name I knew then.

"Emmie!" Mrs. Stoltz sounded surprised when I followed Sue Woehl, the CNA I was shadowing, into her sunny room. "What are you doing here?" she asked, obviously forgetting I'd told her all about my new job the day I was hired.

"Do you have to go to the bathroom!?" Sue was practically screaming at Mrs. Stoltz. We'd come to the room in answer to the call light that had lit up at the nurse's desk.

Mrs. Stoltz nodded. "You don't have to talk so loud. I'm not deaf...yet," she added, a gleam twinkling in one eye. It was hard to tell whether she was making a joke or her eye was simply running like most of the people who lived in this home.

"Sorry." Sue immediately lowered her voice. "I forget who can hear and who can't. You're one of the lucky ones." She patted Mrs. Stoltz's hand. "Let's get you to the bathroom. Do you mind if Emily helps me?"

"That's fine," she replied in her high, squeaky voice. "About the only thing I'm good for these days is to let the young ones learn from me. Might as well be from the bathroom as well as the Bible."

Sue threw back her head and laughed. "You are so funny, Verna."

Verna? Mrs. Stoltz had a first name? And it was Verna? Suddenly I saw her in a way I hadn't before. A little less like my old Sunday school teacher and more like a real person. A person who could still crack jokes. A person who used to be able to use the bathroom by herself. I looked across the room then, not wanting Mrs. Stoltz— Verna—to see the modesty I unexpectedly felt for her.

As Sue began pushing Mrs. Stoltz's wheelchair toward the bathroom of the small room, there was a garbled call from the other bed in the room. "Cooood Iii geeeet soooome waa-er, peees?"

"Emily, would you see what she wants?" Sue asked. "I'd better get Verna to the little girls' room."

Hesitantly, I stepped to the side of the bed. A short guardrail ran from the head of the bed to the middle, making the top half look like a grown-up crib, the bottom half like any other twin bed. Beneath a thick knit afghan lay a woman I hadn't noticed when I walked into the room. Her eyes met mine. One side of her mouth turned up in an attempt at a smile, the other side hung down, not connected to any smile muscles that I could see. "Ha-whoa." With effort she pulled one hand from under the afghan and held it out to me. I wasn't sure what I was supposed to do. A normal handshake seemed like it would crush her frail hand.

I paused a second, then put my suddenly sweaty hand in hers. "Can I help you, Grandma?" I asked, my voice almost as loud as Sue's had been. In the two Saturdays I'd job shadowed, I quickly learned that most of the residents were hard of hearing and that *Grandma* or *Grandpa* were good substitutes for names around here. Thank goodness the staff wore name tags. I hadn't had time to learn the names of the staff. Even though I recognized many people who worked here, more often than not I couldn't drum up a name to go with a face. My head was too full of things to remember. Lift with your knees. Don't give cookies to the diabetics, no matter how often they ask. Keep an eye on the wanderers; make sure they don't get out of the building. I had a million things to remember, and right now learning names seemed like the least of my worries.

"What can I get for you, Grandma?" I asked again.

With effort she shook her head. "Not Graaan-mmmaaa." She flopped her whole hand on her chest. "Mmmy nnn-aaaame iiis Paaaa-gg."

"Peg?" I asked, trying to make sense of her garbled speech. "Your name is Peg?"

She nodded then, the smiling side of her mouth rising again. "Yooo-uu?" She flopped her hand away from her chest, indicating me.

"I'm Emily. Emily Marsden. I'm new here."

Again she nodded. "Iiii knnn-oow." She took a slow, deep breath. "Yooo-uu are vvverrr-yyy prrrre-tyyyy."

I sure didn't feel pretty in the drab-pink uniform the CNAs wore, but I felt myself blushing at the compliment. "Thank you. You are t—" Out of habit I felt myself returning the compliment, only realizing when it was halfway out of my mouth that her long, gray blond hair stuck out in thick clumps across the pillow. Even someone who was only lying in bed had to know they probably didn't look all that great. "Would you like me to brush your hair?" I asked, one of the few duties I felt competent to do without supervision.

"Thaaaa-t wooould be nnniii-ce. Aaaand waa-er" She struggled to lift her head.

"Stay there," I cautioned, not daring to lift her out of bed by myself. After helping her with her drink, I reached for the hairbrush on the dresser near her bed. "I'll fix your hair so it looks nice while you're still in bed."

"Liii-ke Iii-mmm innn a coooff-innn."

Halfway to the dresser my hand froze. Oh, gosh, now I'd done it. Put my big foot in my big mouth. What was I supposed to do now? I turned my head, ready to apologize. Hoping Sue hadn't heard.

"Haaaaaaa-aaa-aaa…" One long breath of laughter from Peg's misshapen mouth. "Goooo-ttt yooo-uu." She laughed again.

"You scared me," I said, joining her laughter, relief washing over me. I picked up the brush. In the two weeks of CNA classes I'd taken, no one ever mentioned to be alert for jokes. Especially not by a resident who, at first glance, looked like nothing more than a helpless body in a bed. I smiled as I began brushing her hair against the pillow. The fact that I'd underestimated her abilities made Peg's unexpected humor all the funnier.

Sue came out of the bathroom. "She's going to take a while," she said, referring to Mrs. Stoltz. She motioned me closer with a crook of her finger. "You stay here, and when Verna's done, help her back into her chair." She lowered her voice, nodding her head in the direction of Peg. "Once you get past her speech, you'll like Peg. Stay on your toes. She's a lot younger and sharper than she looks." No kidding— I'd already learned that. Sue raised her voice again, "I need to check on Edwin. He's not looking good today." Just like that she was gone, leaving me on my own for the first time since I'd started this job.

"Taaaa-lk tooo mmmm-eee." Peg's eyes sought mine, urging me to fill the silence that was her constant companion.

I slowly stroked her hair with the brush, first telling her the easy things…what grade I was in, that I had a brother in college, and that my CNA classes were more interesting than I'd thought they'd be.

"Ssssmaaaarrrt coooo-kieee," Peg said, one side of her mouth bending up.

A curl of pleasure worked its way through my chest as I shaped Peg's hair into pretty, loose waves against the pillow. Up close, I could see the smoothness of her complexion, so unlike the many wrinkled faces around her. She had to be a lot younger than her roommate, and I suddenly wondered if she minded living here. She must have problems and worries just like me. Words came easily then. I told her about my junior year, my longing to be popular, to have Rick for a boyfriend. Peg nodded, her eyes shining as I talked about my teenaged life

"Iiii reee-memmm-berrrr." Almost as though she were reliving her life through me.

I smoothed a few flyaway strands of hair with my hand, letting my fingers brush her soft cheek. It was hard to imagine this bed-ridden woman as a teenager, wishing for a boyfriend as hard as I had. I wondered if she'd ever lost a best friend like I had, too. I hadn't mentioned Jen that first day, but I did later. It seemed Peg knew the pain of that, too.

"Iiiii loooossst mmyyyyy beeeeest frrrrriennnnd." A tear ran down the corner of one eye.

I'd grabbed a tissue and wiped the side of her face where the tear had left a wet stain. How could it still hurt so much after all these years? Would I be an old lady someday still crying over Jen?

A soft hum came from Peg's throat, making way for the words that were so difficult for her to pronounce. "Elll-visss Prrrresss-ly," she'd said. "Weeee daaanced to Elll-visss Prrrresss-ly thaaat fiirrrst daaate." Her eyes twinkled as they met mine. "Heee waaas sooo haaandsooome. Myy boyyfrrrieeend, Iiii meannn." She shook her head on the pillow as if she could hardly believe how cute he'd been. "Ttthe daaay weee got maaarrried heee gaaave mee an Elll-visss Prrrresss-ly reecooord. Fraaamed." She smiled, one side of her mouth lifting. "Heee reeememmmbeeerd." She'd sighed deeply, like she was still in love. "Looove Meee Tennnnderrr." She'd paused, her eyes drifting somewhere I couldn't begin to see. "Heee did love meee. Sooo mmmmuch."

A sudden shiver shook me out of my memory. The car was freezing! I pushed my hands out of the sleeves of my coat and grabbed my backpack from the seat beside me. I knew Peg would listen, but I couldn't very well drive to the nursing home at ten-thirty at night to talk to her.

I stepped from the car, first with my left foot and then with my right. Ouch! Man! Gingerly, I took another step. Pain shot from the front of my right foot up my leg. I could hardly put any weight on my foot at all without wincing. How was I ever going to play in the game tomorrow night? I limped forward another step, tears springing to my eyes. My foot had never hurt this bad. If I hadn't been so preoccupied with the Snow Princess election, CNA classes, and basketball, Rick would have never gotten so upset with me. No wonder he'd felt the need to push me away from him. Just like I'd been pushing him…with my actions, anyway. It was all my fault.

I hobbled another few steps, stopping to let the throbbing subside. Jen and Mike probably felt like shoving me, too. I was a lousy example of a friend. If only I could talk to Peg. She'd help me make some sense of my life. Help me know how to make things better.

I will, too.

I took another painful step as the words danced around my heart. Once again, hot tears slid down my cheeks as I limped through the garage. Two kinds of pain freezing on my cheeks.

How could God be so ready to listen when I'd forgotten about Him? Why didn't He push me away the way Jen had? Or Rick? Could He heal my foot and my heart?

I sure hoped so because right now He was the only hope I had left. I opened the door and hobbled into the house.

"Finally. You're here." My mom stuck a finger into the book she was reading and gestured toward a dozen red roses that stood in a vase in the middle of the kitchen table. "Look! They came just before supper." She plucked a small envelope from the center of the flowers and held it out to me. "For you," she said, a smile playing on her lips.

I set my backpack on the floor and limped forward to take the envelope.

"What's wrong? Did you hurt your leg at practice?" Mom half stood over the table and looked at my leg.

"It'll be fine." I stuck my thumb under the envelope flap, loosening the glue as I spoke. The only thing that could make this day worse would be for my parents to find out what Rick had done to me and blame him. I knew full well it was all my fault. "I just need to rest it."

Mom sat back down. "I'm dying of curiosity. Who sent you the roses?" A mysterious gleam played in her eyes. As if she already knew the answer.

Okay, so this day could get worse. My *parents* could have sent me flowers. How depressing would that be?

I pulled the small card from the envelope. Three lines of type filled the space.

Roses are red,
My eyes will be too,
If I can't have a dance with you.

In spite of this awful day I smiled. The words were corny. Just like something Mike would write. I leaned over and breathed the delicate scent. A dozen red roses wasn't a bouquet someone sent just to be nice. My heart did a curious dance as I remembered Mike on one knee this afternoon, remembered his bashful compliments.

"Oh, okay! So I already know." My mom laid down her book and grinned. "Rick brought them himself."

Libby

I fingered the velvety rose petals that Emily had barely glanced at as she left for school this morning. As nice as the gesture was, I wasn't so sure I liked the idea of Rick giving Emily such an extravagant bouquet. He was too smooth. I wasn't so sure I liked the intentions that might be behind the gift. I shook my head. A dozen roses for a sixteen-year-old. Such a waste.

Kind of like your life? I shook my head, trying in vain to shake away the anxiety that had nagged for months. Each night I climbed into bed, hoping against hope that the morning would bring relief. Each new day was the same…gray and bleak, a knife of worry slicing the hours into a multiplication of minutes that stretched into infinity. Today the anxiety had not lifted. If anything, it was worse. Already this morning the dreaded panic had filled my chest with fear. How was I going to get through this whole day?

You could call Dr. Sullivan. That's what he's there for. Tell him how miserable you are. He's there to help.

What a weakling. You can get through this by yourself. Toughen up. Wimp.

I took a deep breath, steeling myself to face the day. The next hour, anyway. I'd get busy with…well, with something and maybe fool myself into thinking I was normal again. I picked up the vase of red roses and carried it into the living room with me. No use letting their short lifespan go to waste in the kitchen when I planned to spend the morning at my computer. I moved some papers, setting the flowers near my screen where I could keep an eye on them, where their beauty would remind me that some things in this life were still pretty. *In contrast to your life?*

I arranged the flowers slightly, turning the few that had opened the fullest toward the front, where I could see them best once I sat down. A curious mix of bewilderment and joy had crossed Emily's face when she discovered the flowers were from Rick. She'd studied the card and then tucked it into the pocket of her slacks as if a dozen roses arrived every day at supper time. Well, if she wasn't here to enjoy them, I would.

I sat at the screen, poising my fingers over the keyboard, staring at the flowers, waiting for words to come. My column was due today. *No pressure or anything. Nothing like leaving things until the last minute. You're so lazy.* I'd had an idea at the coronation yesterday. What was it?

I reran the memories of yesterday through my mind. I'd pretended very well.

"Aren't you excited for Emily?" My friend Jan had rushed up to me the moment I'd put one foot inside the door of the gym. "Nominated for Snow Princess! You must be so nervous."

I was. But not for Emily. I was more concerned about holding myself together long enough to see who won the crown.

"I just had to come watch," Jan babbled. "April used to babysit for Joey, you know. Of course," she laid a hand on my arm, lowering her voice, "I still want Emily to win. Let's go sit up in the bleachers so we can see everything."

I shook my head, unexpectedly afraid. "No. Umm...I'm waiting for Bob." My nerves zinged, hyperalert, as if doom lurked under the bleachers of the gym. Part of my mind knew nothing was there, nothing to be afraid of in this kid-filled place, but the other part of my brain insisted danger was imminent. As Jan climbed the bleachers, I pushed my back up against the concrete wall of the gym. If my nameless fears were going to get me, it wouldn't be from behind.

"She won!" Bob's soft words filtered through the panic that gripped my chest as I watched the student council president bounce the crown from head to head. I knew I wasn't afraid Emily wouldn't be elected Snow Princess. I reached into my jacket pocket, fingering the small vial of pills I had started carrying with me.

Maybe if you took them as prescribed they'd do some good.

Good? Ha! Those pills are nothing but a crutch. Pull yourself up by your bootstraps, kiddo. All you need is a swift kick, you know where. Weakling.

I dropped the pills back into my pocket. If I *really* needed one, I knew where they were. Right now I had to be happy for Emily. At least that was what my mind was telling me to do.

Smile. Give her a hug. Say congratulations. Tell her how pretty she is. Take a picture.

I went through the motions, doing exactly what I knew was expected, feeling more like a robot than a mother. If anyone knew the effort this performance was taking, I'd be nominated for an Oscar.

Even with all my reservations about Rick, I'd been glad to see him walking toward Emily as Bob and I left the gym. At least she had someone who could give her the adoration she deserved.

I reached up, touching again the red roses he'd delivered the night before.

"I know Emily's at practice..." He'd paused, standing at our front door, a shy smile dimpling his cheek. "...or at class in Carlton, but I wanted her to have these tonight." He'd thrust the bouquet into my hands. Nervous. Hesitant. Young love personified.

Maybe my fears are unfounded, I'd thought, closing the door, pulling the thin plastic covering from the deep red flowers. Lucky Emily. Snow Princess. Star athlete boyfriend. Lots of friends. At least life was good for someone in our family.

And that person wasn't me. I stared at the computer, my mind blank. No, not blank. Frantic, actually. A jumble of thoughts, none of them coherent. Tiny darts of column ideas tried to poke their way through thick walls of worry and self-doubt. I had to write something.

Will You Be My Valentine?

It was an act of pure desperation, a cop-out. The same idea I'd used last Valentine's Day. Listing the letters in the word and typing sappy slogans to fill up the space.

V. Very special is what you are.

A. Always on my mind.

L. Love. *Cliché, but it fit.*

E. *E-gads! Was I really resorting to this?*

N. *No good. That's what your writing is.*

T. *Terrible. Whatever made you think you could write a column, much less a book?*

I. *I'm losing my mind!*

N. *Nuts! You're crazy.*

E. *Everybody knows what a loser you are. No friends. Lousy Mom. Terrible wife.*

I slammed at the keyboard with both hands. "Dasfjfsda;ouierafsjkl." The gibberish made more sense than the thoughts coming from my brain. I had to be losing my mind. I pushed myself away from the desk and retreated to the kitchen. Coffee. A strong dose of caffeine would clear my head. I sipped at the hot liquid, hoping it would burn through the thoughts that cluttered my thinking.

Call Dr. Sullivan.

I closed my eyes, imagining a clean, white hospital room. A sanctuary away from daily life. A shot. A pill. Anything that would make this misery go away.

"The hospital is not a place you want to be."

But I did! I did want to be there.

Quit wallowing. Get tough. Your life will always be miserable. Get used to it.

Miserable? If anyone in Brewster knew you felt like your life was miserable, they'd have a fit—a laughing fit! What do you have to complain about? Your life is the picture of the silver spoon. Loving husband. Good kids. Enough money. Beautiful home. You have the perfect life. Most people don't have near what you have. Quit bellyaching and enjoy it!

If only I could. I knew every blessing I had by heart. I knew even *one* of them should be enough. The fact that I had so many only added more guilt. What could I possibly have done to deserve so much? But somehow thinking about all I was supposed to be grateful for made whatever I was going through that much worse. I felt the heaping coals of kindness the Bible talked about. The coals of mercy that were supposed to make our enemies feel ashamed for the way they treated us. When I piled my blessing upon burning blessing and still felt so rotten, my ungratefulness seared my heart. God knew, I wasn't really ungrateful. I only wished something could free me to enjoy all those blessings I was all too aware were mine. Instead they weighed on me, tons of burning coals, burdens disguised as blessings.

Get a grip! You're the luckiest woman in Brewster. Get over it, already!

I did need to get a grip. Quit wallowing and accomplish something. Emily had a basketball game that evening, and if I didn't get some sort of hold on my thoughts, I'd never make it through the night.

What do you think would happen? You'd lose it? Go nuts? Have a mental breakdown? Now that would be the worst, wouldn't it? Lose your mind. Ooooo… then the folks in Brewster would really have something to talk about. Did you hear about Olivia Marsden, the banker's wife? She's crazy! Ha ha ha…

"Stop it!" I said the words out loud to no one. The awful thoughts receded, hiding who knew where, ready to pounce, to drive me mad when I wasn't watching. I stared around my empty house, looking for demons hiding in corners. Maybe I *was* losing it. The thing I'd valued the most about myself—my mind—was no longer something I could control. My heart hammered in my chest. I had to get out. I couldn't spend a whole day like this, alone with my sick mind.

You have a column to finish, remember?

I can't do it today. I can't.

Oh, that's right. You've never finished anything in your entire life. College dropout! Failed novelist! You're nothing but a loser.

I threw back the last swallows of coffee. I would finish my column. I *would*. At least I'd get one measurable thing done today. I was Olivia Marsden. I was not going to give in to this, whatever *it* was. I set my mug firmly on the counter. Determination pushed aside self-doubt. I half marched into the living room, propelling myself back into the chair in front of the falling leaves on my screen saver. I bumped the mouse, letting the saved text take over the screen. I closed my eyes, embarrassed to think about reading what I'd written minutes ago. Slowly I opened them, quickly scanning what I'd written.

Oh. A full page of words covered the screen. Somehow amid the awful thoughts running through my head, I'd managed to write what appeared to be a normal Valentine's Day column. I read through it again, just to make sure. Where I thought I'd typed sarcasm and criticism aimed at myself, there were words of love and gratitude to my family and friends. I had a vague recollection of writing the paragraphs, but the critical voice had screamed so loud it had drowned out everything else.

A wave of relief washed over me. Maybe I wasn't so bad. Maybe I wasn't losing my mind. Maybe I was just having a bad day. A very bad day. I ran my fingers through my hair, pushing the barrage of self-critical thoughts away. Once again I reread the column, and then I pushed the Send icon, launching my words through cyberspace to the *Brewster Banner* office.

There. I'd done it. I sat back and chuckled, mocking the critical voice that had doubted my ability. I was going to be just fine. I sat straight, reaching for the mouse, guiding the arrow across the computer screen. I left-clicked on Open. I marveled as the screen changed. Whoever had invented this amazing technology was a lot smarter than I was. I scrolled through the many files in My Documents. There it was, buried in the Ns—my novel. *After Anne*. How long had it been since I'd last looked at it?

I clicked twice and watched the words I'd typed so long ago appear. A surge of anticipation ran through me. I could do this. I could finish my novel.

Oh sure, just because you wrote a column, one simpleminded column, now you think you're a novelist. Ha! Just try to write a book. You can't do it. Who do you think you are, anyway? You can't do it.

Yes, I could. I pushed Control and End simultaneously, sending the cursor to the last words I'd written. Page three hundred twenty-two.

See? Look what you've already done. I gave myself a pep talk. I'd already written over three hundred pages. I could do this.

Prove it. Write something. Even if you manage to get it written, who would ever publish it? You don't know anyone in the publishing industry. You live in a little town in the middle of nowhere. You're a nobody, and you'd better face it. Give up. It's impossible.

Arrggghhh! I slammed at the keys. I was going to do this! I could! I wrestled the intrusive thoughts away, forcing my mind to read through the last few pages I'd written, catching myself up with the story that had lain on my heart for so long. The story of Anne's illness. The journey that had turned out to be mine as much as hers. The friendship that had led me to faith.

I'm still here.

The three quiet words stopped me. Oh, yes. Once again I'd forgotten. The gentle voice of God. Calming. Assuring. There, even when I forgot. I laid my hands in my lap, pausing to bask in His tenderness. How I wished I could hear Him instead of the clamor of criticism that constantly attacked. *Oh, Lord,* my heart cried out, *where have You been? Why can't I hear You?*

When I am closest, Satan fights hardest. Though you walk through the valley of the shadow, I am with you. Be strong, Libby. I am with you. Always.

Tears I didn't know were there began to fall. Warm. Cleansing. Hope in a whisper. I'd forgotten how tranquil time with God could make me feel.

Some Christian, forgetting about God! You're not worthy.

You don't have to be worthy. That's the whole point. There's nothing to earn. No one you have to be. You are Mine. No matter what.

For once His voice drowned out the vile, hurtful thoughts. I moved from my computer chair into the seat I used to call my prayer chair. Another thing that had been forgotten amid the chaos of the past months. I sank into its softness, letting prayers from better days caress me now. I picked up my Bible, knowing full well if I had spent more time studying it I might have an inkling of where to look for help. I didn't. I turned to the twenty-third psalm, one of the few comforts of the Bible I knew by heart. Certainly, what I was experiencing now was the valley of the shadow.

My eyes searched the page, falling on the psalm before the twenty-third. "My God, my God, why have you forsaken me? Why do you refuse to help me or even to listen to my groans? Day and night I keep on weeping, crying for your help." I paused, turning the words over in my mind, finding comfort in the idea that someone else had walked my same path. I was not alone.

No, you never have been.

I read on, my writing skills editing the psalm into my own sort of prayer. "I am a worm…mocked at and sneered." And I do it to myself. The person You created. "Don't leave me now, for trouble is near and no one else can possibly help." Except You.

I read through the laments of a person centuries ago who was not so different from me.

I was with him then, and I am with you now.

Oh, the comfort of those words. I sat still, letting God soothe me with a peace I hadn't felt in weeks. Months. If only I could bottle this feeling. Keep it in my pocket instead of the pills I carried. After a time I read on, seeing how the murmurs of discontent gradually changed into praise and promise. "All who seek the Lord shall find him…their hearts shall rejoice with everlasting joy."

Joy. When was the last time I'd thought of that word? When was the last time I'd felt it? Had I ever really known joy? Right now, joy seemed the direct opposite of the state I'd been living in. I was going to hold on to that promise. "Their hearts shall rejoice with everlasting—"

The ringing of the telephone propelled me from the chair, interrupting the promise I'd been determined to claim as mine. "Hello?"

"Mrs. Marsden, this is Mrs. Hoberg. I've got Emily in my office here at school, and we seem to have a bit of a problem."

My mind raced, filling in the blanks while she paused to breathe. Had Emily been so busy with her new job that her grades had dropped and she could no longer play on the team? Had she been caught…I didn't know…smoking? Drinking? Messing with drugs? In the span of a breath I prepared myself for the worst.

"Emily can't walk."

Emily couldn't walk? She'd walked out of the house this morning. Limping a bit on the leg she'd said just needed a little rest. At least that's what I'd assumed.

"What do you mean?" I stammered, confused.

"Her ankle is swollen, and her foot is very tender to touch. I think she needs to have an X-ray."

"But there's a game tonight." It was all I could think to say. I'd seen Emily only an hour ago, walking just fine.

"Emily won't be playing in any game tonight." In the background I could hear Emily's thin voice, "Come get me, Mom." A loud sniffle.

"Uh, okay. I'll be there in a minute."

As I backed out of the garage, I wondered just how I was going to get Emily into the car and into the clinic if she couldn't walk. *Some mother you are! How could you send her to school if she was in such pain?* I was all too aware of my failure as a mother as I drove the few blocks to the school. *A good mother would carry her child if she had to.*

If I *had* to, I supposed I could…but then we'd both need an X-ray. Somehow I'd manage. I turned into the school entry and saw Emily hopping like a one-footed rabbit down the sidewalk. Ah, the agility of youth. Coach Hoberg followed closely behind.

I leaned over and opened the car door. Emily hopped in, said a weak thanks to her coach, and then, as I pulled away from the curb, burst into tears. "It hurts so much, Mom."

"I know," I murmured, knowing she was too upset to explain. There would be time for that later. The best way to help her now was to get her to the clinic.

In Brewster, nothing was more than a few blocks away. If the streets hadn't been icy, Emily could have hopped to the Brewster Clinic as easily as to the car. Emily hardly had a chance to dry her tears before we were there. More hopping, this time with heavy assistance from my shoulder. The receptionist must have recognized the pain in Emily's face. She ushered us immediately into an exam room and promised, "I'll get the doctor."

Within minutes Ellen West, my doctor and sometime friend, walked into the small room. Oh…in my haste to tend to Emily, I'd forgotten all about the fact that I hadn't spoken to Ellen since she suggested I see a psychiatrist for my "issues." But what were my options? With only two doctors on the Brewster hospital roster, I should have known our chances of having Ellen treat Emily were high. I felt my face flush, remembering my anger, the childish way I'd stomped out of her office, still convinced something was physically wrong with me and she'd been blind to it. I wondered if she remembered, too?

"Olivia!" Her smile was genuine. "It's good to see you. How are you?"

Did I detect an ulterior motive behind her question? Had Dr. Sullivan been in contact with her? Did doctors have some sort of radar that alerted them to patients who needed to apologize? I certainly couldn't do that now. Not in front of Emily. "I'm…fine." A loaded word if there ever was one. My eyes tried to tell her the truth. Pleaded for her to let my simple answer stand for now.

Her eyes met mine, an understanding of sorts passing between old friends. "We should do lunch sometime." Ah, her radar was intact. I was unexpectedly glad for her perception and offer of friendship.

"I'd like that," I said simply, smiling a bit. "But I'm afraid it's not going to be today." I pointed at Emily's swollen ankle.

Ellen patted the exam table. "Can you manage to get up here?"

Emily slid onto the table, wincing. "Ouch!"

Dr. West sat on a stool and pushed it to where Emily perched. Gently she undid the laces of Emily's tennis shoe, easing the sock from her foot, revealing an ankle that was thick and bruised. "My, my, you did it up good. What happened?"

Emily sighed, her voice wobbly as she explained. "My foot's been hurting all through basketball. Well, volleyball, too. Something near the front." She pointed to the flat of her foot, just behind her toes. "It's a really sharp pain when I run and stuff." She looked at me, apology in her glance, then turned back to Dr. West. "Yesterday..." She stopped, swallowed hard, and went on. "Yesterday at the Snow Week coronation I had on these new shoes. With heels," she added, gesturing with her fingers at the two-inch height. "And when I was leaving the gym I...tripped." Her eyes darted to me as if seeking confirmation. I shrugged. I hadn't been there then. "Well, I tripped. On the step. And I heard something pop. And then this morning it was all puffed up. Like this." She held her leg out as if it weren't already the center of attention. She took a deep breath and pushed the next words out fast. "Am I going to be able to play basketball?"

"Not for a while, that's for sure." Ellen's fingers probed Emily's foot and ankle. "I don't like the look of this. The ankle is definitely sprained, but I'm going to want an X-ray to see if there's anything else going on. If you've been having pain all fall, it could be a stress fracture."

"*Frac-ture?*" I sounded as though Dr. West were speaking Greek. How could Emily possibly have a broken foot and I not notice?

See? Proof of what a terrible example of a mother you are!

"I'm going to call for a wheelchair." Ellen poked her head out of the room and spoke to a nurse before returning to Emily's side. "While we're waiting, I want to take a look at your arm where we removed that benign tumor this fall. I like to see how my patients heal up." She smiled my way. "Especially my female patients. I always imagine the young girls I stitch up as blushing brides in a strapless gown someday. I try to do my best. Let's have a look."

Emily shimmied her arm out of her sweater sleeve and held it out from her side, the maroon scar clearly raised.

"Hmmm." Dr. West frowned as she fingered her handiwork. "I'm not sure I like the looks of this." She must have caught a glimpse of the blood draining from my face because she quickly added, "It could be just scar tissue, but I want to take a tissue sample and have the lab look at it to be on the safe side."

The safe side? Since when had life started offering a safe side? It seemed this year had been filled with nothing but whatever the opposite of "safe" was. Immediately, the familiar panicked thumping of my heart started. My ears felt like ice blocks. Ellen's voice came from miles away as she called for a nurse to assist with the biopsy and then gave me directions through the small Brewster clinic and hospital corridors to the X-ray department. "Don't worry," she said, placing her hand on my shoulder. "After seeing the tissue, I'm confident it's just from the scar."

Confident? Confident! As if I would believe such flimsy words! In a daze I pushed Emily down the short hallway, stepping into the elevator that would take us to the basement X-ray lab. The doors closed, encasing us in metal. *Emily has another tumor. How could you not have noticed? You were lucky once. There's no way you're going to be so lucky a second time. Cancer. She has cancer.*

The steel walls of the elevator loomed around me, closing in, sucking the very oxygen out of the air. By sheer force of will I pulled air into my lungs. I would surely suffocate before we got out of there. *At least you're in a hospital.* The irony didn't escape my frantic mind.

"Mom?" Emily sat calmly before me, facing the door as if oxygen-deprived elevator rides were something she took every day. "If my foot's broken, does that mean I'm done with basketball for the season?"

Oh, to have such simple worries. I was worried about surviving a one-floor elevator ride. "Probably." I pushed the word from between my clenched teeth. I knew I should offer more comfort, should tell her she had all of next year to play. Something. But all I could do was simply stand there, pretending to breathe, pretending to live. Praying that the solid metal doors would release me soon.

The rest of the morning was a fog of technicians and nurses, another walk down the corridor back to Dr. West's office, where she confirmed the stress fracture diagnosis.

"You need to stay off that foot if you want it to heal properly," she cautioned.

"But," Emily protested, "what about the dance?" Aha, so it wasn't the basketball game she was concerned about.

"No reason you can't *go* to the dance, but no dancing for you for a while, I'm afraid." Dr. West scratched at the back of her head. "There's not a whole lot we can do for a stress fracture. The most important thing is to keep the foot immobilized for six to eight weeks. I'll wrap your ankle, and then I'm going to give you a pair of crutches—"

"Crutches!" Emily's eyes grew big, seeking mine, silently begging for any other form of torture. "What about my new shoes? My dress?"

Ellen took Emily's childish concern to heart. "You can certainly wear your dress, but you won't be able to get a dress shoe on your foot anyway. It's too swollen." Ellen stroked Emily's foot with her hand and began binding her ankle with thick, white tape. "I guess you're not going to fit into Cinderella's slipper tomorrow night. Sorry." She smiled.

Emily didn't. "What about my job?" Her voice was glum.

Dr. West looked to me for an explanation and then told Emily, "Depending on your duties, you should be able to continue. I don't want you doing any heavy lifting, no putting pressure on the front of your foot for at least a month. You should use the crutches until the swelling on your ankle goes down, and then you can wear any shoes that give you good support when you go back to walking. But no basketball, no dancing...nothing that might reinjure the foot for at least eight weeks. If you do, you could risk a more severe injury—chronic problems that will follow you into adulthood."

Emily nodded, her eyes downcast. "Some Snow Week."

I followed as Emily slowly made her way up the long sidewalk leading into the school. After a sandwich at home for lunch, she'd insisted on returning to school even though I'd begged her to stay home. "You need to rest your foot," I said, using her weakness as an excuse to keep my swirling thoughts at bay.

"I want to go back," she'd stated. "At least if I'm busy I won't think about how awful this is." A wry smile turned up one corner of her mouth.

Crutches forward, she took one careful step to catch up, again and again over the frosty sidewalk leading to the school. Slow progress. I hoisted her heavy book bag onto my shoulder, wondering how she'd ever make it through the crowded school hallways between classes in the short time allotted. Maybe Rick would carry her books and carve a path for her. For the second time in twenty-four hours, in spite of my mistrust, I was secretly thanking him for being Emily's boyfriend. I wished I could be stronger for her, but in my current state, holding myself together was all I could do.

I walked Emily to her chemistry class, listening to the collective gasp as she hobbled into the classroom. Mike jumped from his desk, transferring Emily's book bag from my shoulder to his without a word. "Thanks," Emily said to Mike as much as me, dismissing me with a slow blink.

"I can give her a ride home," Mike said, removing a task I hadn't thought of from my list. Emily's car sat in the school parking lot. It would be okay, I decided, for these teenagers to juggle new responsibilities.

As I walked down the long silent hall toward the school office, the unnamed fear that all the activity had kept at bay reared its ugly face. *What kind of mother are you not to have noticed Emily's foot was broken? What kind of mother wouldn't think to check her arm for another tumor? She has cancer, you know. She's going to die. All because you weren't vigilant enough. Cancer…die…it's all your fault. Fault. Your fault.*

Hideous taunts raced through my brain, accusing me of things over which I had no control. But that didn't matter to my mind as I kept berating myself relentlessly. *You're a terrible mother. You're a fraud. If anyone knew just how awful you were…*

Somehow I pulled myself together enough to explain to Emily's coach the details of her injury. "It's a stress fracture," I said, sounding surprisingly in control, but my voice broke like static as it echoed in my own ears. "Caused by too much pressure on the front of her foot. She needs to stay off it. I'm afraid she's done with basketball for this season. She's sick about it, of course."

You're the one who's sick. You might as well wear a mask. You didn't tell the coach that it's all your fault.

I climbed into the car. I knew I should call Bob, but how could I call him when I couldn't even think straight, much less talk coherently? Maybe I should drive to the bank in Carlton and tell him about Emily in person.

Oh sure, fall apart in his office like some helpless woman. Try and drag him into your drama when you know it's all your fault.

I drove around Brewster, not seeing the houses, cars, or people I passed, listening instead to the screaming inside my head. *You're a terrible mother. Emily has cancer. You're nothing. Worthless.* A squirrel darted in front of the car. Automatically my foot tapped the brake, narrowly avoiding the small animal. *You're not safe to be driving around.* It was the only sensible thought that had entered my head all day. I turned down our street, pushing hard on the button to raise the garage door.

Home. I'd go home. I'd take one of the pills Dr. Sullivan prescribed. Two. Crawl into bed. Sleep this horrible day away. Wait until tomorrow to find out if Emily had cancer.

Tomorrow? Tomorrow is Saturday, stupid. They won't call you with the results until Monday.

Panic gripped my chest. I couldn't possibly live like this until Monday. I paused the car in the driveway, waiting until the door was completely raised, then eased the car forward into the garage. Frantic thoughts clamored to be heard. *You're a fraud. A terrible mother.* There, two inches from the wall, just as always. *What a fake you are. Nobody cares about you.* I punched the button to close the door, shifted the car into park, and leaned my head against the steering wheel while the car idled. The vile voice continued to scream at me. *You're worthless. They'd be better off without you. You don't deserve the life you have.*

This would be so easy…

The words crept into my mind, tiptoeing past the frenzied notions running through my brain.

This would be so easy…

A small ringlet of release eased the tightness in my chest. All I had to do was sit here. Let the fumes fill the garage, fill the car, fill my lungs. Ah, it would be so easy. I wouldn't have to listen anymore. Wouldn't have to think. Wouldn't have to *be.* I could be gone. The misery gone forever. Forever.

I sat still, temptation curling around me. Smoky relief crept through the edges of the windows. I'd always loved the smell of gasoline, the greasy, pungent odor carrying memories of summer car trips with my parents when I was young, mowing the lawn in my two-piece swimsuit trying to get a tan as a teenager, waiting in the car on my first date with Bob as he filled the tank. Good memories to associate with something so lethal.

I breathed deeply and listened. The only sound was the well-tuned engine purring relief. The clamor inside my head had stopped, apparently struck dumb by the thought that I might have the nerve to put an end to my misery.

You wouldn't dare. Would you?

My heart thumped wildly. Fear? Excitement? It was hard to know. They felt very much alike.

You wouldn't dare. Would you?

Would I? I breathed deeply again and coughed as the cloudy mist crept down my throat. This was wrong. I knew it, and yet the idea that release was minutes away offered a sort of peculiar thrill. I wouldn't have to live through this anymore.

I knit you in your mother's womb. I had a plan for you even before you were born. I have a plan for you…

Quickly, before I could talk myself out of it, I pulled the keys from the car and dashed into the house, slamming the door behind me as if chased by ghosts. My hands were shaking as I threw the car keys onto the kitchen table. I'd been so close. So close.

Fear, more intense than I'd ever felt before, crawled up my back. A wave of nausea washed over me. I was sick of myself. I stumbled down the hall, up the stairs, and into my bedroom, fumbling to open the sliding door that led to our walk-in closet. I pushed aside the neat row of skirts and slacks that lined the bottom of my half of the closet, folded myself over the row of shoes in front of the hanging clothes, and curled myself into a fetal-like position, my knees tucked to my chest, my back pressed hard against the wall inside my make-believe womb of cotton and silk. Darkness surrounded me. *I'm safe*, I thought. *Nothing can get me here. I can't hurt myself.* I rocked my curled body, back and forth, back and forth, swaying in a combination of comfort and anguish. *I'm safe. I'm safe. I'm safe.*

I had no idea how long I huddled there, hiding from invisible demons. All I knew was that eventually a faint ringing penetrated the cocoon of clothes that surrounded me. From somewhere in the shelter of designer labels, the persistent sound of the doorbell nudged me from my sanctuary. Automatic reflexes took over as I pushed myself from the floor of the closet and hurried down the stairs and toward the front door.

"Ida," I said to my elderly neighbor, as calmly as if she'd called me from the kitchen. I realized my clothes were more than rumpled. I was still wearing the black leather coat I'd worn to drive Emily back to school. Black. How appropriate for almost-funeral wear.

"Oliffia," she replied, taking in all of me in one long glance. "I chust took dis kuchen from the offen. But, my gootness, I tink you neet more important tings den coffee cake. Vhat's wrong?"

I cried then, standing just inside my own front door. Silent tears without words. Mrs. Bauer stepped into my house, set her freshly baked kuchen on the sidetable, then wrapped her coat-shrouded arms around me. "Der, der," she murmured, her thick German brogue offering pure comfort. She was so much shorter than me, but somehow my head rested comfortably in the crook of her shoulder. She released me only to close the door; then with one arm around my waist she walked me to the sofa, sitting beside me as I sobbed. When my tears didn't stop, she pushed herself back into the soft cushions, tilting me toward her until my head rested in her lap as if I were a small child. I continued to cry as her wrinkled hand rhythmically smoothed the hair from my face. "Der, der. Der, der. Tings vill get better."

Eventually her hand stopped stroking my face and rested warmly on the crown of my hair. I felt the gentle pressure of her other hand as she laid it on top of her still hand. "Dear Gott, Father in heffen," she whispered, "I don't know vhat iss wrong here today, but You do. I ask dat You vould touch my precious neighbor witt Your healing handts." She was quiet for a time, then spoke again in German. "Gott im Himmel, hör mein Gebet…" I didn't need to understand the language to draw strength from her heartfelt prayer. I felt it deep in my anguished soul. A balm for my aching heart.

Once again I had no idea how much time had passed. Eventually, Ida patted my shoulder as she slid her soft, round body from beneath my head. She walked to Bob's recliner and lifted the folded afghan from the back, bringing it to me and covering me with its softness. I smiled up at her, my eyes feeling like small, swollen, venetian blinds. Again she patted my head. "You vill get better," she said, then she quietly left the house.

You vill get better. You will get better. I recited the words like a mantra, suddenly remembering Ellen West's words back when I had barely begun this journey. *"Sometimes when we start dealing with these sorts of issues, we might start feeling worse before we start feeling better."* Then I remembered Dr. Sullivan, softly pounding his fist on his desk as he assured me. "*You,*" thump, "*will,*" thump, "*get,*" thump, "*better,*" thump.

Oh, how I wanted to believe those words. Believe Ida Bauer's soft assurance. I wanted to live. I did! Just not like this.

I lifted my head, glancing at the thick Bible that lay on the end table near my head. I didn't need to open it to remember the words I'd read so many weeks ago. The words that had led me to Dr. Sullivan. *"People who are well don't need a doctor! It's the sick people who do!"*

I was sick. Just not in a way anyone could see. I closed my eyes. "Give me courage," I whispered out loud. "Help me to do this." I pushed back the afghan and slowly sat up. My head throbbed. My eyes ached. *Don't do this! Wimp! Weakling!* I slid to the edge of the couch, rising as though I might sit right back down any second. Fully on my feet, I took one step, then another. I knew exactly where I was heading. I paused only when I got to the kitchen phone. *Stop! Don't!* I fumbled through the pages to the Carlton business section. Dr. G. Sullivan. I dialed. *Hang up!* The phone rang…once…twice.

"Good afternoon, Dr. Sullivan's office."

"I can't—" *Hang up you stupid, weak woman.* "I can't—" I stopped as my voice cracked. I took a shallow breath then pushed the trembling words out, "I can't do this anymore. I just can't."

Dr. Sullivan

"Dr. Sullivan?" Elaine peered around the door. I could count on one hand the number of times in my career my office assistant had interrupted an ongoing session. She crooked her finger at me. "I need to speak with you."

It could only be an emergency. "Excuse me." I set my clipboard on my desk, apologizing to my patient. "I'll be right back."

Already Elaine had the phone receiver in her hand, holding it out to me. "You need to take this phone call." She hesitated before pressing the blinking Hold button and added, "It's Mrs. Marsden. From Brewster."

For a quick second I closed my eyes, picturing my client, opening the mental file I kept of all my patients. Competent. Eloquently verbal. Highly functional. Atypical of any depressed patients I'd worked with in the past. Mrs. Marsden was proving to be quite the enigma. Well, I wouldn't solve her problem just standing here. I took the phone from Elaine. "This is Dr. Sullivan."

A tremulous breath. A pause. Then five quivering words. "I can't do this anymore."

She didn't need to say more for me to know she was at a breaking point. I'd seen Olivia weekly for six weeks now. Her condition had remained much unchanged, but at least it had not appeared to downgrade. I'd hoped the new dosage of medication would turn the tide. Obviously, it hadn't. "What seems to be the problem?"

"I can't live like this. Help me. Please."

She wasn't the kind of woman to beg; this was a cry of desperation. "Do you feel well enough to drive?"

"I think so. Yes."

"Go to MedFirst hospital in Carlton. I'll tell them to expect you within the hour." I hung up the phone, knowing I had less than an hour until she'd arrive at the hospital. Less than an hour to finish up my current appointment and make arrangements for Mrs. Marsden to be admitted. Less than sixty minutes to determine just how I would treat this puzzle named Olivia.

Libby

I scrawled a cryptic note on a scrap of paper and left it on the kitchen table. *Had to run an errand to Carlton.* I didn't want to alarm Emily if she found it before Bob. A phone call later would tell him the hard truth. I waited in the car until the garage door was completely raised before I started the engine and backed out.

The late-afternoon streets of Brewster were busy with kids on their way home from school, stomping through snowbanks as they would on any normal end-of-February day. Mothers drove off to the grocery store for last-minute supper ideas. Farmers in pickup trucks headed home with coffee-filled bellies. Automatically, I raised my fingers from the steering wheel, silently greeting whoever might recognize me on my way out of town. A farewell to life as I knew it.

I turned the car onto the highway, pressing the gas pedal as hard as I dared. The faster I could get to the hospital, the quicker I could get cured of whatever ailed me. Before, my mind had tumbled with vile thoughts, but now it was relatively quiet.

See? You're fine. Maybe you should turn around. Maybe you should go back home. The insistent yelling was gone. These were words filled with doubt.

I kept a steady pressure on the accelerator, resisting any urge to return home. My four walls no longer seemed the haven they once had been. Thick, gray clouds hung low in the sky, matching my mood. I sped past farmyards, fields, and pastureland that starkly painted the rolling hills between Brewster and Carlton, slowing only when I hit the outskirts of the city. Even in my muddled state, I wove my way into Carlton as I did every trip, carefully avoiding the intersection where Anne had been killed on her way to the doctor's office.

I didn't need a visual reminder of the scene I'd relived in my imagination too many times. I stopped at a red light, using the brief minute
to plot my path to the hospital. I'd driven there many times, but never
as a patient, only a visitor. Where did a patient go when they were
driving to the psych ward?

Driving Myself to the Psych Ward. For the first time all day, a hint
of humor bubbled in my brain. The phrase sounded more like the
title for a funny column than something I was actually doing. Where
should I park? Short-term parking? Surely not long-term? But not
visitor parking, either. I turned into the hospital parking area. This
wasn't the airport; maybe I wouldn't be faced with such a momentous
decision over something as simple as parking. In the end, I pulled
into the first vacant spot I found, not bothering to look if it was des-
ignated For Crazy Patients Only.

I grabbed my purse and the book I'd thought to bring along in
case I had to wait, and marched to the admittance area, followed by
a cloud of discomfort. What if someone I knew saw me? What if
someone from Brewster overheard I was being checked into the psychiatric ward? What if I got locked in a…a cage? A room with padded
walls? I jutted out my chin. Surely things had changed since the
horror stories I'd read about. What about electric shock therapy?
Every cliché I'd ever heard about psychiatry came rushing at me now.
I should have talked more about this with Dr. Sullivan before I
reached this point. Too late now. I'd find out soon enough. All there
was to do now was to get through it.

"Uh, I'm Mrs. Marsden," I stammered to the admitting clerk.
"I'm supposed to meet Dr. Sullivan. I think."

She ran her blue-shadowed eyes down her computer screen.
"Here you are!" She sounded as though I were checking into a spa.
"Let me get a copy of your insurance card, and I'll get a nurse to take
you to fourth."

Take me to fourth. Oh, so that's the way it was. Even the staff
couldn't say the words *Psych Ward.* Fine by me.

"This way, Mrs. Marsden." A young nurse in white scrubs beckoned from my side. "Follow me." She stepped into the elevator. Every

fiber in my being wanted to walk the other direction, but I doubted that being tackled in the hospital lobby and wrapped in a straight-jacket was a better way to get to the fourth floor than the elevator. I stepped in, too. "My name is Sheryl." She smiled at me as though I were perfectly normal. "I'll be your intake nurse." She pressed the button for the fourth floor. "Can you believe this weather? It's soooo cold!" She chattered until the elevator stopped. "Here we are."

I stepped off the elevator into a carpeted hallway. One long, open hall ran to my right. Cardiac Rehab, the sign read. To my left, two closed metal doors were bisected by two narrow windows. *Psychiatric Care.* For the first time in my life I wished I had heart problems.

Like Lot's wife in the Bible, I looked longingly over my shoulder at what I was walking away from as Sheryl led the way to the left. She pushed open the door and stood aside while I walked through. We stood together in an area no larger than my laundry room. Instead of the familiar washer and dryer, I stood before another set of closed metal doors. Sheryl punched a code into the lock that secured the doors, and they loudly buzzed open, and then slammed tight behind us. Not much different than any prison movie I'd ever seen. *You're not in Kansas anymore.* A small wave of claustrophobia lapped at my throat. I couldn't turn around.

"Let's sit in here." Sheryl led me into a small side room with a tiny table and two straight-backed chairs. It was painted glossy white—an interrogation room if I'd ever imagined one. Certainly not the clear white haven I'd been dreaming this place would be.

"I'm going to go over a few questions with you before we take you to a room."

"The padded room?" I tried to make it a joke.

She smiled. Thank goodness. "People have all kinds of misconceptions about psychiatric work. But sometimes we do need to protect patients from themselves." She pulled out a pen that was tucked into the clipboard. "I don't think you're going to need that sort of care."

She ran through the same questions I'd answered in any doctor's office I'd ever visited. Name, address, insurance coverage, illness history, next of kin.

I looked at my watch. Oh! "I should call my husband." I hadn't even thought of Bob or Emily since I'd left the house. They'd both be home soon, if they weren't already. What would they think? No supper made, Ida Bauer's kuchen on the entry sidetable? Even Columbo would have a hard time tracking me down here.

"He doesn't know you're here?" For the first time she sounded surprised.

"No. I, uh…called Dr. Sullivan from home. Bob—my husband—is…I mean, was, at work. I'm sure he'll be wondering where I am. I left a note, but…" I might have even passed him on the highway on my way into Carlton as he headed home. Little did he know what awaited him that night. For all he knew, Emily had a basketball game. I didn't relish telling him how things had changed in the few hours since he'd left for work that morning.

She glanced at the paper in front of her. "I have a few more questions. I'll only take a couple minutes, and then you can call your husband while I process your paperwork. Let's get to it." She clicked her pen. "Can you give me a brief description of a normal day for you?"

"Before…" I paused. "…all this? Or now?"

"Now."

I quickly ran through my endless days. The stomachache when I woke up, the coffee I hoped would rouse me out of my inertia, the hours I spent at the computer, trying to write. "I've managed to meet my column deadlines." I sounded like a third grader seeking praise. "I belong to a book club that meets once a month. I go to church on Sundays. Basketball games of Emily's." I concluded with my lack of appetite, my restless sleep, the elephant who sat on my chest each day, and the dread that hung over me like a heavy circus tent waiting to fall.

Sheryl wrote it all down and then looked up. "You're very high-functioning compared to most patients I admit."

High-functioning? It sounded like a compliment, but it sure didn't feel like one when I added up my long days walking this path. I shrugged my shoulders, confused about how to respond. "Will I be seeing Dr. Sullivan soon?" All I wanted was a magic shot, some quick advice that would cure me.

"He probably won't be in anymore today. He usually sees patients in the morning. If you'd like you can call your husband now."

So quickly I'd forgotten. About Bob. About Emily. About how they were going to manage at home without me. If I'd have thought of them earlier I might never have called Dr. Sullivan.

A pitcher that is never refilled has nothing left to pour. Maybe it's time to start taking care of yourself. After weeks of listening to disparaging self-talk, the kind words felt as if Mrs. Bauer were gently rubbing my back.

"The phone is right around the corner." Sheryl stood. "You'll want to tell your husband to bring you some clothes. Whatever you wear around home is fine. If you usually wear makeup, he should bring that, too. Keeping up a daily routine will be important for you. We expect you to get up and get dressed, style your hair, put on makeup, and make your bed." I must have looked puzzled. She explained, "Many of our lower-functioning patients have a difficult time with these tasks. Oh, I almost forgot," she sat back down. "I'm going to need to look through your purse. And this…" Deftly she substituted a slip of paper in place of the metal bookmark in the novel I'd brought along. "I'll have to keep this until you leave." She held up the shiny, gold bookmark Brian had given me for my birthday last year. "You're not allowed anything sharp." She was so matter-of-fact, the words took a minute to sink in.

Anything sharp… Oh. All the things I—someone—could do with something metal and sharp. Cut myself. Hurt another patient. Stab a nurse. Jimmy a lock. Chisel out of here. My mind concocted scenarios with frightening speed. And I was high-functioning? What would someone truly disturbed think up?

I looked over my shoulder uneasily. Maybe Dr. Sullivan had been right when he said the hospital wasn't a place for me. Was I less safe inside this cloistered area than I was outside?

"I'll have to keep this, too." Sheryl laid a metal nail file beside my bookmark. "And this." She snapped my mirrored face-powder compact shut. "The glass in the mirror," she explained cryptically. "If you need to use the powder, just ask at the desk." She pulled the brown vial of antianxiety medication from my purse. "This, too. We'll be administering any meds you need. Okay, that should do it. You can use the phone, then I'll show you your room." No bellboys, obviously. But then, who had luggage?

I rounded the corner and picked up one of the three phones hanging from the wall. Apparently privacy wasn't a high priority. Thankfully, we'd subscribed to an eight-hundred number when Brian went off to college. I doubted I'd have been able to maneuver my fingers or my brain around a complicated dialing plan today. I punched through the numbers, wondering just how to word what I had to say to my husband. *I finally lost it. I'm certified.* Nervousness jiggled my fingers as I pushed the last number. *Three guesses where I am?* I drummed my fingertips against the small shelf below the phone as I waited for the call to go through. Busy! I disconnected the line and ran my fingers over the numbers again. Busy. I hung up the phone this time, sighing heavily while I waited twenty seconds to try again. If Emily was hanging on the phone with Jen I might never get through. Maybe Bob was calling my friends Jan or Katie to see where I was. I dialed again and again, frustration building with each busy signal. I slammed the phone down. They didn't need to know where I was! Let them worry! Didn't it occur to them I might be trying to call home? Arrggghhh!

Sheryl put a hand on my shoulder. "It's okay. You have time. Why don't I show you your room? You can come back and try again later." So, there were no phones in the rooms, either. No way to call for help from the outside.

"Here we go." Sheryl stepped aside and let me into the room first.

The color scheme in this room certainly would not be featured in *Better Homes and Gardens*. My eyes took in the putrid tint. I wondered who chose the grayish, pea-soup green. Clean, thin, beige drapes hung from the one window. I couldn't help noticing the chicken wire between the panes. They'd thought of everything to keep their captives inside. Outside, thick snow had begun to fall. If I had been home, I would be lighting the fireplace. A pang of homesickness shot through me. How I wished I were there. Anywhere but here.

"Helloyou'reaprettylady." The voice came from the bed nearest the door. My roommate. One glance told me she had far more problems in life than I'd ever dreamed of. She could have been thirty or sixty—I couldn't tell because of the way her hair stuck out from her head at odd angles and rolls of excess weight stretched the limits of her shabby sweater. Sleeveless at the end of February, no less. Nothing to hide the neat rows of scar tissue that lined the insides of both of her forearms. "It'stimeforsupperI'mgoingtogowatchTV." With that she pushed herself out of bed and left the room.

"That was Vivian," Sheryl explained. "You can have this bed here." She patted the faded lavender bedspread on the other twin bed in the room. I wondered if I had to pay more for the window view— the chicken-wire window view. "You won't be spending much time here. We keep you pretty busy. In the morning you'll see Dr. Sullivan, and then we'll start you in group. Usually after lunch there's free time and then crafts and another group session. But since it's Saturday, we'll be taking a group out to see a movie at the theatre in the mall. I'm sure Dr. Sullivan will give you permission to attend if you'd like."

If the thought hadn't been so horrific, I would have laughed. I could only imagine Vivian and me, along with who knew who else, traipsing into the Carlton mall together. I cringed, wondering what the looks from other shoppers would feel like. Maybe they'd mistake me for one of the staff. Thanks, but no thanks. I'd pass on that bizarre field trip.

"Supper will be served in about fifteen minutes." Sheryl stood by the door. "You got here too late to order what you wanted to eat, so you'll have a general patient tray tonight. If you want to use the phone, now would be a good time. I'll show you where we eat on the way back to the desk."

I followed Sheryl back down the hall, my nerves pulling tighter with each patient we passed. Sheryl greeted each one by name. "Hi, Sheila." Something about Sheila made the word *vacant* come to mind. "Bill, don't forget to eat supper tonight." His laugh was high-pitched and eerie.

I don't want to be here. I want to be home.

"Here's where you'll have all your meals." Sheryl pointed to a large commons area. One half was filled with one long table and several tables for four, the other half with two vinyl orange couches, several chairs, and a loud television set. Vivian sat on a chair pulled three feet from the screen; another woman sat on one of the couches, rocking rhythmically. I would have thought she was odd if I hadn't been rocking myself in a closet mere hours ago. Somehow, I understood. "Everyone eats together," Sheryl explained. "Another thing some of our patients need help with. Routine and socialization. Never a dull moment." She smiled, then nodded her head toward the wall of phones just around the wall from the commons area. I hadn't even noticed the large area earlier.

Once again I ran my fingers over the phone keys, praying my call would go through this time. Someone snatched it up on the first ring. "Hello!" It was Emily.

At the sound of her voice my throat closed. I longed so much to hug her that I couldn't move, much less speak.

"Hello? Who's there? Stupid telemar…"

I heard her begin to put down the receiver. "Emily! No, it's me. Mom."

"Mom? Where are you? I got home from school and you weren't here. Are you still in Carlton? Dad's not home yet. My foot hurts. What's for supper?"

As if it were any normal phone call. Any normal night. How could I begin to tell my young daughter where I was? I couldn't. "Did your dad call home?" My voice was tight, like I'd swallowed bad helium.

"No. What's wrong?"

"Nothing. It's just—well, I need to talk to him." Why wasn't he there? I couldn't tell Emily. I couldn't leave a message. Couldn't tell him to call me. My nerves zinged with a mixture of frustration and panic.

"Mo-om?" Emily's voice rose, half question, half fear. "What's *wrong?* When are you coming home? Where *are* you?"

"I'm at—I'm—" It was too much to tell. There were no words. My voice broke and tears poured out. Loud sobs I could no longer control.

"Mom-*mm?*" Emily was crying, too. "Mommy, I love you!"

I leaned my back against the wall and cried. Silent sobs, so Emily wouldn't hear. Across the large space I could see dinner trays being served, and beyond that the heavy snowflakes continued to fall past large, wired windows. Wet, thick snow, the kind that had fallen the day Anne had died. What if Bob had been in an accident on the way back to Brewster? The thought sent another wave of panicked sobbing through my body. I doubled over, so glad Emily could not see me now, perversely glad I was in a place where I didn't need to be responsible. If something had happened to Bob, I would certainly lose my mind. For once, I was right where I needed to be.

"Daddy!" Bob must have walked in. "It's Mom." I could imagine Emily's tear-stained face, eyes wild, thrusting the phone to him. Imagine Bob standing there still in his deep-brown wool coat, a plaid scarf at his neck. Almost smell his spicy cologne. How I longed to be there now. Cooking supper. Hearing about their day.

"Olivia? What's up?" Smart man—he knew better than to rely on Emily's dramatics for information.

For the first time ever I wished I were mute. If only I didn't have to say these next words. "I—I'm in the hospital. In Carl-ton." I couldn't get any more out before a sob hit me.

"Are you okay? Are you hurt?" In the background I could hear Emily gasp. "What happened?" As usual Bob's voice was level, assessing the problem before making half-baked assumptions. If only he knew.

I shook my head, knowing full well he couldn't see me. "I'm okay. Really." I paused, understanding suddenly that I was okay. Not hurt in any way physical. My shaky breathing began to calm. Things could be much worse. "I'm, uh…I had a really bad day. I called Dr. Sullivan and he admitted me to the hospital. I'm on the fourth floor at Med-First. The—" I stopped and tried again. "The psychiatric ward." There. It was done. I waited. What would he say?

"Okay then, I'll be there as soon as I can. I'll leave now."

"No! Wait!" I looked outside at the thick, heavy snow that swirled outside the window. "Don't come tonight." I wanted him to come and yet I didn't. I wanted his solid presence, but I didn't want to worry about him driving forty miles in a possible blizzard, driving back to Brewster even later tonight. "Stay home. Come tomorrow."

"Olivia." His voice was soft. "I want to see you."

"I know." I stopped as tears closed my throat. I wanted to see him, too. I just didn't think I could live through an hour of worry until he got here. "Please. Really. The weather looks bad. Honest, I'll feel much better if you come in the morning. You know how I am about bad roads."

"The official *nag*igator." I could hear the familiar tease in his voice.

Oh, come. Please. Don't listen to me.

"When you come in the morning, could you bring me a couple changes of clothes and my makeup?" I told him which outfits to bring and where my makeup was. "Don't forget some underwear," I reminded, as casually as if I up and checked myself into psych wards frequently. As if.

I couldn't think of anything else to say. What words could end this sort of conversation? I was quiet, tears waiting to fall as soon as we said good-bye. If I could say that word.

I could hear a deep sigh through the receiver. "I love you, Libby."

That did it. Bob didn't often use the nickname Anne had given me, the name that reminded me of the new person God had made me…was *trying* to make me. I nodded into the wall, hot tears coursing down my face.

"I love you, Lib*by*." Bob's voice cracked. I could hear his uneven breathing through the phone. "I know you hear me. You don't have to say anything. I'm going to hang up now. I love you."

I leaned my head against the wall as I hung up the phone. How had I ever gotten here? How could Bob still love me when I was so broken?

When something is broken, the mended portion is strongest.

I closed my eyes, considering the quiet thought. If I ever got through this, I would be strong as steel. If I ever got through it.

I stood up, wiping my eyes with a tissue from a box near the phones. Apparently I wasn't the first person to ever shed tears here. And probably not the last. I blew my nose. I couldn't possibly eat supper. Not tonight. I went back to my room, laying face down on the bed. Through the thick glass I could hear the winter wind crying along with me. I wanted Bob. I wanted Brian and Emily. I wanted to be home. I wanted to be well.

I must have fallen asleep, my back to the door. A gentle pressure on the side of my bed woke me. In a millisecond I remembered where I was. The hospital. I froze. Was Vivian trying to climb into my bed? The doors didn't have locks; could that weird Bill guy have found my room by mistake? Or, not by mistake? My heart pounded.

"Olivia, someone is here to see you." It was Sheryl, sitting on the edge of my bed, waking me with a gentle touch to my shoulder.

I turned my head as Sheryl slipped away, expecting to see Dr. Sullivan.

"Hi." Bob was standing at the foot of my bed, his brown wool coat unbuttoned, his plaid scarf in his hand, a sheepish grin on his face. "I was in the neighborhood…" He stopped, shrugging out of his coat in one quick motion. He eased himself onto the bed beside me, whispering, "Move over a little."

"Is this legal?" I whispered back, scooting over.

"Sue me." He wrapped his solid arms around me.

"Where's Emily?"

"At the basketball game."

"I told you not to come." My eyes filled again, glad with all my heart he was here. "How were the roads?"

"Shhh." He slid one of his firm hands to the back of my head, threading his fingers through my hair, massaging away my questions.

I could feel my muscles relax at his touch, muscles that had been taut for months. I melted into his embrace, pushing our odd surroundings from my mind. For once I would try to embrace the moment. Embrace my husband. Not imagine what lay ahead.

"I didn't think you'd come," I murmured into his chest, turning my head to kiss the crook of his neck where his white shirt was unbuttoned. I lifted my head and looked into his eyes. "I'm glad you did."

He was quiet for a moment, his fingers kneading my neck, moving across my shoulders. "Me too," he whispered, gently pushing my head back onto his chest. "Me too."

Emily

"Where's your tiara?" It was the first complete sentence Jen had said to me in weeks.

I reached up to touch my head, pretending I'd forgotten to wear my Snow Princess crown. "Oh!" I said, faking it. I didn't want to tell her it was on my nightstand on top of the pile that always was there. It wasn't that I wasn't glad to have the crown, wasn't glad to be Snow Princess, I just didn't feel much like royalty with crutches under my arms, one foot in a pretty shoe and the other wrapped in thick athletic tape. The nude-colored bandage on my arm covered the two stitches where Dr. West had done the biopsy, but it didn't look very princess-like, either. Finding out the night before that my mom was in the hospital hadn't helped any, and when she wasn't there to take pictures before the dance…to insist I wear my crown…

"She doesn't need a crown to look gorgeous." Rick tried to wrap one arm around my waist, but it bumped my crutch, causing me to wobble on my one good foot. "Oops…sorry," he said as he moved his arm to my shoulder, giving Jen a quick grin.

"Too bad you can't dance." Jen eyed my crutches and then my boyfriend.

Her attempt at fake sympathy was as thin as the sheer fabric that covered her stomach. The fake jewel in her belly-button ring winked at Rick. I wondered when she'd gotten it pierced. Just weeks ago Jen and I had fantasized about the day we'd turn eighteen and not need our parents' permission for things like piercings and tattoos. I was willing to bet she faked her mom's signature. Everything about her seemed bogus lately.

"Do you care if Rick dances with me?" Well, at least Jen wasn't trying to hide her motives. "He should have some fun, even if you can't."

Of course I cared, but I shrugged one shoulder, knowing Rick would turn her down. He'd told me lots of times he thought Jen was turning into a sleaze.

"I don't think I should," Rick said…but he sure didn't sound very convincing. I looked at him out of the corner of my eye. Maybe he secretly liked her skanky look. My parents would never let me out of the house dressed like Jen did these days. But my parents hadn't been home when I left; I could have worn something sexier than my black skirt and sleeveless silver turtleneck top. I thought about the pile of clothes lying on my bed. Nothing looked good with crutches and athletic tape.

"Oh, come on." Jen grabbed Rick's hand and pulled him toward the gym stage where the speakers were blasting some techno-sounding rap. "Just one dance won't hurt."

I limped my way to the bleachers and sat down on the bottom bench—the same place I'd probably be sitting all next basketball season if my foot didn't heal right. The big, colorful Snow Week poster still hung across the back of the stage, one corner starting to fall down. Normally, I would have gone and pressed it back to the wall, but the places under my arms where my crutches rested were already aching. I set my crutches on the floor near my feet and leaned back against the next bleacher, trying to act cool, like I needed a rest from my wild night instead of sitting all alone because my former best friend was dancing with my boyfriend. I couldn't ignore the way Jen was gyrating in front of Rick. Or the way he was watching her.

I looked again at the wrinkled Snow Week sign, noticing now that Mike was the DJ, his collection of CDs piled high in front of him. Leave it to Mike to wear his silly Snow Prince crown. I almost felt like smiling. Almost.

"This next song goes out to a special friend of mine." Mike didn't look at me, but I could tell he meant me. I felt a flush begin in my neck and move to my cheeks as the beginning notes of a Norah Jones song filled the gym. Apparently Mike remembered how many times in a row I'd listened to that CD when it first came out.

As the bluesy notes played out, I waited for Rick to come ask me to dance. I couldn't dance the fast songs, but I could certainly sway in his arms to this slow song. As if in slow motion, Jen slid her arms around Rick's waist and laid her head against his chest. Rick's head turned my way. If he was looking for permission to continue dancing with Jen, he wasn't going to get it from me. His eyes met mine, and he held out his hands as if to say, "What am I supposed to do?" Then he wrapped them around Jen.

I could have told him what to do if it hadn't been for the lump in my throat. I turned my head, pretending to be fascinated with the advertising signs that lined the upper wall of the gym. No amount of decorating ever seemed to hide them completely. Between the paper snowflake cutouts that hung around the auditorium I could read clearly…Victoria's Café, German food every Wednesday. Ken's Gas Station, free vacuum with oil change. So, so interesting. State Bank of Brewster, where you bank with friends and neighbors. I felt as if I didn't have any friends tonight. Certainly not Jen and not even my boyfriend.

I blinked rapidly, looking above the signs, trying desperately to keep the tears inside my eyes. This day had lasted forever, and it wasn't over yet. My eyes roamed the gym, looking everywhere but at Rick and Jen. I held my chin up, trying hard to look like I hadn't been dumped.

"One night the, uh…prince couldn't get to sleep…" Mike's voice filtered over my right shoulder as he slid a couple feet along the varnished bleacher to my side. "…so he went for a walk along the roof of the palace. As he looked out over the, uh…*gym,* he noticed a woman of unusual beauty." He grinned, his crepe-paper crown at a goofy angle on his head. If he was trying to make me feel better, it worked.

I smiled. "What's that? Some butchered fairy tale?"

"Actually, it's a butchered Bible verse. Second Samuel, as a matter of fact." He nodded his head like some sort of actor taking a bow. "Do you like the music?"

"Yeah." I looked down at my lap, remembering the time Mike had taken me to the radio station after it was off the air for the night and played the whole new CD over the speakers at the station. We'd sat on the floor together, drinking Cokes, letting the music surround our comfortable friendship. I felt that calm again now. "Aren't you supposed to be up on stage?"

"Norah's sitting in for me." He nodded toward the equipment on stage and the Norah Jones CD covering for him. "I'm taking a well-deserved break." Mike crossed his arms and leaned back against the bleacher, looking out at the dancers swaying together. I was sure he was watching Rick and Jen just as closely as I was. Their bodies couldn't get any closer together. I was surprised Mr. Morgan hadn't tapped them on the shoulder and told them to break it up.

Having Mike sitting beside me was nice. I didn't feel like quite as big of a loser now that I had someone next to me. Why couldn't it be Rick? A second Norah Jones song began to play. Rick and Jen didn't miss a beat. I wondered if Rick even remembered I was here.

"Kind of a bummer night, huh?" Mike had that right.

I looked up at the ceiling, blinking at the sudden stinging in my eyes.

"My night hasn't been so great, either." Mike seemed to know I couldn't talk. "When I was at the station after school, Ruthie told me she might be closing KBRS. That means I'll be out of a job. And probably out of my pickup."

I stared at Mike. Even before he had his license, he'd saved for the down payment on his used truck and counted on his job to make the monthly payments. I'd counted on him for rides to school for the past two years. I couldn't begin to count the number of times we'd cruised around Brewster together, complaining about school, laughing about everything, dreaming about the day we'd graduate and leave our little town for good. I couldn't imagine Mike without his pickup. "What will you do?"

"Try and find another job, I suppose. Hey, maybe your dad would let me be a repo man. You know, the guy who goes out and collects on bad loans. I could repossess my truck and still drive it for work."

I bumped Mike with my shoulder. He could put an upbeat spin on anything. I stared out at the dance floor, wondering what Mike would say about Rick and Jen. I couldn't think of one good thing that was even sort of funny about the way they were pressed together.

"A beautiful woman lacking discretion and modesty is like a fine gold ring in a pig's snout."

"Ha!" I burst out laughing, leaning forward, half wishing Jen could have heard Mike's comment about her sleazy behavior. She probably wouldn't care.

"Old King Solomon was pretty wise, huh?"

"You are, too." The smile left my face. It was good to have Mike understand how I felt. Suddenly I wanted to tell someone about this whole rotten week.

You can tell Me.

I knew Mike would be the first one to tell me to talk to God, but I wasn't so sure God wanted to listen to someone as confused as me. Mike already knew about Rick and Jen—I wouldn't even have to explain that part. "Can I tell you something?"

"Always."

I leaned back against the bleacher again, angling myself so I could see Mike as I talked. "There's more than just Rick bumming me out tonight." I stopped, glancing out at the dance floor and then back to Mike. "I have to drop out of basketball for the rest of the season so my foot can heal, the doctor is running another test on that lump in my arm, and my mom's in the hospital in Carlton."

"Wow." Mike sat forward, leaning his elbows on his knees. "This Snow Prince and Princess stuff isn't all it's cracked up to be, is it?" Before I could even smile at his remark, he asked, "What's wrong with your mom?"

I shook my head. "I'm not completely sure. Dad didn't say much. We just found out last night. He went to Carlton before we even ate supper to go see her. He seemed pretty worried. Mom's been acting weird for a while. Crying a lot and stuff. I kind of wondered if things were bad between my parents. Dad's gone so much at work and all. But now she's in the hospital, so maybe she's really sick and has been upset about that. I don't know, but *it scares me.*" Tears cloaked my last few words.

"Me, too." Mike reached over and grabbed my hand, squeezing it tight. "I'll pray for her. You, too." He didn't try to explain away my feelings the way Rick had when I'd told him about my mom on the way to the dance.

"I'm sure there's nothing wrong," Rick had said, not even looking at me as he drove into the school parking lot. "She'll be fine." He shifted the car into park and turned off the motor. "Ready to boogie?" he'd asked, smiling big, forgetting that fast about my mom and my foot.

Norah Jones sang through the silence as Mike and I sat side by side, our eyes converging on Rick and Jen out on the gym floor.

"You don't deserve to be treated like this, you know." Mike's gentle words cut through my memory.

I was quiet, staring at a spot on the wooden gym floor. What could I say? That Rick had given me flowers? That he'd apologized in school yesterday for pushing me and promised not to ever do that again? That he'd walked in the door to my house to pick me up for the dance, wound his arms around me and whispered in my ear, "I'm so sorry, Emily. I love you. You know that."

It was the first time Rick had said those words to me, and somehow they made everything better. Until Jen had made her move.

"It's Jen's fault," I said to Mike. "Rick is just trying to be nice."

Mike rarely used sarcasm to get a point across, but this time he did. "Yeah, I can tell, he's trying really hard." He let go of my hand and pushed himself off the bleacher, and then he stood and stared down at me for a long moment. "You don't deserve to be treated like this."

I couldn't meet his gaze any longer. I stared at my bandaged foot instead. Mike didn't understand that this was all part of being in love. Didn't all the songs he played at that country station talk about how sometimes love hurt? Rick couldn't help it that Jen was being so aggressive. He was just being nice to her. I knew he wasn't purposely being mean to me. "You don't understand how it is," I mumbled toward my lap.

"I guess you're right…I don't." Mike stuck his fingers into the edges of his khaki pockets. "I've gotta go give Norah a break. If you want to talk later, call me." His voice was soft as he added, "Or if you need a ride home, I've still got my pickup."

I watched as Mike walked away. He reached up and pulled the silly crown from his head, dangling it from one finger as if he didn't have a care in the world. I knew how much his job at the station meant to him. Besides the money, he had a gift for what he did. I couldn't think of a job in Brewster that would be better for Mike than the one he already had—and might lose. Maybe I should be the one praying for him. As Mike passed the garbage can that stood near the foot of the stage, he twirled the crown off his finger into the black opening.

An image of the rhinestone crown I'd left in my room at home filled my mind. It was lying directly on top of the devotional book Mom had given me for Christmas. The one I'd vowed to read every day this year. I could count on one hand the number of times I'd opened it. Maybe if I'd read it more, my life would be better. My mom wouldn't be in the hospital. My lump might not be cancer. My foot wouldn't be broken.

Or my heart.

Dr. Sullivan

My Monday started off with an eye-opener. Olivia Marsden came into my office at the hospital jabbering a mile-a-minute. I could see this was what had thrown me off all along.

I expected the weekend in the hospital to calm her down. Taking her out of her routine would let the stresses of daily life take a back burner while the increased dosage of Prozac took effect. I had confidence that the chemical imbalance she was experiencing would soon right itself and Mrs. Marsden would realize this whole episode was under control. Apparently, I'd made my assumptions too soon.

"You've got to do something." Olivia sat down heavily in the chair across from my desk. As usual, she looked as though she were ready to attend an important luncheon as soon as she left my office. Her black slacks and black sweater might have looked gothic on anyone else. On her the look was classic. It was the pearls, I decided. "I haven't slept since I got here. My roommate snores louder than Bob. I still can't eat. My skin is crawling, and those craft sessions are a waste of time." She rolled her eyes. "Do you really think making a bowl out of coiled rags is therapeutic? Give me a break. If anything, it's enough to drive a person nuts." Catching the irony, she added, "*More* nuts."

I couldn't help but chuckle. Olivia, while a puzzle, was a refreshing change from most of my patients, who were often non-verbal and compliant as clay. The ones who weren't inclined to violent outbursts, that is.

"You must understand," I said, matching the glint in her eye, letting her know I'd caught her joke, "those crafts can be challenging for many of our patients."

"They make me feel like I'm in kindergarten." She crossed her arms over her chest but then realized her action was typical of a five-year-old. One corner of her mouth turned up as she uncrossed her arms and folded her hands in her lap. She crossed her legs and leveled her eyes at me. "What am I going to have to do to get better? I can tell you for a fact that paint-by-number pictures aren't going to do it."

Once again I chuckled. She was an aberration. An anomaly from the classic description of depression. One would think a doctor of psychology would be alert to such deviations. Instead, I'd been trying to push her into a preconceived mold. I expected someone who was truly depressed to play the part, to present herself as noncommunicative, responding in syllables, not paragraphs. I had to give Mrs. Marsden credit; she had thrown me for a loop.

Her frantic call for help sent me scrambling through textbooks and through my brain. A phone call to a colleague had helped me gain perspective. I was ready for her today. At least I hoped I was.

"I'm going to be changing your medication, Olivia. I don't believe Prozac is the drug of choice for you."

"Now there's an understatement." She raised her eyebrows, challenge in her eyes. Her voice softened as she looked down at her hands. She breathed deeply, expelling air as if it were weighted. "Thank you. For trying…something."

Her tender words made me flustered. Patients rarely thanked me for merely doing my job. "Well…yes…" I looked through notes the weekend nurses had made. "You said you're not sleeping, but the nurse noted you were resting well Saturday night. Last night, too."

"Just because my eyes were closed doesn't mean I was sleeping. Did they also note I sat out in the lounge and watched late-night TV at three in the morning?"

"Yes, that's here, too."

"For the price I imagine I'm paying for this stay, I would think you could afford to get cable on this floor." She licked her lips. "I'm not begging for pills, Dr. Sullivan, but could you give me something to help me sleep? If I could just get one good night's sleep, maybe I could cope." Her eyes lit for a moment. "Who knows? I might even finish that lovely rag bowl."

I finally recognized that her humor was what had deceived me. It distracted me from my usual analytic mind-set and made me think I was dealing with a colleague rather than a patient. A mental sparring that threw me off course. I sat back and templed my fingers. "I think you'll find this new medication has a bit of a sedative quality. Let's give that a try before we add any other medications to the mix."

"You know," she said, running her fingers rapidly through one side of her hair a couple times, "I keep racking my brain, trying to think of some reason all this is happening to me. If I could just put my finger on what started it all, I could understand and move on." She leaned her head into her outspread fingers, massaging her forehead. She looked up. "What is it?"

I rested my fingers on my chin. "I'm glad you asked that. I want to talk about something you mentioned at our last session."

Olivia rubbed the back of her neck with her hand. "That appointment seems like ages ago. I hope I can remember."

"You mentioned that your current medical issue—your depression—reminded you of Job. In the Bible," I added quickly, even though I knew Olivia probably didn't need the prompt. "I found that analogy interesting."

I wasn't about to add that I had to scour my shelves to find a Bible, finally resorting to opening a box of books Margaret had left behind. I found it there but then had about as much trouble finding the story Olivia had referred to. I hadn't realized the narrative took up an entire book or even that it was simply called "Job." Obviously, my Bible days were few and many years past. Eventually, I stumbled upon the book within the Bible. I poured myself a glass of Merlot and settled in my study, intending to skim the story, hoping to find a nugget that would help me relate to my patient.

Possibly forty-five minutes later, I paused from my reading to take my first sip of wine. Quite a psychological study, that man Job. No wonder Olivia had been captured by his story. I wasn't sure I quite believed it all as gospel, but the way the events were laid out made for an old-fashioned thriller Agatha Christie could have had fun with. It wasn't so much a whodunit as a whydunit. The very question Olivia struggled with. Why was this happening to her?

I took another sip of the garnet wine and read on. I was anxious to see how this miserable tale of Job ended.

Ah, just as Olivia had indicated, all was restored to Job in the end—in abundance. No wonder Mrs. Marsden found a kernel of hope here.

I sat the book in my lap, leaning my head against the high back of the navy leather chair—the one Margaret had given me for my home study as a gift on our twentieth anniversary. I was so pleased at her thoughtfulness, and I imagined buying a matching chair so we could enjoy evenings in my favorite room, reading together. I never got around to it. And then—well, maybe there was a reason. An empty chair would only serve as an unwelcome reminder of better days. I picked up my wine glass and spun the liquid around, reminding myself that living in the past did nothing to improve the future. I took a sip and forced my mind to return to the issue at hand. Job's dilemma. The interesting read had reminded me of something I'd forgotten as I searched for an explanation to Mrs. Marsden's problem. It seemed so simple but so true.

I said it to her now. "Olivia, you need to understand that sometimes these things don't happen for any particular reason. Sometimes they just do. Our task is to learn to overcome the situation, to become better in spite of it. Maybe *because* of it."

Did you hear what you just said, Doctor? Heed your own advice. I pushed the thought aside. "Much like your friend Job." I paused, remembering how easily I'd found myself identifying with the put-upon man. He, too, lost his family. With only a juggling of semantics, I could put myself in his shoes. Unlike Job, I hadn't lost Margaret so much as I'd pushed her away. She was as good as gone. He lost his children. How long had it been since I'd thought about the miscarriage Margaret had during our sixth year of marriage? Margaret and I had never been blessed with more children, regardless of how hard she had pleaded with God. I let her do all the begging, telling myself a career could be just as fulfilling. Now I was nearing the end of that without a wife to speak of, or children. Soon, I'd have no job to fill my life, either. Certainly, the book of Job had more to say to me than I'd been searching for. Much more.

Sometimes these things don't happen for any particular reason. Sometimes they just do.

As if she'd heard my thought, Olivia slowly nodded her head, squinting her eyes at me. "I might need to think about that for a bit, but are you saying that we might not find a reason—something hidden, say…deep in my past—that's causing this?"

"That's exactly what I'm saying. Your depression and anxiety may be a chemical imbalance that has nothing to do with anything in your psyche."

Olivia put a fingernail into her mouth and chewed on the tip, almost as though she were chewing on my words. When she spoke, her words came slowly. "So…like Job… who'd done nothing to warrant his misery…I might be…being…tested? By God?"

I held up one hand. "I don't know if I'd go so far as to blame God for—"

"Oh!" she interrupted. "I wouldn't be *blaming* Him. It would be a…a *blessing* of some kind…to think He was using me in that way. Testing my faith. Making me into a stronger Christian." She paused. "Maybe I shouldn't take the new medication."

She must have seen my eyebrows shoot up.

"It was a joke," she said.

Once again her humor zipped past me so quickly that I'd taken her seriously. This woman was a challenge. I wasn't sure if I should envy or feel sorry for her husband.

"I fully understand that God put doctors on this planet for a reason," Olivia continued. She held out her arms as if expecting shots. "Medicate away."

This time I caught her joke. "You can put your arms down," I said. "I think you have basket weaving before meds time." Two could play this game. I had a feeling she'd like the banter.

She smiled wryly. "You're so thoughtful. But if you really cared, you'd knock me out completely so I wouldn't have to attend."

"Go on." I waved her away with a chuckle. "We'll talk tomorrow, after you've had a night on the new medication."

Olivia stood, brushing at her neatly pressed slacks. She headed toward the door but then turned back. "I want to thank you," she said softly. "I feel better knowing I have a man of faith for a doctor."

Before I could set her straight, she was gone.

I cleared my throat, reaching up to adjust my tie. Suddenly it felt too tight. *A man of faith.* That was a laugh.

I'm not laughing.

I wasn't either. I thought about the Bible lying on the end table by my chair at home. I could see exactly where I'd left it open, waiting for me when I returned tonight. I found it fascinating that the sorry book of Job was followed by the book of Psalms. The classic book of lament and hope. Wasn't that precisely what my job entailed? Listening to laments, offering hope?

I found myself looking forward to the evening of reading I had planned. Maybe I'd learn something that would offer hope to me.

Libby

I closed the door to Dr. Sullivan's office, breathing a sigh of relief. When I talked to Dr. Sullivan I was fine. Witty, almost giddy. Matching wits with my intelligent doctor. So unlike the way I had spent my long days at home. Some mysterious placebo effect seemed to take place in his presence. During the short time we talked, I had a bit of my normal life back. I walked down the stark hall of the hospital to my room. I imagined the way I felt around Dr. Sullivan must have been how people had felt in the presence of Jesus. Their hope for healing. Only He was no placebo. He was the real deal.

I entered my room and breathed a guilty prayer of thanks that Vivian was out. Her simple, long-winded chatter grated my already frayed nerves. Pretending to listen to her was almost as difficult as listening to the thoughts that roiled through my mind when she wasn't talking.

I climbed onto the bedspread of my twin bed. The bed I'd made at seven-thirty this morning. "Part of the socialization schedule," Nurse Nancy had reminded a grumbling Vivian. I leaned myself against the brown veneer headboard and pulled a pillow across my lap. The short walk down the hall was just long enough for the familiar oppression to begin closing in.

You're such a failure. You're lucky Bob is sticking with you. You weren't home to take pictures of Emily going to the dance. Her Snow Princess dance! You're not even going to be home to get Emily's test results. You're a terrible mother. Terrible. You'll probably end up like Vivian, unkempt, mumbling gibberish. No one in the world cares about you. Serves you right. It's all you deserve.

Where was Dr. Sullivan? Why couldn't he hear what was in my head now?

I hear you.

I bowed my head into the pillow, trying to remember the story of Job. My misery was certainly less than his, but it didn't feel that way this morning. Tears pushed their way from between my eyelids. Where was God?

"Time for group!" Sheryl, my favorite nurse, poked her head into my room, sounding as though she were calling me for ice cream instead of therapy. Her eyes registered my tear-stained face. "Not a good morning, huh?"

I shook my head.

She walked over to the bed and rubbed my back. "Can I do anything to help?"

A silent sob shook my body before I could speak. I hiccupped. "My daughter, Emily, had a biopsy on Friday. How could I find out the results?"

"That's simple." Sheryl clicked her pen. "Where was it done?"

"At the Brewster Clinic. Dr. West. Ellen West." I wondered if Ellen had any idea where the business card she'd given me had led.

"No problem," Sheryl said. "Now you need to get to your session. I'll walk with you." She helped me off the bed as if I were in the hospital for a broken leg instead of a disturbed mind. Still, her arm around my shoulder felt good. Simple comfort. I'd take what I could get.

"Who would like to share some good news this morning?" The perky voice of Jamie, the young social worker who was leading this session, set me on edge. Her enthusiasm was better suited to an aerobics class than this dismal group.

I looked around the circle. A ragtag bunch if there ever was one. Vivian's hair was positively electrified this morning, jutting out with unusual flair. Bill sat slumped in his orange plastic chair, his frown blending into his gray-specked goatee. Three other glum faces I didn't have names for were followed by a nicely dressed woman who looked completely normal. Her dark hair was discreetly highlighted in a way that screamed "expensive." She must be another social worker, sitting in on the session. Or a doctor. We locked eyes. She nodded in greeting. I hoped she thought I was a colleague.

"Ihavenews." Vivian raised her hand as if we were in grade school. "IwenttothemovieonSaturday." She giggled, looking at me.

Oh man. I averted my eyes. I didn't want to be any sort of friend to my strange roommate. More guilt.

"Thank you for sharing, Vivian," Jamie gushed. "It feels good to go out and do something fun, doesn't it?" Vivian bobbed her head like a toy dog in the back of a car window.

"Anyone else have news to share?" There was a long silence. "Anyone?"

The well-dressed woman spoke. "My weekend at home went really well." She looked down at her lap, glanced at me, then focused on Jamie. "I'm hoping to be released from the hospital sometime this week."

The woman I thought was a doctor was a *patient?* My heart thudded at the realization. She looked like someone who could be my friend, not some crazy person.

Talk about the pot calling the kettle black. I bit back a smile at the irony of it all.

"That is good news, Krista." Jamie smiled. "Would you like to share a bit about your weekend?"

"Well…" She breathed in slowly, sorting her thoughts. "I was really worried about what going home again would feel like. You know, to see the kids and my husband, back where it all started." She paused and then added, "Almost ended." Again, she breathed deep. "It was…okay." She smiled at Jamie and glanced again at me. "It really was. I didn't break down crying in front of the kids like I'd feared. I felt as if I'd been off visiting my sister instead of…here." She unfurled her clenched fingers for a second. Another deep breath. "I think I'm ready to go home. This time."

She'd been here before? She looked so…so…normal.

So do you. It's not what's outside a person that I care about; it's what's inside.

"That's great, Krista, just great." Jamie tried to make eye contact with the others in the group. Most were staring at the floor. She locked on me. Quickly, I looked away. I had no good news to share.

"Krista," Jamie said, turning her attention back to a willing victim, "could you tell the group some of the coping skills you've learned during your stay here? Some things you found helpful while you were at home this weekend? Something others in the group might benefit from knowing?"

Krista smiled for the first time. She was beautiful when she smiled, as if she didn't have a care in the world. I wondered if I'd ever get to that point. "That's easy," she said. "The 'stop sign' technique." She made small quote marks in the air.

"Ah, yes," Jamie said, "many clients have found that helpful. Could you explain it for those who are new here?" Again she looked at me.

Was I the only new person here? Certainly they weren't going to waste the time of the whole group just so I could hear this.

You are worthy.

No I'm not.

You are worthy.

I closed my eyes, trying to believe the inner words I was hearing. I didn't feel worthy at all.

"It works like this." Krista sat up straight, holding her fingers together in a mangled octagon shape. "Whenever I start to hear that negative self-talk inside my head, I immediately picture a big STOP sign instead."

As I listened to her explanation, a gigantic red sign appeared in my brain. STOP! For a second I couldn't think of anything but the imaginary sign. Oh. That was probably the whole point. STOP thinking destructive thoughts. I had a name for them now…negative self-talk. Perfect description. If I had been a cartoon character, a light bulb would have been flashing above my head. Ah-ha.

Krista went on, directing her words to me, the only attentive pupil in her makeshift classroom. "The next part has been the hardest for me to put into practice, but I'm getting better at it. It's…" she paused, glancing at Jamie, who nodded encouragement, "re-languaging my thoughts."

"Huh?" I blurted what I was thinking, which wasn't much.

Krista laughed. "I thought that too the first time I heard it. What it means is to take the negative thought you've had and *re-language* it. Say it in a way that is honest and positive."

I leaned forward, placing my hands on my knees. I felt a trembling inside, as though a huge new space were opening inside of me. A scary place, full of new possibilities. "Can you give me an example?"

"Sure." Krista rolled back her eyes as she thought a moment. Jamie folded her arms and relaxed, a satisfied smile on her face. "For instance, I always used to think, *You are such a terrible mother.*"

A freezing chill swept through my arms as I recalled the many times I'd thought that same thought about myself. I leaned forward even more. I was anxious to hear every word.

"When I walked into my house with my husband on Friday night, neither one of the kids were there to greet me. I have a boy and a girl," she added.

Just like me.

"Right away I started thinking, *They hate you. They don't want to look at you after what you tried to do to yourself. You're a terrible mother. A terrible person.* I stood in the doorway, ready to turn around and come back here. Then I said to myself, *STOP.* And there it was, the STOP sign. The thoughts stopped just as my husband said, "I didn't tell the kids you were coming home…just in case the doctor decided you couldn't. I'll go get them. They're going to be so excited." Krista closed her eyes and smiled to herself as if remembering their faces. "While I waited for my husband to round up the kids, I re-languaged what I'd thought. Instead of thinking, *They hate you,* I thought, *Your children love you. They might be angry about what you tried to do to yourself, but they love you.* Instead of thinking, *You're a terrible mother,* I substituted, *You made a mistake, but you're only human. You've learned from this and are growing into a better person. You love your children with all your heart."* Krista's eyes filled as she spoke. *"You are a wonderful mother."*

My eyes filled too as I imagined saying the kind and generous words to myself.

"Thank you for sharing that," Jamie said. "It's a lesson we all can benefit from. I like to remind people that we often say things to ourselves that we would never think of saying out loud to a friend. Can you imagine saying to your best friend, 'You are a terrible mother?' Of course, you'd never say something like that. And yet, as Krista shared, we say those same sorts of things to ourselves. We need to treat ourselves with the same respect and courtesy we give to others. We are worthy."

A chill ran down my spine as Jamie repeated the words I'd just struggled with.

"But it takes practice," Krista added, rising to her role as teacher. "It's hard at first. Really hard. But it gets easier every time you do it."

I stared at Krista, marveling that a patient in this surreal place would have so much to teach me. Three days ago I would have judged her harshly. Anyone who had apparently attempted suicide was not someone I wanted to know. That was three days ago. Before I contemplated wearing those shoes myself. Now I found myself listening closely to what she had to say, knowing she'd walked my path ahead of me.

"The thing is," she went on, continuing to focus on me, "you can't give up. You will sometimes forget to say *stop*, and you won't always be able to think of a thing that will make your negative thoughts into something better." She clenched her fist, pulling it in toward her chest. "You've got to keep trying. Keep thinking. You can do it."

I found myself nodding at her as though she were a preacher preaching only to me. I hadn't realized how intent I'd been until Jamie said, "Thank you, Krista." As I sat back in my chair, I felt a sort of tension leave my body. For the first time since I'd arrived at this place, I had something I could grasp on to. Something I could *do* to get better. Jamie turned her attention to other members in the group while I tumbled the words Krista had spoken around in my mind.

"When did you get here?" Krista was standing by my chair. The group members were dispersing, and I was holding court in the circle by myself.

I stood, my height a near match for my comrade here. "On Friday." I stuck out my hand. "I'm Libby."

Krista shook my hand, her grip firm. "Sorry I wasn't here to welcome you." She raised one eyebrow. "The Welcome Wagon around here can be a bit surprising."

"Well said." I fell into step beside her as we walked back toward our rooms. "I appreciated what you said back there." I tossed my head in the direction of our group room. I was afraid to ask the question, but I had to. "Does it really work? That technique you talked about?"

"It does," Krista said with resolve. "It really does. But you have to practice. It doesn't happen overnight. But then," she paused to sigh, "none of us got this way overnight, either. I don't know why we expect to get better so much faster."

I matched her stride, thinking about what she'd said. It was true. I'd spent months or even years telling myself how rotten I was. Logic told me a habit that ingrained wouldn't disappear overnight.

"I've got another technique to share with you, but…" she looked at her watch. "…a friend is meeting me here for lunch, and I've got to get going."

A friend was meeting her here for lunch? I couldn't help it, I snorted disbelief through my nose. Maybe she *was* nuts and here I'd been eating up her advice. "Ok-ay," I said, unsure how to act.

"No, really." She put her hand on my arm. "I have a pass off the floor to meet a friend in the cafeteria downstairs for lunch. They let you do that if they…well, if you're able to handle it."

"Well, okay, then." I felt better somehow. I stopped at the door to my room. "This is where I…live." I waved a hand at my humble abode. "Have fun, I guess."

"I'll talk to you later. We're not supposed to go into each other's rooms. Will I see you at crafts?" Her eyes twinkled. "I got roped into macramé. Pun intended."

"Rag bowl," I answered back. She nodded her understanding, making a date with a dip of her head.

I stepped into my room and suddenly stopped. A flower shop had apparently set up business in my room while I'd been gone. Almost every available surface held some kind of bouquet.

"They'reallforyou." Vivian sat on her bed with her arms crossed and her chin pushed into her chest.

I walked around the room, fingering the delicate blossoms, pulling fragrance through my lungs, reading small cards tucked inside miniature envelopes. *Get Well Soon! Andrew, Lisa, and family.* My brother who lived in Minneapolis. How had he found out I was here? *Hope to see you back in church soon. Friendship Circle.* My women's group from church. *Didn't you read this month's book? You're excused, but only this time. Get better…fast. The Bookworms.* My book club from Carlton. *I'm praying. Talk to you soon. Love, Katie.* How had any of these people found out about where I was? I'd sat home for weeks, for months, convinced no one cared about me, and here was living proof, refuting those thoughts. I pulled a card from the middle of a vase of showy calla lilies. The unusual flowers were beautiful in this ordinary room. *Love always, Bob.* My throat closed.

You don't deserve his love. You're nothing but a drain on Bob's career. Just think what he could do without you!

STOP! A large red, octagon appeared in my brain. What was it Krista had said to do now?

"*I re-languaged what I'd thought.*"

I took a deep breath, forcing my mind to reexamine the thoughts I'd just had. *You don't deserve Bob's love.* Yes, I did.

No, you don't! STOP!

Yes I do! *Help me with this, Lord! I'm only human and I'm going through a hard time just now. It doesn't make me unworthy of love.*

You're right, it doesn't. I felt myself relax as the affirmation took hold. I repeated it to myself, *You are not unworthy of Bob's love.*

Mine, either. Goosebumps pimpled my arm as realization dawned. Without even knowing, I'd felt unworthy of God's love, too. He created me, and I'd done nothing but rip at His creation with my awful self-talk. If I had felt at all worthy a moment ago, I didn't now.

"Forgive me, Lord," I whispered into the soft, white flowers. "Forgive me. Help me to treat Your creation with…tenderness."

"Ilikeflowers." Vivian's petulant voice cut through my prayer.

She's Your creation, too, isn't she, Lord? I looked over my store-like stash of flowers. "Would you like these?" I couldn't quite bring myself to share the calla lilies Bob had sent, but I knew Katie would be the first to share her gift with someone less fortunate. I picked up the vase of orange tiger lilies. "How about if I put these on your nightstand?"

Vivian smiled, her crooked teeth reminding me once again of how much I already had going for me and how little Vivian had. "Thankyouit'stimeforlunch." She paused by the door. "Comeon." She held out her hand.

She's My creation, too.

I had no choice. I reached out and grasped her hand, turning the thin line of horizontal scars that lined her forearm toward the floor. I didn't need to be reminded what a thin line separated me from Vivian.

Emily

I was the reason my mom was in the hospital. She was depressed because of me. My sneaking out, my crummy foot problems, the lump on my arm. All my mom ever did was to try and make life good for me, and look where she ended up. In the hospital. I was a loser with a capital L.

I tugged at the latch of my school locker. As usual, it stuck. Harder than necessary, I banged the door with the heel of my hand. It popped open, revealing the mess inside. Kind of how my insides felt. I rolled my eyes far back into my head, trying to keep the stinging there from turning into tears. Even my talk with Peg yesterday hadn't made me feel better.

Just in case anyone was watching, I leaned my crutches against the locker next to mine and poked at the papers sticking from between books stacked in front of me, pretending to be organizing my mess. Instead I was remembering…

Even with my crutches I could walk faster than most of the residents at the nursing home. I felt guilty as I passed several slow wheelchairs on my way to my favorite resident's room. I'd waited until my dad had left to go visit my mom, and then I hopped in my car and drove to the nursing home. Maybe I'd go see Mom after I talked to Peg. Or after I stopped back at home to see if Rick had left a message on the machine.

"Hi, Peg," I called, limping my way into her room.

"Emmee," Mrs. Stoltz, Peg's roommate, said in greeting, her voice high and whispery, "Peg isn't feeling well this weekend. The flu is going around. You probably shouldn't be here."

"I work here," I answered, even though I wasn't clocked in today.

"Well, then…" Mrs. Stoltz fluttered a hand near her chest. "Could you pour me some water? I'm not feeling so good myself."

I poured the water, watching as Peg slept soundly. I wouldn't wake her if she was sick, but oh, how I wanted to talk to her. Tell her about all that had happened. About the lump on my arm, my terrible night as Snow Princess, and about my mom being in the hospital. Somehow talking with Peg was like writing a Dear Abby letter to a newspaper. Just saying the words out loud helped me think more clearly.

"Hey, Emily!" Jen stood by my locker, jolting me back to reality. "Jason's having a big party on Friday night. You coming?"

I bent over, rummaging in the bottom of my locker for my lit notebook. It was only Monday; how could anyone be planning a party for Friday already? The kind of party Jason would throw wouldn't be the kind he'd send out invitations for. Everyone in school knew Jason did drugs. The kind of parties he threw were word-of-mouth only. Whispered words. I wondered if Jason had any idea Jen was broadcasting his event to anyone who had ears.

I also wondered why Jen was telling the news to me. Since when did Jen care whether I was going to a party or not? I knew the answer to that. Since she'd started to steal my boyfriend. I straightened and answered, "I doubt it."

She tossed her straight hair over her shoulder. "That's not what Rick said."

Oh, so she'd already talked it over with him. If that was the case, why was she double-checking with me? Or was she trying to point out that Rick told her things he hadn't told me? I turned my back to Jen, pretending to fuss with my hair in the small mirror I'd stuck in the door of my locker. I bit at my lip. Why would Rick tell Jen he was going to the party before he talked to me? Or did he plan to go without me? "I haven't talked to him since last night," I said over my shoulder. Actually I hadn't talked to Rick since he'd dropped me off from the dance on Saturday night. His distracted peck of a goodnight kiss was far from his usual good-bye. Even then I wondered if he was planning to go somewhere after he dropped me off.

I waited by the phone that night, secretly hoping he'd call to say goodnight or something. Sunday I pretended we didn't own a phone. But that hadn't worked so hot. Pretending something doesn't exist is hard when you're staring at it.

At least I'd had two hours in the morning as a reprieve. Church and youth group. But even that time had been filled with angst of its own. I'd silently hoped two hours in church would take away some of the guilt I felt about sending my mom to the hospital, but it had only made me feel worse. Pastor Ammon had started his sermon quoting a Scripture about the sins of the parents being visited on their children. I wondered if the Bible had anything to say about the sins of the children?

Even Mike's good-natured bantering during youth group couldn't shake the blame I felt. I couldn't concentrate on our lesson. Instead my mind filled with images of ways my mother had shown her love for me. Sitting in the bleachers at every game I'd ever played. She'd never missed one. Even my dad couldn't say that. She made me sandwiches to take on the bus to away games when she could have just tossed me some money and told me to buy a greasy slice of pizza when I got there. I remembered all the times she waited up for me when I stayed out late, making sure I got home okay. Times, I thought now, when she'd rather have been sleeping. I'd thought her vigilance was some sort of punishment; now it seemed like a grand sort of love. But the memory that kept returning to my mind was from when I was little. The night before school started in fourth grade.

"I can't sleep," I whined as my mom switched off my light.

"You haven't tried," she answered calmly.

I squeezed my eyes shut hard, trying to go to sleep in a nanosecond. "I can't," I said again.

My mom walked to my bedside, taking a seat on the edge, putting her hand on my cheek. "You're just excited," she said. "Going into fourth grade is a big deal."

I nodded, hugging Mutt, my ragged, stuffed sidekick harder than ever. Then I said it—the thought that had worried me the whole month of August. "What if I can't remember how to write cursive?" My heart pounded with the notion.

"Turn over," Mom said, gently pushing at my side. She lifted the back of my pajama top, running her flat hand over my back as if it were a chalkboard. Then, with one finger, she lightly traced a course across my back. "What's that?" she asked.

It had taken just a second for me to understand what she was doing. I smiled into my pillow. "An E?" I questioned, knowing full well it was the cursive version of the first letter of my name.

"Exactly right!" Mom had answered. She drew another letter, then another. I didn't miss a one. At the end of the whole alphabet, she drew an A+. "Go to sleep, smarty pajamas." She kissed my cheek.

All I could think of now was that I'd never even said thank you.

I was a terrible daughter. The worst.

Dad and I had gone to Vicky's Café for lunch after church. "I'm going to drive over to Carlton this afternoon to visit your mom," he said. "Want to come along? I know she'd love to see you."

How could he not know? How could I visit her when I was the reason she was there? I imagined the way her eyes would narrow when she saw me, then how she'd look away. My heart clenched at the thought. No, thinking of her there was painful enough. I didn't need to see her with my own eyes. "Rick and I have plans," I lied, pushing the green beans on my plate into the mashed potatoes I couldn't eat. "Tell her hi." I pushed my plate away. I was done.

"So," Jen interrupted my memory, her obviousness irritating, "do you think you'll go to Jason's party?"

I pushed both sides of my hair behind my ears. Who did I have left besides Rick? I wasn't about to let Jen get her hands on him. Then who would I have? I turned to face her. "Yeah," I smiled with confidence I didn't feel. "Rick and I will be there."

"Great!" I'd known Jen long enough to hear the fakeness in her voice. I suddenly had no doubt she'd been hoping I'd say no, giving her a whole week to work on getting Rick there by himself.

The time had come for someone to call her bluff. "Who are *you* going with?" I asked innocently, stepping away from my locker as she stuttered for words.

"Mindy," she mumbled, looking over my shoulder, at the floor, anywhere but at me. She knew me well enough to know I saw through her flimsy invitation.

"*We* will see you, I guess." There, now she'd know Rick and I were a couple. She could quit dreaming about him. He was mine. I flipped my hair over my shoulder with one hand, tucked my crutches under my arm, and pegged away from her. Acting righteous with crutches and schoolbooks was hard.

My eyes searched the faces in the hall. I needed to find Rick and make sure I had a date for Friday night.

Libby

That's what I got for living in a small town. Brewster—ha! Trusting Ellen West with Emily's life? I should have known better. On Wednesday I still hadn't heard the outcome of Emily's biopsy.

"A part broke on one of the machines they need to read her test," Sheryl reported before she went off duty on Monday. "They're waiting for a replacement. Hopefully tomorrow," she added, leaving me alone in my stark hospital room.

You're an awful mother. There was the thought again. *Any decent mother would have insisted on results sooner. Any decent mother would have noticed the lump on her daughter's arm long before it had a chance to—STOP!*

My thoughts stopped in their tracks. For two long seconds. *What kind of mother are you? You—* With every ounce of concentration I had, I pulled the STOP sign into my head again. I took a deep breath, blowing air out of my mouth as if trying to blow my thoughts away. If only it were so easy. I closed my eyes, conjuring words to reform my vile thoughts into something not so contemptible. A doctor's words I'd heard during Anne's illness came to me now. *If your test results are what we're hoping, a few days won't make a difference. If they're not what we're hoping…a few days won't make a difference.* Even knowing the grim results Anne's tests had brought, those same words comforted me now. A broken piece of equipment wouldn't change whatever Emily's outcome would be. A thankful sigh escaped my lips.

I use all things for good.

Those words had comforted me on Monday, but the "tomorrow" Sheryl had promised had turned into Tuesday and then Wednesday morning. I could have *walked* Emily's tissue samples to Carlton for tests by now—if I hadn't been in the hospital. A stab of guilt pulsed in my chest. I tried to rationalize it away. Small town economics was what we were dealing with. Waiting until the old testing machine broke before replacing it, while in the meantime people's lives hung in the balance. Trying to skimp on equipment that could save my daughter's life. *Or not.*

I felt the familiar panic begin to rise in my chest. Anxiety was still dogging my days, but the new medication Dr. Sullivan had prescribed had definitely helped my insomnia. I'd spent my Tuesday session with him talking with my eyes at half-mast.

"Good morning, Olivia," he said, his voice much too hearty. "How did you sleep?"

"Like the dead," I'd intoned, a sleepwalker disguised as awake. He chuckled. "I figured you might. How do you feel?"

"I'll tell you when I wake up." I tried to force my eyes open a millimeter. "What was in that stuff?"

"It has a sedative quality that your body will adjust to in time."

For all the complaining I'd done about not sleeping, I hated to say anything now. I did anyway. "I don't think I can live like *this.*"

For once he didn't ascribe serious, psychological meaning to my remark. "Give it a couple days, Olivia. I promise you the side effects will subside. For now, enjoy the chance to sleep." He sat back in his chair and adjusted his tie. "Tell me how things are going otherwise. Have you been attending the group sessions?"

"As if I have a choice." Even I had to laugh. My days here were as regimented as military school.

Dr. Sullivan caught the understatement but explained anyway. "Routine is an important part of dealing with depression."

"I understand that," I sighed, not wanting to talk about what was really weighing on my mind. Worry overcame my reticence. What was I paying for after all? Might as well spill my guts and get my money's worth. "Emily hasn't come to see me yet." I twined my fingers together, pressing my thumbs together until they turned white. "Brian's called me twice from college, but Emily…" I swallowed, tugging at a wrinkle in the fabric of my slacks. "She was right here in

Carlton last night for CNA classes, and she didn't even st-op." My voice cracked.

"Why do you think that might be?"

I shrugged as if I didn't know. I really did know, but I struggled to say my thoughts out loud. "She's mad at me for missing the lump on her arm and for missing her big night as Snow Princess. No one was there to take pictures." I ducked my head, glancing at my doctor from lowered lids. I looked at my hands clenched so tightly my fingers were red. "She's ashamed that her mother is in a psychiatric hospital."

Dr. Sullivan's deep sigh matched mine. "Do you know what I think?"

Why did he keep talking in questions? His habit was driving me nuts.

You already are nuts.

STOP! Even though my conscience had a keen sense of humor, instinctively I knew the thought did no good. I re-languaged my thought into the question I should have asked in the first place. "What do you think, Dr. Sullivan?"

Before speaking, he picked up a pen and twirled it between the palms of his hands, and then he held it flat in one hand as if measuring his words. "I think you need to cut yourself some slack."

Oh! My tired eyelids rose all on their own. I'd never heard him speak quite so bluntly.

"For one thing, Emily is a teenager, and if you know anything at all about psychology, you know teenagers are wrapped up in themselves. For Emily to drop everything to sit by your side in the hospital when you aren't terminally ill would be unusual. It would also be unhealthy—for both of you. You need this time to recuperate, and Emily can use this time to become more independent. This can be a win-win situation if you let it."

"But—"

He held up his hand. "One of the hallmarks of your illness, depression, and anxiety, is the tendency to personalize events, to put the burden of any outcome on yourself. It's called all-or-nothing thinking. If a depressed person is having a bad day, *every* day from here on out will be bad. At least that's what they think. In a more logical frame of mind, we know that some days are better than others, and your task is to learn to understand that and not be overcome by your thoughts." He put down his pen, adjusting himself in his chair so his hands were free. "Let's look at your concerns with Emily. Without even talking to her you've imagined her," he held up one finger, "angry with you," he held up another, "ashamed of you," and another, "blaming you for a growth on her arm that you didn't even know was there." He put his hand down. "Now, let's look at the facts. You haven't talked to Emily. For all you know she could be studying for a big test, she could be trying out for a class play—"

"The play was this fall." If he was talking facts, I couldn't help but throw in my two cents.

He pressed his lips together. "I think you get the point, Olivia. This might not be about you at all. And if your concern holds some truth, then you and Emily will need to work that out when you get home. The world is not your responsibility."

I hung my head. "I feel like it is most of the time." I didn't tell him about the long days I'd spent at home in Brewster, worrying about Bob's commute to work in Carlton, about the paper Brian had due for his economics class, about the fact Emily didn't like what I'd made for supper the night before…as if somehow my worry, my vigilance, would keep my family safe from anything bad.

Dr. Sullivan sat back in his chair, letting my morose words hang in the air. He rubbed the back of his neck with his hand then sat forward again, picking up his pen. "I don't usually do this with patients, but I'm going to make an exception in your case. I know you are a woman of faith, so I'm going to tell you a story about Moses. Here was a man who talked directly to God. Face-to-face. And yet, even *he* was swayed in the wrong direction by the very people he was leading. Cut yourself some slack, Olivia. You're not God. You're only human. And, unlike Moses, you don't talk to God face-to-face." Dr. Sullivan leaned back in his chair. "I think God will understand if, occasionally, you're not perfect."

He had no idea how much I wanted to believe what he'd said. What release there was in the idea that God could be in charge, not me. Old habits died hard. "But—"

"No 'buts' Olivia. I want you to think about what I've said." He stroked his chin, then smiled. "Now I need to apologize."

"For what?" I puzzled my eyebrows together.

"I took up most of your time standing on my soapbox. I'm going to get down now." Slowly he shook his head. "Usually this is a time for my patients to unload, not me. I'm sorry."

"Can I charge you for my time?" One corner of my mouth turned up.

So did his. "Sorry, it doesn't work that way. You'll have to consider it pro bono work. Volunteer." Dr. Sullivan folded his hands together and laid them on his desk. "I want you to think about something else. Other than my monologue, I mean." He raised his eyes to me. "I'm thinking about releasing you in a day or two. Do you feel ready for that?"

My heart took up a thumping I was sure Dr. Sullivan could hear. Did I feel ready? No. Yes! No. He'd talked about facing the facts. "I'm not sure." That was the fact.

"That's why I wanted you to think about it." His voice was kindly. My doctor, Mr. Rogers. "We'll talk about it at your session tomorrow." He looked at his watch. "I need to get to the clinic, and you need to get to group."

"Yippee." I twirled my finger in the air.

He chuckled. "I guess we both have an exciting day ahead of us."

"I guess." I didn't tell him how I'd come to look forward to my ragtag group. How Krista and I had formed a quick, unlikely friendship within the confines of these strange walls. How Jamie had morphed from a too-perky, aerobics-like instructor into a young woman who was wise for her age. I pushed myself from the chair, standing over him behind his desk. "You've given me a lot to think about." My heart still pounded at the thought of being released.

The thumping felt like fear, with a small measure of anticipation thrown in.

I turned at the door. "In between thinking, I'll keep praying for you." Praying was the least I could do. Small payback for all he'd done for me.

~

That was Tuesday. Wednesday started off badly. My body had not adjusted completely to the new medication, and simply waking up felt akin to rousing from Rip Van Winkle's epic slumber. I sleep-walked to take my turn in the shower room, realizing once I'd undressed in the too-large, cold room that I'd forgotten to request a razor to shave my underarms and legs. I felt close to tears as I redressed and walked the long hall. *They treat you like a two-year-old. STOP!*

I was getting better at catching my thoughts before they spiraled out of control. *They are not treating you like a toddler by making you ask for a razor; they are protecting the patients who might harm themselves.* A proud shiver patted me on the back as I accepted the forbidden razor from the nurse.

Showered and smooth, I dressed for the day, realizing I'd also forgotten to request my blush compact, which held a potentially dangerous mirror. As if I were an audience of one for a dull melodrama, I pursed my lips into the tin-like mirror that hung in the shower room. "Ooooo, scary." Another walk down the long hall, another moment of feeling babysat. "Could I use my blush, please?" I applied it in front of the nurse. No use marching back and forth down the hall for such a mindless task. I was chaffing at the bit to get my old routines back.

I looked in the forbidden mirror, brushing blush across my cheeks. *Maybe you are ready to be released.* My heart danced a crazy jig at the thought just as it had lurched every time I'd contemplated the idea. Going home? In some ways I felt as if the idea had never crossed my mind, and yet in some secret place the thought had been tucked in my heart all the time.

I handed the green compact back to the nurse, walked into the for-once-empty TV lounge, and perched on the edge of the couch.

Was I ready to go home? I looked around this odd hotel. The weird walls of the hospital served as insulation for those of us here. A safety net from the world. And yet they also kept out many things I missed. Random phone calls from my friend Katie. Oh, she could call me here. She had, in fact. But without phones in the rooms, the calls were fraught with a formality that was so different from our usual chats. I missed Bob, but his late-afternoon visits each day gave us almost more time to visit than when I was home. In some ways my stay here had warmed a place between us that had been cooling. I missed Emily, teen mood swings and all. *She hates—STOP!* The red sign flashed in my mind. I couldn't think about her without the old degrading voice screaming in my head. For right now, I wouldn't think of her at all.

What else did I miss? How about privacy? Rooming with Vivian was a challenge I would be glad to forfeit. But even the unexpected routine of nurses stopping in my room at all hours kept me unsettled, not to mention Pastor Ammon tapping at my door on the heels of Bob's late-afternoon visit, offering prayer while I tried to shush Vivian's nonstop chatter.

I missed my computer, e-mailing my brother, and the challenge of working on my column and my book. I'd timed my hospital stay just right. So far, I hadn't missed the deadline for my twice-monthly column, and if I was released soon, I'd have time to jot something quick. I doubted my time here would ever be fodder for column material, but I'd think of something. Was I ready to face all that again?

You wouldn't be thinking of what waits outside these walls if you weren't ready to face it.

"Olivia?" Sheryl walked into the TV area. "Dr. Sullivan was called away on an emergency. He's hoping to be back in to see his patients later this afternoon, but he won't be seeing you this morning."

What kind of emergency could a psychiatrist have that he couldn't handle at the hospital? As usual, I blurted out my thoughts. "What's he doing? Talking someone off a ledge?"

Sheryl laughed. "I love you, Olivia. I wish half our patients had your sense of humor." She sat down beside me. "I believe Doctor Sullivan was called out on a family emergency."

Oh. I'd never ever thought about my kind doctor as having a personal life. I hoped everything was okay. "I guess I'll excuse him then."

Sheryl smiled. "I guess that means you have some free time between now and group." She put her hand on my back. "Maybe you want to go work on your crafts." I didn't miss the twinkle in her eye. She winked. She knew exactly how I felt about that lame exercise. "Or, you can have some private time in your room. Vivian is having some tests done on another floor of the hospital today." She knew how I felt about Vivian, too. "Or, you can sit here and watch television."

"Then I'd really lose my mind." I exchanged glances with Sheryl. She got my joke.

"Don't forget to eat breakfast," Sheryl reminded. The makeshift kitchen adjacent to the TV area held all the ingredients for a do-it-yourself breakfast. Another part of the cure for patients whose mental abilities were far below mine—teaching them to eat regularly and fend for themselves.

I slid a slice of bread into the toaster. While I waited for it to toast, I poured myself a cup of coffee. I continued to be surprised that they served regular coffee here. The anxiety on this floor could fuel a space shuttle; caffeine couldn't help matters any. But I was learning that coping skills came in all forms, and caffeine was one of the more acceptable ones. I sipped the strong brew, wishing Krista would wander in and join me for breakfast. I found her an odd role model, considering the circumstances. But her willingness to share her techniques for coping with her depression and anxiety provided me a shortcut to wellness. I learned almost as much from her as I had from any of the doctors and counselors I'd seen. My suggestion that she submit a bill to my insurance carrier for her services had lit up Krista's face.

I ate my toast alone, pouring myself another cup of coffee just as a man I'd never seen walked in. If he noticed me, he didn't acknowledge it. One look told me he was a new patient. Disheveled clothes, unkempt hair. Maybe he was the guy who had wakened the whole floor at two A.M. with his ranting and hollering. The nurse doing her late-night rounds had whispered that the commotion had been the police bringing in a patient. She apologized for the uproar and assured me the man was being supervised, planting the scary idea in my mind about what would happen if he weren't.

I eyed the man as he poured himself a cup of coffee and stared into the fridge. He closed the fridge, grabbed a slice of bread from the bag on the counter, and consumed over half of it in one big bite. He had a familiarity with the kitchen that gave me the feeling he'd been here before. He scratched under his arm and then stuffed the rest of the bread into his mouth, reaching into the bag for another slice as he chewed.

Time alone in my room suddenly seemed like a good idea. "Excuse me," I muttered, pushing myself up from the table. I really wanted another cup of coffee to take back to my room, but I wasn't about to cross paths with this guy. I tossed the Styrofoam cup into the trash on my way out.

I climbed onto my neatly made bed, propping my back against the thin pillow. I wrapped my arms around the top of my bent knees, laying my chin in the crisscross of my hands. What was I doing here? In this strange place? The image of the odd new man in the kitchen haunted my thoughts. Why was I here when other people so obviously needed help more than I did?

I use all things for good.

I corralled my thoughts and closed my eyes. This might be a good time to talk to God about going home. *I'm scared, Lord.*

I am with you always.

I'm afraid of being alone in the house. Of having my anxiety come back the second I set foot in the door. Already I could feel the thump in my chest at the thought.

I am with you always.

What if I can't cope? What if Emily doesn't talk to me? What if she ignores me? Ashamed of her poor example of a mother…

I wasn't sure just when my prayer turned into a worry session, but by the time Sheryl came to call me for group, I had worked myself into a clammy sweat, agonizing about all the awful possibilities a return home could bring. Emily's cold shoulder. Bursting into tears in the grocery store. Fleeing from church in the middle of a service. Forgetting Katie's upcoming birthday. What if Brian died during some weird college hazing? What if Bob decided he couldn't stand my anxieties and decided to leave, taking Emily with him? What if—

"Time for group," Sheryl called into my room, her voice serving as a STOP sign all its own.

"I'll be there in a minute," I told Sheryl, my voice conveying none of the angst I felt. I took a deep breath, bowing my head in shame. *I'm sorry, Lord. I meant to pray. Forgive my wandering mind.* I sighed in frustration. *I don't know why I can't keep my mind on You, why I can't pray anymore!*

The thought came gently, between my troubled prayer. *Now is the time when others are praying for you.*

My burden of worry fell from my shoulders. I knew Katie was praying for me, and Pastor Ammon had told me many from my church were as well. I hoped Emily mentioned my name to God even if she was mad at me. Bob was a man of few words when it came to faith matters, but I felt safe in assuming he'd lifted me in prayer more than once this past, long week. I bowed my head, humbled by the reminder of prayer by others. *Oh, Lord, help me to pray and not to worry.*

⁓

"Today I want to talk about handling worry." As if God had forwarded my prayer to Jamie, she picked up where my mind had stalled this morning. "I discovered a great little book when I was getting my master's called *Hope and Help for Your Nerves* by Dr. Claire Weekes." Jamie looked around the circle, making eye contact with anyone who would meet her gaze. "How many of you struggle with worrying?"

Even the group members who appeared not to be listening, raised their hands.

Krista reached over and touched my arm. "You've got to read that," she whispered. "It's great. I think this is the technique I wanted to tell you about."

I turned my attention to Jamie. If Krista recommended it, I wanted in.

"Much of our battle with anxiety is caused by worry that gets out of control. We start thinking one *small* thing…" Jamie wrinkled her nose and held her fingers a quarter inch apart. "…and before we know it, we've expanded that thought *this* big." She stretched her arms as far as they would reach.

I wondered if Jamie had been a mouse in the corner of my brain just minutes ago. She was describing the very thing I'd done. Her visual demonstration was a perfect illustration of how one little worry had grown to take over my prayer.

"Just like you do with the STOP technique, you'll need to practice this, but I can guarantee that if you master it, worry will practically vanish from your life."

Krista was nodding her agreement while just about everyone else but me stared at the floor. If no one else was interested, this time I didn't care. I wanted all the help I could get before I stepped outside these doors.

"This is a variation of the STOP technique. You need to have a slip of paper handy," Jamie explained. I side-eyed my group members. I doubted everyone here could write complete sentences, but Jamie treated us all as equals. "Every time you start to worry about something I want you to say 'stop.' Stop that worry in its tracks. Then, you may have noticed this…" Jamie caught my gaze. "…sometimes your mind won't let go of the thought. You feel afraid to stop worrying about it. Something might happen if you don't." I found myself nodding in recognition. "What I want you to do then is to write down your worry on a piece of paper. Keep a list, all day. Every time you start to worry, write it down. Then you need to pick a 'worry time.'" She used her index fingers to strike quote marks in the air. "Sounds goofy, I know. But trust me, this works." Jamie leaned forward, her hands tucked under either side of her thighs, her face a picture of concentration. "Krista? What would be a good time for you to do this?"

"I usually try to do it between three and three-thirty, right before the kids get home from school."

In a beat I realized that because Emily would no longer be playing basketball, the same time would be good for me. Even though I hadn't heard the whole concept, I'd already bought the premise. I leaned forward to hear the rest.

"Okay," Jamie said. "At three o'clock you need to grab your list, find a favorite chair, sit down, and start worrying. You have a whole half hour. You've got all your worries written down, laying right in your lap. Gentlemen. Ladies." She looked around the group. "Start your engines." She smiled. "Start worrying."

I felt one eyebrow start to rise. "I thought you said we were going to learn to eliminate worry? Now you're telling me *to* worry?"

Jamie raised one finger and pointed it at me. "I'm glad you brought that up, Olivia. It does seem counter intuitive to what we're trying to do. I can't explain exactly why it works, but it does. For some reason the brain seems to have a hard time worrying on command. Try it." She put a finger on her chin, and like a carnival barker she said, "Pick a worry. Any worry. Go on, bring to mind one of your favorite worry topics."

Picturing Emily was easy.

"Now, start worrying," Jamie instructed.

I closed my eyes and tried to twist my mind around the picture of Emily. Tried to produce the thoughts that were so automatic, they were almost second nature. I opened my eyes. "I can't."

"Exactly." Jamie sat back and crossed her legs. "I'll admit worrying is hard in a group setting like this. It makes my point easy to prove. When you get back home, you might find your normal worry habits harder to break. At first you might be able to sit and at least contemplate thoroughly all the items on your list. But I've found only a rare individual who can sit there and stew for the full thirty minutes.

As time goes on, and I'm talking in terms of days, not weeks, you will find your worry time shrinking."

Krista interrupted. "It starts to feel like such a waste of time."

"Bingo!" Jamie pointed at Krista. "It doesn't take long to realize that you didn't worry about something all morning, and now it's afternoon and nothing bad happened by not worrying. So why spend a half hour sitting and worrying when it doesn't do any good anyway?"

Krista raised her hand, catching Jamie's attention. "I've gotten pretty good at this the second time around. Every time a worry comes into my head, I don't even need to write it down anymore. I turn my worry into a quick prayer and send it on its way."

"Excellent point," Jamie concurred. "For those of you with a faith system, prayer can be an outstanding substitution for worry."

"At least prayer can accomplish something," Krista added. "At least that's what I believe."

I did, too. I was anxious to try this lesson I'd learned. I could hardly imagine a life without worry. My new motto would be, "Prayer, yes! Worry, no."

"For those of you who don't have a belief system, this method still can be very effective." I had the feeling Jamie had been coached to be politically correct. "Now," she held up her arm, looking at the watch on her wrist, "I believe it's lunchtime. Thank you for a great session."

Prayer, yes! Worry, no. Prayer, yes! Worry, no. I repeated the mantra to myself even as Krista walked and talked me down the hall.

"I need to go to the bathroom," Krista whispered as we neared the TV and lunch area. "Save me a spot."

I was surprised how quickly people formed cliques even in a setting like this. In the five days I'd been here, I'd already formed a small group of compatriots, as had most of the patients. Vivian scurried to her usual table, sitting with three friends who had more in common with her than I did. She waved. I wiggled my fingers back to her. Underneath her odd mannerisms lay a heart of marshmallow crème. She was the first of the people here to reach out to new patients, put an arm around a shoulder and say, "You'regonnagetbetter." I'd found myself on more than one occasion wishing I had her transparency. Overanalysis was my middle name. If I could accept situations and people as simply as Vivian, life would be a whole lot less complicated.

The kingdom of God belongs to those who have hearts as trusting as children.

A pastor had come to the hospital on Sunday and spoken to those of us who made up his curious congregation. No doubt he had someone like Vivian in mind when he picked that Scripture. If Vivian was getting the kingdom of God, I wondered what my inheritance would be.

I took a seat at the table Krista and I had adopted as ours. I looked around for Maxine, the schoolteacher who made up our threesome. She hadn't been in group. Maybe she had a doctor appointment this morning. Or maybe she'd been released. Once again my heart jumped at the word. Surely Maxine would have mentioned that at supper last night. Then again, like me, maybe the idea was mixed with such trepidation it was better left unspoken. If Maxine didn't show up soon, I'd ask Sheryl what happened to her.

One of the aides pushed in the lunch cart. Plastic trays were layered on the cart, laden with plates covered with stainless steel domes. I got up to get my food. From my short experience, I already knew not to expect much when I lifted the dull silver lid.

Fish sticks. Oh, my. I hadn't eaten fish sticks since Emily had been…what? Five? My appetite had been getting better, but the sight of the greasy coating, combined with my bad mood of the morning, flipped my stomach around. I looked around at the other tables, making sure this food was everyone's lot in life and not just mine.

Oh, great, all I needed—the strange man I saw at breakfast was headed my way. I ducked my head, concentrating on my sorry food with energy I didn't feel. *Please sit somewhere else. Please sit somewhere else.*

Without a word the man set his tray across from me. Taking in his eccentric appearance, I gulped at the lump of fish stick stuck halfway down my throat. With any luck I'd start choking and have a good excuse to run from the table. Where was Krista? A strength in numbers might overcome the feelings I had sitting alone with this man.

Prayer, yes! Worry, no.

I risked a glance at the man. Wild eyes stared back at me. I concentrated on my food again and felt the uncomfortable chemistry of not acknowledging my tablemate. He was a person, after all. A patient in this hospital, no different than me. Well, not *that* much different.

"What's your name?" I asked, trying to be polite. His eyes shimmied in the sockets. He wore a pair of thick black-rimmed glasses— the sort that look hip on kids in their twenties and dorky on anyone older. He was older. He reached up and scratched vigorously at the scraggly gray-streaked goatee on his chin with his fork and then dug into his fish sticks. Apparently social etiquette classes weren't on the fourth floor schedule.

"You gonna use those?" The man pointed to the three packets of tartar sauce lying beside my plate.

"No." I had more or less lost my appetite. I handed the packets over.

"Hmm-hmm," he mumbled—a thanks of some sort, I guessed. He picked up one packet, tore off the top and tilted his head back, holding the packet above his mouth as if it were a bag of peanuts and we were at the ballpark. In one quick squeeze he emptied the gooey mass of tartar sauce into his mouth. I tried hard not to gag. He reached for the other packet and I quickly looked away. Soon three empty packets were lying on his tray.

"Stan," he said, offering his name as a kind of dessert.

"Stan the man," I blurted, in awe of the stomach this man must have. "Nice to meet you." Always polite.

He threw back his head and laughed, loudly, his mouth open wide, tartar sauce lining the inside. Suddenly even the bland mashed potatoes on my plate seemed unappetizing. I slid my plate to the side. "You're not gonna eat that?" Stan already had his fork poised.

"Go for it," I said, sliding my tray his way. I imagined this would be a note on my chart. *Patient not eating.* If Stan was going to be my dining companion during the rest of my stay here, I just might end up in an anorexic clinic instead of back home. But then again, if Stan ate all my food and I pulled the tray back in front of me...who would know I hadn't been the one to clean my plate? *Devious behavior.*

What was it about this place? Just when I'd start thinking I was getting better, something would happen to make me feel vulnerable again. I was getting crazier by the minute. Catching it from Stan, apparently.

"Hi, Stan." Krista set her tray on the table and pulled out the chair on my right.

"You've met?" I didn't even try to keep the surprise out of my question.

"This is Stan's table," she explained. "He just lets the rest of us sit here to be nice. Right, Stan?"

"Mmm-hmm," Stan mumbled. "You gonna use those?" He pointed to Krista's tartar sauce packets. Oh, please, no. I didn't know if I could stomach his act a second time.

Krista put her hand over the packets. "Yes, Stan, I am." She sipped at the glass of apple juice on her tray. "When did you get here?"

"Last night. You?" Without looking at either of us, Stan shoved a pile of my mashed potatoes into his mouth.

"I've been here three weeks. I think I might go home pretty soon, though."

"Good for you." Stan didn't look up as he pushed half a bun into his mouth.

By their comfortable conversation it was apparent they understood each other. As if they were old friends of some sort. "Do you know each other?" I asked.

"Stan and I go way back." Krista picked up her fork and cut a small piece off her fish stick. "We met...when was it, Stan?" She chewed, waiting for Stan to reply.

"Four years." He said the two words as if he'd been keeping track all along. "Three times in four years we've been here together. Now it's four. Four for four. Ha!" He swallowed the entire contents of his apple juice in one large gulp.

I gulped, too. I turned to Krista. "You've been here four times?"

She dipped a piece of fish stick in tartar sauce, then paused with her fork in midair. "Five, actually. I was here one time when Stan wasn't."

Oh. I pasted a pleasant smile on my face, but my heart was off to the races. Somehow I thought one stay here was all that was possible. Two at the most. Once you went through the paces, received the right medication, and learned the techniques, you'd surely be done with a place like this. I watched as Krista cut a slice of canned peach with the edge of her spoon. She looked so normal. So much like me. I imagined us as friends outside of the hospital setting. If someone like Krista ended up back here time and again, who was to say I wouldn't?

Suddenly I really did feel sick. "I'm not feeling well," I said, pushing myself away from the table as Stan replaced his now empty plate with mine. Let him have it all. Let them have each other. "I'm going to go lie down for a while." I felt the need to run from this room. The walls seemed to close in on me.

I pulled air into my lungs as I hurried down the hall to the safety of my room. A sudden flood of panic rose in my chest. I threw myself on my bed, burying my face in the pillow, trying to block my raging thoughts with feathers.

I wanted to go home and yet I didn't. I was afraid to leave the safety of this place and afraid to stay. Even more afraid of leaving and then coming back. The thought of going through everything all over again was more than I could bear. The days and weeks, the months of anxiety. Crying over nothing. Spending my days staring at a blank computer screen. Worrying over Emily, Brian, Bob...anyone who came into my mind. Wrapping myself inside clothes in my closet. Fearful to drive the car into the garage just in case I wouldn't turn it off. *STOP!*

STOP! The huge red sign twirled through my mind, knocking my wild thoughts askew but not away. With every bit of effort I could muster I said aloud, "STOP!"

Hot tears began to flow from my eyes into the pillow. Sobs shook my shoulders. This was too hard. I wanted to be home, but how could I ever leave when my emotions were still so raw?

You're not getting better at all. You'll always be like this. You'll—
STOP!

In spite of this bad morning, I knew I was getting better. Little step by little step. I could feel it.

Two steps forward, one step back. A revised version of the old cliché sang in my head as I curled onto my side, tears still flowing. Why did the backward steps feel like giant steps and the forward steps seem so small?

You…will…get…better." The voice of Dr. Sullivan so many appointments ago rang in my ears. If only I could believe those words. If only.

I felt the outside edge of my bed sag with the weight of someone. Whichever nurse it was, I didn't feel like talking to her, explaining one more time "how I was *feeling."* I clamped my eyes shut, pretending to be asleep. Even if I didn't have her fooled, I didn't care.

I waited for her to give up and go away, to leave me alone just this once. My shoulders tensed as I tried to lay still. Then, ever so softly, I felt a hand reach out, touch my shoulders, and begin to rub small circles into the middle of my back.

"Youwillgetbetter," Vivian whispered. "Youwillgetbetter."

Angel words if ever I'd heard any.

I only hoped they were true.

Dr. Sullivan

I tossed my pen onto my desk, exasperated. Olivia Marsden had left our Tuesday session with her usual exit line, "I'm still praying for you." Or some such variation. At this point in her therapy I could hardly lay all the blame on Mrs. Marsden for the way her words always seemed to send my thoughts on a tangent. To Margaret.

I'd worked in this field long enough to quit expecting simple, pat answers for the way a person's mind worked. Reading the Bible, for instance. I'd begun my quest in that book in an attempt to meet Mrs. Marsden's needs, but something more kept pulling me back to where I'd left off the night before. That thick book contained more solid psychology than most of the textbooks lining my office.

As I'd told Olivia not all that long before, things didn't always happen for a particular reason. Sometimes they just happened. Sometimes the way life played out was a mystery.

Or God.

Rather than push the thought away as I might have even a week ago, I let it hover for a bit. The notion that I wasn't in this world completely alone, that God was really here, was unusually comforting.

Margaret is here, too.

I smiled. Another thought I would not push away any longer. Not after yesterday.

Well, alone or not, I needed to get to work. I tamped together the many sheets of paper that made up Mrs. Marsden's file, straightening the corners with my fingers. Her stay here in the hospital would be shorter than many. I'd had no doubt all along that with the proper medication she'd be well on her way to wellness. The trick had been finding the right combination of medicine. Thankfully, that finally seemed to have happened.

I lifted the top piece of paper into my hands. I'd missed my appointment with Olivia yesterday. I wanted to review the nurse's comments from Wednesday before I saw her this morning and made my final decision to release her from the hospital.

> Morning agitation. Didn't eat much lunch. Tearful episode in room before afternoon group session. Participated well in group. Socialized well during evening meal. Husband made daily visit after supper. Patient appeared upbeat after visit. Slept soundly throughout the night.

I rubbed my chin. Olivia's morning agitation was not unexpected. Mornings were often a hard time for people dealing with depression. Serotonin, the vital brain chemical that regulated mood, was at its lowest level in the early hours. Daylight, activity, and medication worked wonders if given the chance. But I knew Olivia's agitation probably had more to do with the idea I'd planted on Monday than with her depression. Many patients chafed at the thought of leaving this facility…some, almost as much as they'd chafed at the idea of coming here in the first place. I was well aware of the safety net these walls provided. I'd purposely previewed the idea of discharge to Olivia on Monday to give her time to prepare herself for release. The fact that by afternoon she'd settled back into the expected routine told me she was ready.

The question was, was I ready to let her go?

I removed my glasses, cleaning them with a tissue from the ever-present box on my desk. Olivia Marsden had tested me. No question about that. But in ways my colleagues would never guess.

Her assumption that I was a doctor with faith was left uncorrected. The words, "No, I'm not," would not leave my lips in her presence. As much as I fought with her accusation, I was challenged. The fact that she struggled so with God and with her faith in light of her misery intrigued me. Most patients in her frame of mind were ready to abandon ship. Toss overboard whatever might be causing their pain. God was often the first to go over the side along with old friends and sometimes spouses.

You should know. Ouch. I did. But I could change that.

I blew on my glasses, wiping them again, convicted by the thought. The drive I'd made yesterday was much too fresh in my mind.

"I have a family emergency," I'd told Elaine, noting the raise of her brows. She knew the only family I had was my wife. The forbidden topic in my office. "Could you call the hospital and have them reschedule my rounds?" I didn't feel the need to explain to Elaine that this was an emergency of the heart. That was between God and me.

The drive to the Brewster nursing home was not one I'd made often. In the two years since Margaret's stroke, I'd managed to travel this direction very few times. Seeing her drooping face and hearing her slurred words had been a reminder of all my beloved wife no longer was.

Oh, I'd told myself all the platitudes. *She's still the same person inside. You're a doctor—you should be used to people with limited abilities. You made a vow.*

I'd also repeated all the excuses. *Her care is not your responsibility. You can't. You have a medical practice to run. "For better or worse" didn't mean this. You shouldn't have to live with half a wife.*

But I wasn't living with half a *wife*; I was living half a *life*. My life without Margaret had been one-dimensional at best. Work had not turned out to be the panacea I had hoped. Meals eaten alone were food for the body only. My soul had withered these past two years. I'd forgotten I even had a soul until Olivia Marsden's struggles began a resurrection of sorts.

I was almost wishing for a Xanax as I followed the nurse to Margaret's room. Placing her in Brewster had seemed like a smart move at the time. The facility was known for its excellent care of residents. Anyone who knew Margaret would understand why I'd moved her there. "The best care possible," I repeated when asked, patting myself on the back for my thoughtfulness. Over time, the inquiries about

Margaret had gotten fewer. Making the discouraging trip less frequently had been all too easy. Less disheartening when I didn't have to be reminded of her incapacity so often. Almost forgetting I had a wife became easier and easier. Some of my colleagues seemed to have forgotten. More than once I'd been offered an introduction to an available woman. At least that was one road I'd not walked.

"She's in here. She hasn't been feeling well." The retirement home nurse led the way into a surprisingly homey room. Margaret's roommate sat in a comfortable recliner, crocheting something beige. I nodded, not sure if this was the same woman I'd nodded at when I'd visited Christmas Day.

"Peg," the nurse called loudly. "Your husband is here to see you."

I didn't miss the surprised look on the face of her roommate. I turned to Margaret, waiting to see her eyes meet mine. I'd quit calling her Peg the day I'd admitted her here. Distancing myself was easier when I didn't recall the affectionate nickname I'd used for the woman I no longer recognized.

"Peg!" the nurse picked up Margaret's limp hand and patted the back of it. "Wake up. You have a visitor." The nurse stepped aside and turned to me. "Maybe you want to try."

I hesitated. One reason I'd gone into psychology was because it didn't require much in the way of bedside manner. Most of my patients were upright when I saw them. Give me facts and theories and the precise measurements of prescriptions, and I thrived. Face me with a pale woman I hardly knew anymore, and awkwardness was all I knew.

Lord, help me. I hadn't prayed for a long time, but the plea felt as natural as breathing.

I stepped into the place where the nurse had stood and picked up my wife's hand. It was cold, so cold.

I felt a flash of anger. How could they let her lie here and freeze? Why hadn't someone put an extra blanket on her? Rubbed her hand until it was pink with warmth? I began rubbing her hand. "Margaret, it's me. Wake up."

If anyone does this to the least of my people, they do it as for Me. I felt a warm current begin somewhere deep in my chest.

Bible words. Words I'd all but forgotten until Mrs. Marsden had sent me searching. I rubbed Margaret's hand harder. "Please. Open your eyes…" The word caught in my throat. I swallowed and tried again. "*Peg.*"

I reached up and stroked her hair. It had grayed since I'd seen her. She had always been so meticulous about her appearance. I recalled the first gray hair she found, and the way she plucked it out and held it up for both of us to examine.

"Would you look at that?" she said, and then added, "Take a good look because it's the last one you'll see." She tossed her head like a shampoo model when I returned from work that night. "Miss Clairol and I are new friends," she announced, smiling, fluffing her thick hair just for me.

Suddenly, I wanted very badly for Peg to wake up. I wanted to look into her blue eyes. "Please, Peg." I was surprised at the emotion in my voice. I didn't care. I just wanted to *see* her. I lifted her hand and kissed it. I put my hand against her soft cheek and simply held it there.

Oh, Lord, I found myself praying, *please…please…* I was a novice. Unpracticed. *Forgive me. Please hear me. Heal her. Heal me.* I asked so much in so few words. Far more than I deserved to have answered.

Peg's eyelids fluttered. She coughed.

"Peg? Can you hear me? I'm here. Look at me. Please." I wasn't above begging.

Blue. The bluest of blue. Sky. Ocean. Eyes—Peg's eyes. The eyes that, in spite of all the other changes that had happened to her body, had never changed. How could I not have seen that before?

I wanted to cry. I wanted to shout. Instead I leaned over and kissed her lips.

She smiled. "Yourrrrrre hhherrrre."

"I am," I'd said, suddenly so glad I was. "I'm here, Peg." I was surprised how easily her name came to my lips again, by how much I wanted to stay by her side. "I'm going to come back tonight." The miles between Carlton and Brewster were nothing. Why had they seemed so far? Suddenly I felt awkward, assuming she wanted me here. Maybe after all this time she didn't. A thudding began in my chest. "Is that all right?"

One side of her mouth lifted a little. She nodded, then licked her lips. They were dry. I reached for the water glass near her bed, then slid my hand behind her head. "Here," I said, lifting her head gently.

"Mmmm." She licked her lips. "Gooooood." Her eyes closed, then opened. "Thhhhaaaaank yoooooou."

"Anytime," I answered.

"Foorrrrrr coooommmmmminggg."

Oh, she hadn't been done speaking. No matter, I was going to have plenty of chances to get used to the way she talked now.

Many waters cannot quench the flame of love, neither can the floods drown it.

Goodness knew, Peg and I had been through the flames and the flood. It seemed just yesterday I'd been struggling through med school, our finances thinner than fine china. Peg worked two jobs in addition to typing term papers in her "spare" time as she counted the days until I opened my practice. In my quest to become a doctor, I took her devotion for granted. The amount of attention I gave her during those long years hadn't been much more than what I gave her these past two.

I rubbed at the bridge of my nose as memories flooded back. Trying to start our family had been a wondrous time. A time of reconnecting with each other and our passion. Until each month brought disappointment. Time and again. Then the joy of pregnancy. How Peg had glowed during those short months. I'd felt her joy as mine. Until the miscarriage. We never made a decision not to have children; somehow it had been made for us. I turned to work. What had Peg done? Tried to be the best wife she could…I could see that only now. What had been my thanks? I left her alone at home or in countless hotel rooms as I rushed off to meetings, so impressed with my own importance that I'd not seen hers. Backing me up. Always there, no matter how often I abandoned her. She'd ironed my shirts for thirty years. I'd sent them out for two, hardly missing the love that had been pressed into the cotton…until now.

And then her stroke. I thought I would have years to make up to her all the time I'd spent away, only to have her taken from me by a tiny clot of blood. The stroke was no fault of hers, and yet I'd blamed her. Blamed God. Pushed them both from my life as if I truly could.

My eyes watered now as conviction burned. Flood and flame. If only I could have another chance…I'd do things so differently. *Please, Lord. Please.*

"I'm so sorry, Peg." There was so much more to say, and yet nothing more. "I love you, you know."

"Iiiiii lllo—"

I put one finger over her lips. She didn't need to say it. I already knew.

~

I was a different man since that visit. Maybe no one else could see the changes yet, but they were boiling inside me as ardently as the bubbles in the caramels Peg used to make me for Christmas each year. She knew they were my favorites, and I missed them so much my mouth watered. Where was her recipe? I wondered what would happen if I tried stirring up a batch…if I took them to Peg? Would she smile as she recognized the memory along with me, or would she spit out the burned mess I'd probably make? Either way, I had no doubt she'd laugh.

Well. I straightened my tie. That was a project for a different day. Right now I needed to focus on Olivia Marsden. The woman whose struggles had unlocked my frozen heart. Telling her how her case had changed me was hardly appropriate. I could only hope the help I'd offered her was payment in kind.

"Good morning, Olivia." As usual, she was impeccably dressed. I had no idea how she managed to look so put together in this unfashionable hospital setting, but she did. Much the way Peg used to dress up each morning even if I was the only person she'd see all day. *You should buy her a new outfit. Something stylish.* I blinked hard. Why was it every time I saw Mrs. Marsden, my professional mind-set went out the window? "How did you sleep last night?"

"Great," she said. "Either Vivian has quit snoring or I'm dead to the world." She took her usual chair. "Sheryl told me you had a family emergency yesterday. Is everything okay?"

I cleared my throat. Patients rarely took an interest in my personal life. "Yes. Yes." I cleared my throat again. "Things turned out very well. Thank you for asking." I needed to get the focus back on her. If I let Olivia continue with her questions, I'd more than likely be lying on the couch before our time was up, confessing my guilt about the past years. Confessing would come later. To God, not Olivia. Not that I hadn't spent a good hour on my knees last night. I needed more time to talk things over with Peg. With God. But not now. "How was your day yesterday?"

She wobbled a hand in the air. "So-so. It started out kind of rough, but guess what?" She sat up straight, a big smile on her face. "Emily's biopsy finally came back. The sample was benign. Just scar tissue...praise God."

I still wasn't completely comfortable with her transparent faith, but I couldn't question the impact it had had on me. "Yes," I answered, checking if my tie was straight. "Good news, indeed." I sat back in my chair, knowing that what I was going to say next might open Pandora's box. "I want to discharge you today."

Her eyes grew wide. "Today? Oh." She leaned back as if the wind had been knocked from her. "I was thinking tomorrow or Saturday."

"You've progressed very well, Olivia. Jamie tells me you've been her star pupil in group. Many behavioral techniques can be very helpful in dealing with anxiety and depression, and Jamie is an excellent teacher. You've apparently learned quite well."

"Thank you...I guess." She took a deep breath and leveled her eyes at me. "I'm scared."

"So are soldiers, but still they fight." I removed my glasses and set them on my desk. "Do you know the definition of courage? It's action in spite of fear. Soldiers are afraid, but they continue to move forward. I find people who battle depression to be some of the most courageous people I know."

"That wouldn't be me. I'm half German-Russian, part Scandinavian, and the rest Chicken."

I openly laughed. Her dry wit no longer threw me. "There's another quality that will serve you well. Your sense of humor."

"I wasn't joking." Her eyes twinkled.

I pointed a finger at her. "Oh, yes, you were. Laughter does good like medicine, you know." Here I was, quoting the Bible to her. I recognized the irony.

She grew serious, looking at her hands as they folded and unfolded. I'd learned to wait in times like these. Some things weren't easy to speak aloud.

"All I want is to feel happy again. To feel some measure of joy!" The words burst from her as if frustration and volume could substitute for what she didn't have.

I took in a slow, measured breath, templing my fingertips under my chin. How quickly the tone of this meeting had changed. "You're a smart woman, Olivia," I said. "Tell me, just what do you think *is* the measure of joy?"

One side of her mouth turned up. "You never let me off the hook, do you?" She crossed her arms for a moment, then pulled at the lobe of one ear, thinking. "That's a good question. I've never thought how to measure joy. The Bible says heaven rejoices when a sinner repents, but goodness knows I haven't caused that yet."

I wasn't ready to tell her how wrong she was.

She bit at the corner of her lip. "There's joy in the Lord." Once again her eyes penetrated my gaze. "I don't know about you, but I have a hard time wrapping my arms around that. How do you measure joy?"

"Maybe we can't. Maybe joy is an emotion so deep it's unfathomable." Where were these words coming from? "Maybe we're not meant to measure joy, but to let it come to us."

"Well, I wish it would hurry up."

"My guess is that you already have joy…you're just not seeing it. Depression can do that sometimes. Cloud our vision. Think about your children, your husband, and your friends. Your home, your faith." I nodded as if pointing at her. "There's a difference between happiness and joy, you know. Happiness is momentary; joy is something much deeper. More lasting."

She was quiet as she considered my words.

"Thank you," she finally said. "I needed to hear that. I'm not going to try to measure joy; I'm going to try to accept it. I'd forgotten, joy is a gift of the Holy Spirit, and rejecting a gift is impolite." There was that smile again. "Maybe I should write a thank you note to God."

"Now there's an idea." It might be good therapy even for this doctor. Again, something to consider later. I picked up my pen, twisting it between my fingers. "Let's talk about you going home. What do you think you'll do now?"

"Clean the house." She gave a fake shudder. "I don't even want to imagine what it looks like after being gone six days. I'll have my work cut out for me."

"After that," I prompted. It was good for my patients to have a plan. A goal.

She thought a moment, pushing one side of her hair behind her ear before speaking. "I don't know. Finish my novel?"

A big thing she was picking. Maybe too big for someone still so raw. I found myself wrinkling my nose. "I don't know if you want to do that. Publishing is a hard nut to crack. It can be very discouraging. I don't know if you need that just yet."

"Finish college?" She wasn't asking me so much as herself.

"Is that something that interests you?"

Her brows furrowed, then relaxed. Her voice was tentative. "I think it does."

We talked a bit more, exploring what the coming days might bring. "Life is all about change," I reminded her. "Everyday we're a little bit different. It's not something to fear but something to embrace. We have a chance each day to become someone new.

Someone better." I realized I was maybe saying these words as much to myself as to Olivia.

She smiled, her eyes light. "Watch for her soon…" She splayed both hands on either side of her face. "The new and improved Olivia." She put her hands back on the arms of the chair, her face growing serious. "I didn't mean to make light of it. That's an interesting idea. That we're always changing. Always coming closer to becoming the person God created us to be. I can almost hear Him whispering, *You are becoming…*"

Olivia's voice trailed off, but I could tell her sentence was complete. I finally broke the silence. "Well, good." I was suddenly, surprisingly pleased with the new person I, too, was possibly becoming.

"I need to remember what you said about the soldiers," she said in closing. "About putting on the shield of faith, carrying the sword of the Spirit. To stand boldly, without fear. Maybe with…" She paused, her eyes light. "…joy," she finally said, smiling.

I hadn't said any of that, but I wished I had.

"Godspeed," I found myself saying as she left my hospital office for the last time. I knew I'd see her again at follow-up appointments, but this meeting brought a sense of finality I hadn't anticipated. I had a feeling we'd both be different people the next time we met. "Godspeed."

Go with God.

Words I may never have said but for this woman. I found my head bowing, my eyes closing. *Go with her, too, Lord. Go with her.*

Libby

One time in the summer when the kids were little, Bob and I took them to a street fair in Minneapolis. Blocks of streets were lined with booths full of vendors and crafts people, all with something to sell. Bob and Brian had been struck mute by the array of food, chewing barbecued turkey legs as if they were their last meal on earth. Emily and I, however, had forgotten all about our stomachs. Instead, we feasted our eyes on a thin man who spun elaborate creations out of molten glass.

As I stepped into my house for the first time in six days, I felt very much like the glass bubbles the man had blown and shaped. Small as sand, thin as glass. A fragile crystal masquerading as a person.

"Well, how does it feel?" Bob stood in the middle of a sparkling kitchen, proud as any king who'd ever loaded his own dishwasher.

"Good," I said, spotting the new bag of Starbucks coffee by my coffeemaker. Bob's way of welcoming me home. "The kitchen looks nice."

"I can't take much credit. Emily did most of it." He grabbed my suitcase. "Let me take this upstairs."

I ran my hand over the shiny countertop, noting the way the hard-to-clean stainless steel sink gleamed. I wondered what kind of psychological insight Dr. Sullivan might note about Emily going to such lengths to please me when I hadn't set eyes on her in six days. The clock on the stove read two-thirty…she'd be home from school soon. Was I ready to face her? I'd have to be.

I walked into the living room, my eyes caressing my favorite chair, my computer, and the afghan I threw over my shoulders on chilly mornings as if they were long-lost friends. Oh, I'd missed my home. Even the screen on my computer had been wiped clean of any dust. When had Emily had time for all this? Maybe Bob had done more than he was taking credit for. He'd already taken a rare afternoon off from work. He even offered to cook dinner or go out to Vicky's Café—my choice. Bob offering to cook? I'd missed my chance to take his temperature before I suggested we order pizza. My first meal at home in so long would be awkward enough. Pizza in a cardboard box in the middle of the kitchen table seemed the perfect icebreaker.

"So." Bob joined me in the living room, rubbing his hands together as if they were cold. "How does it feel?"

He'd asked me that once already. His nerves were showing almost as clearly as mine. There was a shy awkwardness between us I hadn't felt since we dated.

"Good." I'd said that already, too. "Weird. I've never been gone from home this long before. It's strange to…" It was hard to put into words. I sat on the couch. I didn't quite dare tell Bob how scared I felt. I was afraid if I said the words out loud they might come true. Bring the anxiety rushing back. Overwhelm me with panic. Send me running to the closet—STOP!

My heart rate had increased as my thoughts whirled out of control. Jamie would be proud of how quickly I'd recognized the pattern. I was proud of me.

I patted the couch. "Sit beside me."

Bob sat close, his arm over my shoulders. Safety. Security. All the things I didn't feel by myself. He pulled me into his chest and whispered, "This feels good." He kissed the top of my head. "I'm glad you're home."

"Me, too." As I relaxed in Bob's arms I couldn't help but think of the friends I'd left behind in the hospital. Krista, Vivian…even strange Stan had been a comrade of sorts. Was anyone there to hug them? *Bring them healing, Lord. Continue Your healing in me.* This was one of the first times in so long I'd been able to pray for someone else's troubles. The prayer alone felt like healing.

We sat quietly, the silence a balm between us. If I were at the hospital now I'd be on my way to crafts. The fact I was missing such lameness was cause for rejoicing all by itself. "How about I make some cookies? Chocolate chip?" How good it felt to choose something I *wanted* to do.

"You said the magic words." Bob hugged me, then released me from the couch.

He followed me into the kitchen. My afternoon shadow, it seemed. I was glad for the company. I pulled my mixer away from the wall and grabbed the chocolate chips from the drawer by the fridge as Bob pulled out a kitchen chair and sat down. I began cracking eggs and measuring sugar.

"If you think you'll be okay tomorrow, I might run into work for a couple hours," Bob said over the hum of the mixer. "We've got that strategic planning session in Carlton over the weekend."

He'd mentioned that meeting ages ago, a lifetime ago. I'd forgotten all about the meeting that might decide whether we moved from Brewster. I poured one cup of flour into the bowl and then a second—and then felt a pain, a warning in my chest. The idea of moving wasn't what I feared; instead, I feared the terror the idea might trigger. I breathed deeply, monitoring my emotions. So far, so good. I was okay. "I'll be fine," I told Bob, sounding more confident than I felt.

"I told them I might not be around for much of it, but I should get a few things organized for the others to review."

I stopped the mixer and turned to him. "You need to be there."

"No, it'll be okay. They can get along without me."

"You're the CEO. How can they have a strategic planning meeting without the CEO?" Just the fact that Bob was willing to miss such an important meeting made me generous. Brave. "I'll be okay. Really. Dr. Sullivan wouldn't have discharged me if I wasn't fine."

"It's a two-day meeting." His voice was cautious. "They rented out The Prairie Place, that executive retreat center way outside of Carlton. The whole board is planning on attending. It's supposed to be quite the spot."

"Sounds nice." I turned the mixer back on, spooning flour into the bowl. My heart thudded. *You'll be fine. You can write this down and worry about it later.* "Don't worry about me. You plan on going."

Bob rose from his chair and wrapped his arms around me from behind, nuzzling my neck with his lips. It was so good to be home.

~

I was pulling the last batch of cookies from the oven when Emily slowly walked in through the kitchen door. I'd forgotten all about the crutches she was using. *How could you forget about that?* I pushed the negative thought away. I put the cookie sheet on top of the stove, smiling to myself, waiting for her reaction. Chocolate chip were her favorites.

"Cookies!" she exclaimed, sounding very much as she had when she was ten. Her eyes fell on me. "Oh, hi." It was as though a mask had dropped over her face.

"Hi," I said, trying to sound cheerful in spite of my disappointment. She hated me. *She doesn't hate you; she's a teenager and doesn't know how to act around you just now.*

"Give me a hug?" I held out my arms. She leaned her crutches against the counter, limping toward me as if walking to the gallows. "Oh, this feels nice." I squeezed her hard. "You smell good. New perfume?"

She shrugged as she stepped out of my embrace. "Can I have some cookies?" Her voice was flat, almost as if she were trying to keep any enthusiasm from her tone.

She hates you. You've been a rotten mothe—STOP! I was not going to let myself fall into that trap. I took a deep breath. "You'd *better* have some cookies. I made them especially for you." I could see the crinkle at the corner of her eye as she poured herself a glass of skim milk. If she was pleased with my gesture, she wasn't going to let me know. With the spatula I transferred two very warm cookies to a plate. "Careful, don't burn your tongue."

"Mo-om," she said in two syllables, reminding me she didn't need the reminder. "Ouch!" She grabbed the milk and took a big swallow. Even she couldn't suppress the sheepish grin that followed. "They're good." She blew on her cookie, then took another bite.

I poured myself a glass of milk, pulled a cookie onto a napkin, and sat across from her. "Tell me about your week."

I was answered with the teenage shrug. The move that said everything and nothing in one giant lift of the shoulder. "It was fine."

"How's Jen?" My question was met with a level stare. Whatever that meant. "Mike?"

"Okay." She took a bite of cookie. "He might lose his job." It was as if Emily wanted to talk and yet the words wouldn't come.

"Really? Why?"

"The radio station might close."

Oh. Bob hadn't told me about that. But then I guessed he'd had more on his mind this past week. A problem wife was probably more pressing than a problem loan.

"What about you and Rick? You two still hangin' out?" I hoped that was the right term these days. I never could distinguish what the difference was between "going out," "hanging out," or what we used to call "going steady." According to Emily, the difference was *huge*. I hoped I'd chosen the right term this time.

"Sure," she answered, downing the last drops of milk. "Why wouldn't we?"

If she could answer with a shrug, so could I. I lifted one shoulder. There. She could interpret that however she wanted. "Any plans for the weekend?"

She picked up her empty glass and tilted it to her mouth. "Probably just hanging out with Rick. Watch some movies, or something."

Not much had changed in a week.

"Sounds fun," I said, getting up and rinsing our glasses in the sink. Nothing I couldn't handle without Bob.

See? You're fine. Life isn't so hard, is it?

Emily pushed her chair away from the table. "I'm going to go do my homework." She hopped on one foot over to her backpack lying by the door. She swung it over her shoulder, then tucked her crutches under her arms. The maneuver didn't look easy. She made her way to the doorway and paused. "Thanks for the cookies," she said without turning around.

"You're welcome." A warm glow filled my chest as I stacked the cookies I'd baked into a Tupperware container. It was so good to be home. So good to talk to Emily again—if you could call what just happened "talking." I squirted a drop of dishwashing liquid onto each cookie sheet, quickly scrubbing the crumbs away with a stream of hot water. The awkwardness between us would pass. I'd been gone a week. To a teenager that could feel like a whole lifetime.

In many ways I had been gone a whole lifetime. *What if you can't cope here at home? What if Emily—?* Quickly I dried my hands and grabbed a tablet of paper lying near the phone.

Worry List, I wrote at the top.

1. Coping.

2. Emily.

3. Bob gone for the weekend.

I looked at my watch. It was almost four. An hour past the worry time I'd picked at the hospital. Should I wait until tomorrow? What if I couldn't wait that long? What if—*STOP!* Good grief. Here I was worrying about worrying.

No time like the present. I tore the paper from the pad and went into the living room, settling into my favorite chair.

Gentlewoman, start your engine...

Within ten minutes I'd exhausted myself. Worrying on command was hard. A waste of time if ever there was one. I wasn't accomplishing anything but trying to wrap my brain around nonexistent problems. I could almost hear Jamie say, "Bingo." I could almost hear Krista say, "I like to turn my worries into a prayer. Then let them go."

Krista's method seemed a lot more effective. I picked up the Bible lying by my elbow and thumbed to the Twenty-third Psalm. Perfect. "The Lord is my shepherd...He restoreth my soul...though I walk through the valley—" A quick beat of my heart. God knew, I'd been through the valley. The good thing about being in a valley was that I had nowhere to go but up.

Unless you fall into a hole. The thumping began again, harder than ever. What if I couldn't handle being at home? What if—?

I will fear no evil. Thou art with me.

Oh, how badly I hoped He was.

Emily

"Be home by midnight." I mimicked my mom's parting phrase as I backed out of the driveway. I'd spent a whole week without her warnings and somehow survived. Amazing. I rolled my eyes as I scowled into the rearview mirror.

I expected more of an argument when I suggested leaving my crutches at home this morning. All Mom said was, "Use them today, and I'll call Dr. West and see what she says." Dr. West said I could start walking on my right foot as long as I was careful. Without my crutches I felt free! I was going to celebrate tonight with Rick or without him. I hoped it was *with*.

I turned my old silver Taurus onto Main Street. I was too early to go to Jason's party, but I needed to leave the house early so Mom would think I was watching movies at Rick's.

"Is Rick coming over tonight?" she'd asked as I'd poked at the meatloaf she made for supper. Dad had left for his overnight meeting before I got home from school.

"Umm, I'm not sure yet." It wasn't exactly a lie. I wasn't sure what Rick's plans were. I'd barely talked to him all week, and when I mentioned Jason's party, Rick had said he might have to help his dad with calving. Farm life was something I didn't quite understand, so I had to take his word for it. He said he'd let me know, but he hadn't. I had good reason to be a bad mood on wheels.

I'd waited for Rick to stop me in the hall or call me to make plans for tonight. The longer I'd waited, the madder I got. Forget him! I wasn't going to spend the night alone and depressed, crying along with my Norah Jones CD. I'd dressed carefully in my new blue jeans and white cotton shirt. I'd curled my hair, too. If Rick did decide to come to town, I wanted to make sure I looked my best. The pair of shoes I was wearing had heels higher than I was sure Dr. West would approve, but Dr. West wasn't going to be at the party tonight.

Three cars in a row came toward me on Main. I honked at all three, easily recognizing Mike's green pickup and Scott Dosch's old Chevy. I wasn't sure who was in the third vehicle, but I didn't want anyone to think I was stuck-up. I only hoped they didn't think I was a big loser for driving around alone. I headed for the end of Main, ready to make a U-turn and drive the well-traveled route again.

A pair of headlights flashed in my rearview mirror—the Brewster teen's universal sign to pull over and talk. I turned off of Main, drove halfway down the block, and glided to the curb. I could see Mike's truck follow me and then pull alongside my car. I rolled down my window. The cold March air blasted into the car. We weren't going to be talking too long in this weather. I turned the heater fan on high as the electric window on the passenger side of Mike's vehicle slid down.

"Hey!" As usual, his grin was warm. "Are you alone? Want to ride with me?"

I had at least an hour to kill until I dared to show up at Jason's alone. The party would be well underway by then, and I hoped to sneak in without anyone making a big deal about it. I didn't usually go to Jason's parties; they were the stuff of too many Monday morning whispered gab sessions in the halls at school. But if Rick did come to town, I knew he'd head to his football buddy's house. I was not about to let Jen get her hands on him. Mike stayed away from Jason's parties, too. Driving around with Mike would be an easy way to waste an hour. I'd tell him I was going to go home and watch movies with my mom, and then I'd head to Jason's by myself.

"Sure!" I rolled up the window, turned off the car and hopped out. Ouch! Without the crutches as a reminder, I'd forgotten about my foot. I limped the few steps to Mike's pickup.

"You look great!" he said as he shifted into gear.

I wondered how he could tell what I looked like with my heavy coat on. Still, the compliment felt nice.

"How's your mom?" Mike asked whipping his pickup around the corner, heading back to the main drag.

Mike had been the only person I'd told that she'd been in the hospital for depression, but I knew the Brewster grapevine must have been having a field day. "Why? What are people saying?"

"That your mom is in an anorexic clinic in Minnesota." At least I could count on Mike to be honest.

"Oh, for stupid." I looked out the side window as the familiar Main Street of Brewster passed by. "She got home yesterday."

"That's good. She's better then?"

"She made chocolate chip cookies." As if that was proof of anything. I was too ashamed to tell Mike that I'd hardly talked to my mom since she got home. Every time I looked at her I was reminded that my problems had sent her to the hospital. I wanted so badly to apologize, to tell her I was sorry about sneaking out, causing her to distrust me. Sorry for all the times I'd talked back, sorry I hadn't mentioned my foot problems earlier and had to drop out of basketball. My mom lived for my games. I knew the growth on my arm hadn't been any fault of mine, but somehow I felt like it was. I wanted to tell her, too, about how things were with Rick and me. How I was afraid I was losing my boyfriend. How I was scared to be with him and scared not to be, too. But how could I tell my mom any of those things when I hadn't talked to her in months? Tears filled my eyes as I stared out the side window into the night. How had my life gotten so crummy so fast?

Blurry blocks of houses slid by as Mike took a detour off of the highway through Brewster. He wove through the side streets, slowly working his way back and forth through the grid that was our town.

"Guess I might as well tell you my news." Mike spoke into the silence. I hadn't noticed how quiet he'd gotten. It wasn't like Mike to be silent for so long.

"What?" I blinked rapidly before I turned his way.

"At work tonight Ruthie told me she's definitely closing the station in a couple weeks. I'll be out of a job."

Mike could join the crummy-life club, too. "What'll you do?" I knew Mike needed a job to make his pickup payments.

A grin spread across Mike's face. "With this gift of gab?" He pointed a thumb to his chest. "I'll talk myself into something. Until then?" He put both hands on the wheel. "Trust." His voice held no doubt. I knew he meant trust in God.

I wished I had even a fraction of the confidence in God that Mike had. God and I hadn't had much to say to each other lately. Well...*I* hadn't had much to say, and if God had been talking, I hadn't been listening. I knew I should be praying more, reading the Bible, and all that stuff. But when it came to holding on to Rick, just praying and reading wouldn't do it. Tonight I wasn't leaving anything to trust. I was going to make sure, all by myself, that Rick would still be my boyfriend tomorrow.

"Do you want to stop by Hannah's? She said she was going to have some kids over to play Taboo."

A knife-point of worry began to twist in my stomach. I looked at my watch. Only a half-hour had passed since I'd jumped in the pickup with Mike, but what if Rick was already at Jason's? I knew Jen wouldn't waste any time moving in on him if I wasn't there to tell her to back off. "I should get home," I said.

"Okay." Mike did a U-turn around the gas pumps at Kenny Pearson's gas station. "Say 'hi' to your mom," he said when he pulled up beside my car.

I put my fingers on the door handle. "Are you going to Hannah's now?" All I'd need was for Mike to see my car parked at Jason's. Already my lie was beginning to rub.

"Yeah. I guess so. Nothing much else to do." One side of his mouth turned up. "Unless you want to change your mind about going home?" Mike didn't give up.

I shook my head. "I'd better go. Have fun."

"You, too."

I drove around the side streets of Brewster for another fifteen minutes. Part of me really did want to go home and be with my mom, to make the lie I'd told Mike come true. I wanted to sit beside her on the couch and let her lightly tickle my arm while I talked to her about all the things that were making my life so awful these days. Talking to her had been my comfort when I was ten. She'd had a way of making everything seem better. What had happened? Had she changed? Or had I? I didn't need to look too deep to know the answer to that.

I punched at the buttons on the radio. The sappy song that was playing was just what I didn't need to hear. There. The loud thumping of a bass guitar filled the car, fueling the part of me that was trying to get up the nerve to go to Jason's by myself. Even as I pulled to the curb, wedging my car into the line of vehicles near the end of Jason's block, I knew I should pull out of this space and drive home. The only good thing that could happen at Jason's would be if Rick would show up, realize what a jerk he'd been to me all week, and apologize and promise his undying love.

Yeah, and you're Britney Spears. Dream on.

I took a deep breath and jumped out of the car before I could change my mind. Ouch! My stupid foot. Why had I worn these shoes with high heels?

Because you wanted to look cool.

Oh, yeah. I turned and quickly threw my bulky jacket back into the car. I'd rather be cold than uncool. I limped down the sidewalk, feeling the music pulsating from Jason's house. Did his parents let him play his stereo that loud all the time?

Duh, his parents aren't home.

Go home, Emily.

I stopped at the turn in the sidewalk leading to Jason's. It wasn't too late to go back to my car. No one had seen me. I wouldn't look like I was running scared. If I didn't go home, I could always stop at Hannah's. I knew her group of friends would welcome me even at this time of night. Through the front window of the house I could see a mass of bodies crowding the room. Some were moving as if trying to dance, some were trying to simply move through the crowd, holding beer bottles high in the air. I wondered if Rick was inside. I hadn't seen his car, but then I hadn't really looked. Maybe I was afraid to know for sure if he'd come here without me.

This is nothing but trouble. Go home, Emily.

I wrapped my arms around myself. I was cold out there without a coat. I should just go home. But what if Rick was in there? What if Jen was smiling up at him, laughing at whatever he said as if it were the funniest thing she'd ever heard? I couldn't go home. I had to go in there and make sure Jen wasn't stealing my boyfriend. I took one step toward the door and stopped. A rock settled in the bottom of my stomach.

Don't go in.

I had to.

No. Go home.

"Hey, gorgeous." An arm wrapped around my shoulder. I jumped. I hadn't heard a car door slam, hadn't heard anyone crunching on the light layer of snow behind me. "Need a date for the party?"

The voice was familiar—and not, all at the same time. The warmth of his arm was welcome. I turned my head. "Pete?"

"Emily?" His arm dropped from my shoulder. "What are you doing here?"

"It's a party," I said, as if that explained it. As if I came to these kinds of parties by myself all the time. I could have asked him the same question. Pete West's mom was my doctor. Pete had been one of my brother's best friends in junior high. He practically lived at our house until he started messing with drugs. He was way too old to be at a party full of high school kids. He had to be Brian's age at least. Twenty? Twenty-one? I saw the case of beer he had tucked under one arm. Make that twenty-one.

"You've grown up." Pete's arm was around me again, pulling me along with him toward the door. "Nicely, I might add."

At one time I'd thought of Pete as an extension of our family. Almost like another older brother. But I knew he wasn't. His words felt creepy and delicious all at the same time. Maybe if Rick were here and saw me walk in with Pete, he'd see that I wasn't going to mope, waiting for him to come around. There were other guys on this earth besides Rick. I pushed my chin forward. I'd walk in with Pete and check out who was here. If Rick wasn't, I'd slip out quickly.

Don't go in.

I hesitated in the doorway until Pete pulled me inside. A couple of the senior guys quickly took the beer from under his arm, pushing a fistful of money into his hand. The fact that what he'd done was illegal didn't seem to faze Pete one bit.

"Here." Pete handed me a beer, one of the two he'd somehow grabbed as part of his payment.

I held the cold can as if it were diseased. If anyone reported me holding this, I could lose all of the awards I'd earned at school this year. Even though I hadn't been able to play basketball for much of the season, I was still eligible for a letter award. I'd be getting one for volleyball, too, and for playing piano for the choir. I looked around for a place to discretely set the can down, but couldn't find a spot that wasn't already filled with people or empty cans. So, I'd hold it. Holding it didn't mean I was drinking.

"Come on." Pete grabbed my free hand, maneuvering me through the mash of kids. It didn't look as though I had to worry about anyone reporting me for drinking; everyone here had a big head start on me. A few kids said hi, and a few looked surprised to see me. Mindy, Jen's new friend, looked the other way when I walked by, pretending to be totally engrossed in some geeky-looking guy from Flander that I knew she'd never spend two seconds talking to if she hadn't spotted me coming her way.

My eyes searched the noisy crowd. If Mindy were here, Jen couldn't be far away. I stood on my tiptoes, trying to see into the corners of the room. I couldn't see Jen or Rick.

You should have gone home.

Pete stopped in the middle of the room, talking to some kids from school that I knew were younger than me. I looked toward the front door, wondering if I could get back and get out. I saw Pete reach into his pocket and pull out a small plastic bag. Money changed hands as one of the kids took the bag. Someone blew a puff of smoke into my face. Phew! I turned my head, trying to breath clean air. Everything I'd ever learned about secondhand smoke tumbled around in my brain. The loud music and crush of people suddenly seemed more oppressing than exciting. I just wanted to get out. Again, I glanced toward the door.

My heart stopped and then pounded. Look who just walked in. Rick and Jen. Together. No wonder Mindy hadn't dared to look me in the eye. She knew they were off somewhere together. I lifted the beer to my mouth and took a long swallow, suddenly wanting nothing more than to have Rick see me with my accidental date, Pete. I turned my back. Let Rick be just as surprised to see me as I had been to see him. I was already practicing the nonchalant look of surprise I'd give him when our eyes met. *See? I've got someone else, too.* Let's see how he'd like it.

I took another swallow and then another. Courage in a can. Pretending Rick wasn't here was hard when the corners of my eyes tracked his every move. Pete moved me around the room almost as if he knew enough to keep his distance from Rick. I finished the can of beer, letting Pete replace it with another wet can. Someone bumped me from behind as I lifted it for the first swallow, spilling beer all over my white shirt and down my new jeans. I gulped at what was left. I'd hardly eaten anything for supper, worrying if Rick would call and wondering what I'd tell my mom so I could get out of the house without explaining why Rick wasn't picking me up. The cold beer was filling an emptiness I felt, and not just in my stomach. I watched Rick bend to hear something Jen was saying to him and watched his eyes casually dance across the room. I knew they'd land on me before long. I took a long swallow, tossed back my head, and laughed loudly at whatever it was Pete had just said. I wanted to make sure if Rick was noticing, he'd have no doubt I was having a great time. Without him.

"Having a good time?" Pete leaned over and smiled near my lips. Was he going to kiss me? Right here?

"Um-hmm," I said, lifting the beer between us, forcing him back a little bit.

"Here. You've got—" Pete leaned in again and with his thumb dabbed at a drop of beer that hung on the edge of my lip. He licked the bead from his thumb. He was so close he was fuzzy, like some romantic movie scene. I hoped Rick was watching.

The music that had been pounding through the room switched to something slow and dreamy. Pete wrapped his arms around me, pressing his cold can of beer near the top of my belt loops. I laid my head on his shoulder and closed my eyes. Whoa! The room tilted slightly. I stumbled.

"Hey, careful." Pete held me up. I lifted my head to look into his eyes. He leaned towards me. I closed my eyes, lifting my chin, picturing Rick watching from across the room. "Come on." Pete took my hand and wove his way through the crowd into the empty kitchen. He backed me up against the counter by the sink and stood in front of me, one leg on either side of my legs as if to keep me upright. I didn't need the assistance; I knew perfectly well what I was doing. Getting back at Rick.

"Now," he took the beer can out of my hand and put it on the counter, placing his there, too. "Let's try this again." He put his hands on either side of my waist, leaning toward me. I knew better than to shut my eyes; my world was already spinning enough. His kiss was soft. "There." He pulled back. "How was that?"

I grinned, goofy like. Nodded. I couldn't help it. No wonder they said revenge was sweet. So what if Rick was here with Jen? I had someone new, too. Pete reached into the pocket of his jeans and pulled out a small plastic bag. I could see an assortment of pills inside. Part of my brain wondered if he'd gotten them from his mom. She was a doctor—my doctor. But I knew better.

Pete opened the bag, reached in and pulled out a few of the multicolored tablets and capsules, cupping them in the palm of his hand as if they were a gift. "Want one?"

I hesitated. This whole night was feeling like some kind of weird dream. It was scary and forbidden and secretly thrilling. What would one little pill hurt? I stuck out my finger, pushing the tablets around in Pete's palm as though they were tiny, misshapen marbles. They were pretty.

"Go on, take one," Pete urged. He picked a blue one up and tossed it into his mouth, swallowing it down with a gulp of beer. "It's okay." He held the pills closer to me. "You'll feel good."

I picked up a pink tablet, turning it between my fingers as though I could see the magic it held.

Leave! Now!

I wished that stupid voice that sounded so much like my mother would be quiet. I examined the pill some more and picked up a yellow one.

What are you doing? Remember your brother and the mess he got in from huffing? Are you an idiot? Drop it. Now!

I'd almost forgotten. How devastated my parents had been. How mad I'd been at Brian for causing so much trouble and heartache in our family. How stupid I'd thought he was to do something so dumb. I dropped the yellow pill back into Pete's hand. I had enough sense to shake my head and say no.

"Whatever." Pete closed his fist on the pills, leaning forward to kiss me again. I had a sudden image of my brother. The way he'd looked when he was home for Christmas. Like some kind of guy model for American Eagle. Not like some college dropout pushing drugs to high school kids.

I turned my head. Pete's kiss landed on my cheek. "I need to go home." I felt sick. Was it the beer? Or simply sick of who I'd become these past months?

"It's early." Pete's whisper near my ear was no longer thrilling. His breath was damp, filled with beer and smoke. "I really like you." He inched closer, pinning me against the kitchen counter. He placed his finger on the side of my cheek and turned my face to his. He smiled. "Brian's little sister." As if I needed the reminder. "Not so little anymore."

No, I wasn't. I was big enough to know this wasn't what I wanted. "Please move." I could hear the slight note of panic in my voice. I had to get out of here, to get home, away from this place I should have never come to in the first place. I put my hands on Pete's chest, pressing him back. "Please?" Why was I being so polite? As if manners mattered to someone like Pete. "Move."

He leaned closer. "You're so pretty."

"You heard her." Rick's voice was a growl. I hadn't heard him come into the kitchen, but there he was. In one swift motion he shoved Pete away from me. The pills that had been in Pete's hand went flying across the floor as he scrambled for footing.

"Hey man, chill." Pete tapped at the air with both hands, his eyes darting around the floor, spotting his contraband.

Rick took a step toward him and pushed him again. "Stay away."

"No problem." Pete kept one eye on Rick as he bent to retrieve his loot. So much for really liking me.

Rick wrapped his thick fingers around my upper arm. Tight. Too tight. "What do you think you're doing?" He pulled me roughly toward him, then pushed me away. My back hit the counter. He grabbed my arm again and yanked me toward the back door. The too-high heels on my shoes slowed me down. I couldn't keep pace with Rick when he was fueled by fury. His hold on my arm tightened even more as he half-dragged me out the door. He pulled me down the three back steps. Ouch! An ice patch sent my sore foot flying askew.

I screamed, not sure which hurt more, my foot, my arm, or the way I was being treated. "Let go of me!"

"I'll let go when I'm ready to let go." Rick threw my arm away from him as though it were a baseball and this were a game.

I lost my balance and fell to the ground. Rick reached for me again. I cowered, listening to the sleeve of my shirt ripping from the force of Rick's grasp as he tried to pull me up. Damp snow soaked into the knees of my jeans as I kneeled on all fours, debating the wisdom of getting up.

Oh Lord. I prayed into the ground. *Please help me.*

"Get up!" Rick was standing over me, hands on his hips.

Help me, please!

He took a deep, deep breath, blowing loudly into the cold night. His voice was lower now, more threatening. "Get up, Emily."

I was scared. I shook my head, leaning back onto the heels of my feet, unsure of whether I should stand. Or if I could. Tears came as my foot throbbed from the pressure of my body. Tears of pain and disillusionment over this sorry night. My sorry life.

"I said 'Get up!'" Rick bent toward me.

"Don't...touch...her." Mike's command stopped Rick's hand in midair. Mike pushed open the back door of the house and took the three steps down in one big leap.

Mike was almost as tall as Rick but thirty pounds lighter, maybe more. His scrawny frame was no match for Rick's athletic shoulders. If there was going to be a fight, Mike wouldn't win. But Mike didn't seem to care. "Back off," he said, moving closer, his tone leaving no doubt he meant it.

"Get out of here, Anderson." Rick glared at Mike. "This is between Emily and me. Get lost." He reached for me again.

"I said, 'Don't touch her.'" Mike put his arm out, stopping Rick's hand in its track toward me. Rick slapped at his arm.

Mike's down jacket absorbed most of the blow. "Yeah, that's better, if you're gonna pick on someone it might as well be someone who will fight back." Rick shoved at Mike with both hands. Mike hardly moved an inch. "Go ahead, use *me* for your punching bag, Wynn. Pretend I'm Hannah or Emily. Hit me instead." If Mike wasn't careful, he'd be down on the ground with me. Rick shoved at him again. Mike shoved back. He was stronger than he looked. Rick took two steps back. Mike pushed him again. "How's it feel to get pushed around? You like that?"

A low growl began in Rick's throat. He drew back his right hand and threw a punch straight at Mike's jaw. Apparently Mike had been anticipating the move. He ducked at the last second, bending and thrusting his shoulder smack into Rick's stomach. They both went sprawling onto the snow-covered ground.

"Fight! Fight!" In a matter of seconds the house emptied. The backyard was filled with kids. Rick had flipped Mike over onto his back. He reared his right fist back, then threw his shoulder along with the blow, hard into Mike's face. Mike groaned as blood spurted from his nose. Mike twisted away from the second punch, using Rick's changing balance to slide out from under him. Mike leaped to his feet and threw his coat on the ground. He backed up, back bent forward, arms curved, ready at his side as if this was a championship wrestling match. With a roar, Rick charged at him like a bull. Mike sidestepped, Rick went flying into the crowd. Kids laughed as they pushed Rick back into the circle.

"You're dead, Anderson." Rick faced Mike, shifting his weight from foot to foot, planning his attack.

I looked at Mike, his hair sticking out from his head at crazy angles, his nose dripping blood onto his denim shirt. And yet he was still standing, ready to take the punishment that might have been mine. How could he offer himself up for this kind of beating?

All of a sudden I felt as if I'd been wearing sunglasses at night. The past months with Rick seemed pitiful compared to what Mike was doing for me.

"Get him, Mike!" I jumped to my feet, balancing on my good foot.

At the sound of my voice, Rick looked my way. His puzzlement at my cheer quickly turned to anger. Mike used the diversion to land a punch to Rick's lower jaw. Rick's head jerked to the side, but he quickly threw another punch at Mike, tripped him as he staggered back, then jumped on him as he fell to the ground.

"The cop!" Almost as fast as the house had emptied at the news of a fight in the backyard, the yard now emptied as kids dropped their beer cans and ran to their cars. Watching a fight wasn't illegal, but a minor in possession was.

Rick scrambled to his feet. "You'd better watch it, Anderson." His words were tough, but they were tinged with the sound of defeat of a different kind. He disappeared into the alley without even a glance back at me.

Mike lay on the ground, breathing heavily.

"Are you okay?" I asked, limping over to him.

"Oh, yeah. I was just thinking of making a snow angel as long as I was down here." Except for his messy hair, his torn shirt and all the blood, he looked really cute.

I stuck out my hand. "We probably should get out of here." Beer cans littered the snow-covered lawn. If Brewster's crabby cop really was on his way, we needed to leave.

Mike grabbed my hand and sat up.

"Oh man," he groaned. He blinked his eyes, wincing as he gingerly touched his nose. "World Federation Wrestling has to be easier than this." He pushed himself off the ground. He stood for a moment, looking himself over as if checking for damage. "I think I'll live. Are you okay?"

I nodded. "My foot really hurts. I can hardly walk on—"

A flashlight beam blinded me as Brewster's only full-time policeman stepped through the back door. "You kids stay right there."

Libby

Something was wrong. I could feel it.

I closed the book I'd been trying to read for the last hour and glanced at the clock on top of the piano. I didn't expect Emily home for at least another hour. I ran through my usual list of uneasy worries. Brian at college. Bob at his planning meeting. Emily was the only unknown.

She'd left alone—an odd occurrence as of late. Rick had replaced Jen or Mike as her usual sidekick. I sighed, trying to imagine Emily watching movies at Rick's house on the farm. I'd never been out there, so I couldn't get a mental picture of where she was. Even if they hadn't stayed at his house, Rick was big and strong. If they'd gotten stuck in a snowbank, he'd more than likely be able to push them out. But she had left alone, her plans vague at best. Something was wrong. Mother's intuition.

Write it down.

How could I write something down when I didn't even know what it was? And besides, my worry time wasn't for another sixteen hours. Anything I had to worry about would be over by then.

That's the point. Worry won't change anything.

I wished Bob were with me. If nothing else, he could listen to my fears. Just saying them out loud helped sometimes. More often than not my fears sounded foolish when put into sentences. I thought of Krista's wise words in the hospital, "I turn my worry into a prayer, then let it go."

Well, that I could do. I bowed my head, trying to articulate to God what I couldn't to myself. *Lord, something doesn't feel right. If anyone in my family needs You right now, be there. Protect them. Give them safety in Your arms. Be especially with Emily, with her friends. Teenagers are so vulnerable—*

My mind started drifting to all the trouble that lay outside these four walls. Drinking. Sex. Drugs. Accident—*STOP!*

Okay, Lord, You can have these worries, too. I give them to You. I opened my hands on my lap, letting the palms of my hands release my fears to God. I sat in silence, the hum of the refrigerator in the other room a comforting friend. Everything was all right for now.

I opened my book, searching for the place where I'd left off. No, not there. There, either. Obviously my mind had been wandering for sometime. I turned back a couple pages to catch up with the story.

Again, the nagging unease. Why hadn't I insisted Bob stay home with me tonight? I'd only been out of the hospital one day. *One day!* What had I been thinking to volunteer so quickly to let him go to his meeting, leaving me alone to deal with whatever Emily concocted tonight?

I can't do this. I paced the floor, the thumping of my heart a steady backbeat to my escalating worry. *What if I lose it? What if I end up back in the hospital? Why was I so stupid to think I could—STOP!*

I literally stopped in my tracks. I was doing this to myself. For all I knew, nothing was wrong. Everyone and everything was probably fine. I took a calming breath, re-languaging my thoughts. *You're okay. You aren't losing it. You are simply wondering where Emily is at and who she's with. Every mother worries about that. You are home from the hospital because Dr. Sullivan knows you are able to handle things. You are fine, Libby. You are just fine.*

The pep talk did its magic. I sat back down in my chair, determined to read at least one chapter before I let my mind roam the world again. "*You* are Lord," I whispered, reminding myself He knew where Emily was even when I didn't.

Bare seconds had passed before I heard the outside door leading into the garage slam shut the way it always sounded when Emily was on her way in. Ah, a feeling of relief spread through me. This had been the cause of my angst. I could relax now. A quick glance at the clock told me not much must have been going on in Brewster tonight. She had at least a half hour before I expected her home. "Thank You, Lord," I said out loud.

More than one pair of feet made their way up the three steps leading to the kitchen door. No doubt Rick was walking her in. That was sweet. I guessed a goodnight kiss might be part of the evening, but I walked into the kitchen anyway. I wanted to see this child I'd worried about so much tonight as soon as I could. I stopped in the doorway, waiting for Emily to come inside.

Without a pause on the steps, the kitchen door opened and Mike stepped in. Emily stood behind him. Before I even had time to gasp at their ragged appearance, Mike held up one hand as though he were a traffic cop and said, "We're fine. We might not look like it, but we're okay." He turned to Emily, bending his shoulder down so she could put her arm around his neck and hop into the house. "Well, except for Emily's foot," he explained. "She can't really walk on it at all."

I was speechless as I took in the two bedraggled young people standing in my kitchen. Mike was covered with blood from his nose down. His hair stood up in clumps that might have been fashionable on a stage at a rock concert but not in my kitchen. A couple buttons had been ripped from his shirt and it hung open in a way that looked nothing but chilly for an early March night.

Except for the absence of blood, Emily didn't look much better. Her carefully fixed hair was a mess. Mascara rimmed her eyes in a bad imitation of Tammy Faye Bakker. If she had other makeup on earlier, it wasn't there now. Emily's eyes met mine. Fat tears formed a puddle in her eyes and began a slow crawl down her face.

My heart began to pound as the realization of what might have happened to Emily dawned. A car accident? Rape? *NO! STOP!* I couldn't even think about that.

I can't do this. I can't handle it. I can't. My heart hammered in my chest as panic rose like a flood from a burst dam. A numb, ringing sensation filled my ears. *I can't handle this.*

I needed Bob here. Right now. Whatever had happened, I couldn't do this alone. I would snap. I'd end up back in the hospital.

Why had Dr. Sullivan let me come home? I wasn't capable of handling this alone. I wasn't. I—

You aren't alone. I am here with you.

The thought was like one of those tiny bandages I'd sometimes used to comfort Emily when she had a paper cut on one of her little fingers. Hardly big enough to wrap around even the tiniest of pinkies, but balm all the same.

I was shaking. *You can do this, Olivia. You can.*

"Your new blouse," I said. Strange words to pick to comfort my daughter. I held out my trembling arms and took a step forward. Two steps. With Mike's help Emily limped into my arms as I walked into hers. "What happened?"

She cried then—sobbed. My tears fell along with hers, crying only because my daughter was. If she hurt, so did I. Over Emily's shoulder I looked at Mike, waiting for one of them to tell me what happened. Mike looked to the floor, swiping at his eyes with the back of his blood-spattered hand.

"I'm sorry, Mom. I'm sor-ry." Her head was still buried in my shoulder. Her apology a mystery to me.

"It's okay," I said, patting her back, rubbing it hard, as if I could push away the pain.

I let her cry as my mind went on a journey, imagining every terrible thing a mother can conjure up in a matter of seconds. Fear of the unknown circled overhead, waiting to drop. My personal fears rose to join the flight pattern. *What if Emily tells me she was raped? I'll fall apart. I know I will. I'm too fragile emotionally to offer her support. I'll fail her. I can't do this. I can't.*

You can. I am with you. I am your strength. Trust Me.

I closed my eyes, took a calming breath, and put my hands on Emily's shoulders. One shoulder was covered with her shirt, the other side had been ripped away. I saw four finger-sized black and blue marks streaking her upper arm like faded tattoos. A shudder of cold fear filled me. I didn't want to hear whatever was coming, but I had to.

I am with you.

I moved my hands to her face, cupping her cheeks in my palms. Her eyes were inches from mine. "What happened?"

She poured out her heart then. Tears and words. First, the story of the night. Rick going off with Jen. The party at Jason's. The beer Emily had downed in an attempt to show Rick she was cool.

I knew better. It had been an attempt to drown hurt feelings.

Pete West had come along—Brian's old friend, someone Emily should have been able to trust. Instead of being trustworthy, he'd offered her pills.

Pills! I wanted to scream, to shake the kid who would offer something so lethal to my child. Instead, Mike and I helped Emily into a kitchen chair. I sat knee-to-knee with her, holding her hands as she told the rest. How Rick had walked in on Pete and her together, how Rick had pushed Pete and pulled Emily outside, torn her shirt, and tossed her on the ground like garbage.

No! My insides cringed at the thought of Emily being treated that way.

"It's not the first time he's done that, either." Mike had joined our circle of safety. Pulling a chair near us, he added his version of the story. "That's why Hannah broke up with Rick. He treated her that way, too." Mike looked at Emily. "Remember? I tried to tell you. That's why—" He stopped, glanced to the floor, then back at Emily. "That's why I always tried to kind of hang around where you and Rick were. That's why I showed up at Jason's tonight." He looked to me. "Rick's bad news when it comes to girls."

"Thank you, Mike." I laid my hand on his. Squeezed hard.

"Ouch!" Instinctively, Mike pulled his hand into his chest. "Man, that hurt. That's the hand I punched Rick with."

Once again I looked over these two tattered young people. Children who had turned into young adults in a night.

I am with them. I am with you. Always.

I'd heard the words…Emily's and Mike's. I hadn't fallen apart. In some way I felt stronger, as if I had in some way taken on their pain and been fortified by the listening. I sat up straight. Was that the way God got His strength? By taking on our hurt? Our pain?

I felt an unfamiliar sort of warmth filling my body. I could do this. With God's help I could do it. I leaned forward and hugged Emily as I put my hand on Mike's knee and held it like a prayer. "Okay." I sat back, putting both of my hands on the tops of Emily's knees. I knew what I had to do next. "I'm going to take you to the hospital."

Emily nodded as if it was someplace she already knew she needed to be. Mike chimed in, "I'll ride along."

I tapped his chin with my finger as I stood up. "You need to get checked out as much as Emily. I wouldn't be surprised if your hand was broken. Your nose, too." I pushed my chair under the table, feeling stronger by the second. "I'm going to go get Emily's crutches. You call your folks and tell them to meet us at the hospital."

~

"Too bad I can't give you a three-for-one special." Ellen West was the physician on call for the weekend and had come into the large emergency area located at the rear of the Brewster hospital. Emily and Mike, cleaned up now, were propped on side-by-side examining tables. They had yanked back the dividing curtain between the two examining areas as quickly as a nurse had pulled it forward. Emily and Mike had been through too much tonight to be separated now.

Dr. West tucked three X-rays onto a panel hanging along the wall. She flipped a switch, illuminating the bones as if they were a feature film. Tonight they were. "I'm going to have to wait for the radiologist to read these for the final report, but Emily, it looks to me like that foot is broken for sure this time. And Mr. Mike..." She looked at his mom, then back to the X-ray. "You're the lucky one tonight. A broken nose *and* a bone in your hand. You really hit the jackpot."

Mike grinned. "My pleasure." His mom rolled her eyes, but smiled. Mike's gift of gab had already saved Emily and Mike from a ride home in Brewster's only squad car. He'd somehow convinced Eddie, our local Andy of Mayberry under his gruff exterior, that he'd been defending Emily from an angry boyfriend. Most likely Eddie had heard enough stories in his twenty-five years patrolling these streets to let them off with a warning to get home.

I drove them to the hospital, leaving Mike's pickup parked in our driveway. Emily's car was still at Jason's. We could get things back where they belonged another day. Right now, all I wanted was to tuck my precious child into bed.

Dr. West applied a dab of salve to a small cut under Mike's eye. "I'm surprised Pete wasn't in on any of this," she muttered to me. "He's got a knack for this sort of thing."

Emily, Mike, and I exchanged quiet looks. I would have a private conversation with Ellen later. Mom to mom. Tonight held enough heartache already.

"All patched up." Dr. West tossed the last of the bandage wrappings away. "Time to call it a night."

Emily smiled at Mike as she maneuvered down the hospital corridor on crutches and a blue cast. "Thanks," she said to him in the understatement of the year.

"The least I could do for the Snow Princess," Mike said. He waved his hand, encased in matching Badger blue, in an elaborate gesture, turning it into a deep bow. "Oww," he said, standing up quickly, fingering the butterfly bandage across his nose. He smiled at Emily. "It was worth a headache."

"See you tomorrow." It wasn't a question.

"You bet." Mike saluted, clunking himself in the head with his cast. "Oh, great. I suppose I'll give myself a concussion next."

Relief mixed with laughter as I tousled Mike's hair. "Come over for supper tomorrow night." I nodded at his broken right hand. "We'll spoon-feed you if we have to." It was the least I could do.

⌒

I followed Emily up the stairs to her bedroom, ready to catch her if she wobbled backward on her crutches. We were both tired. "I'm going to get my pajamas on. I'll come say goodnight," I told her as she went into her room.

"Okay," she said, her voice raspy. How well I knew how tears could do that.

⁓

She was lying on her back, looking at the kitten poster that had hung on her ceiling for years. "I should have Brian take that down," she said.

I sat on the edge of her bed and stroked her hair. Tonight had pushed her way past kitten posters. "I'll ask him next time he's home." I dug my fingers deep into her thick hair, massaging along her scalp. "You okay?"

Tears formed in her eyes. She blinked and shrugged one shoulder against her pillow. "Tickle my back?" she asked, turning away from me onto her stomach.

I pulled up her pajama top, her fair skin smooth like a slate. Lightly and slowly I ran my fingers over her back. Smoothing. Soothing. I knew sometimes words came easier when they weren't face-to-face. I waited.

"I'm sorry." Her voice was barely a whisper.

"Hmmm?" I said, questioning, leaning closer. I'd been expecting a retelling of her night, a healing repetition and release of the trauma. "You have nothing to be sorry about." Surely she didn't blame herself for Rick's abusive behavior. "Rick needs to learn to control himself. He can't go around—"

"Not that," she interrupted. "I'm sorry I—" Her voice caught. She sighed. She started talking, her voice tight. "I'm sorry I broke my foot. I'm sorry about my arm. I'm sorry for how stupid I've acted around you this year. And I'm sorry I—" A sob filled her throat as she stumbled on. "And I'm sorry I didn't come visit you in the hospital. I wanted to. I'm sorry I made you go there." She was crying as she spoke. "I feel so terrible. I made you sick—and I couldn't even go see yo-ou."

I opened my mouth to deny her words, but she kept talking.

"And then tonight when Mike was fighting Rick—" Again, she stopped to cry some. "I just felt so ashamed. I'd trusted Rick when all along Mike was looking out for me. The same way God never left…I just ignored Him. Both of them. I feel so stupid. And…sad."

"Oh, Emily." I pressed the flat of my hand against her back. Leaned over and hugged her from behind. "God knows it all. I think Mike probably does, too."

She nodded into the pillow, not squirming at all in my embrace. I laid my head in the crux of her neck and shoulder, thinking about the last conversation I'd had with Dr. Sullivan. Could it have been just yesterday afternoon? It seemed like ages ago.

"Remember when we talked about discontent being the cutting edge of growth?" Dr. Sullivan had templed his fingers under his chin, a gesture I'd learned meant something important was coming. "Let's talk about what you're growing toward."

I'd been waiting for Bob to come get me from the hospital. Somehow the car I'd driven myself there in had made its way back to Brewster. I was glad Bob would be bringing me home. I'd fixed my hair, borrowing hairspray from the nurses' desk, as if I were getting ready for a first date. In a way I was. My first time away from this place since I'd been so broken. Dr. Sullivan had knocked at my room saying, "I thought of something I'd like to add to our previous conversation before you leave." He took the chair near my bed, where I was waiting. If this was growing, it felt a lot like standing still, simply holding together. "I'm not sure what I'm growing toward," I answered honestly. "It's hard to think of that now."

"I read something over lunch," he said. "I'm thinking it might be helpful for you to think about." He stroked his chin. "It was in the book of John—the story about the vine and the branches. I'm guessing you're familiar with it."

I was, but maybe not as well as I should have been. "Yes?" I urged him on.

"It compares God to a gardener. Are you familiar with the way a gardener will trim a tree, sometimes cutting off whole branches? You'd think the tree would die, but the surprising thing is, it gets healthier. Stronger. In fact, the part where the wound is deepest ends up being the strongest part of the tree." He folded his arms, shook his head a little. "Amazing how that works in people, too."

It was a lot to take in when all I'd thought I was doing was waiting.

He stood, held out his hand to shake mine. He kept a firm grip even when our handshake was done. "You know pruning is an ongoing process. It's not something that's ever really 'done.' But it keeps us growing." He let go of my hand then. "It's been a pleasure. I'll see you in my office in a couple weeks. Be well."

I squeezed Emily tight, lifted my head from her neck, and sat up.

"Be well," he'd said. I struggled to understand how I could be well after this awful night, and yet I was.

I wiped my hand across Emily's back, then took one finger and drew a fancy curl in the middle. I waited.

"I?" Emily finally asked.

"Um-hmm." I drew another letter, then another, until I was done. I pressed my hand against her back, waiting. Had she fallen asleep?

Finally she spoke, her voice soft, warm against the night. "I love you, too, Mom."

Funny how it had come when I least expected it.

This.

Now.

My measure of joy.

Goodness and Mercy...

Epilogue

One year later

Emily

"Mom! Are you ready?" I ran into the house from school. We only had a few minutes or we'd be late.

"Emily, you don't have to yell. I'm right here." Mom was pushing her chair away from her computer. She ran her fingers through her hair as if making room to listen to me. Mom had practically lived at her computer this past year. I should have known she'd be right there. She looked at the clock on top of the piano. "Oh, goodness, is it that late?" She jumped up from her chair. "Give me two minutes."

I ran up the stairs after her, throwing my backpack on my bed. A note fell out of the side pocket and fluttered to the floor. I picked up the scrap of notebook paper.

Wherever you are right now, I'm thinking about you. M.

Mike. I smiled to myself. He didn't need to write his initial—I'd know his handwriting anywhere. I also knew he was thinking about me even without a note. If Rick had been half the boyfriend Mike had turned out to be—huh! I didn't want to think about what half of Rick would be like. Not much, that was for sure.

After their backyard fight, Rick and Mike cut a wide path around each other. Not easy to do in a school the size of Brewster High, but somehow they managed to keep their paths from crossing. Rick almost seemed afraid of Mike, although to look at the two of them, it should have been Mike who avoided Rick. But, as Mike said in his half-kidding, half-serious voice, flexing his skinny arms like some kind of superhero, "When you wear the armor of faith, who wouldn't be afraid?"

I hardly saw Rick after he graduated. Someone said he was playing football for a junior college in Minnesota. I hoped he had learned to get his aggression out on the field instead of on people.

I leaned into the mirror over my dresser, fluffing my hair with both hands. I couldn't wait to bring Mom to the nursing home with me that afternoon. She was finally going to meet Peg. I picked up my eye shadow and opened the lid.

I'd asked not to be scheduled to work after school that day. They were celebrating the April birthdays of the residents, and Peg had invited me to be her guest. We found out months ago that our birthdays were only a day apart when I told her I would be turning eighteen.

"Praaacticallly twiiiins," she said. Her real birthday had been last week, just like mine, but somehow this felt more like the celebration I'd been waiting for.

I dabbed at the pale brown eye shadow, blinking at myself in the mirror as I put it on. I was amazed when I thought about all that had happened since I'd first met Peg more than a year ago. Back then I was sort of afraid of her. I could hardly understand anything she said. Now I barely noticed her slow speech. Of course, Peg had changed almost as much as I had in this past year.

I glanced down at my feet. I'd never thought to be grateful for matching shoes until I spent eight weeks in a cast. My foot had healed slowly. But that slowness had given me a chance to slow down in another way.

I had to drop out of my CNA classes for a while. Even though Mike had offered to drive me back and forth from Carlton, my parents and I had decided I needed time to heal from more than just a broken foot.

Getting over Rick was easy, but getting over the damage he'd done to me was harder. Why I'd ever thought his cutting remarks were a kind of love, I might never understand. But I'd learned that his cruelty, verbal and physical, wasn't love at all, but rather an attempt to make himself feel powerful by making me feel weak. What was scary was how easily he had done that to me.

At least I didn't have to worry about him anymore. But I did have to worry about getting to the birthday party on time. "Mom! Let's go!"

"One more minute," she called from her bedroom.

I picked up the small wrapped package on my dresser. I'd gotten Peg a pearl necklace. Well, not real pearl—not on my part-time budget. The director of nursing had been really good about scheduling my work hours around things at school. I finally passed the CNA test in the middle of last summer and worked full-time until school started. She'd been great about scheduling me a lot less once school started. Between volleyball last fall and basketball all winter, I hadn't worked all that much lately. But even when I wasn't scheduled for work, I tried to stop by and say hi to Peg. She'd become almost like a mom-kind of girlfriend to me.

Unlike Jen. I was still trying to figure out what had really happened between Jen and me. Our brief exchanges in the halls at school were awkward. I longed for the days when we didn't even have to speak to know what each other was thinking. Now we exchanged polite nods and fake smiles. She often rode around Brewster with Pete West. My heart ached to think about how innocent we both had been in the days when we swore we'd be "friends forever." At one time, I was convinced Jen and I were sisters, like in the *Parent Trap* movie, separated somehow. That dream was long gone.

I looked at the devotional book lying on my bed. The one Mom had given me in memory of my piano teacher, Anne. I closed my eyes, remembering how I'd felt playing her favorite song in church this fall in memory of her birthday. "Jesus Loves Me." The same version I'd played as a ten-year-old at her funeral. I was surprised at how much of it I still had memorized. Playing it again had been part of my healing. Remembering who I'd been back then, who I was becoming now.

I laid one hand on the devotional. A photo of Jen and me together more than a year ago marked my spot. A daily reminder to keep her in my prayers.

"Ready?" Mom poked her head around the door. "Oh," she said, her eyes on the small package in my hand, "I should have gotten Peg a gift. I didn't even think about it."

"Mom, you don't even know her."

"I know, but still… Let me grab a card." She headed down the stairs to her desk.

I followed, watching as she quickly wrote "Happy Birthday" and a short greeting in a card with her favorite silver pen. She licked the envelope.

"Too bad your book isn't done. Peg loves to read."

Mom ruffled my hair. "I wish I had as much confidence in my book as you do."

"Will you let me read it?"

"It's not done yet. But maybe. Sometime. We'll see." She picked up her purse and car keys from the kitchen counter. "Let's get going."

I followed her into the garage. "You'll never get your book published if you don't let someone read it."

"I won't get it published if I don't finish it either. But I'll worry about that after I'm done with it. Right now I've got enough on my plate." She backed the car out of the garage and shifted into drive.

I knew exactly what Mom meant. She was going to be graduating from college in a month—the same week I'd be graduating from Brewster High. She'd been commuting to Carlton almost every day this year, completing a degree in psychology. She'd threatened to room with me in college if I didn't pitch in and help around the house so she could get her schoolwork done. I knew she was kidding, but I was glad she was getting her degree before rooming with me was an actual possibility. Dad was, too. He said having three college tuition bills was not something he'd planned on when he only had two kids. Mom just laughed. He did, too. I could tell Dad was proud of Mom's four-point last semester. He grinned as big as she did.

I was hoping my college path would be quicker than my mom's. She told me about how she started college shortly after her dad had died, dropped out, started again, met Dad, and got married. Over the years she'd taken a class here and there, accumulating enough credits to be within one full-time year of her degree. She shook her head in amazement every time she talked about it.

We pulled into the parking lot of the nursing home. I could see Mike standing on the sidewalk waiting for us. Peg had invited him to the party, too. I often brought Mike along when I stopped in to see Peg. If she had been younger, I might have had to worry about her stealing my boyfriend. They had become friends fast. His new job at the *Brewster Banner* had mushroomed from sports writing to covering other community events. He had a knack for interviewing that had landed his stories on the front page of the weekly paper more than once. He hoped to find a story at the party this afternoon. If not, we'd have fun anyway.

I was looking forward to having fun with Mike for a long time. He'd recently decided to attend NDSU along with me. He was going to major in speech communications and journalism. Right up his alley. I was still deciding what my major would be. Sometimes it bothered me that I didn't know what I wanted to go into. My mom reminded me that I had plenty of time to decide what I wanted to be when I "grew up."

"It took me more than twenty years to finish college," she told me. "I have a feeling you'll do it in a lot less. Keep praying."

I was.

The three of us walked through the wide glass doors into the home. Faint sounds of a drum and an accordion playing polka music called us into the birthday party.

There was Peg! Across the room, she sat in her wheelchair, looking beautiful in a new blue dress. Even from here, I could tell it matched her eyes. I waved. Slowly she lifted her hand and waved back, her crooked smile full across her face. As it had been for the past year, her hair was dyed a soft ash blond, styled in a short, funky cut that made her look years younger than when I first met her. I'd thought she was ancient but found out she was only turning sixty-two. Her stroke had aged her quickly, but I'd learned love could heal in a way physical therapy couldn't.

There was her husband, proud by her side. I'd met him a bunch of times. He mostly visited in the evenings when I was working. He was cool, bringing Peg new clothes and books, and candy to share with me. He waved, too, when he saw me, his eyes darting to include Mike and then stopping on my mom. His brows furrowed. Of course, he didn't know who she was. I could solve that.

"Come on." I pulled Mom by the hand. "You need to meet Peg and her husband." Mom's feet moved like they were glued to the floor. "Come o-on."

There was a small round of applause as the two-man band ended their song. "Let's all sing Happy Birthday now." The activities director stood, lifting her arms as if she were a choir director. The drummer rolled his sticks as if this were an awards ceremony until the accordion player found his keys. "Happy birthday to you…"

We sang as we walked to meet Peg and stood awkwardly beside her while the last lines of the song were sung. I could see Peg's husband eyeing my mom and my mom giving him a puzzled smile back.

"Happy birthday to you-uuuu!" Mike pointed at Peg and she laughed as everyone clapped for the birthday residents.

"Dr. Sullivan." My mom stuck out her hand.

"Olivia." Peg's husband took my mom's hand in both of his.

My mouth was hanging open. I snapped it shut.

"You two know each other?"

Dr. Sullivan

I watched as three familiar faces walked toward Peg and me. Emily. Her friend, Mike. And Olivia Marsden, of all people. I didn't need to be Sherlock Holmes to notice the similarity between Emily and the woman who had to be her mother. So, Peg's young friend, Emily, was Olivia Marsden's daughter? I could have thrown back my head and laughed. God had been astounding me in all sorts of ways this past year.

The number one way was the renewed love I felt for Peg. I'd been blind. Steel walls had encased my heart. I felt ashamed to think about the quick way I'd dismissed her faithful love toward me simply because she'd had a stroke. So what if her abilities weren't the same as they were before? She was still the same person inside. God helped me see that in a way my own human eyes couldn't. And for that I had Olivia Marsden to thank.

"Olivia, don't tell me Emily here is your daughter!" I couldn't hide the laughter bubbling in my throat. The coincidence, if you could call it that, was too unexpected not to laugh.

"One and the same," she replied, a bit of puzzlement still in her voice. "And you're…?" She paused.

"Peg's husband." Odd how proud I felt, considering the way I'd so carefully tucked my wife away these past years. "I hear Peg and Emily are quite the friends."

"So I hear." She turned to Peg. "I should introduce myself. I'm Emily's mom. Libby." She reached for Peg's hand, not shaking it, rather holding it between her two hands, a caress of sorts.

"Thaaank youu for shaaarinnng yourrr daaaughterr with mmmee."

"No." Olivia bent at the knees, squatting down so she could look Peg in the eye. "Thank you for being such a good friend to Emily. I was…" She stopped, her eyes darting to me, back to Peg. "…ill for a while, and Emily needed someone who could listen to her like a…like a mom. You did that for her, and I've been wanting to thank you."

I'd always prided myself on being able to remain detached from my patients. Unfortunately, that detachment had spilled over into my everyday life, too. I'd managed to quell my love for Peg by distancing myself from her. Emotions were not something I had to worry about. Until lately—until that moment, for instance. Hearing Olivia thank Peg for being something like a mom to Emily—while I'd been treating Olivia for her depression—brought a lump to my throat that all the swallowing in the world wouldn't budge. How God masterminded this plan, I had no idea. But I liked it. I liked it a lot. Move over Freud. Step aside Jung. I was finding God was the master psychologist.

Olivia stood and turned to me, keeping a hand on Peg's shoulder. "This was a surprise," she said. "A nice surprise. How are you?"

"Good. Very good." I nodded. I hadn't seen her for at least six months. Twice, under my supervision, she'd tried to wean herself from her antidepressant medication with unsuccessful results. She finally came to terms with the thought that she may need to be on medication for life. At her appointment early last fall, we agreed that an annual visit with me to check on things would be fine. She looked wonderful. But I knew with Olivia, appearances could be deceiving. I had to ask. "And how are you?" My look told her it was more than a polite question.

"How much time do you have?" She was serious long enough that I briefly wondered if she wanted to turn this surprise visit into a therapy session. But then she laughed, the twinkle in her eyes telling me her sense of humor was alive and kicking.

She was still catching me off guard. "So, things are good?"

"Very good. I'm going to be graduating from college next month."

"You are?" I knew she had enrolled in some classes, but… "My, that was fast."

"When I put my mind to something, I like to get it done."

"I can see that. Congratulations."

"What about you?" Leave it to Olivia to ask me questions. "Are you still chasing demons?" Odd, her choice of words. She had no idea that the demons she'd sent me chasing were not hers but mine. My time with Olivia may have helped her, but it changed me.

"Actually, I have some news, too." I hesitated to tell her here in the nursing home. Announcements like this were better left to a conversation in my office, or at the very least, a letter to be read in the privacy of a patient's home. News like this could be upsetting to my clients. But maybe this was the perfect spot after all. In the nursing home where God had brought us all together in such an unexpected circle. I put both my hands on Peg's shoulders. "I've decided to retire. I'm going to be moving Peg back home with me."

"You're *leaving?*" It was Emily who took the news hard. She was staring at Peg, a mixture of surprise, joy, and sadness streaming across her face. She dropped to her knees and threw her arms around Peg. "I'm so…so…sad…and happy." Tears were in her words. "I'm going to miss you. So much."

Slowly, Peg lifted her arms around Emily. Tears were in Peg's eyes, too. "You'lll beee at colllllege, I'lll beee inn Caaarlllltonn. We'llll stiiill beee friennndss."

"I'm going to work through the summer," I added, feeling the need to explain somehow. "I'm having some work done in the house so Peg will be able to manage better. We're going on a cruise in the fall." I lifted one hand, palm up. "Retirement celebration. It's long overdue." I squeezed Peg's shoulder. She bent her head toward my hand, nestling it in the crook of her neck.

"Awesome," said Emily.

"Iiii thinnnk ssso, toooo." Peg smiled.

I thought so, too. "Maybe we should go have some cake." I nodded my head toward the dining room, where most of the residents and guests had moved. I led the way, pushing Peg in her wheelchair.

Making the decision to retire was surprisingly easy. I'd been toying with the idea since I'd been fifty-five. My psychiatry practice had been lucrative, allowing Peg and me to dream of all sorts of possibilities for the years ahead. A summer in Europe, a lake home in Minnesota, winters spent somewhere far from North Dakota blizzards. All those dreams had disappeared after Peg had her stroke three years ago. I'd blamed Peg. I'd blamed God. I'd never thought to blame myself for putting limits on my dreams that weren't there after all.

I threw myself into my work instead, mistakenly thinking it would provide what a wife, what a relationship with God, couldn't. I'd been so wrong. My work had done nothing but help pass time. Oh sure, some days, some clients provided a sense of accomplishment. But most days I felt the true limitations of being merely human. I couldn't heal people any more than the false gods in the Bible could.

In part, Olivia had sent me on my search. Her struggle to find meaning in her misery, her attempt to hold on to her faith in spite of her pain, had launched me onto a similar path. I came to understand that even Jesus didn't heal everybody. Only those people who came to Him *seeking* healing were restored.

I came to see that my clients may not have been so different from those in biblical times. In part, their healing took place because of their desire to be well. Their faith was as much a part of the cure as Jesus' touch. Perhaps God had designed us to work that way. Meet Him halfway. He created us with free will—free to choose to reject His healing or accept it.

That realization helped me relieve myself of much of the burden I'd been carrying. Many of my patients I couldn't fix. They struggled continually, regardless of the medication or therapy we tried. I'd grown discouraged, especially these past few years. Studying Jesus' healing ministry had helped me understand that I was not in this alone. My responsibility was to do my best at what I could. Then I needed to let the patient, and God, do the rest. Somehow, that seemed like a huge relief.

This past year, I realized I'd done my work as faithfully as I could. I was now being called to something new. I'd met God halfway and

He'd been right there, waiting all along. Ready to show me what was next. Loving Peg wouldn't be so much a new career as it would be a gift. I didn't feel worthy, but the gift was mine all the same. Imagine that.

"To new beginnings." I raised my glass of punch as the two-man band began to play a waltz.

"And nneww frieeennnnds."

Mike jumped up, leaning down towards Peg. "I think we should celebrate. May I have this dance?"

Peg laughed, her blue eyes catching mine as Mike pulled her wheelchair from the table and spun it around once before heading to the makeshift dance floor near the band.

"Hey!" Emily jumped up. "No fair stealing my boyfriend, Peg." She ran after them, putting her hands on Mike's hips as if they were starting a conga line.

I turned to Olivia. "Are you really as well as you look?"

She looked at her chocolate cake, then at me. "I really am." She hesitated, took a sip of punch, then said, "Can I ask you a personal question?"

I braced myself. "Sure." With this woman I never knew what to expect. But then, that had been part of the challenge of treating her. Her questions had led me far beyond any formal training. The challenge of treating Olivia had earned me a new degree entirely. A degree of faith. I took in a deep breath, readying myself for her question.

"All this time I've been curious…" One side of her mouth turned up in a half smile. "Your name. Doctor G. Sullivan. What does the 'G' stand for?"

That was it? That was her burning question? This one was easy. Finally. "George," I said. "My name is George."

Libby

He said his name was George. *George!* I smiled to myself as I climbed into bed and slid over to snuggle beside Bob. George. Imagine that. Such a simple name. Old fashioned. Plain even. Not the name I'd imagined for someone who had done so much for me.

How surprised I had been to see Dr. Sullivan standing beside Emily's friend Peg. I'd never seen him outside of an office or hospital. Picturing him with a regular life and a wife was difficult for me.

I had seen no pictures in his office. No talk of his personal world—only mine. I had simply never asked. How selfish. How unselfish of him to devote his life's work to listening to troubled people like me. I closed my eyes. *Thank You, Lord, for Dr. Sullivan. And Peg. Bless their new time together.*

I moved over to my side of the bed, turning onto my stomach, scrunching my pillow so it supported my head just the way I liked.

It was only then, a little more than a year after my depression had started, that I could start to unravel the tight ball that had formed my insular world for so long. Dr. Sullivan had helped tug at those threads, loosening them enough for me to get at them and pull some more. I'd learned that part of the nature of this illness was an intense focus inward. Something I'd been doing on some level since my dad had died when I was a teen. It had been Anne who had so gently broken through the walls I'd built that I'd hardly realized what she'd done until she was no longer around. After she was gone, I was left to deal with life on my own. Without Anne. Without walls. Without God.

Goodness knew, I tried. The faith I found after Anne died had been the only thing that kept me from giving in altogether. But even my newfound faith hadn't been enough. Given time, some people could free themselves from this force that pulled like gravity. I wasn't one of those people.

Instead of unraveling, I'd wound tighter and tighter, isolating myself first from my friends, then from my family, and finally from God. I formed a tiny world of my own making, thinking safety was somehow inside me. I was convinced that my mind, which I valued above all else, held the secret to my misery. If only I could find it.

It had been profoundly humbling to finally understand that my brain required medication to function normally again. To think clearly. To pray. I couldn't do it on my own. But I had to be willing to accept the healers God sent to help.

The other me had gone, not leaving so much as merging, her watchful eye no longer judging. She was no longer my harsh critic but rather a calming, quiet ally.

"You're different now," Katie told me over lunch one day in Vicky's Café. "I can't quite put my finger on how...more direct, maybe? Stronger? I don't know." She picked up her spoon and stirred her coffee. "But you're still the same." She leveled her gaze at me. "Do you feel different?"

"Oh my, yes." I stirred my coffee, too, even though I didn't use cream or sugar. I needed time to think. I lifted a shoulder. "I can't describe it, either. I just have this...feeling inside of...strength? Or something. I'm the same, and yet I'm not." I smiled. "I know this doesn't make sense."

"It does." Katie smiled, the comfort of our friendship going beyond words. "I can see it in you. It's more a feeling than something concrete." She picked up her cup and swallowed a sip. "But then, isn't that what faith is all about? You can't see it, but you know when it's there."

And, oh, how I'd needed my faith these past months. It had taken nearly two months to wean myself from the antianxiety medication. A quarter milligram less of those tiny tablets each week. I would have never guessed lowering my dosage by such a tiny amount could send me shaking for two days as if I'd overdosed on coffee. Big-time.

With Dr. Sullivan's supervision, I tried going off my antidepressant medication, too. Not a good idea. I crashed twice. Going back to that dark valley was something I never wanted to do again. I finally came to the conclusion that depression may not be a whole lot different from any other chronic disease. A diabetic took medication to stay well, to keep their body functioning normally. If I had to take my medication every day in order to think normally, in order to pray, I would. Once I made up my mind, swallowing those pills was no longer a battle I had to wage each day.

I turned onto my back. Sleep was not coming easily. Seeing Dr. Sullivan so unexpectedly had set my mind in motion, reliving, assessing, taking stock. Thank goodness this sleeplessness wasn't like the long nights during my depression. I felt soothed as I looked back and saw how far I'd come. How far we'd all come.

I smiled, remembering the wedding Bob and I had attended last month. His coworker, Paul Bennett, had married Ruthie Hammond, Mike's former boss at the radio station. During the vows at the church, Bob had wrapped his hand around mine, holding on tight, as if just then he understood how close he'd come to losing me. Losing us. I'd looked at him out of the corner of my eye, watching him blink rapidly, emotion working at his jaw. I'd leaned over, putting my head on his shoulder. He released my hand, putting his arm around me, pulling me close as Pastor Ammon said, "You may kiss the bride." Bob looked down at me as if he just might...kiss *me*, that is.

And, there it was again. Joy. Small measure. Filling my cup.

More, later, at the reception when across the table from us, Mike whispered something into Emily's ear. She laughed, her face unclouded by the uncertainty she carried the year before. They got up to dance, Mike leading Emily onto the old wooden gym floor, taking her into his arms, trying to find the tentative steps that would carry them across the floor and into the future.

I didn't know what was in store for them. Good friendship? Something more? I didn't need to know as long as God had a plan for each of them.

I closed my eyes, letting the mist of sleep cover me. Tomorrow would be here soon enough. I'd wake up, set my feet on the floor, and say, as I did every morning these days, "This is the day the Lord has made, I will rejoice and be glad in it."

Some days were easier to rejoice in than others. But I was going to keep trying. Only God knew the purpose of all I'd been through. All I had yet to face. Maybe it was simply to teach me to rely on Him. Maybe there was something more. If He could use it for good, I guess I'd find the reason in heaven. Until then, I had to content myself with the mystery of it all.

I felt as if I'd fast-forwarded through the summer. One minute it had been spring, the next it was almost fall. The late-August sun was well over the horizon. I looked across our king-sized bed. Bob was already quietly off to work. I'd slept too late, the birds outside halfway through breakfast, no doubt. I turned onto my back. I'd lie there just a moment more, enjoying the coolness of the early morning, the soft prickle of sun-dried sheets. Funny how much I enjoyed sleeping now…and waking up. So different from my nights almost a year and a half ago when I dreaded bedtime, frightened by the hours until morning, and then woke, if I'd slept at all, fearing the long day ahead.

I tossed back the covers, anxious to get on with my day. Emily and I were going to the nursing home later this afternoon to say goodbye to Peg. She was moving back to Carlton the next day, and Emily was leaving for college in a week. Another goodbye.

Emily wasn't calling it goodbye, exactly. Neither one of us were calling her leaving much of anything. Whenever the subject came up, we both blinked a lot these days, our tears replaced by nervous giggles when our eyes met. At one time, both of us had been anxious for the day she was old enough to be off on her own. Now that it was here, I wanted time to stop for just a bit longer.

I swung my legs over the side of the bed, stretching like a worm being tugged from the grass. I was glad God was in charge of time, too. If I were the one to decide, Emily might never leave my nest. And I knew God had a better plan in mind than that for Emily.

I had too much to do to wallow in what "might be" in the days ahead. *It's Yours, God,* I prayed as I hurried to get dressed. I was anxious to get to my computer. This was the day I would finish my novel. I could feel it. So close.

I tugged the load of clothes I washed the night before from the washer tub and then carried the heavy basket outside. I didn't even have to peer across the street to see the clothes I was sure Ida Bauer already had swinging on her backyard clothesline. Just once I'd like to have my clothes on the line before my elderly neighbor.

I set the basket on the ground, running a cloth over the white vinyl line to clean off any dust. How many times over the years we'd lived in this house had I wiped off this line? How many times had I hung clothes outside only because the women living on either side of me had their clotheslines full? I'd resented the task, wanting nothing more than to toss the wet clothes into the dryer, waiting for a buzzer to summon me to fold the clothes instead of a sudden rain cloud or the setting sun.

I bent, pulling Bob's yellow cotton shirt from the basket, shaking out the wrinkles as best I could. I pushed my hand into the clothespin bag. The wooden pins knocked each other softly as I took out two. The dampness of the cloth was cool against my fingers as I pinned the shirt to the line. I looked up into the sky. No rain today. Nothing but the pale blue of an early-morning, late-summer sky. How many times had I stood here, simply completing a task, not noticing how beautiful it was? I stooped to the basket again, selecting my favorite summer dress. There wouldn't be too many more days to wear it this season. I held the moist fabric close to my nose and breathed deeply. Freshness. Soap. Water. Memories of a wonderful summer. If smelling something like that was possible, here it was. I pinned the dress to the line, filling my lungs again. Dew. Grass. Sun. I paused, my hands on the clothesline, my world suddenly too perfect to move. Goosebumps of joy pimpled my arms. A bird sung out in the tree overhead.

The Holy Spirit finds words to speak to God when you can't.

Well, there.

I smiled. Let the birds sing praises while I hung out clothes. Somehow this morning their tune echoed my thoughts exactly. Slowly, I emptied the basket, bending and straightening, pinning and smoothing, the dreadful task turning into a dance of praise in the morning.

I returned the basket to the laundry room, almost wishing I had another load to hang out.

Almost.

I knew I had the same clothes to take off the line later. Folding and ironing was a dance I'd be doing this afternoon.

I poured a cup of strong coffee, fortifying myself for the hours ahead. In between sips, I picked up the stack of photos that were lying on the counter near the coffee pot. I leafed through them, pausing only when I came to the family photo taken at my graduation from college three months earlier.

There we were, the four of us. Grinning into the camera held by a stranger. My cap was slightly askew. Emily's face was smushed up against mine. Brian somehow between Emily's grin and mine, Bob's arms embracing us all. My imperfectly perfect family.

How hard I'd wished for joy. How long I had taken to understand I'd had it all along. Just because I hadn't felt it didn't mean it wasn't there. Just like God. He'd been there, too. Waiting for me to notice. There, even when I doubted.

I flipped to the next picture, completely out of sequence. I stood in the bathroom at home before the ceremony, pinning and repinning my graduation cap. It hadn't looked decent at any angle. That morning I'd imagined Anne's voice. Heard her laugh in my mind. *"Libby, stop it! You look great. Go, already."*

She should have been there.

I put the photos down. I'd frame one soon. Right now Anne was telling me of something more important I had to do. I picked up my coffee mug and headed to my computer. I'd learned keeping to a routine was a good tool in the treatment of depression. I needed to write that morning, as I'd been doing almost every morning all summer. Hearing Anne's voice urging me on. *"Tell our story."*

I hit the Control and Home keys, sending the cursor back to the beginning to write a prologue I hadn't lived back when I'd started this book.

> *After Anne...left, I thought I had two options:*
> *One. Go crazy.*
> *Two. Die of loneliness.*
> *It turned out there was a third option I hadn't imagined. But then, that's my story.*
> *Our story.*

I could see now that it had taken losing what I valued most—my mind—to acknowledge that God's power was greater than mine. He could do what I couldn't.

Only if you lose yourself will you find Me.

Our story. Mine, Anne's, and God's.

It was a relief to know He was in charge, not me.

I pushed the Control and End keys and typed some more.

> *If I wouldn't have lost Anne I might never have found God. And I could hardly wish that either. After all, discovering faith turned out to be my third option— the one I hadn't known to imagine. The one option I couldn't imagine living without.*
> *But then Anne knew that all along.*

I stopped typing, sat back, and stared at the screen.

So this was the cure. Cobbled together with medicine and doctors, exercise and schedules, work, friends, family, and faith. It was a process, not a place. Losing Anne. Brian's brush with drugs. My marriage. Emily. The cut places were where I'd be the strongest.

Incredibly amazing.

But then, so was God.

I reached forward once more and typed:

The End

But I knew it wasn't an end, only a beginning. It was hard to remember exactly who I'd been when all this had started, and exciting to imagine who I might become. I knew this was only the beginning of the next step in God's plan for me.

I picked up my coffee cup and lifted it toward the screen. Took a sip. I planned to count it all as part of my measure of joy. Part of becoming the Libby my friend, Anne, had seen all along. Part of becoming the Olivia God had planned from the start.

A Note from
Roxanne Sayler Henke

Dear Reader,

At one time, the topic of this book would have sent me running. I would have gladly confessed to any other ailment than anxiety and depression. I valued my mind too much to admit the darkness I sometimes felt. The despair and worry that filled my days. How could I be depressed when I wrote a humor column? When I loved to laugh? Yet, I finally couldn't deny my depression any longer.

The apostle Paul had a thorn of the flesh. Depression is mine. It was a walk through a valley I wouldn't wish on anyone, and yet I wouldn't change a step of it. God was there, along with many others. I am a different person, a better person, for the journey. God had a plan all along. He is so amazing!

I wrote this book to bring light to a dark subject. To bring understanding and offer hope. If, after reading this book and thinking about the discussion questions, you'd like to share your thoughts with me, you can write or e-mail me at:

Roxanne Sayler Henke
c/o Harvest House Publishers
990 Owen Loop North
Eugene, Oregon 97402-9173

roxannehenke@yahoo.com

or contact me through my website at:
www.roxannehenke.com

Becoming Olivia
Conversation Questions

1. "I'm depressed." Discuss what those words mean to you.

2. In what ways did *Becoming Olivia* give you a better understanding of clinical depression? Did any of the symptoms surprise you?

3. Depression and anxiety are closely linked. Discuss the connection.

4. Clinical depression is not something that happens overnight. Talk about the gradual progression Olivia experienced. Can you understand why she might have thought, at first, that she had a physical illness? Why was it so hard for her to accept the fact that she was suffering from clinical depression?

5. "Pull yourself up by your own bootstraps" is a phrase we often hear. Discuss the reluctance of many people to take medication as prescribed, or to seek help.

6. Why is it so hard to admit we need help?

7. Emily is determined to be popular at all costs. What price did she pay trying to achieve her goal?

8. Teenagers are often reluctant to talk to their parents about their problems. What can a parent do to overcome this natural reticence?

9. Discuss Emily's friend, Mike, and his persistent friendship. Have you ever needed a friend like that? Have you had one? Have you been one? Talk about the benefits of that sort of friend. Discuss Peg's role in Emily's life.

10. The issue of date abuse is seldom talked about. Why? What are some of the reasons Emily accepted the way Rick treated her?

11. Talk about the role work played in Dr. Sullivan's life. What was his intense focus keeping him from?

12. How did having Olivia as a patient change Dr. Sullivan?

13. Think about your own career (motherhood counts!). In what ways are you affected by the people you work with? In what ways do you affect those around you?

14. People who are depressed are often so focused on keeping their own life together that they end up pushing others away. Talk about how this affected Olivia's relationship with her husband and with Emily.

15. Discuss how hard times can cause us to question our faith. How hard times can increase our faith. Have you ever experienced either of these times? Share what you learned.

16. Why does the idea of having a mental illness, as opposed to a physical illness, have such a stigma attached to it? Did this book help you understand the illness of anxiety and depression better? In what ways?

17. Talk about Olivia's friends Katie and Jan. How did their reaction to Olivia's illness affect Olivia? What are beneficial ways friends can reach out to those who are hurting? What do friends sometimes do that is not helpful?

18. Dr. Sullivan talked about discontent being the cutting edge of growth. Talk about this concept. How can unhappiness lead a person to something better?

19. At one point all Olivia wanted was a "measure of joy." What is your measure of joy?

20. *Becoming Olivia* is the title of this book. Discuss what it has taken for you to "become" who you are. What events in your life have shaped you? Can you recognize difficult times in the past that God has used to change you for the better?

Hope and Help for Your Nerves by Dr. Claire Weekes (New York: New American Library, 1969) is mentioned in *Becoming Olivia*. It is a real book and one of the best I've found on the topic. If you are dealing with anxiety and depression, I encourage you to seek out a copy.

Other books in the
Coming Home to Brewster series:

After Anne

When Anne Abbot moves to Brewster, Olivia Marsden immediately dislikes her. She finds Anne's perkiness and the open way she talks about her faith very irritating. Meanwhile, Anne prays for a deep friendship and is somehow drawn to the aloof Olivia. Finally drawn to the faith Anne shares, will Olivia turn to God when Anne's life is threatened by cancer? Misunderstandings, death's shadow, and a beautiful new life play out in this story of a friendship forged by fire and inspired by God.

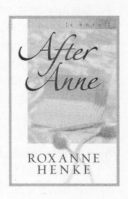

ISBN 0-7369-0967-2

Finding Ruth

After high school, Ruthie Hammond was moving to a big city...anywhere but Brewster. Surely God had a plan for her, and it wasn't in this small nowhere town. Years have passed, and now Ruthie's back in Brewster with her boyfriend, Jack. She's given up on God—and if she ever wants to have a life in the city, she'll have to do it solo. But when her first love, Paul Bennett, moves home to Brewster, Ruthie wonders if happiness really does lie in this podunk town.

In this second novel in the Coming Home to Brewster series, Roxanne Henke offers another wonderful story about relationships, choices, and spiritual growth.

ISBN 0-7369-0968-0

Coming Soon...

the fourth volume in the
Coming Home to Brewster series:

Jan Jordan is having a BIG birthday. She's turning...um, uh... well, that's the problem—she can't bring herself to say the number. She's been dreading this birthday since she learned to count. The day only means one thing...that she's officially *old*. Surely, life can be nothing but downhill from here.

Kenny Pearson is old enough to know better, but he doesn't care. As long as he can still knock a softball out of the park, drive anything with a motor as fast as it will go, and brag about it over a beer with the guys afterwards, life is good.

His wife and three kids? They have a different story.

Ida Bauer is old and she doesn't mind saying so. She's earned her wrinkles. Every one of them. Her husband is gone and so are most of her friends, and, she has to face it, soon she will be, too. Does she have anything to offer in the time she has left?

God has a plan for all these people...if only they will listen.

Roxanne Henke's fourth book in the Coming Home to Brewster series deals with the topic of aging in ways that will have you smiling, nodding your head in recognition, and maybe, just maybe, learning about the joys that can come along with turning older.